The Dancing Murders

Portia of the Pacific

Volume 6

A Literary Historical Mystery

JAMES MUSGRAVE

ISBN: 978-1-943457-46-5

Published by EMRE Publishing Fiction
San Diego, CA

The Dancing Murders

By

James Musgrave

© 2021 by James Musgrave

Published by English Majors, Reviewers and Editors, LLC

English Majors, Reviewers and Editors Publishers is a publishing house based in San Diego, California.

Website: emrepublishing.com

For more information, please contact:

English Majors, Reviewers and Editors, LLC

Interactive and Multimedia Enhanced eBooks

EMRE Publishing is now selling completely "enhanced" versions of its books through the unique Embellisher Multimedia Stream platform. Simply register inside the eReader to have access to the variety of titles. They contain relevant historical videos, music, interactive content, and a complete audiobook edition in many of the great titles.

Visit https://emrepublishing.com/new_embellisher-ereader/ to see what's available. Enter your email and a password to register and view. Buy your future digital copies of this Portia of the Pacific Historical Mystery series at reduced prices here: https://books.bookfunnel.com/portiaofpacific

DEDICATION

To my dear wife, Ellen Anita, who enjoyed historical fiction, especially mysteries. She died from Lewy Body Dementia in 2017, and I began writing this mystery series in her memory while we cared for her. I believe the combination of research, literary creativity, and Judaic mysticism would have pleased her, as she was also a college professor, and she taught many popular courses, one of which was "The Bible as Literature." It was from her that I first learned about Asherah, the lost goddess of the Hebrew tribes. I hope her fellow Jews, and non-Jews, enjoy this work in her memory.

Other Works by This Author

"The Israelites were polytheists. And God had a wife." (God & Bible & Old Testament & Gods & Elohim & Asherah)

"You cannot buy the revolution. You cannot make the revolution. You can only be the revolution. It is in your spirit, or it is nowhere."— Ursula K. Le Guin

"As to the American tradition of non-meddling, Anarchism asks that it be carried down to the individual himself."— Voltarine De Cleyre

Table of Contents

Chapter 1: Vagabonds

Sadie

I understand. I cannot testify for or against Wyatt. You plan to interview each of us, right here, where it all happened? The mayor foots the bill, you say? Will Hunsaker is paying for our transportation? I know him. He was District Attorney before he became mayor last year. He ran as the Workingmen's Party candidate. Why did you speak for this party? Ah, because they support suffrage? Good for you! You know, the mayor represented Wyatt in Tombstone, when he was the U. S. Marshal. He and Mr. Fitch, I believe that to be his name, represented my husband on a few cases, including the other murder trial. Yes, the OK Corral shooting against the Clanton gang. You know, they were never shot inside the corral. That's a myth. Honey—that's what I call him--was the Tombstone lawyer out there. He showed us around San Diego when we arrived last year. He now has three lovely daughters and a strapping son with his wife, Florence.

This is your daughter? What's your name, darlin'? Bertha May is a strong woman's name. Wyatt is always calling me Sadie, but I hate it. He gets a wicked grin, under that seagull mustache of his, whenever he calls me Sadie. He knows my name is Sarah, and I'm a Jew. You can call me Josie, or Aunt Josie, if you prefer. Do you prefer Bertha or May? All right. Bertha *and* May it shall be! Your mama must be very proud of you being able to take shorthand for her, Bertha May. I never learned a clerical trade myself. I always wanted to be an actress or a singer. I traveled out to the Arizona Territory with the Pauline Markham Theater troupe. After the cad Johnny Behan left me, to chase renegade Apaches, I met Wyatt, and my singing and dancing career was over. After we left Tombstone, we caught the gold and silver fever, and we haven't stopped yet. I suppose you could call Wyatt and me a couple of wayward vagabonds.

All right, Mrs. Foltz, I shall tell you what events presaged this murder. I presume you've already obtained information from Wyatt. I have lived with a law man for many years now, and I have also been closely acquainted with attorneys. Thus, I understand how your minds work, and I shall endeavor to explain to you in a manner that you can use to explore possible theories which might exonerate Wyatt from this predicament. I know full well you cannot use my testimony, or me, on the stand, but you can certainly avail yourself of what I have to say now.

Oh, why thank you! No, I have never attended college. However, I do enjoy reading and listening to many of my learned acquaintances. My father always taught me that the most developed intelligence is what one can experience with the senses and not from just books. The great artists succeed most grandly when they are able to learn from life through trial and error. Born artists are too rare. Most are hued from life like totem spirits. Each person must discover his or her meaning alone, but experiences with others are of primal importance.

I have always given life the risk it deserves. You can take a chance on love, or on friendship, but you cannot live to the innermost fulfillment unless you explode with curiosity. An inquisitive mind combined with a passion for risk evolves into a higher being. I believe that. That's also what my father taught me. My family did not attend *shul* in San Francisco. My father was my only rabbi, and he took his role very seriously. I was his only daughter, and I almost broke his heart when I left to go down to the Arizona territories.

I understand. I shall return to the reason we're here. I believe the good Rabbi Sonenschein was murdered because he discovered an unspeakable secret and was condemned to die. Secret? Yes, this secret is from beyond, and yet it's right here, and it has the same vibration which powers the cosmic physical reality all around us.

Correct. Exactly the way Ida would describe it. She was the

rabbi's lover and student. Did you know? Oh, yes, she was searching for something far deeper than that which the mystic from Europe possessed. She told me she would know the person she needed to meet by the tremendous light emanating from him or her. No, not the brilliance of the sun, although it's there also. I mean the flash of light that arouses the inside of the brain. Satori, Enlightenment, or the Abyss, it makes no matter. The Great Paradox becomes evident. The single Atman, Adam, or Atom is contained inside the single human, and so do the infinite possibilities outside the barrier of the self. Then, as a final twist of miraculous fate, the process is reversed. A vision of Paradise and the Tree of Knowledge illuminates your body, and everything you touch is affected in this incarnation and into the infinite possibilities of love and agony, colliding in karmic passion.

It was I who told Wyatt that Rabbi Sonenschein was not an authentic Kabbalist. My father was an intuitive, or authentic type. This fellow was the intellectual type, the poisoned and twisted type. Why? My father stated it most succinctly, as one would imagine from where such wisdom emanated, when he told me, "An intellectual hides in a hole of prejudice and arrogance, even though that hole is located above the senses in an ivory tower." Sonenschein made his living as a scavenger of men's souls, creating tricks of illusion and a game they can play, for a price, to reach some kind of miraculous state. Each state of being, of course, is synchronous with both the inner realm of subjective reality, and the outer realm of objective reality.

Each level of the human senses and consciousness, becomes more advanced, gradually evolving, taking on new energy from experience and inward searching, until, one day, in the future, the most evolved of humans is extant. The Buddha, the Christ, the Prophet, the Redeemer, and the Creator, Destroyer and Preserver, are awakened from their hiding places. You see, the intuitive knows, while the intellectual does not know, how the life's energy travels from the lowest bowels of the scrotum or labia, upward, through the penis and uterus wall, held captive inside the heart to get the spark of life and the kiss of death, until the spiritual achievement is reached. One can no longer stand the pressure from the billions of lives lived on Earth or in some other planetary or light existence. One must pierce the top of the hierarchy and out into the stars of infinite expanses, or stay imprisoned forever within the Samsara of the mental intellect.

My father wanted that, and he tried to get me enthused about the inner life of the Kabbalah, but I merely listened, held transfixed by the sound of his words. I did learn the mesmerist's trade from my father, and this has helped me with those who can be placed into trances. But I knew I was more interested in the words themselves as arbiters of the truth and not just suggestions to hypnotize. Others often heard my father's words as nothing more than praise for his handsome form and his regal bearing, which made him a potent avatar for life's energy. I saw that same light inside Wyatt's blue eyes. However, unlike the energy of my father, Wyatt's power over me came from how he behaved, his actions. My Tribe's most valuable essence is not gold, which is the bigot's understanding of my religion. The most valuable essence is the light of the Truth that our Lord is One. Once obtained, whether from an inner quest or from activities in the world around us, this essence of singular brightness and optimism will propel one into an infinite state of energy. This energy is the only creative force needed in the universe to keep everything together, allowing the continuity to unfold, as these creatures of the light portray an infinite array of identities in beautifully agonizing images, sizes and shapes. I knew that to Wyatt I could be this generator of energy, and he was my intuitive light to see the final Truth.

I understand. I do sound esoteric. However, this is truly what happened that night, as far as I can remember, and I do remember things very well. For example, I remember reading that you had to leave your lover back in San Francisco. Detective Isaiah Lees. Have you perused the territory in San Diego for possible beaus, Mrs. Foltz? As you might be aware, from your years in San Francisco, when the newest discovery of a precious gem or metal is made, or even the prospect of selling to those who pursue such dreams, the light of that moment heats up and the greed boils upward, frothing over everything, until only lust is left, but the women are few, and these women are passion itself, and they solve the immediate problem. Oh, so you *do* understand our little game. Women, or whatever passes for a woman, because gender identity is a fickle reality, become the keepers of that initial spark of rebellion in the Garden. Remember? We were blamed for our impetuous behavior when the snake figure, most likely symbolizing intuitive wisdom, gave us that forbidden fruit and told us we could live forever by knowing what God knows, and speaking as God speaks, forever and ever, amen. Just pierce that fruit with our teeth. Swallow those delectable juices of good and evil until you gag on bliss. That's what I thought when my father told me this. That's what Rabbi Sonenschein should have thought, but he was not intuitive, as I stated before. He was the intelligent male, the one who believes his introspection can shield him from the Truth. To him, there was no ultimate Truth or Higher Power. There was only what the intellect could create. Shakespeare said it, didn't he? "There is nothing bad or good than thinking makes it so." Intellectual, the thinker, the follower of rules and the giver of the senses. I only believe what I can see, touch, taste, hear, and smell. But, what about that inner light? You know, the one inside that keeps you awake at night, wondering when it will go out, leaving you in the darkness. It is, after all, Death, which you, the intellectual, fears most. Why? Because the mind goes blank. Without the light there is only perpetual fear and the blackness of the abyss.

So, I followed Wyatt, for better or worse, because I knew he was my only chance at redemption from the barren life I had lived before. I am going to tell you my truth, as I believe that Wyatt has now crossed over to the forbidden level of consciousness. He made a bet with Mr. Anthony Comstock, about fulfilling a secret desire they both had. How do I know this? Believe it or not, Mrs. Foltz, what I will now tell you can singe the hide on young girls. Could you please send your daughter out of the room for a moment? No, I suppose you won't have this written down for the record. But you will know, won't you? Only the reader will be unaware. I think it makes the process rather enjoyable. Have you read that new tale by Sir Arthur Conan Doyle? Sherlock Holmes, his detective, turns to cocaine and opium because his mind moves too quickly. That is the dilemma, is it not? We who are more intellectual need something to slow down that mind because it travels so fast—moving from one possibility in an infinity of possibilities, to the next—until our time has run out. There was nothing more we could comprehend. It was one long race to fulfill desire and then there was nothing.

What was the wager? I hope you do realize the darker aspect behind intellectual Kabbalah. This is the aspect Wyatt and I share, and why your daughter cannot be in here. We share the highest consciousness in Kabbalah, the awareness of how the joining of bodies—no matter the sex—in a loving coital passion, brings ecstasy beyond human despair. What happens? We see ourselves bathed in the Universal Light, the *ein sof* itself. Indeed, this was to be the prize for Wyatt and myself once we created this passionate wonderland from Anthony Comstock's book. She did? Ida Bailey understood about the perversity of it all? How nice! I know her profession is to arouse the passions in the best way possible, but what Wyatt and I were creating was much more than just sexual arousal and physical fulfillment. We were duplicating what this Grand Inquisitor of the Flesh secretly wanted to experience. Rabbi Sonenschein was merely the one who became Comstock's foil, his momentary antagonist, and it was my husband who was being used as the scapegoat, and I became the figure of Beatrice, leading these two poor Dantes out of their personal hell.

I shall. I shall tell you. I just did not want your young daughter to overhear, lest she believe that our secret power in life is to lead men astray. She probably is taught this in school. What? Why, that women tempt and betray men, in the negative sense; but the truth is that it is their wifely duties that are the evil side, and no teacher ever tells them that. But *I* do! And, Bertha May, lovely, pristine Eve that she most certainly is, has no reason to hear of that right now. Only we older women, we women with the wily old smiles, and easy, open corsets. We, the *femme fatales*, the ones who can propel men into states of unrelenting lust, with our words and with our bodies. Yes, please go get her. Once she returns, I shall tell you the story of the Passion of Anthony Comstock. This shall be for your record.

Thank you. Now I can continue. This is a murder story meant for the darkest nether regions and lower levels of the Kabbalah's Tree of Life and a human's mind. It was within this loamy and abundantly lusty soil, where Comstock's unconscious mind was controlled, which made him afraid of the power being held over him, but he knew not what to do to make it stop. Why should he not ask the Marshal of the Intuitive Joy to help him recover from his night sweats and his vivid, raving dreams of pubescent boys and girls, cavorting unclothed in the lush green hills of his native New Canaan, Connecticut? We told Mr. Comstock about the New Promised Land of his dreams, where he could run with these children as he once did as a youth, with Miss Pricilla Warren, daughter of the town's parson. He told us he ran deep into the forest, where they both plunged onto a pile of fall leaves, and he saw her auburn hair mix with the brown, yellow and crimson hues of the season's sacrifice, the season's Thanksgiving of wonders he could never experience today in his adult life. We would provide these passionate young creatures for him, in Tijuana, where he could romp with abandon, and his love for them would not be forbidden, the way it is in the States. After all, Wyatt and I told him, his secret desires were the Alpha and the Omega, and we were going to explain how he could live out his fantasies forever, with our guidance.

Of course, it was all possible in Mexico. This is the dark land between the greed of San Diego, and its real estate boom, and the corrupt officials in Tijuana, is it not? What am I telling you? I'm telling you that Wyatt killed the rabbi because he was going to expose the real truth behind our enterprise and who was controlling it. Ida Bailey's dance was the precursor to this expose. Sonenschein knew half of San Diego's government was attending the 100-Round Fight, and he was about to announce to them all what we had provided to Postmaster Comstock and to the other men who had such aberrational fantasies. No, this was not the only reason Wyatt shot him. The rabbi was also planning to destroy Ida Bailey and her house of ill repute, the Canary Cottage, as well as all the other bordellos in San Diego. This was his personal path to release the *ein sof* inside them. He believed the divine light had to be rescued from sin and debauchery. How do I know this is fact? Because Rabbi

Jerome Sonenschein was not alone. He had formed a secret cabal of followers, and Wyatt and I discovered this when Dr. Charlotte Baker told us about its existence after she discovered Ida Bailey had become a member. You see, Dr. Baker treated all the prostitutes in San Diego, free of charge, as she wanted to convince them to see the light and to get out of the profession forever. Dr. Baker also founded the Young Women's Christian Association and was the new President of the Women's Christian Temperance Union. She told us it was her goal to close down the Stingaree district forever. Who was behind our business venture in Tijuana? Is it not strange how life often goes in circles, Mrs. Foltz? Our dear friend and benefactor, Mayor Honey Hunsaker, was our main contributor, and he was behind many other similar enterprises across the border.

Chapter 2: Phantoms

Tijuana, Mexico, May 6, 1888.

Ida

Thank you, Mrs. Foltz, for allowing me to describe what happened that day. However, because of the phantom nature of my thoughts, I cannot vouch for the authenticity of what I experienced. Your daughter, Bertha May, appears pleasant enough. She squints a bit when she writes, so you may want to have her vision examined. You have guaranteed that what I tell you will not be given to the newspapers or other press sources. This testimony of mine is for legal purposes only. I understand. Your job as the defense attorney is to gather testimony of eyewitnesses to this murder. My testimony is being used by the prosecution as well? I see. There were four of us who saw this murder being committed? Can you tell me the others' names? We shall surely meet if we are called into court. I probably already know them. Believe it or not, I am quite the society gadfly, despite the nature of my occupation.

Josephine Marcus? Of course. I do know her very well. We have self-same interests, although she never likes to admit her past experiences in my line of endeavor. I understand. Sadie's common-law husband, Wyatt Earp, is your client, the accused. I did not realize Sadie was there, actually, because I was under the influence at the time. Mr. Elias Baldwin? Lucky! I also know him. He gambles quite a bit, and he has visited my cottage upon several occasions. I understand he knows Wyatt quite well, as they are both investing in our real estate boom. I do recall seeing him on the night of the big boxing event in Tijuana. It was before I took the drug. He had purchased one of my lovely escorts, Marie, for the evening. Did either of these two know Mr. Sonenschein, the victim? I am so sorry.

I have a very inquisitive nature, as you shall see. Who is the third fellow witness? You? You must be in jest. I see. You were there reporting the event for your newspaper. That is quite understandable. Why did I not see you, I wonder? You were where? Up in a tree overlooking the arena? You also had a box camera? Quite ingenious. I can understand that. Many other journalists were trying to get photographs, and you decided to take to the trees like our monkey relatives! We women must be especially daring to compete, do we not? Of course, I shall continue my narrative now.

I must stipulate at the outset that much of what I shall describe to you shall be of an internal variety. It is the nature of the hallucinogenic ingredients contained in the peyote cactus, to give the user a way to appreciate the common interdependence of living beings and not their antagonisms, which are usually caused by the ones in control of the social rules and obligations.

On that day, my vision, both externally at the scene around me, and internally, at the comparisons I was making in my mind, was acutely attentive due to my ingesting the cactus buttons, peyote. My self-importance and cultural identities began to melt from my body. I became a cyclops, and my all-consuming spiritual power made me see things around me as if I were the microscopic lens of that part of me, which is connected to you all, and my attention was held rapt simply by my being close to the object in my purview.

If you have already placed me in a negative category of your mind, I understand. I warrant that not many in my profession of harlotry have vocabularies as advanced as my own, and not many have studied books in the library as frequently as I have. When you are born without papers, orphaned by the mother who gave you life, you begin to experience the reality of living inside the world of poverty. The vow you make to yourself is that you will never experience such mental depravity and physical squalor again if you can prevent it. The first escape route I saw was to be able to mimic the grand community leaders who would visit Our Lady of Guadalupe Catholic Mission Orphanage on Fifth Avenue. A large vocabulary was at the top of my list.

The male benefactors, many of whom would gaze down at

us girls, had glittering, pale-colored eyes darting in their sockets. Their eyes were like Mrs. Ortega's when she would read to us about Little Red Riding Hood's grandmother in bed. "Oh, Grandmother. What big eyes you have! exclaimed Red."

Even though these men had wolfish eyes, I eventually learned how they spoke, and what they found important, so I could convince them to pay attention to me. I was no longer simply in the genus of orphan and species of a female human, required to gather around their legs like a reverent doll, a prayer of thanks on my lips, ready to bow and curtsy for their favors. I was Ida Bailey, the little red-haired riding hood pursuing the wolf. I wanted to avenge my literary grandmother, whom I envisioned was held captive inside their full bellies.

My imaginary grandmother, as I knew her, had no hereditary lineage to trap one inside a traditional family way of life. As I viewed these outdated kinds of women, they were raised to become subservient and fashionable powder puffs out in society. However, at home, they were kept as a functional ovulating machine, ready to procreate at the whim of their lord and master. They kept the home free of dirt, grime, and grit, tending to the daily chores of "mother," which was a job invented by men to trap their women inside the dangerous wheel of torture and pain, with little or no time for what these women desired.

My grandmother was billions of years old, who had, as in Darwin's *Origin of the Species*, evolved from the same tribes of monkeys and apes that first appeared in this magnificent Garden of Earthly Delights. More than that. My grandmother taught me I was born from the stars above, as were all of us, and the only power I needed was from the sun. I looked around me at this world I was inhabiting, and I knew I had come from a time and a place that knew no boundaries or restrictions imposed from the outside. My origins allowed complete freedom on the inside. The memories which were poured into one's brain by the institutions were not the source of real knowledge. Real understanding takes place after the human mind has been freed from all interference caused by the selfish social realm into which one is born. The power from the stars is enough to allow the unconstrained mind to channel the full radiance of true freedom.

From the women's magazines, in the San Diego Library's reference section, I was learning which dress to drape upon my developing body, and what words to speak to woo the male star-gazers. I knew my glow of freed intelligence must appear alluring to these tall men who wielded so much power. They had candies and coins in their pockets. They could whistle and sing, play harmonicas, and even dance jigs! They, who smelled of European linen and the best cologne, smoked long cigars from Cuba and drank bottled water from artesian wells. They owned the key to the door of Our Lady of Guadalupe and my salvation.

I was, in my post as Madam of the Canary Cottage, Horatia, the female version of Hamlet's best friend. Instead of dying in a tragic duel, I won, by teaching Hamlet how to dance with his father's ghost instead of fearing him and going murderously mad. I taught these important men how to truly enjoy us, their women of leisure. We, who catered to their every fantasy, their every carnal desire, were the same women who laughed and pointed at the passing lines of Suffragettes on Broadway, demonstrating for equality, not understanding that it was not an equal that men desired but a reflector of their greatness.

They knew their wives were pliant and submissive, creating concern over family matters. I and my ladies, in counter-response, became fussy about *them*. We learned to dress in opera gowns, smoke from long Parisian cigarette holders, drink champagne from our corsets, dance on velvet red table cloths, our bodies revolving under the spinning, multi-colored overhead chandelier. The band played *Dreamland*: "Down upon the silent waters, floating on the crystal stream ..." as we danced for our breakfasts, lunches, and dinners, at the best restaurants in town.

Riding in private black carriages, the windows tinted black, these important men pulled up to my Canary Cottage, or, depending on their intoxication, to other San Diego Stingaree houses of ill repute. Except our Canary fantasy dreamland gave us access to their bodies and their minds, and this is where the fun begins, isn't it, ladies and gentlemen? According to my Fairy Grandmother, who was living inside these wolfish men, who had devoured her long ago, I am billions of years in the making. I can channel pure energy, so what I say and do break the boundaries of time and space. A completely free mind is the direct source of eternal light, whose waves of flowing atoms transform into physical shapes, on the way toward the first stimuli of infinitesimal life forms.

The men who came to my Canary Cottage knew I provided what they needed to fulfill themselves as real men. To be completely forthcoming, I also provided "special real men" to some of these real men. We cater to any fancy. Women seeking women. Men seeking men. I stop at children and animals. Why? Not because of the Bible or other holy text. I stop because, since ancient times, children and animals have been protected from outside harm. Until recently, in our part of the world, if you stole a person's horse, you could be put to death. And children, according to the Romantics, have come from the angelic spheres, so their innocence must be kept intact until their minds can determine a personal identity.

Our young children, and the animals they imitate in games, pantomimes, and stories, should never be used for any carnal or capital purpose. True. This is not the rule the world over, as different habits and customs can become unique inside each of our brains. The grave mistake, I know, comes about when these thoughts become laws, and the corrupt group's adherents grow in number, and loyalty to cultural values and laws eventually controls their minds. Society establishes the rules, and they are repeated every day, in the schools, in the bedrooms, in the boardrooms, until these rules are second nature. Dr. Freud of Austria, according to Rabbi Sonenschein, calls it the "unconscious," deep inside the brain. The unconscious rules the conscious, and is many times greater, as it is a repository for all the billions of sensory impressions we receive every day. Whereas, if each brain could remain pure and free from these societal pressures, then the pure love energy of intelligent purpose might become our collective salvation because it obliterates these strict rules of convention and replaces it with Eros, sensual freedom.

I believe it is this love energy of intelligent purpose that keeps me yearning for each day to begin again. Perhaps men like

13

Secretary and Chief Special Agent of the New York Society for the Suppression of Vice … What was that you said, Mrs. Foltz? And Post Office Inspector? Quite right. The fact is, men do not simply enjoy largesse in their affairs, including their status titles, they also enjoy women who can feed them their fantasies of lust one delicious tidbit at a time, one exhilarating moment at a time. These men want an unlimited expansion of the senses. My women and I are what I like to term "Traps for young men" and their unconscious cravings. For, you see, my ideas for creating my Canary Cottage came from the pages of this little book, with the same title, written by Sodom and Gomorrah's Postal Inspector, Archangel from Heaven, and dry goods salesman on Earth, Mr. Anthony Comstock.

As you know, Attorney Foltz, I am only one of your four eyewitnesses. I am also probably the least valuable to your investigation. As we have discussed at length, on the day and location of the murder in Tijuana, wherein we have now returned, I was under the influence of the two Peyote buttons which symbolize, to me, my ancient Grandmother's eyes. This means that when I did my belly dance what I saw was streaming directly from the pure energy of our Creator, Preserver, and Destroyer, the *Ein Sof*.

What I shall describe will not be understood by normal readers educated in the prison schools of American society. Although, perhaps a few might be able to puncture the veil of my symbolism. As some readers of Mr. Carroll's *Through the Looking-Glass* know so well, the phantom Alice inside the mirror is also a part of the human Alice standing in front of the mirror. As I will demonstrate, Alice merely needs to believe in her magical ideas to step through the mirror to make them real. Even though the magical world of uniqueness makes your surroundings strange, the ultimate freedom it gives you is worth the temporary maladjustments.

After I read Mr. Comstock's book, what I saw were not chapters filled with "thou shall not." Instead, I created my version of "thou shall," from my Fairy Grandmother's imagination. These ideas were certainly not coming from my old life, as I was seen by most San Diego citizens as a poverty-stricken maiden, who, except for the transient beauty and impetuous nature of a wild red vixen, was condemned forever to struggle within a menial existence.

Of course, that was until I read about Mr. Comstock. This gentleman protector of virtue, my Walrus Prophet, and his little book of "shall not," gave me the very personal pattern I needed to seek my vein of golden providence in California. The fact that he was also witnessing this murder is neither here nor there. Having read about Mr. Wyatt Earp's "Hundred-Round Fight" in your newspaper, *The San Diego Daily Bee*, Mr. Comstock was here to entrap me and my clients in one of his clever artifices. I am certain he will have his tale to impart, so I shall not muddy the waters of your investigation with my prejudices against the man. You must be aware that he does figure into my description of what I witnessed. You, as a journalist and lawyer, must surely understand the impossibility of being completely unbiased when using fickle symbols such as words. It is your job to put together these different viewpoints to arrive at the truth, is it not?

Grand Jury, you say? I understand. These are upstanding members of our San Diego community who are charged with determining whether there are enough tangible evidence and unbiased witnesses presented to bring an accused to trial for First Degree Murder. No, I am not familiar with the role of a witness. There has been only one murder committed in my place of business, and I was not in the room when it occurred. Yes, the murderess was the wife of one of my clients, who came searching for her husband one evening at the behest of her four children. That was *her* excuse, of course. I, as the proprietress of the Canary Cottage, do not ask my clients about their personal and familial relations. Why should I? I create a fantasy world, like Alice's Wonderland. I inform each of my employees, whether man or woman, that he or she is charged with granting wishes that make each client the happiest. These clients come to us because they cannot, for one private reason or another, fulfill these wishes elsewhere in society.

I see. You have your own experience with brothels. Miss Ah Toy in San Francisco. Did you represent her as an attorney? I know this is neither the time nor place, but I would certainly enjoy speaking privately with you about your experiences. Perhaps at a later date? Very well. I shall continue.

I realize another lie. There were five witnesses to this murder instead of four, as you told me previously. Oh. I can now see more deeply. It was, you believe, Mr. Comstock's secret fantasy that set in motion the events leading to the murder of the Jewish Mystic, and itinerant, Jerome Sonenschein. He is why there became five witnesses. The fifth witness, however, is an antagonist of at least one of the other eyewitnesses. How many more tentacles of negative energy were there between these linchpins of justice and their societal prey, you ask? These are the heady questions only you can answer, Mrs. Foltz. Call you Clara? Very well, I shall.

What I observed that night was a phantasmagorical vision. I did not know I was seeing someone being murdered. To me, as you will soon realize, as did I, the evening was divided into two halves. The first half, when I came to the party before the main event, what Wyatt Earp had billed as the "100-round Fight," I was checking on my four girls and one young man, who were contracted to work that night as escorts for privileged clients. They first saw my employees when I took my Canary Cottage bandwagon out for a spin down Broadway, along the business mile of banks, saloons, restaurants, and hotels.

The men knew my business plan. Each woman and one man wore a different color: red, green, blue, yellow, and brown. The first client to bring a poker chip of that color to me at the Canary Cottage could take my employee to the big extravaganza across the border into Mexico. Yes, Clara, I was also part of the main attraction, and this was how I came to make the acquaintance of the victim, Rabbi Jerome Sonenschein. He was the immigrant who journeyed from Brody, in the Ukraine, where his people were being persecuted by Austrians, on one side of their border, and Russians on the other. His city had lost its status as a tax-free commercial hub, in 1879, and was being taxed. Not only that, the rabbi told me, upon our first meeting, but his Jewish brethren, who made up eighty-eight percent of Brody's population, had turned against his Kabbalah teachings and marked him as a "blasphemer and idolater." They believed his strange teachings had turned the Russians and Austrians against them.

THE DANCING MURDERS

The rabbi came to New York City by boat, not a penny to his name. From there, he joined a caravan of settlers traveling to California, and he settled in San Diego, after roaming for weeks with a contingent of Mormons, who were sympathetic to his plight, and who thought of themselves as one of the "lost tribes of Israel." When he heard that some also practiced polygamy, he believed he had indeed discovered a long-lost tribe of brethren.

I spent the spring studying with Rabbi Sonenschein. I remember because my ladies had ventured up into the Anza-Borrego desert to harvest wildflowers for our cottage. Come to think of it, the rabbi called my workers and me human wildflowers, and the rains that were so necessary to the desert blossoms' growth applied to us as well in the form of real estate storm's excesses. These land speculators and builders were our best clients, as they were to all of San Diego, yet we in the flesh and spirit trade had to capture their viscera before we could allow them to use our outsides for their pleasures.

Yes, I'm coming to that. Rabbi Sonenschein explained to me that his religion was based on his ability to see through the seven veils which cover us from the Divine Light, the *Ein Sof*. He always wore the same suit, an old black frock, similar to those worn by priests in the missions. But on the surface of this long frock, and also etched upon the round *kippah* on his head, were hundreds of letters and numbers of many languages, fonts, and sizes. When I asked him what they were, he went into what I was later to learn was his deepest meditative unconsciousness. His lips moved under his black beard and riveting, yet staring raven eyes. I can hear his words any night when I'm alone, and the sounds of the nocturnal carnal escapades have finally disappeared. There is only me and his words, whispering, the letters taking form, dancing in the light of the window where the stars poured in their luminescence.

"Behind the seventh veil of the world's illusion lies a direct connection with the infinite mind of our Creator. My coat is an attempt to capture the name of this Creator in symbolic form to allow us to contemplate it and to realize it. This is possible if one has lost consciousness completely and can follow this Creator's instructions down to the last detail."

I am an intelligent young woman, Clara. I must admit, however, that I had no inkling as to what this mystic was telling me. What of these seven veils? I knew of Salomé, the Jewess stepdaughter of Herod Antipas, and her stepmother Herodias. Salomé's mother was Mariamne, the daughter of Simon, the Jewish high priest. Herodias took offense when John the Baptist, the prophet, said she was disobeying God's law. She had married her husband Philips's brother, Herod Antipas, while Philip was still alive. Herod, on his birthday, wanted to see Salomé dance her specialty number wearing the seven veils.

Each veil, in its seductive order, was removed by her, as she swirled and leaped in front of the campfire to please the king and his entourage of nobles. When I told the rabbi about this, he laughed. He said behind her last veil was the Truth of the Divine Light. It was not carnal pleasure, as many philosophers believed, and it was not some passage into the hell of temptation, lust, and murder. For, as we know, the biblical Salomé had promised her mother the head from John the Baptist, who had insulted her marriage to the king. Herodias convinced Salomé to tell her husband she would dance for him at his palace revelry. In return, the king must cut the head from the false prophet John's shoulders and bring it to Herodias.

Now, I shall enumerate the explanation he gave me, which eventually evolved into the horrendous murder of the rabbi in Mexico. Many artists and philosophers of the Enlightenment were sympathetic to the dancer, Salomé. Herodias was an evil witch to force this impressionable and artistic young woman into doing what she did. Salomé was completely innocent, and her stepmother was to blame.

But then, in our present Romantic Era, the same assortment of literary and philosophical experts changed their minds. It was the time when each person was believed to have a unique and completely free will. Therefore, the Jewess could have refused her mother. She could have been courageous and stood up to her insulted parent. Instead, Salomé disobeyed her moral compass, which was controlled by Jewish law, and she danced a most wickedly vile and magical enchantment that cost John the Baptist his head.

At this moment, the rabbi grabbed me by my shoulders so abruptly that my head wobbled. His black pupils were slightly enlarged but were riveted in a concentrated stare into my windows of the soul. He explained the symbolism of each veil Salomé used in her dance, as it corresponded to his doctrine of finding what he called "The Zohar," the Divine Light of the Creator, Preserver, and Destroyer of this mystical realm. He said this dominion became illuminated once this final cataract veil was lifted from our eyes.

His words are also marked upon my brain as the Ten Commandments were marked upon the stone tablets by Yahweh, the unnameable. I shall always remember them. Especially now that the rabbi is dead. Before I began my dance that night here in Mexico, before I took my drug, Rabbi Sonenschein explained my purpose.

He told me the first veil I must cast off allowed the meditators upon my body to begin to work in the wisdom of internality, which is sweeter than honey and nectar, opens the eyes, and revives the soul. It allows you to find a hidden delight, sweet as the light to the eyes, and good for the soul, refining and illuminating your brain with good and upright qualities, tasting the flavor of the hidden Light of the next world in this world through the wisdom of *The Zohar*.

The second veil that I must loosen from around my undulating form, and allow to drift away on the evening's breeze, allowed viewers to feel the light and the future reward within their bodies. Their flesh would begin to tingle, their loins begin to moisten, and their brains would become infused with my brain. Their faces would come alive with new radiance and with an appreciation of all that was around them was infinite.

My third veil would be difficult. It must remain around my body the longest, clinging with static energy that seems to be welded to me most diabolically. I will curse and spit upon it, and still, it clings, like the first man who raped me in the orphanage, his orange body hair shaking particles of some secret earth mineral upon my nakedness. He had been digging for his fortune deep inside a hellish mine. Once I can repel the third veil, it will disintegrate, with a flash of lightning, and the viewers will be able to view the false façades worn by all humans in this dark world of trickery, shadows, and light. Their insight into the character and mental cruelties will be rejuvenating and will satisfy their urge to become omniscient and yet they will still cling to the passions of this life. There were three more veils to destroy before the ultimate goal was attained, he reminded me.

The rabbi's voice now sounds raspy in my mind. For it is not me, nor is it my subconscious brain that now remembers his instructions. No, it is his voice and his brain, even from the land of Sheol, of Forgetfulness and Death, which make me confess to you once more.

I was ordered by him to dance into the fourth realm in a circular spiral towards the infinite Seventh Seal veil, in the white-hot center core of my being. He said I would suddenly hear a female voice from outside my meditative cocoon. Are you not aware, voice, those female-loving men, when shown photographs of women, of similar beauty, will always select the ones whose pupils have been enlarged by mydriasis drugs? Such as peyote. This was what I used in my dance that night, voice. Voice? You are Clara Foltz, the attorney? Oh, there you are, and your lovely daughter, Bertha May.

The fourth veil I would cast off gave the audience a vision of the magnitude of the Creator's Dominion. Planetary solar systems would fill the sky in their minds. It was a moving, rolling tapestry that never stopped whirling, pulsing outward and then pulling inward once more. Expanding and constricting, spiraling galaxies, streaking comets, and exploding stars. To my audience, my legs would be seen moving beneath my final three veils. I was that vision of loveliness conditioned by billions of my sisters of the past, who, over the millennia, had learned to harness nature's neurological Eden to give dancers like me power over these hunter males.

Rabbi Sonenschein, the mystic, told me the gender of the dancer and watcher means nothing. Male watching female. Male watching male. Female watching male. Female watching female. It was the symbolism of what was behind these important veils, not the lust the dance might provoke in the heat of the moment. Although lust *was* a part of my appeal, in the beginning, he explained that the purpose of my dance was to transfix and reveal a deeper meaning to them. Men were usually much larger, much more conditioned by pain and their chosen role as tribal protectors. The continuing passage of infinite galactic possibilities, caused by shedding the fourth veil, will make my mouth water from thirst. I will know I still had to continue to dance for three more rounds, and my body will begin to sweat, the beads forming on the surface of my arms, legs, and torso like droplets on desert sands.

The fifth veil, he said, would create a frozen moment in time and space. Each of my observers would be able to fantasize about whatever it was made them happiest. It was as if the prospect of reaching the seventh veil made a fissure that created a dream within the mind that was not controlled by one's chronological age. Instead, the reality of seeing this thin, red piece of silk brush against my skin for the last time was a passageway to a moment of existential joy beyond the usual pain and suffering of the world's dramas. He said, if I watched them carefully, I would be able to notice a smile on each of their faces. It might be caused by a childhood toy or the first kiss during a spring shower. No matter what the moment was, it would suspend the viewer in a wonderful rapture. After I cast it aside, the person who caught this veil would be able to have the first wish he or she made come true.

I understand, Clara. That is a good description of what I was experiencing. I felt like I was in *A Thousand and One Arabian Nights*. Now that a murder has been committed, I wish I could go back in time and tell the rabbi I could not dance for him. Wait one moment. I don't remember. Did Shahrazad survive her ordeal of telling stories to the king? Yes? Thank you, little miss. I suppose there is hope for me yet.

I am not speaking too quickly for you to copy, am I, Bertha May? Does your mother employ you in her business quite often? You once pretended to be mad inside the Stockton State Insane Asylum? How exciting for you! I hope you won your case. I see. This story of mine is also becoming quite extended. Only two more veils, and then I can tell you what happened after I took the peyote.

I know as I reach the final veil, the reality of what happened while I was dancing was not in the realm of sensory perception. That is why I am attempting to explain the meaning of each according to the victim. When I tell you what I saw when I was hallucinating under the control of the drug, you will be able to compare and contrast these details with what your other witnesses experienced. I must emphasize the fact that it was my choice to take peyote and not Rabbi Sonenschein's. The fifth veil diverged most from what he told me would happen. I understand your analogy very well, Clara. Finding the truth is quite like peeling the layers from an onion. I shall now explain what I saw from the perspective of my state of hallucination while dancing to reveal the fifth, sixth, and seventh veils. I understand. The rabbi was shot during the reveal of the seventh veil, and I was also quite naked. Can you now understand why I believe my testimony may not be valuable to you? I was in the center of the onion, which, of course, has no center. Be prepared to set your sacred Suffrage Movement back at least two thousand years. Now I shall begin.

Chapter 3: Murderous Intent

Home of Drs. Fred and Charlotte Baker, Pt. Loma, San Diego, California, May 7, 1888.

Clara Foltz took the small sailboat that the Bakers used when commuting to San Diego from their house on Pt. Loma in Roseville. Theirs was the only residential property, and they had it built shortly after arriving in San Diego from Socorro, New Mexico, in January 1888. They had two children, Mary Caroline and Robert Henry, both of whom were attending boarding school in Massachusetts.

She knew both doctors were tireless supporters of their new community, and this necessitated the break-up of their family unit. However, as her client, Wyatt Earp, required some corroborative information concerning his role in the alleged murder of Rabbi Sonenschein, she was ready to seek out all possible avenues of discovery to make her defense clear inside a court of law.

The interviews with Ida Bailey and especially Wyatt's common-law wife, Josephine Marcus, were filled with some very mysterious elements, not least of which was the idea that the victim, Jerome Sonenschein, could have been the leader of some kind of nefarious cult out to destroy the houses of prostitution wherein his members worked.

Wyatt's only possible defense was to prove what Josephine told her was true. That her husband had shot the rabbi before he, or one of his cult members, could shoot him. It was completely self-defense. She was not going to ask the Bakers concerning the allegation by Josephine that Charlotte had informed Wyatt's wife about the connection between Earp, the rabbi, Ida Bailey, and Will Hunsaker. She wanted to discover if it were true during her investigation. Dr. Charlotte Baker, she knew, had just become a member of the local Purity Committee. The goal of this group, of mostly women, was to shut down the Stingaree District's prostitution, gambling, Chinatown opium sales, and other nefarious activities.

Clara also knew that as a female physician, Dr. Baker treated these prostitutes for their venereal diseases to protect the populace; so, she was, most likely, intimate with the madams such as Ida Bailey. Clara wanted to discover if Sonenschein's cult included other prostitute members, in addition to Ida Bailey. She also had an inkling that her client and Josephine Marcus were in contact with one or all of these madams to procure workers for their scheme to blackmail or pander for other dignitaries in San Diego, most especially and ironically, Anthony Comstock, the Postmaster of the United States.

Clara had recently written a rather scathing editorial, in her *Daily Bee*, about the Stingaree and how it was ruining lives. She knew what could happen to a community when the established officials kept such depravity under wraps, as had been done in San Francisco when she lived there. However, these activities of graft and crime were extremely profitable to their investors, and many of these same investors, she was discovering, partook of these same vices, with apparent gusto.

It was just such flagrant "gusto" that led to the murder of Rabbi Sonenschein. This was the "bigger picture" she wanted to prove to the court to save her client from the hangman. However, since first-degree murder required specific and malicious intent, and malice aforethought, on the part of Wyatt Earp, she might be able to show the jury how her client's actions were not malicious. If the person or persons behind his pulling the trigger on that day were responsible for the alleged malice, then Wyatt Earp was protecting himself from harm. Therefore, it would demonstrate to the jury that her client was defending himself and his wife and not performing a cold-blooded murder.

As the grizzled and paunchy captain, Juan Ramirez, sailed the twenty-foot boat into the breezes off the coast, Clara was below decks, and she was reading an article in the Southern California

Medical Society journal, written by Dr. Charlotte Baker, concerning what she termed the "medicine show atmosphere" prevailing in San Diego:

It is advertised that over half the people in this city are consumptive. They come here to escape the wet climates in other states. As a result, San Diego has more than its share of charlatans, who sell their nostrums, inhalators, and cures, such as a 'diet of dog meat.' It is in this climate that the local medical society struggles to legitimize its profession.

Clara also wanted to determine what was behind her client's relationship with Postal Inspector Anthony Comstock. Not only was the negotiated erotic fantasy with Comstock legally questionable, but if this diabolical enterprise were somehow connected to Sonenshein's group, then she might be able to formulate a defense for Wyatt. She did understand that the inferior sophistication of the law in San Diego was a far cry from what she experienced in San Francisco, so she supposed since the Comstock-Earp contract was to first take effect in Tijuana, Mexico, along with Earp's Hundred-Round Fight promotion, then the agreement could be legal.

The weather was superb in May, and as she was given a helping hand from the captain to step off the ramp onto the pier, she noted that there was no morning fog the way it had been for her years in San Francisco. There was, however, a frequent marine layer of dark clouds that came ashore in the evenings, which hampered visibility.

She thanked Captain Ramirez and gave him an additional quarter after the Mexican drove the buggy up to the Baker residence. She wore what her daughter, Trella Evelyn, in San Francisco would call "an ancient relic" dress, a yellow, full-bustle affair, with chiffon lace at the sleeves and neck and a matching bonnet to cover her reddish-brown hair, swirled in its usual bun and fastened in the back with one of her friend Ah Toy's Chinese dragon hair combs. She was missing her separated family already, but her purchase of the daily newspaper, and her need to earn a living in the burgeoning real estate boom, had caused her to relocate.

She now had her office in the Nesmith-Greely Building on Fifth Avenue between E and F Streets. She spent her time working on her newspaper, such as it was, and doing her legal work. This Earp case would help pay the bills so that she could wire some money to her daughter, Trella Evelyn, who was still in school at Berkeley in San Francisco, majoring in Dramatic Arts.

The house was a white stucco A-Frame, two stories tall, with a white picket fence and chickens pecking inside the yard. Behind the house was a barn to keep said chickens, along with a small adjoining shack that served as a smokehouse for curing meat, she surmised, from her own experience on the farm in Iowa.

Those were her teaching days when she was plopping out her children, one by one, serving as a prize Holstein for her Civil War veteran husband, Jeremiah, who later deserted her and her five children, and thus began her slow, trudging accomplishments leading to her law degree. She had been the first woman in California to be admitted to the California Bar, and she always joked that if the population had not been five males to one female, she may not have been chosen. She could see her five children from the window, standing on the sidewalk, and the five male bar examiners that day were so astounded to watch her pass the examination the first time that she was given the certificate to practice the same day, without ever having attended a day of law school.

She saw Dr. Charlotte Baker standing in the shadows behind the screen door. As the woman swung the door open, the wide, beaming smile on her face was quite welcoming. Clara stepped inside to see that her husband, Fred, the other doctor, was standing in the foyer as well. They were both expecting her, and had, most likely read about the case in the community newspapers, of which there were over twenty, the largest of which was the *Union*. Her husband, she noticed, had a copy of this paper tucked under the arm of his brown frock coat.

"Mrs. Foltz! Did Captain Ramirez keep our boat steady for you? I trust you didn't get seasick. He tries to keep close to the coast, but we can get some rough seas in our not-so-passive Pacific. Come. We must sit down. I shall bring out the tea and biscuits. We want to hear all about your case. Freddy and I have read about it in this morning's *Union*. It's quite ghastly. Never have we had such a tragedy that involved so many prominent citizens in our community."

As she sat down on the long leather divan in the small living room, she smiled over at Freddy, who had maneuvered himself into his favorite rocker beside the roaring fireplace to their right. He took out a black briar pipe, brought some matches from his vest coat pocket, and twisted one off, struck it against the sandpaper, and it burst into a flame. His walrus mustaches looked as if they might also ignite, but he twisted his upper lip to the side, just so, and he was easily able to puff on the pipe. While the flame found its proper home inside the bowl, she could soon smell the sweet aroma of cherry-flavored tobacco, which reminded her of her father's brand. Her husband, Jeremiah, had smoked cigars, which, to her, was a much more uncivilized practice.

"A woman attorney. I must say, no females are practicing in the courts of San Diego, about whom I am presently aware. You must be quite proud of your accomplishment, Mrs. Foltz." She noticed that Dr. Fred did not exactly have the same wide smile as his wife. His forced grin resembled more of a boy's teenage smirk.

"Don't mind Freddy. He also believes my being an obstetrician is one small step above a midwife, even though I graduated first in my medical class, and Fred was in the last quarter of his. Isn't that so, darling?"

Charlotte set the tea tray down on the mahogany table in front of the divan and began to immediately pour the steaming hot liquid into two cups. After she had placed the two cups and saucers in front of each of them, she handed her a plate of ginger snaps and nodded toward her husband. "Freddy already had his black coffee. He also abhors ginger snaps. Says they can harm the lining of the colon. Have you ever heard such nonsense?"

"Thank you, Mrs. Baker. You and your husband have such a nice home. Do you mind if we begin on a first-name basis? I feel I know you both already, after having read your biographical information at the library and learned from Madam Ida Bailey that you both have treated her ladies in the past."

Clara noted they both wore spectacles, and at 35 and 34 years of age, they had the youthful and optimistic attitudes of two people who took their lives and occupations quite seriously. Fred, a general practitioner, had helped found the San Diego Zoological Society and the Marine Biological Institute near the beach on San Diego Bay. He kept many species of animals and was known to do a lot of dissection, blood work, and other research to prevent diseases in these animals. As for Charlotte, she was prominent in the local Suffrage Society, as well as being the first woman elected President of the San Diego Medical Society. Clara hoped that her proposal would not be too startling to their refined characters. However, she did note that Charlotte had spent her internship working to help women in trouble in Michigan, where she obtained her medical degree.

Clara leaned forward to make her proposition. She hoped her instincts were correct about the Bakers. Whether they agreed to participate in her investigation to formulate an alibi for her client, Wyatt Earp could mean the difference between convincing a jury of his innocence and allowing social prejudice once more to quash her courtroom experience in Criminal Law.

"As you perhaps are aware, my client, Mr. Wyatt Earp, was a man of the law. He was a Marshal who, quite often, because of the nature of frontier life, had to confront other men who believed they could make their laws, for their benefit. I understand you are scientists and medical professionals, and that you must also confront a society that has little or no technical experience with how medical treatments have evolved on the East Coast."

"Yes, we both face those challenges daily. As you know, our community of bachelor miners, real estate speculators, and gamblers outnumbers our female population by quite a bit, even though I am personally attempting to remedy the strength of our women in my way." Charlotte smiled. "Freddy is with me on this as well, even though he finds more interest in the animal kingdom than our homo sapiens."

"I don't believe Charles Darwin was correct when he said we had made the leap from chimpanzee and gorilla to mankind. Many of the men I treat have tarried a bit too long in the jungles of this Wild West to be readily tamed." She saw that Fred Baker had that schoolboy smirk again.

"My client has been accused of the intentional murder of Rabbi Jerome Sonenschein, a gentleman who made his living from harboring several ladies who were, quite possibly, in the employ of the madams who ran houses of ill repute inside the Stingaree District. Are you familiar with these madams, by any chance? I was only able to interview one of these women, and her name is Ida Bailey. I must admit that my interview with Miss Bailey did not give me much in the way of hard evidence for my client. She spoke more about her personality and history as an orphan than she did about what occurred on the day in question. I intend to resume my inquiry with her shortly."

Charlotte picked up her teacup, blew across its hot liquid, and sipped delicately, her lips not moving nor did she make any sound. She then set the cup back on its saucer on the table and smiled at Clara.

"I am well known to those in the Stingaree, as you call it. I prefer calling that vicinity by its proper name, Sodom and Gomorrah. The only reason I treat those poor women is that I know if I did not, then the diseases they might pass on could inflict the scarcity of established families we have in San Diego. Not all men are like my Freddy. They tend to stray from the nest when they believe they can do so without being caught in the act. Many of these men, the sailors and roustabouts, and the Chinamen, simply prey upon the wealthier visitors to that neighborhood, including, I am told, your client, Mr. Earp, who owns and operates three gambling halls in that area." Charlotte frowned. "I do not envy your predicament, Clara. What makes you believe he is innocent?"

It was her turn to frown. "I am an attorney, Charlotte. I am not predisposed to believe one way or the other. It is the law that says he is innocent until proven guilty. As his sworn representative in a court of law, I must defend him to the best of my ability, unless he is proved to have lied to me. Then, and only then, would I recuse myself."

"Why are you here, Clara? What can we do to help your client?"

It was Fred who seemed to be receptive now. She turned

toward him.

"I believe Wyatt was in more trouble than he even knows. His wife told me about a scheme they had to provide Postal Inspector Anthony Comstock, and possibly others, with some kind of erotic playground in Tijuana. They executed a contract to that effect, and I believe the victim, Rabbi Sonenschein, and his cult members, many of whom were prostitutes, were threatening in some way to blackmail or even kill Earp."

Charlotte gasped. "My goodness! Such depravity exists in San Diego?"

She nodded. "Yes, and what Sarah Marcus told me about this Sonenschein made me want to investigate his group more completely. If I can establish an alibi of self-defense for my client, by questioning these former members of the Kabbalah sect, and perhaps tying them to the contract between the Earps and Anthony Comstock, then my story just may be enough to convince a jury of his innocence."

Fred Baker laughed. "You want to bring out a story concerning some erotic blackmail scheme against the United States Postmaster? You'll be driven out of San Diego, Clara. This is not San Francisco. The police officials, and even the mayor, Hunsaker, might be keeping the Stingaree District in business, but they would never admit it. I am afraid your client, Wyatt Earp, Madam Ida Bailey, and the Jew victim, Sonenschein, and their relationships, will have to remain a secret. That is if you wish to remain employed in this town."

She noticed Charlotte stir in her seat on the divan.

"Now Freddy. Don't be so harsh. What is it you want from us, Clara? I do know many of these madams, and I also treat the people of Chinatown. How does our medical expertise involve us in your plan? Frankly, I believe it would be in the best interests of San Diego if we could pull back the shroud of infamy over what goes on in the Stingaree. I, for one, am willing to help you."

Clara smiled at her. "You understand my ambitions completely, Charlotte. I do believe what we might discover could go a long way to show this community exactly why the Stingaree should be exposed for what it is. If San Diego wants to become a civilized place for families to grow and prosper, then we would be doing the town a favor with our investigation."

Fred also stirred. "I am afraid I cannot participate. You see, these gentlemen, and especially the mayor, Will Hunsaker, would not support me and my effort to establish the Zoological Society. I want to bring us into the larger world of educated enlightenment. Only people like Hunsaker can make this happen, I am afraid." He stood up, puffed twice on his pipe, placed his right hand on his lapel, and walked off into his den in the back of the house.

"Go on," said Charlotte. "I want to help. Don't worry about Freddy. I shall bring him around. You know how these things are, don't you, Clara? We women must endure."

Clara clenched her jaws. "I am happy he left us for the moment. I want to explain some intricacies of the law to you. I have not won a case yet because I have always refrained from fighting the way my best friend and fellow lawyer, Laura de Force Gordon does. This time, I shall take the bull by the horns, so to speak."

"Well? Is there room on your bull for me?" Charlotte's hazel eyes behind her spectacles widened with anticipation.

"I believe there is. You see, the burden of proof shall be on the prosecutor. He, or she, must prove to the twelve male jurors that my client not only shot the victim, Rabbi Sonenschein, but there must also have been a malicious intent on his part, what's called 'malice aforethought,' in legal terminology. We shall endeavor to show that his intent was not there on the day in question."

"How exciting! And, why was Mr. Earp not malicious when he shot the poor rabbi?" Charlotte pursed her lips.

"I believe that, as we used to say back on the farm in Iowa, there was a bigger bull in the herd. Wyatt shot him because there was something even more threatening about being exposed. Something bigger than both the Kabbalist and the gambler. The rabbi was posing a direct threat to Mr. Earp's life, and he shot him in self-defense. We must discover what that something is, Dr. Baker. Because, if my woman's intuition is correct, it could be a threat to our entire community here in San Diego."

Chapter 4: Ida Speaks Again

New Town, San Diego, CA, May 8, 1888.

It was Clara's concern about going into the Stingaree District that caused her to ask Dr. Baker about hiring a possible tour guide and escort. As her companion worked there quite regularly, treating the variety of prostitutes who plied their trade therein, the doctor was, immediately, quite accommodating. During their luncheon at the Grand Horton Hotel, they were discussing family and, of course, the present trial discovery into the murder of the Kabbalah rabbi, Jerome Sonenschein.

A *Union* newspaper reporter, Rand Paulson, had already seen them together, that morning, walking from the horse trolley down Fifth Avenue toward her office inside the Nesmith-Greely Building. The scribe immediately wrote a feature article, and Clara was reading it, as her son, David Milton, had purchased a copy of the afternoon edition, and he brought it to her inside the hotel. He grinned wickedly, as he handed it to her and sat down at their table.

Her effeminate and overly dramatic son was one of the three children living in San Diego with her. Now age seventeen, he was an inch taller than she, and he was very handsome. His reddish-brown hair was pomaded into a rakish pompadour, and he wore mascara, rouge and a pale-rose lipstick. He wore a Chinese red *changshan*, a body-length shirt with gold parrots emblazoned upon it, and his Civil War veteran father, Jerimiah, had given him the incongruous black cavalry boots that were crossed at the ankles beneath the table. At home, she permitted David to wear female attire, as her psychologist friends advised it was best to give him psychological comfort.

Bertha May, eighteen, her stenographer, was seated to her right, wearing a blue spring frock with white lace and a matching bonnet. Virginia Knox, now twelve, was attending the local public school. Her two eldest offspring, Trella Evelyn, twenty-two, and Samuel Cortland, twenty, were living with her life-long friend, Ah Toy, on Nob Hill, and attending Berkeley College in San Francisco.

David had been kidnapped, last year, along with First Lady Frances Cleveland, during her case in Washington D.C. He was enamored of the actress, Sarah Bernhardt, who had befriended him during that case, as she was also kidnapped later on in the ordeal, along with her legal partner, Laura de Force Gordon.

During their lunch of veal cutlet, wine, and fresh salad greens, David summarized aloud to her and Dr. Baker about the article, even though she was now reading it. "This cad, Mr. Paulson, calls you both the female Sherlock Holmes and Dr. Watson of the Wild West." He looked up into the rafters of the hotel, inhaled, rolled his brown eyes, and exhaled. "Shortridge Foltz and Dr. Baker. As my good friend, the Divine Sarah Bernhardt would say, *son très spécial*."

They all had quite a laugh about the story during their walk back to her office. The street was busy with the usual assortment of horse-drawn trolleys, merchant carts, and buggies. The odors of sewage from the migrant hordes living along the San Diego River wafted, seemingly ever-present, in the air. This pollution control problem, along with the Stingaree, often came up at the City Council meetings headed by Mayor Hunsaker.

She and Dr. Baker were alone inside the office once more, and they continued with their business discussion about how to maneuver their investigation of suspects inside the Stingaree. When she again asked about the possible escort, Charlotte smiled and adjusted her spectacles. Clara could see a humorous twinkle in the doctor's hazel eyes as she pulled out a photograph from her purse and slid it over to her on the desktop and said, "Why, of course! I have just the person for this task. His name is Li Wei. He lives on Third Street, in Chinatown, and he does a lot of my medical deliveries to these bordellos and shacks along the waterfront. I have read about your Barbary Coast in San Francisco. We have its twin right here in San Diego."

She leaned forward to address the younger woman. At thirty-seven, Clara was tall, and she still wore bustles to aid in countering her wide hips, protruding stomach, and most especially her puckered and veined legs. She believed her premature deformities displayed the "curse" of being a fifteen-year-old bride and child-bearing wife on the frontier farmlands of Iowa and Indiana during the post-Civil War years.

"Yes, I am well aware of this. The small Chinatown you have here currently has around two hundred citizens, and there is also a much smaller community of Japanese, is there not?"

Dr. Baker nodded and pointed to the photograph in her hand. "Mr. Li is my favorite delivery person in the Stingaree. Many such bicycle delivery people are employed to carry food and medicines back and forth from New Town San Diego into the slums of sin and debauchery. Li Wei, whose name means 'great,' actually comes from a very literate and wealthy family back in China. We enjoy sharing tidbits concerning Chinese and American medical practices, as he formerly studied to become a doctor in Hong Kong at one point."

"How interesting," she said. "My former law partner, Laura de Force Gordon, defended a San Francisco Chinatown midwife, last year, during her criminal trial for manslaughter. The case concerned the death of a sixteen-year-old, half-Navaho, pregnant child named Penelope Farmer. The poor girl died during a botched abortion treatment. The midwife's medicine included the use of acupuncture, which proved to be the evidentiary difference between the woman's guilt and innocence during the trial. And, the key witness for the State was this midwife's supervisor, a Dr. Liu Wei."

"Why, yes, the name is quite common in China. Acupuncture is exactly what Mr. Li and I discuss. He is well versed in Chinese medical procedures and the ancient science of hypnotism. I recently gave a presentation to my group of doctors on the use of this mesmerist treatment on victims of consumption, of which there are many cases in San Diego."

Charlotte reached out to accept the returned photo from Clara. "He is quite handsome, don't you think, Clara? For an Asian. He just turned forty, so perhaps you might find him interesting enough to have him escort you to one of our many dance halls some evening—in New Town, of course. He is quite popular with many of the ladies, as most of these men in San Diego are more interested in enjoying the pool halls and gambling dens and seeking out the women inside Ida Bailey's Canary Cottage. But I digress. When would you like to leave on our tour?"

"Can you ask Mr. Li Wei if we can do it tomorrow morning? Would nine be all right? I must complete my interview with Ida Bailey this afternoon. Bertha May will be going with me, of course, to transcribe." She smiled. "I'm afraid I don't have much free time to cavort in the evenings. But thank you for thinking of me."

Dr. Baker stood up. "I believe that will be fine. I shall check with him, and on my patients in the Stingaree, while you are interviewing Miss Bailey. I would be extremely wary of what that woman tells you. In my opinion, she is quite daft, and she would bed down with the Devil himself to protect her coven of harlot witches from any danger."

She stood up and walked her new partner to the door. Instead of feeling like Holmes and Watson, however, she was beginning to feel more like Don Quixote and Sancho Panza.

"I thought you were concerned about your patients, Charlotte. Even the females who work in the world's oldest profession, for Ida Bailey. Most likely they are there because of their social downfall caused by being ruled over by these lusting patriarchs."

Charlotte turned to confront her as she opened the door. "Quite right, Clara. I do sympathize, but my Christian faith and my wifely duties—especially as concerns my Freddy—make me constantly wary of how far these women—especially their leaders—will go to get their way with men. It is not the women, per se, whom I distrust the most, but the way they can break up families who are the ultimate victims of such activities. Some men even marry these wenches, can you imagine? Good day to you, and don't believe what you read in the newspapers. We shall prove them all wrong; don't you think?"

Clara smiled. "I will tell you once this case is over. I will meet you both here tomorrow morning, a little before nine."

***

C lara told Ida Bailey to meet her at the City Library, where she had reserved a private room. When she and her daughter arrived, there the madam was, sitting inside the enclosed room, which was not much larger than a police interrogation enclosure. If she were on the correct trail, Miss Bailey might be able to give her some clues to track down the party who might have caused this mayhem to take place.

"Ida, I am so happy you could come. Have you been waiting long?" She sat down across from the young woman, and Bertha sat down in one of the side chairs. Her daughter immediately took out her stenographer's pad, and had her pencil poised, ready to take notes.

The madame looked clear-eyed, as she nodded and smiled, so perhaps her elocution might be better than it was the day before in Tijuana. Although, after what Dr. Baker was telling her, Ida's condition might be in a psychological state of flux. Either way, she would heed the doctor's warning about Ida's proclivity to tell tales in order to protect her business. She must get to the heart of what she needed to know for the sake of her client, Wyatt Earp. She assumed her new "de Force Gordon" legal aspect, flexed her jaws, and began.

"First, I wish to thank you for the information you gave me yesterday. Have you been able to make your memory any clearer about what you witnessed? As you recall, my eagle's eye vantage point above the arena was not conducive to a good look at what took place. Since you were right there in front of the crowd, on the stage, I would imagine you could see much more clearly what happened." She folded her arms across her chest and took a deep breath. "Try to finish your story, to the best of your ability."

She now knew that Ida's testimony thus far was quite different from Josephine Marcus's. According to Miss Bailey, it was Anthony Comstock who had come to Tijuana to entrap Ida and her ladies, possibly to arrest them. However, Josie and Earp had told her that they were there to carry through with their plan to proceed with their secret contract with Mr. Comstock to allow him to frolic in some kind of erotic playground. She needed to get to the truth of the matter once and for all. Will Hunsaker may also be suspect in profiting from Earp's plan.

The harlots of San Diego might also be employed in this scheme. Rabbi Sonenschein, who was, according to Bailey, her lover and the leader of the Kabbalah cult, wanted to save the prostitutes from being used in any sexual ventures, including her own. Jerome Sonenschein, conceivably, was there to stop Wyatt Earp and his plan to profit from the erotic fantasies of Postmaster General Comstock and any other of the town's interested parties to this vainglorious scheme. She needed to prove that Wyatt was indeed protecting his own life when he pulled the trigger of his Buntline special.

"I was not clear-headed that day, as I told you. When I was doing my veil dance, I was looking right at Rabbi Sonenschein. I could see his smile, under his black beard. That meant he was pleased with my dance, and that was all that mattered at that moment. I was what one would call 'transfixed.' I did not see Mr. Earp fire the shot if that's what you wish to know. I would assume you have police who shall determine that fact for you, correct? What I saw in my addled mind's eye was my teacher's head exploding with a burst of skull, blood, and brain expanding. To be quite honest, I thought he had become another galaxy, at last, just the way he taught us girls. He told us when the *ein sof* was realized, it would empower one to create an entirely new universe of personal existence."

The mix of objective, quite graphic description, and fantastic delusion made Clara wary. However, since she had never experienced reality from within the delusion of a drug such as peyote, she did not know if Miss Bailey was hallucinating properly or not. She made a mental note to ask either Dr. Baker or to wire her friend, Dr. McFarland, concerning its actual effects.

"I understand. How many members were there of the sect which followed the rabbi? Could you make a list of names for me? It's rather important to my case representing Mr. Earp. Also, it may be of interest to you, I am being accompanied in my investigation into the Stingaree by Dr. Charlotte Baker. She has agreed to assist me, and she can help me verify your list, among other, more technical and strategic duties."

Ida Bailey's face turned crimson. Her pale blue dress became an instant contrast, as she stood up, flailing her arms and knocking her bonnet from her curly-red hair onto the floor of the library conference room. She did not pick it up. Instead, she whirled around, stumbled against the door, fumbled for the gold doorknob, and pulled the creaking door wide, so violently, the glass pane trembled. She screamed, "No! Not my dancers! I am Asherah!"

"Where are you going, Ida? I have not finished my questioning. Are you refusing to help me? I shall get a court order if you refuse. You do understand that, don't you? Who is Asherah?"

She stood up, but to no avail. The woman who had been so talkative and vociferous about her fabulous history, the day before, now had become a grim picture of defensive anger when asked to give personal information about prostitutes, or others, who might have been members of Jerome Sonenschein's cult. What could that secrecy mean? Was she attempting to protect their honor? Hardly. She must know the court would force her to testify, even if it was for the State. No. There was something more sinister at play here, and Clara knew it. It would take some exploration with Charlotte Baker, and there was also the testimony of Josephine Marcus concerning the possible antagonism between this cult and what the Earps and perhaps Mayor Hunsaker had negotiated with Anthony Comstock.

"Come, Bertha. We must be home before twilight. Your sister will be waiting. I also have a job for you and David Milton. I dare say, it will appeal to your adventurous spirits. I shall tell you what it is on our walk to the trolley."

As they walked out of the library, Clara kept picturing the figure of young Ida Bailey, sitting at a table in the back, alone, pouring over the books and magazines, imagining her revenge against the wolfish men in San Diego. Ida's tale about the Red Riding Hood Grandmother, devoured and living inside those wolfish gentlemen, reminded her of the fantasies of poor Penny Farmer and her Navaho Skinwalker witches of revenge. Was Ida Bailey another, perhaps more mentally deranged, version of a witch? The possibility was certainly there, and so she would be closely monitoring her responses from this moment forward.

***

The next morning came after fretful tossing and turning during the night. Clara's children were so anxious about their new employment in this case, at her behest, they kept her awake much of the night, climbing about their room inside the small, one-story house on Fourth Avenue. They were getting their disguises prepared for the assignments. David was especially irking, as he would dash into her bedroom at strange moments to show what he had chosen to wear.

She had researched what Ida Bailey had called herself in the library. Asherah. It was the name of the ancient female consort to Yahweh, the Hebrew God. Could this have any special importance to her case?

Now, as she rose from her drowsiness, the two of them were standing at the foot of the four-poster bed, ready for inspection. It shouldn't have been such an arduous undertaking, as all they were going to be doing was delivery work inside the Stingaree. As bicyclists, it would be their duty to visit specific houses of ill repute to see if they could overhear any gossip concerning members or prospective members of the current or former group known as the Kabbalah Mystical Society. Besides, they were also to keep their eyes and ears attuned to any mention of experiences in Mexico concerning the erotic playground mentioned in the contract between Wyatt Earp and Post Master General Anthony Comstock.

Finally, and she did not believe this was very probable if her children heard about or even saw any of the following gentlemen: Mayor Will Hunsaker, Anthony Comstock, Police Chief Bill McCormick, or Dr. Fred Baker. Yes. She had listed Dr. Baker, as she had become suspicious of him because of her earlier interview at the Baker residence at Pt. Loma in Roseville. He had acted strangely, and she also sensed there was some antipathy going on between the two doctors, even though Charlotte seemed to be in a state of denial about something.

"I think you both look marvelously outfitted! However, I don't believe you shall require the road cap and goggles, David. You are not Bertha Benz on the first road trip in Germany. There is dust in the road, but I think plain glass spectacles will suffice. You must have a clear vision to see peripherally if you're going to be my spies in the field."

"But, mother, they match brilliantly with my leather flared Jodhpurs. I shall be drummed out of the delivery corps for my *gouache accouterments*!" Her son, with some disdain, took off the black leather cap with goggles and tossed them onto the bed. "I don't need any!" He crossed his arms across his thin chest.

"You are almost eighteen, David. Be more reflective. Bertha has the name of the aforementioned female road warrior, but she has chosen correctly. You both look dashing in your Jodhpurs. Dr. Baker told me that's what all the delivery personnel wear. It sets them off from the *hoi polloi*."

"Very well. Our mission is to keep a record of anything we hear about those named gentlemen you gave us. Should we follow them if we see them cavorting amongst the damsels?" David's eyebrows rose and fell. "By that look, I would say not. Come, Bertha, my dear. We may have time to get an iced cream at the day's end."

She kissed them both and watched as they rode off down Fourth Avenue, on their red bicycles with the large wheels, and then they turned right onto India to go over to Fifth, the main thoroughfare. It was comforting having them willing to take time off from school to assist in her case. She was, at first, hesitant, as David had been the victim of the recent kidnapping, as had Bertha, during her portrayal as an insane child at the Stockton State Asylum case. The fact was that she did not have the money to pay any professionals, and her children were more than eager to assist her.

As she was standing at the door, she saw Charlotte and a man coming up the road in a one-horse black buggy. The horse was black, but the man was, of course, Chinese. She had always wondered about the racist affixation of these people as being the "Yellow Peril." The racist Chinese Exclusion Act was still being enforced by President Cleveland and his administration, and the public and press had often taken it upon themselves to characterize the ancient Chinese people as backward pagans and superstitious and yellow-complexioned gamblers and purveyors of illicit narcotics.

The man at the reins of Charlotte's transportation was neither yellow nor was he abnormally slant-eyed or Mongoloid. He was probably the most handsome human specimen she had ever laid eyes upon. She almost practiced a dance step or two as he stepped down from the carriage, walked around it, his smiling face riveted upon hers, and helped Dr. Baker down to the ground, which, to her way of thinking, was beginning to tremble a bit.

After being carefully escorted into the buggy's carriage by this man with the dark, slicked-back hair that glittered in the San Diego morning sunshine, she composed herself. She knew at this point in her investigation everyone was considered a possible suspect; or, at least a potential informational conduit. Therefore, she remonstrated her inner passions and spoke to him.

"Hong Kong is one of the most progressive cities in Asia, is it not? The British have always shown an interest in its successes from what I've read. You must be proud to be educated there." She watched his face. It reminded her of her girlhood fantasies while reading about the Kings and Princes of the ancient Forbidden City of mainland China. His straight-backed, yet interested nods, as she talked to him, made her corset feel looser, and her mind began to wander, her eyes moving slowly, as he spoke, to those slightly swollen lips and the small mustache riding so regally above them.

His British accent was so startling that it made her cross her legs beneath her bustled dress in protective anxiety.

"Yes. Quite so. However, as I am certain you must be aware, there are those in China who have continued to exploit the Han in the south, and they make a mockery of justice. These poor emigrants are beaten down by both sides until they are creatures without a home. Ex-patriots searching with their minds and hearts to find some meaning and purpose in life. Not the kind of social bearing one expects of new citizens to a country that prides itself on accepting all those who can become integrated into a freedom-loving nation."

She recalled her long discussions with Ah Toy, the bordello Madame, and artist of San Francisco's Chinatown. Her Uncle Pete was certainly one of those Tong gang overlords about which this Li Wei was referencing.

"Mr. Li wants to begin a medical practice of his own someday," Dr. Baker pointed out. "He has learned quickly from me. My husband first met him in England, as he was assisting Dr. Bruce, a research scientist there. I believe he can now recite most of the remedies and treatments I recommend for the usual maladies we confront here on the southwestern frontier. Yes, he is quite a quick study, and I would be more than happy to recommend him to the board someday soon."

He smiled, and his white teeth were straight and glassy. "But today I am helping the famous detectives, attorney Shortridge-Foltz and Dr. Baker. I have lived in the Stingaree for twenty years, as I came here at nineteen. Mrs. Baker has helped me continue my medical studies, and I have been diligent in my assistance to her."

She smiled. "I am so happy you can take us on this tour, Mr. Li. It is very crucial to my client's defense," she said.

"Sadly, we must keep the bodies healthy of citizens who, through no fault of their own, are found to be caught in the vicious and sinful snares of Sodom and Gomorrah," Charlotte reflected.

Li Wei continued in his lilting tone, "If like Lot, the people who manipulate the sins in the Stingaree make evil choices, then they will lose in the final battle of Siddim. And, just as Lot was kidnapped and forced to leave, they must also not look back when commanded to leave, as Lot's wife did, because God will turn them into pillars of salt, or of opium, or lust, or of dice. These are all symbols, Dr. Baker has told me, of the practices which can destroy a civilized community. I have come to America to be free, yes, but freedom without responsibility for others is antithetical to my values as a person from China and as a new citizen of this wonderful country."

Clara understood his passion. It was the same passion Ah Toy showed her, and, to a lesser extent, her former lover, and former Englishman, Captain of Detectives, Isaiah Lees.

"Lead on, then, Mr. Li, or should I say, Mr. Lot! Into the den of iniquity!"

***

The Stingaree District, San Diego, CA, May 8, 1888.

She decided not to inform Dr. Baker about what her children were doing. As a conservative and proper medical practitioner, Clara thought it best that she did not risk showing the woman her more impetuous and daring side. At least, not at this juncture in the case. If they were able to uncover the information she hoped would lead to a not-guilty verdict of Wyatt Earp, then she would certainly inform her. Also, since it was Josephine who had informed her about Charlotte Baker telling Wyatt's wife about Ida Bailey and the other prostitutes being part of the Kabbalah group, this Christian Temperate might even be anti-Semitic, which would not be conducive to an impartial discovery in their case.

"Ladies, this is the southwest corner of Fifth and K. So now begins the Gaslamp Quarter or what we insiders call the Stingaree. Why, might you ask, is it called this? For most of us, including the Chinese fishermen who first landed in the 1870s, the docks at the end of Fifth were where the first whore houses existed. It is said that the sailors who would partake of the sins therein, would roll off the cots in a drunken stupor, only to be awaked by the sting from the flashing barbs on the tails of the small rays, which flowed by the dozens, over their bodies, when the tides came in. Ergo, the place was named Stingaree because later, when the sailors and others were rolled for their money, in the bars that also grew on the waterfront, they were being stung differently!"

"Mr. Li, we need to see as many of the places where the men might go to entertain themselves. I want to get a clear picture of how my client, Wyatt Earp, would have ventured out and become acquainted with these businesses, such as they are." She looked out at the scenery, and as they drove past the rougher areas, she could see several swaying sailors, and men in dirty frock coats, clutching at lampposts, bottles in hand, cursing or singing loudly at the passing carts, horses, and buggies, including theirs.

The odors of beer, urine, and fried foods wafted over them, and it was so pungent that it made her eyes water. She could hear music coming from the saloons he pointed out, and they were certainly not lyrics that made you think of romance unless the proclivity was to be besotted and ribald.

As they passed over to Island, and down to the L Street tidelands, Li stopped and pointed toward a group of shanties near the ocean. "Those are the L Street tidelands, and they go to the foot of Eleventh, near the old Gumbo Slough. See those shanties and wooden cabins? They teeter on stilts above the water. That's Pirates Cove, where people live on bread and barracuda."

"Real pirates?" she asked.

"Only the best money can buy. The Stingaree can be dangerous. They say the guano poachers, the longshoremen--who shovel sand ballast for a dollar a day--and other denizens of the cove, can make a night at the Stingaree appear to be a lemonade soiree. However, if you amble down these unlit dirt tracks, laced with smashed bottles and wee hours' vomit, you may never amble back."

"That's not an exaggeration. My husband and I have treated many such victims of the skullduggery that goes on here," Dr. Baker pointed out.

"Ever since Alonzo Horton built a $50,000 wharf at the foot of Fifth in 1869, I was told, there have been saloons at Fifth and K. In the early 1870s, Johnny Petty's Last Chance, that rough-hewn long bar with few amenities, is still over there, on the southwest corner. The whiskey tastes like sweetened turpentine. Those of a more health-conscious bent can chase shots with water drawn from local wells. But a glass of that aquatic is browner than the liquor."

"How many houses of prostitution would you suppose there are?" Clara asked.

"In the Stingaree? I would expect there are now one hundred and ten to one hundred twenty. Most are just lean-to-shacks near the waterfront, with the names of the girls on the door outside each one. Of course, I'm not including the high-class houses of Ida Bailey and Mrs. Goldstein. These are the boom years. The Stingaree has so many saloons they need gimmicks to stand out. Madam Mamie Goldstein's The Turf, right over there, is a bar with an upstairs parlor house, and it offers culture. Goldstein hires the organist from the German Lutheran church to play familiar hymns to exude a moral uplift."

Both women laughed.

"And here it is, the end of the tour, and we have returned to the New Town section of San Diego. The Canary Cottage of Ida Bailey." Li pointed toward a yellow, one-story house with a white picket fence surrounding it. It was right next door to the classiest hotel in San Diego, the Grand Horton. Clara didn't realize Ida had her place outside of the Stingaree.

"Do you take care of all these whore houses?" She turned to address Dr. Baker again.

"No. Fred assists me, and I do employ nurses. But Li is my only medical courier. I trust him to get the orders correct from the pharmacy, as it can be a matter of life and death with some of these cases." Charlotte frowned. "You won't believe the myths that crop up here in the Stingaree. Many of these poor girls are former slaves and immigrants. Chinese girls. Girls from the Caribbean Islands, Haiti, the Dominican Republican, and the Philippines. They might speak different languages, but coitus is the only language these men understand, and this is what they pay for. In more ways than one."

"More ways?" She was unexpectedly naïve, considering her friendship with a Chinatown madame for thirty years.

"Why, the diseases of the trade, of course. Gonorrhea, the consumption, and the worst of them all, syphilis. I try to get them to use prophylactics, but many of the poorer girls get more money from their Johns if they allow them to enter without protection. It's a vicious and deadly cycle for these women." She could see Charlotte's eyes tear up. Her opinion of the doctor began to change.

"I want to tell you something, Charlotte. I expect you might have thought me too outlandish and irresponsible, but I think I must inform you so we can be on equal footing during this case." She leaned forward.

"Yes? Very well. You can tell me anything, dear. I am a doctor and a confidant about more things than you can imagine, probably in your wildest dreams." Charlotte's eyes grew wide and expectant.

"My two children are spying on the houses, acting as delivery drivers, just like Mr. Li. I need to find out who are members of Rabbi Sonenschein's group and if any city officials might be involved."

She started, as Charlotte slapped her on the knee, quite hard. "I should have known as much! You are also a journalist and public speaker. What better way to insinuate yourself into our sin city than to enter it with food deliveries? As you and I know, being around women and men when they eat is paramount to being at a family dinner table. You will, indeed, strike gold. Good for you, Clara Foltz, attorney, and detective. Good for you!"

As they drove up Fifth Avenue, toward her house on Fourth, she felt better. Perhaps she and Dr. Baker *could* become investigators to rival the fictional Holmes and Watson. Her mind was already forming some ideas that made her believe Wyatt Earp's neck might be swaying away from the noose waiting for him outside the City Hall.

As the carriage came up to the house, she saw both her children coming at her on their red bicycles. David was waving at her, and Bertha May was shouting something. She was assisted by Mr. Li to the ground as they rolled up to her, out of breath and excited.

"Mother, we have news!" David said.

Bertha May shook her head. "Don't be dramatic. Some men were taking young girls from the orphanage. Most were immigrants."

"Yes, but then Dr. Baker came up with another group to confront them! They began to shout at one another most vociferously and violently." She knew David was prone to hyperbole.

"Freddy was there?" Charlotte said.

"Bertha, what were they saying? Please, word for word if you can." She was pleased when her daughter took out a piece of paper from her messenger uniform pocket and began to read.

"Dr. Baker said, 'You cannot take these children to Tijuana.' The other man answered, 'I have instructions from the mayor. Look, he signed here.' And he gave Dr. Baker a sheet of paper."

David pushed in front of his sister.

"Dr. Baker waved his hand and screamed at them. 'You are the tyranny of the State upon society! A plague upon you!' I swear, Mother, this is true. There then came a cloud of wings overhead, and hundreds of bats began to circle and dive at us. The men were so frightened they forgot their job and left. Dr. Baker was exultant, and he raised his fist into the air!"

Charlotte nodded as if this were something she'd experienced before. "He has trained them. The harmless free-tails from Mexico. We do it whenever we demonstrate for our cause."

Clara was looking at Mr. Li, who also began nodding his head in agreement. She turned back to address her assistant.

"What cause is this?"

"Oh, it could be several groups. The Knights of Labor. The Workingman's Party. The World Suffrage Movement. We do a lot of organized work, and it usually comes to nothing. You may want to see if that group was taking those girls to work for this contract between the Earps and Anthony Comstock. You did say the mayor might be involved as well, did you not?" Charlotte said.

"That must be it," Clara nodded. "Children. Thank you very much. That is important news. We now must get ready for dinner. I shall add this important information to my file."

Chapter 5: The Golden Faun

New Town, San Diego, CA, May 9, 1888.

Unknown to him, Anand Prabhakar, 19, wandered into the lives of the women who worked for Heaven Riendeau in the house next door to the Canary Cottage. His arrival from India was a re-birth, so to speak, as he had given up his life as an initiate assistant to the great Yogi and Swami, Kamasutra. Anand's job was to assist the guru of the ancient left-handed practice of Tantra, which was the coital joining of members of the opposite sex for purposes of spiritual *moksha*, or "God Consciousness." This practice, Anand discovered, almost too late, was rife with charlatans. When he watched his beloved guru staring back at him from behind the bars of the British stockade, he knew his first fact of life.

Because of Anand's youth, the court decided to exile him from Delhi, rather than imprison him. His master's arrest occurred during an actual "spitting" confrontation between Yogi Kamasutra and the beloved and iconic spiritual leader, Swami Vivekananda. This occurred during a train stop beside a small village just outside Rajputana.

Strangely, the argument the gurus had did not concern the sexual nature of Swami Kamasutra's Tantric teachings, about which Vivekananda was certainly opposed. Instead, it was about whom had first purchased a bowl of curried potatoes from a passing vendor inside the crowded train car. The two gurus began shouting at each other, and then their argument devolved quickly into spitting at each other like angry Billy goats. Anand finally had to shield his master from further spraying by placing his body between them, thus feeling the major portion of the Yogi's expectorant against the back of his neck and on the lime green shoulders of his new Jodhpuri suit, which his master had purchased for him in Delhi, to appear worthy of accompanying him on the journey.

His ride across the seas was uneventful, and he was able to earn his journey by working as a cabin boy for the fifty crew members of the merchant steamer *SS Porterhouse*, and they arrived in San Diego Bay on schedule.

Anand was staring at all the frying, sweating, chicken bodies rotating on electric spits inside the Moonbeam Café and Tavern next door to what the sailor on the ship told him was the Canary Cottage. He was tarrying a bit before entering the yellow cottage on the alleyway, tucked away like a hidden treasure, as the sailor told him he could find work there.

He stood before a wide front window of the restaurant facing the street, gritted his teeth, and his black eyebrows furrowed together over his flaring nostrils, and tears rolled down his cheeks. Even though he was hungry, his faith bade him to eat no flesh of any animal, including the eggs or other products of said animals, even their milk, as is the case of the cow. In fact, he grew-up sleeping with these wandering Brahman cattle out in the fields on the sweltering summer nights in northern India. Their combined perspiration felt cool as the breezes came down from the mountains later in the evening.

"Young man? Are you famished?"

The voice came from the person attached to the hand he felt on his right shoulder. When he turned, the woman who was touching him smiled, and he immediately returned the grin, as he was trained to follow and not lead. She was wearing a violet dress that was crushed velvet, and the small plumed hat was the same material. Her collar was a ruffled appendage from the white blouse beneath, and as she turned to move toward the door to the restaurant, he smelled the most exquisite odor from her person. It reminded him of the lavender incense his guru used to light before instructing the proper ritual of the Tantra.

"I shall buy you anything you want to eat, young man," she said, pushing in on the swinging doors. "My name is Heaven Riendeau. Are you from the Indian continent, by chance? I adore your ways! I could tell by your expression that you are quite repulsed by our evisceration of animals. I understand. I do not abide by their slaughter either, as I am vegetarian. Would you like one of Chef Chavez's famous salads? He puts green chilis, cilantro, and scallions on top of the mixed greens, avocado, garbanzo beans, and fresh oil and vinegar on the side."

"My name is Anand. Anand Prabhakar. Pronounced *Prab-ha-kar*. I just got off the *Porterhouse* out in the harbor. That salad does sound quite appetizing." He waited. She smiled again and motioned to him with her right hand.

"Come with me, lad. My treat." She pushed on the two swinging doors into the restaurant, and he followed her inside.

He felt his stomach begin to rumble after the lady described the salad, and he followed closely behind her gently swaying bustle into the restaurant booths in the side room. Four men, who looked like miners, were seated at a table in the tavern portion playing a card game. They turned from their activity to watch them.

One grizzled old man pointed a tobacco-stained finger and remarked, "Heaven's treatin' the chicken to a meal before she plucks his feathers!" The entire group laughed, and one of them spat a stream of brown juice into a gourd-shaped copper receptacle next to his chair. Anand winced in revulsion.

"Don't bother about those men. Tell me about yourself. What interests do you have? Besides eating, that is," she giggled. He liked the way she smiled and her eyes looked deep into his, rather than the usually squinty-eyed or wide-eyed looks he received from his new countrymen.

"I suppose I enjoy soccer. Not much of that here, I see. I like different philosophies and religions as well. But I must admit, it's work I need right now. I haven't been getting any wage since I was aboard the ship."

Her eyes looked down at her hands, and then she raised her head again. "You know, I'm sort of in business next door to the Canary Cottage around the corner. I got sponsored by Mrs. Wyatt Earp. I need somebody who can clean up after women and such. Can you cook?" She again smiled that calm way, and her voice was very gentle.

"Yes. I cooked for Yogi Kamasutra. I was … what do they call it here? His valet? I took care of the house also." He watched the young waitress come up to the table. She was not much older than him, and she also had a contagious grin. He smiled up at her as if she were going to produce the salad from out of the air. Instead, she looked over at Miss Heaven.

"What'll it be, Miss Heaven? The usual? Do you want to try the ginger wheatgrass tea? Made a batch this morning. Supposed to keep scarlatina away from children, and the croup. Ask Dr. Baker. She knows."

"Miss Kai Krissy Wong, I want you to meet Mr. Anand Prabhakar. Did I pronounce that correctly, Anand?" He nodded. "He has just landed after a long journey. He's from India."

The waitress, an Oriental with dark hair, finally looked at him. She seemed curious.

"Do you talk to spirits? Are you a telepathic sort? I heard some of your kind can sleep on a bed of nails and not feel a thing." She laughed, a full-throated, youthful, and rumbling sound that made him laugh in response.

"Don't mind Krissy, Anand. She has an extremely fertile imagination. She was working as a personal maid for Rabbi Jerome Sonenschein before she came here." Heaven covered her lips with the tips of her fingers. "Oh my! Did you know about the murder of the rabbi in Tijuana?"

"That's all well and good, Miss Heaven. If the young gentleman doesn't know about the murder yet, he will soon enough. Did you know that Dr. Baker is working with the attorney who is defending Mr. Earp in court? Her name is Mrs. Clara Shortridge Foltz. She owns the *San Diego Bee*. She was at the scene of the murder. It says in the newspaper."

His stomach again began to gurgle, much louder this time. Kai looked down at him. "I'd better get this young man some grub!" She laughed, turned around, and hurried away toward the kitchen.

"If you do come to work for me, you will have to maintain discretion. My work requires this. Do you understand, Anand? You must not tell anybody what goes on inside my house."

He noticed that as she began talking about her business, she took on a different demeanor. It was similar to the way his yogi changed when he worked with his clients. The voice became somber, and the words used were chosen carefully.

He decided to comfort her. "I worked for a Swami in India, and he supervised the ancient practice of Tantra. Do you know of it?"

"Is that the joining of male and female in a sexually symbolic act or some such erotic discipline?" She did not blush.

"Not exactly, but you are quite close. My employer was arrested because of our business, and I was told to leave Delhi, and this is why I am on these shores today." He looked down at this plate. "I am very familiar with the rooms where sexual cohabitation takes place. I cleaned them up, I washed them, and I took care of such ceremonies, but I am not proud of it."

When the waitress Kai returned with the food, she paused while placing the plate for Miss Riendeau before her. He could hear her whispering, but all he could make out were two words. *Josie* and *tavern*.

Her benefactor smiled after both plates of salad were in front of them, and the steaming tea had been poured. She raised her porcelain cup.

"Here's to a mutually beneficial relationship. I want your stay in this new country to be one you shall remember for the rest of your life. I believe you will make a fine American, Anand, and I will endeavor to teach you how to be one."

He saw that she wanted him to touch his cup with hers, so he raised it by the handle and did so. Some of these Americans might be gracious hosts after all. Time and hard work on his part would tell. He could feel his karma changing, as his fork plunged deep inside the monstrous salad.

***

It was 5 PM when Heaven pushed into the wide swinging doors of the Nightingale Saloon on Fifth Avenue. She was meeting her patron, Josephine Marcus Earp. As the wife of the accused murderer, Wyatt, the owner of this tavern, and two other bars, Heaven knew she could have never been able to open her bordello without their financial help. However, it was Mrs. Earp who knew her next-door neighbor, the Madame of the Canary Cottage, Ida Bailey. She was meeting Josie to get her final blessing and to find out what Ida needed to keep her and her ladies in the senior business woman's good graces. Heaven expected it concerned Josephine's husband and the upcoming murder trial, but she was not certain.

Josephine Earp burst out of the back room and into the smoky confines of the tavern. The men in the room, mostly gamblers, sailors, and merchants, watched carefully as she walked toward Heaven. By the looks on their surprised faces they seemed to have never seen two women engage with such emotion and frivolity. One of the men, an older gentleman and merchant, with wide gray sideburns and a cough, waved at the barkeep.

"Pete, give these ladies a drink on me. Maybe they won't cause such a ruckus with a shot of whiskey in their bellies."

The rest of the men laughed uproariously as Heaven took Josie's hand and was guided into the back room to confer at a small table amid the liquor bottles, beer kegs, canned pickled eggs, and a barrel of cracklings, or fried pork skin.

Heaven smiled at Josie. The older woman was the first person she had written to about her business proposal, and she knew she needed to see if the money to finance the beginnings of her enterprise would still be forthcoming now that her husband had been arrested.

"Miss Riendeau, we meet at last! I was so impressed by your letters that I supported you sight unseen. Now I can meet you in the flesh, and I like what I see. Thank you for coming." Josie pushed a bottle of burgundy and a wine glass toward her. "Please, help yourself. We have business matters to discuss. A cordial will enliven our spirits. Complements of Bud Randolph. He's a regular here."

Heaven nodded, and poured herself a half-glass, and then poured her hostess one. After they both sipped, the tension of never meeting before seemed to seep from their consciousness like morning dew drying in a field of clover.

"I was so aghast when I read about your husband! How long before he goes on trial? It must have been a matter of self-defense. Please, tell me all about it." Heaven leaned forward in anticipation of Josie's response.

"We have employed two women to investigate. Mrs. Clara Foltz and Dr. Charlotte Baker. Foltz was quite a successful barrister in San Francisco, and she moved here to work and to run her newspaper, the *Daily Bee*. I believe we have an advantage with her as our counsel, as she was also at the scene of the alleged murder. As for Dr. Baker, she has been in communications with all the parties with whom we suspect may be behind the conspiracy to make Wyatt appear to be a murderer."

"Conspiracy? Who would do such a thing? What is your attorney's plan to defend him?" Heaven took another, and longer, pull at the wine. She was happy to put off her real reason for being there, which was to obtain more money to pay for her new employee, Anand Prabhakar.

"I don't know Mrs. Foltz's plan. I just know she's working on obtaining witness testimony and possible evidence for the trial. As you might understand, I cannot divulge any facts in the case, as it may prejudice my husband's chances at an acquittal." Josie smiled. "He's been in these scrapes before, you know. I'm not afraid of his holding up. It is I who is most affected. What did you wish to talk to me about, Heaven?"

She knew this was the moment of truth. Should she tell this woman what she was wanting to do, and how she had been involved with the cult of Rabbi Jerome Sonenschein? Not yet. If she was asked by the attorneys, then perhaps. This was her business at stake right now.

"Josie, I appreciate your loan. My brothel is a bit different, as you now know, and yet you still wanted to back me. How coincidental was it that we both read the same book by Mr. Ritter von Leopold Sacher-Masoch, *Venus in Furs*? Wasn't that an astonishing insight into what I will be doing for profit? Yours and mine, of course!"

"It is amazing, but it is not without its attraction in many spheres of influence. Men, as a rule, tend to be more visually stimulated than we women. This would lead one to assume, depending on their proclivities, they can be coaxed into activities upon which this book alludes. Do you have any concrete ideas at this point? If so, I am ready to listen."

Heaven was enjoying this more with each moment. She understood the Earps were wealthy, having invested in local property and untoward activities such as she was presenting. But with the trial at hand, she did not expect Mrs. Earp to be so open. Could she be into even more such investments of which she was not aware? If so, perhaps even more money could be had, if she played her cards right.

"My girls are ready. I expect they will be most admired with the accouterments of leather gowns, whips, and some boots I have ordered from the Prussian Army. These war-hardened gumboots come up to the knees, and my ladies' legs shall be bare, of course, and the government gave me a reduced price, as my women have small feet."

She enjoyed it when Mrs. Earp laughed. "Oh, my goodness! And what dramatics do you have in store for your clients? I would suppose some could be purloined directly from novels like that of *Venus in Furs*. These men in San Diego, although they may have heavy wallets, have less than heavy reading matter."

"Yes. I have quite orderly routines worked out for each of my specialists—for that is what they shall be—and the gentleman callers will have a menu from which to choose. I believe we will be able to advertise discreetly in the men's periodicals as well." She reached into her handbag, pulled out an ad she had worked up, and handed it across to Josephine. She picked her wine glass up and took another drought.

"I see. You have cleverly couched the language of sport into a call for sadomasochistic pleasures. 'Do you enjoy chasing after the sleek doe at daybreak? Watching her white tail shiver from the dewy cold? And what if that doe should transform into the fearsome stag, ready to defend the forest? What then, my sportsman? Come and sit by our hearth to enjoy the sweet music of the celestial and natural realms. Listen to tales of feminine strength and conquest over male aggression.' Quite good, Heaven! I applaud you."

"Thank you, Mrs. Earp. I might add, I have one woman, Miss Rosie Daniels, who invented her rueful character. She will portray Joan of Arc, the French warrior of the Middle Ages. I was able to procure a very alluring ensemble for her to wear, you may be certain." Heaven knew it was time to broach the subject of Anand, her new employee. "I must say, however, because of these added dramatics, and these many changes that must be made throughout an evening's festivities, the need for extra help has arisen."

"Extra help? You mean, extra cost?" Josephine frowned.

"I have met a young man just off the steamer, and he's from India. Like me, he is a vegetarian, and he eats very little. And, as luck would have it, he was a valet for an employer who was also working in the sex trade, although his art form was much more ancient. Are you familiar with the practice of Tantric Yoga?"

"I know of yoga, but as it pertains to spiritual meditation and calling upon an inner soul of some kind. This Tantric is not familiar."

"To be brief, it involves the sexual intercourse of male and female. However, the ultimate goal is to achieve what they term Enlightenment. The *moksha* state of consciousness whereby one becomes one with the universal power. It supposedly gives the body a powerful infusion that can when done correctly, literally explode light through the top of the craniums of the two persons involved."

She watched Josephine's expression. She knew this would affect her, as her people were known to be mystically inclined, as was the case with Rabbi Sonenschein.

"I love it! Can this young man assist you in creating such a mystical practice? What would you charge for these rites?"

The money was out in the open. Heaven knew she could come in for the final conviction to seal the deal with her employer.

"If you loan me the funds to hire this young man, I believe he can be convinced to train some of my girls to do this practice. We could charge, say, five dollars for each visit? Of course, I would tell the men that if they took what they learned back home to their wives, it would be even more powerful magic!"

Josie laughed even more loudly.

"You are full of mirth today, Heaven! I like the way you think. I have the perfect man in mind for this particular connivance. Have you heard of the gentleman by the name of Lucky Baldwin? My husband and I have been into a few business dealings with him, both here and in San Francisco. He's now sixty but full of vim and vigor."

Heaven nodded vigorously. "Oh, yes! He attended my establishment quite often when I was in San Francisco. How do you want Mr. Baldwin involved?"

Josie's dark eyebrows furrowed. "Elias was one of the witnesses to the murder that evening in Tijuana. He also became an investor in another scheme we devised to trick the Postmaster-General, Anthony Comstock. I don't doubt he shall be a witness at my husband's murder trial."

It was Heaven's turn to become reflective, as she knew this meant her involvement with Rabbi Sonenschein might put her under investigation by the legal authorities, and she was wary. She picked up the wine glass and drank, staring at Josie over the rim. When she put her glass back on the table, she was filled with rebellion.

"Don't you believe it might become dangerous to have Mr. Baldwin involved in another sexual scheme if that's what you were referencing concerning Anthony Comstock?"

Mrs. Earp leaned over and took Heaven's hand. The pressure from her grip was significant until Heaven winced in pain.

"I want there to be a distraction in this town when my husband goes on trial. Quite honestly, I don't trust this attorney, Mrs. Foltz. She is much too frilly and feminine, and she has decided to partner with Dr. Charlotte Baker. You know how much trouble she makes for us in the Stingaree?"

Heaven nodded. "Yes, I am aware. I had a long discussion about Dr. Baker with my new next-door neighbor, Ida Bailey. Although she treats our girls for their female problems, she is trying to shut us all down, eventually."

"Well, Charlotte's husband is no prude, according to Bailey.

He's a regular visitor to the Canary. He even sends milk goats, cats, dogs, and other animals to the whore houses by his Chinese messenger. He even sent Ida Bailey one exotic species from the Amazon, an armadillo, I think it's called. Dr. Fred Baker traveled to Brazil himself, I was told, rather like Charles Darwin."

"Yes, we received two nanny goats, three hens, a rooster, and an armadillo as housewarming gifts. The delivery messengers were a young girl and boy," Heaven said. "He even works with me to help the working conditions of my ladies and the other lower classes. Are you aware of the international labor movement to unchain the workers of the world? Dr. Baker, me, and the victim, Rabbi Sonenschien, contribute money to their cause, and we have demonstrated against this country's governments, city, state, and federal. Our movement is growing all over the world. Perhaps I can send you some literature?"

"I don't get involved in those kinds of politics. My husband and I support many workers with our businesses. The Bakers, I know, are known philanthropists. It is my intention with you and this new hire of yours that we have the chance to distract the male population in San Diego enough to allow me to do my investigations into the real cause of my husband's arrest. I have my suspicions that Mr. Baldwin may be behind some of the plotting involved against my husband and me."

She was worried now. Did Mrs. Earp also know how her involvement with the victim, Rabbi Sonenschein, came under the purview of this ever-widening mandala of conspiracies? Would this Clara Sherlock-Foltz, as they called her in the press, be questioning her?

"We will do our best, Mrs. Earp. I thank you for this loan, and I do believe we shall be able to make a tidy sum from it. I will contact Mr. Elias Baldwin. Hopefully, we can distract him before your husband must go to trial. Our efforts will, of course, increase once the trial has indeed begun, you may be assured of that!"

Heaven stood up, took a deep breath, and adjusted her velvet hat.

Her employer also stood, but before escorting her out, she

first walked to the back of the supply room where there was a black, cast-iron safe. She entered the combination and swung the door wide open.

When she returned, she held what appeared to be a small sack. She transferred it into Heaven's hands, and it was quite heavy.

"It's gold. Better to use it, rather than bills, which can be traced. Tell Elias where it came from, and keep half for your new enterprise. He will, no doubt, supply you with the rest you need to establish our ruse of interference during the coming trial. Also, ask him about the Amazon Natives and their potions."

***

As fortune would have it, Elias Baldwin was next-door at the Canary Cottage when Heaven returned to her abode. Her Rosie was sitting on the front porch of Ida's yellow cottage as Heaven walked up the path to her house.

"Miss Heaven! Howdy," she grinned. Rosie was from Texas, so her drawl was pronounced. "They's having a shindig in there," she said, pointing backward with her thumb to the Canary's wood-frame confines. "Lucky Baldwin's payin' fer everything!"

Anand was in the parlor getting acquainted with her other six girls. He seemed to be their center of attention, as they had little experience with those of the swarthy skin, since most of the Negroes and Chinese had no money to visit a bordello, so the young man's physique was both lean and attractive to them. She knew their daily task was having to cater to all the pot-bellied businessmen and the tobacco-spewing miners. Anand must have been a welcome reprieve.

Janice, her blonde from Tennessee, was flexing the boy's arm as if she were priming the water pump out back. Alexa, the eighteen-year-old redhead from Washington State, was sitting next to the boy on the divan. The other four, Bobbie, Rosanne, Michelle, and Fern, the new girls with whom she had yet to become acquainted, were standing before him as if he were the Prince of Egypt.

When the boy saw her, he stood up at once and weaved his

way through the crowd to greet her. His brown eyes were glowing but downcast and furtive.

"Miss Heaven! I am so sorry. The ladies were showing me what I will have to be doing around here."

"I can see that. I have some important news for you all, but first I must go next door. Anand, you are now an official employee of mine. When I return, I will explain your new duties, and they shall include some very responsible activities that will incorporate your experience in India. I will be choosing three of your girls, as well, to be part of my new promotional offering here at the Golden Faun."

Janice stepped forward and giggled. "Golden Faun? You mean, like the baby deer?"

"Yes, I came up with the name as I was writing our advertisement to be placed in the daily press of San Diego. You ladies and gentleman will be very proud of what you will be doing, and ours will indeed be a special place of refinement and grandeur. I want to re-decorate it as well, and we shall have trees, a pond with Oriental spotted koi, and lush, azure bushes enveloping us as if we were welcoming Hansel and Gretel into our home made of gingerbread in the woods!"

The youngest girls squealed and began to dance with Anand around the parlor.

"Please! Calm yourselves now. I must leave for a while, so finish showing Anand his duties, and stop toying with him, felines. He will be showing us a new way to make love, so he is very important to our future here."

As she opened the door to leave, she heard the ladies' voices, as they giggled and whispered.

"New love!"

"Clean my room first, Anand."

And, "What do you know about love-making, young boy?"

She knew she would soon have her hands full watching after this group. As she walked over toward the raucous sounds coming from inside the Canary Cottage, Heaven Riendeau knew she was at last in her primal element. There was a murder, there was intrigue, and she had a large sack of gold inside her crushed velvet purse.

What more could a woman ask for, other than perhaps a rendezvous with a man with whom she had once had intimate relations in San Francisco? The connivance Josephine Marcus Earp wanted her to perform may not end up the way she believed it should. Elias was indeed a ladies' man, but Heaven knew a secret about him that she hoped the investigators would never know. It was this secret knowledge that she was going to use to extract even more profit from the so-called trial distraction Josie wanted her to devise. It was, in fact, a new drama, which, if all went well, would also include Krissy Wong, the waitress, and Rabbi Jerome Sonenschein, himself, back from the dead.

Choose Your Suspect

Naturally, a population is drawn together from the adventurous classes of the world, imbued as it was with excitement and far from conventional trammels, contained and developed a store of profligacy and vice, much of which found its way into official, business, and social life. Gambling was open and flagrant; games of chance were carried on at the curb-stones; painted women paraded the town in carriages and sent out engraved cards summoning men to their receptions and "high teas;" the desecration of Sunday was complete, with all drinking and gambling houses open, and with picnics, excursions, fiestas and bullfights, the latter at the Mexican line, to attract men, women, and boys from religious influence. Theft, murder, incendiarism, carousals, fights, highway robbery, and licentiousness gave to the passing show in boomtown San Diego many of the characteristics of the frontier camp. Society retired to cover before the invasion of questionable people, and what came to be known as "society" in the newspapers, was, with honorable exceptions here and there, a spectacle of vulgar display and the arrogant parade of reputations which, in the Eastern States, had secured for their owners the opportunity and the need of going West. (Walter Gifford Smith, Story of San Diego)

Dearest Reader,

The author has placed before you all of the suspects that could have the means and motive to initiate the murder of Rabbi Jerome Sonenschein witnessed inside the pugilistic arena on May 6, 1888, in Tijuana, Mexico, by the gun hand of retired Marshal Wyatt Earp, the accused.

Since this is not the Nineteenth Century, we can allow you

to follow the various plots of these suspects, to see if your choice is correct. The author has strategically developed his mystery in this format to allow his readers to experience the same chronology of events from four different suspects and their points-of-view. This frame may be familiar to you if you've viewed the classic film, *Rashomon*, by Director Akira Kurosawa. In this film, the same rape and murder are told from three different witnesses' viewpoints. Authors who use this stream-of-consciousness technique are Henry James, Virginia Woolf, William Faulkner, Marcel Proust, Jack Kerouac, Dorothy Richardson, and James Joyce. In this unique novel, the reader will first read five chapters in the conventional format. Then, the narrative becomes a journey into the mind of each of the four suspects. You choose which one to explore, as the action takes place during the same chronology. It will be like a *Groundhog Day* mystery, where the only difference is the unique perspective and psyche of the suspect you choose. You should be forewarned, however. Unless and until you read all four suspects and their unique perspectives, you won't understand the complete ramifications of the plot and its movement into the next mystery. Even if you choose the correct suspect, the "macrocosm" of the overall mystery may surprise you. Happy reading!

Suspect #1: Josephine Marcus Earp
Go to page 65.

Suspect #2: Wyatt Earp
Go to page 115.

Suspect #3: Miss Ida Bailey
Go to page 170.

Suspect #4: Miss Heaven Riendeau
Go to page 219.

Josephine

I hope Wyatt's allergies do not sprout forth in this dusty tomb. Wyatt and I are on the committee that is in charge of constructing the new courthouse next year, on this same spot. God willing, my poor darling husband will be here to take part in the ground-breaking. Honey Hunsaker says we supply a necessary aura of protection here in San Diego because of Wyatt's reputation as a federal marshal. The East Coast still calls San Diego the "Wild West" in their ludicrous penny presses. The population is over 30,000 now. A small city, if you ask me.

I see Wyatt upfront, at the Defense table, seated with his attorney, Mrs. Foltz. His hair is slicked down with that gooey Brilliantine I hate. We have all been working together to mount his plea of self-protection, as this is what our attorney calls it, and although I will not be called to the stand during this trial, my husband certainly shall be. We will contend that Wyatt is defending us from the violent group of fanatics, under the direct leadership of Rabbi Jerome Sonenschein, and the witnesses for his defense will build the truth underlying his innocence.

As our attorney explains it, the prosecution must prove, beyond any reasonable doubt, and with most of the evidence, that it is Wyatt's vendetta against the "good" rabbi that led to his pulling the trigger of his Buntline Special that day in Tijuana. They must also demonstrate that Wyatt, in some manner, has preconceived malice or specific intent to kill this man. Without this "malice aforethought," according to Mrs. Foltz, there can be no conviction by the jury of his peers that there is a murder in the first degree. And, because this is the only charge being brought forward against Wyatt, as long as we can show his act is justified in some way, then there can be no malice in his action.

The District Attorney, Archibald Richardt, our adversary, is fiddling with his notes on the other side of this creaky old barn at the prosecution's table. As he speaks, his waxen bush of a mustache is twitching at his co-counsel, a slimy little man in a gray suit and wide, red suspenders. The authorities have allowed this small building to become crammed to the rafters with out-of-town journalists and just plain gawkers.

Foltz and her companion, Dr. Charlotte Baker, have been working tirelessly these last few days, but since the prosecution, and the entire world, it seems, has such a blood lust for this case, we are rushed into court. Mrs. Foltz's attempts at obtaining a continuance have fallen on probably the literal deaf ears of this old judge, Smithfield Parker, who is called out of retirement to officiate this case. He must be the modern brethren of the biblical Methuselah, as Dr. Baker told me he was a lawyer in the eighteen forties and fifties when San Diego was trying to tame the savages in Mission San Diego, and stealing land from the Mexicans.

I have begun my investigation into this murder, and my assistant, Heaven Riendeau, has started her unique enterprise to distract the male population during this trial. I see Mrs. Foltz coming toward me. Perhaps my ruse is having an effect.

"Have you been here long?"

She takes my hands into her own and stares at me. Should I tell her about my plan? I think not.

"I want to stay out of Wyatt's view," I say, stretching my neck to see around her wide hips at what he might be doing. His wrists and ankles are locked together by chains. "They didn't chain Wyatt during his trial for shooting Frank McLaury and Billy Clanton in Tombstone. Later, after he killed Frank Stilwell at the train station in Tucson, Wyatt told me he is most proud of getting Stilwell, as he is the one he suspected of killing his brother, Morgan Earp."

"I understand. Your husband told me. The prosecution will be calling their four witnesses this morning. The policeman at the scene of the murder will testify that the rabbi was unarmed, and he was shot from point-blank range, a bullet in the forehead by a very efficient shooter." Mrs. Foltz makes no lady-like grimace. She has tried a murder case before, in San Francisco.

"I don't suppose you have evidence to challenge that," I say.

"No, I don't need to accomplish anything with these witnesses. They are the State's witnesses, policeman, coroner, forensics' expert, and Mayor Hunsaker. I was thinking about Hunsaker's involvement in your contract with him concerning the sex game to trick Postmaster Comstock, but this morning's not the time for it. I'll bring it up with this afternoon's parade of witnesses, one of whom will be Comstock himself." The attorney smiles. "I will be weaving a very sticky web around this aspect of the conspiracy. I hope to trap quite a few men if all goes well."

I am thinking about all the men Heaven and her ladies will be trapping at the Golden Faun. She tells me they are coming in every day, like lambs to the slaughter. Ida Bailey is quite jealous, so she has begun her promotional binge of parading her ladies down Broadway, in broad daylight. I don't believe the Stingaree has ever experienced so much seductive activity in its history.

I am not enjoying this prosecution very much. I need to do something productive. My husband's life is at stake here! I shall get to the heart of who is really behind the murder of Rabbi Sonenschein. Who better than a fellow Jew to solve this mystery? My father taught me well about charlatans, and I suppose I may have learned my lesson too well. While Wyatt put all his investment eggs in the basket of property and gambling dens, I invested in the minds of men, which is a far more dangerous and yet, potentially, a much more profitable endeavor.

What is the commotion going on up near the judge's bench? All the attorneys are up there, along with some police. I must find out from Mrs. Foltz what is happening. Could it be Heaven and her girls have crossed the line too far with their distractions? If she has spoken about my role as a financier, it could hurt Wyatt's case. Let me see if I can get up there to speak to her.

"Excuse me, I must see my husband's attorney. Please, let me pass." These reporters are animals. No respect for a lady when it comes to their newspapers. "Get the hell out of my way or I'll run you down!" There. I can get past.

"Mrs. Foltz!" I yell to get her attention. She is still conferring with the judge and all the other men. The police have formed a barrier around them. When she finally sees me, a strange expression comes over her face. I have only seen that look once before. A small child ran up to me after seeing her pet run over by a stagecoach coming into town. Our lawyer has the same visage of fear and pity.

"Must you arrest her now?" Mrs. Foltz says, just before one of the policemen breaks ranks and marches toward me.

The young copper grabs my wrists, and I jerk away from him. He looks back at his group, pleading for assistance. One woman is too much for him. Damned right! This one woman is.

Mrs. Foltz crashes through the group and comes up to me. "Let her go, Officer," she instructs the young man, who nods and walks back to his circle of other men in their navy-blue, San Diego uniforms.

"What's happened? Why are you all congregating up here like pigs at a trough?" I am going to get to the root of this imposition. I must continue with my investigation to free Wyatt.

"Mrs. Earp, you failed to inform me of your dealings. Now the prosecution has concrete evidence to place you under arrest for being an accessory to murder. Why didn't you tell me about your relationship with Miss Heaven Riendeau from San Francisco?"

"Riendeau? I don't know what you mean. I have never had any dealings with this woman," I lie, hoping my employee has yet to tell them about me.

"Riendeau has not said anything about knowing you. Mayor Hunsaker's office has the proof that you have been running at least twelve bordellos in San Diego, beginning when you were a working girl in Tombstone. You told me yourself that the mayor was your husband's attorney, but you never told me you were running brothel businesses throughout your journeys in California, Utah, and Oregon. Hunsaker knows, beginning in 1874, at the age of 14, Josie Marcus fell in with a San Francisco madam Hattie Wells. Late in November 1874, using the alias Sadie Mansfield, you arrived in Prescott, Arizona, and began working in Hattie's brothel."

I want to grab Foltz by her porcelain neck and wring it like a turkey. "That's a lie! I never worked in a brothel. Honey has gone berserk from the sex parlors he visits. He's trying to protect his investments, by god!"

"You learned the trade, and it seems, according to all the documents Hunsaker has collected, you have perfected the business to a rather high art form. The last agreement came when you spoke to Miss Riendeau in your tavern. Do you not remember your exchange with her?"

How in the hell did they find out I spoke to Heaven? Nobody was there. Unless.

"One of your regulars, Mr. Budreaux Randolph, was there, and he works for Mr. Hunsaker's office, part-time. He overheard everything you told Miss Riendeau. However, that's not the last of it."

"Last of it? Which *it* do you mean? You're being quite vague for a lawyer, aren't you Mrs. Foltz?" I know where she is headed, and I don't like it one bit.

"Because you worked these bordellos in absentia, so to speak, you had to create written agreements. Hunsaker has collected all these agreements, and this last oral agreement has caused all your chickens to come home to roost, I am afraid."

Wyatt's lawyer has the most vacuous eyes I have ever seen on a woman.

"Agreements? My husband and I have signed hundreds of agreements. We never know what we've signed, most of the time. What does this prove?" I am now grasping at straws to save myself.

"The mayor has sworn evidence from several of the bordello madams throughout your travels, ending in San Diego, and including Ida Bailey. In each of these places, you not only became an investor in their duties as prostitutes, but you were always followed by another person who was trying to stop you from these investments."

I am aware of her now. Hunsaker is behind this, I realize. This is his way of keeping them from investigating his contract with us concerning the Postmaster General and the prepubescent playground in Mexico.

"Who is this other person, pray tell?" I ask, arching my eyebrows for effect.

"Rabbi Jerome Sonenschein. He followed you wherever you

went. It was his sworn duty to stop you from ruining these women and their lives as children of God. The Grand Jury has written out new charges against you, as a co-defendant in this case, as a murderess in the first degree. They say you wanted the rabbi dead more than Wyatt did, and that you are the main instigator in his assassination because Sonenschein wanted to stop your exploits and bawdy experiments, the likes of which this country has never seen before. Before I can represent you, we must have a very long talk. Is that clear, Mrs. Earp?"

As they drag me away, I know I must say something for my honor. "Hunsaker is behind all of this! I told you about our contract with him to create Comstock's garden of earthy delights in Mexico. Why don't you tell them now? You are not a lawyer. You are a prude and a poor suffragette. Is Dr. Baker behind this as well? You and your kind. Always putting the image of society before the truth of the evil that always lurks behind all the prim and proper attitudes and hypocritical religions."

Mrs. Foltz keeps nodding at me, like a calm school marm watching her best student being punished.

"You will all find out! I shall not stop my investigation until I can show you all what is happening here!"

When they slam the doors on the police wagon, I am comfortable in the darkness. I see the face of my dear father, and he takes the place of Mrs. Foltz, nodding patiently at me, encouraging me to stay the righteous course of the true Kabbalist.

***

And so, it is my arrest that gives me the information about what I knew would eventually be the case. The State's key witness is no longer Miss Ida Bailey, the Madam of the Canary Cottage. In light of the new evidence, the new main witness is going to be Mayor William Jefferson Hunsaker. Wyatt's defense attorney in Tombstone is now the lodestone to send both of us hanging from our necks for the entire town to witness.

This is certainly never going to happen as long as I can take a breath. The jailhouse food tastes like cats urinated on it.

"Walton! Bring me more bread. This pork and beans are not fit for human consumption." I already know my jailer's name, as he may prove to be my messenger if I can play my cards correctly in this game of murder and mayhem.

As the tall and stooped-over old man fetches my bread, I begin to make my plans before Mrs. Foltz comes to give me her reckoning.

I keep thinking about the fact that I am now facing death, but it is strange. I hold a real fear about somehow not being able to prove that Bill Hunsaker isn't the foul, woman-crazy intellectual I know him to be. He always sniffs around me, when Wyatt isn't looking, or when he is out playing marshal. Honey believes he is more appealing to me because he has read literature, and he has a legal mind, qualities Wyatt does not possess, but he needs very much to survive the rigors of being a man of the law in the West.

That's why Wyatt and Doc Holiday get on so well. They balance each other like I balanced Jerome Sonenschein. Nobody knows how close Jerome and I were, not even Mrs. Foltz. For all her interviews, she was never able to ask the one man who knew my inner nature the best. The truth she has right now is that Sonenschein and I are enemies, both as fellow Jews and practitioners of the ancient rites and mystical conundrums of Kabbalah, but not the reality of being what Heaven Riendeau calls Tantric opposites. Together, Jerome and I became a pair of archetypes, beyond time and space, past all humans who are mired inside a desperate good and evil universe. Ours was a battle to the death for the souls of all mankind.

"Thank you, Walton. This is much better." The pumpernickel is fresh. I don't see where I'll get my protein for the day. Perhaps I'll take a small bite of Honey, as he passes by, going up to the witness stand.'

"Mrs. Earp, the bailiff is here from the court. I believe you need to go now." Walton's raspy voice irritates me. I am so used to Wyatt's slow, deep, and frequent drawl.

The short man in a black suit and bowtie has a pair of handcuffs draped casually across his forearm as if he were bringing a corsage to wrap around his date's wrist instead of steel bracelets. First Walton's voice, and now this man's smile under a walrus mustache, make me feel nauseated.

"We must be in court before seven. Judge Parker's orders." The creaking door on the cell opens, and I stand up, thrusting my wrists toward the man.

"Can you keep them loose? A lady must have freedom to touch up her face and fix her hair." Of course, I have no handbag, but this ape will follow my instructions anyway. The grin on his face tells me he is not the sharpest knife in the drawer.

"Not to worry, Mrs. Earp. With those delicate appendages, these are going to fit real fine."

I walk ahead of the dolt, who doesn't give me his name, and I am not going to ask. We ride together in his one-horse surrey to the courtroom on Front Street. There are citizens lined up to get into the trial, as this is the big day for the prosecution side of the case. I suppose they are hoping to hear about all the sexual allure that has been added to this case, thanks to yours truly. A few of the journalists I know turn toward me as Mr. Dolt takes my hands and helps me down from the surrey.

"Josie! The *Union* wants to know why Mayor Hunsaker has turned against you both. What happened between you and him?"

I remember this man. Mr. Val Gordon. He writes the most libelous stories I've ever read, about any topic under the sun. The cat sunning herself in the window of the Canary Cottage is not safe from his vicious rumor mill. I am not about to give him any more information to exaggerate for his paper.

"You'll have to ask the mayor, young man," I tell him, and I march up the steps behind the bailiff.

I am led inside the defense counsel's office, to the right, as we enter. I know this will be the big speech from Mrs. Foltz. The one about how I kept all of this secret bordello business from her. Most especially, how my relationship with the rabbi makes me implicated in this shooting in Tijuana on May 6.

She is sitting at the end of the table, and there is her daughter again. What is her name? May? Yes. Bertha May. And, hiding in the corner, working on her knitting, is Dr. Charlotte Baker. The only emancipated woman who knits. Mrs. Clara Foltz, Attorney-at-Law, rises to greet me.

"Bailiff Whitmore, you may leave her. Good morning, Mrs. Earp. I have already talked with Wyatt, and you will remain separated in court, on either side of our table. I'm afraid because you have now both been accused of a capital crime you must keep those ungodly handcuffs on. Wyatt has anklets as well, so I suppose there is some feminine grace left in San Diego. We don't do things this way in San Francisco. We keep two guards but no manacles."

"I don't care. I've been cuffed before. I am no stranger to these halls of justice. Just tell me what you need to say before we listen to those lies from the mayor. If Wyatt were still a marshal, you can guarantee, the tables would be turned on that poor excuse for a gentleman." I sit down hard, and I feel my corset ride up the sides of my legs. I still wear the blue dress from yesterday, and I need a bath like most of the men in San Diego.

She takes out some papers from her folder on the table. She shuffles the pages, reading, reading, and then she looks over at me.

"You told me in the first interview in Mexico that Ida Bailey is Rabbi Sonenschein's lover. Was that a lie? Were you his lover?"

I feel a gag reflex in my throat. "Lover? That little Jew toad? Not on your life. He is my sworn enemy!"

"There must have been something very serious going on between both of you. Why would you lie about your relationship? Our entire case is built on self-defence. Wyatt, supposedly, is protecting your honor, and we are going to show that the mayor is behind the sexual skullduggery you all concocted to milk Mr. Comstock and others out of their money. Now they have turned the tables on us, have they not? They have these contracts from all over the territories and states you visited." She holds up some of the papers.

"I make business arrangements. Yes. That is no crime in these United States. My husband buys property for his saloons and gambling parlors. I buy into my own investments. All of the towns we visit allow for such investments, even if they have to change the wording in those contracts you're holding." I nod at the papers, pointing my handcuffed hands at them.

"You never told me about how Sonenschein was following you to stop you. Why didn't you tell me that fact?" Her usually feminine voice takes a sharp tone. "We must now transform our defense, and I need to ask you some key questions before we hear the State's key witness this morning."

I hear Dr. Baker's knitting needles hit the table hard. "We interviewed most of the prostitutes in this city! They knew about the rabbi and his crusade against these dens of iniquity. I know it was Rabbi Sonenschein's moral purpose and duty to save these women from a life of disenfranchisement and debauched reputations."

"I see. Then I suggest you turn the tables on them by questioning Miss Ida Bailey once again. Except, this time, why don't you ask her about *her* relationship with the good rabbi, and what they are *really* trying to do? Oh, and while you do this new exploration, ask her about the good doctor's husband, dear Freddy, and his unique appetites."

I watch Charlotte carefully. If she has never bathed nude in a sauna before, the heat vapors emanating from her rotund body at this moment make her appear as if she has just stepped out of one.

"Why, you lying bitch!" Dr. Baker stands up from her chair, holds her knitting needles forward, and lunges toward me.

"That's enough! Both of you!" The attorney shouts. "I am actually planning to do just that. But, Charlotte, this is a fact that must also come out when I cross-examine Mayor Hunsaker. It is a revelation I discovered when I interviewed your husband and his doctor, Wayne Riley."

"Wayne? What reason did you have to confer with him? Is my Fred ill?"

Mrs. Foltz searches in her folder again and extracts another sheet of notes. "Yes, he is. But his illness, I am afraid, has a lot to do with what Josephine has just related. Your husband's carnal appetite."

There is a kind of silence in the room that only women understand. It is the silence of the unspoken realities that have, throughout the ages, turned women into lesbians, perhaps, and even witches. At least, that is my father's theory. Murder victim Rabbi Sonenschein also had a theory concerning the malady about which I know Clara Foltz is going to speak. He believed this disease is a curse directly from the soul of Judaism, the feminine *Shekhinah*, which is the presence of Yahweh in this world. This curse of the *Shekhinah*, supposedly, brought down the Tower of Babel, and it destroyed those twin cities of sin, prostitution, and corruption, Sodom and Gomorrah. Was this what Mrs. Foltz, the dead rabbi, and this crestfallen doctor and her husband are trying to accomplish? The destruction of the source of evil itself? I know this to be impossible, and it will be my job to show them why.

***

There is that raspy bailiff's voice again.

"Do you swear to tell the truth, the whole truth, and nothing but the truth, so help you God?" I take quick looks at Wyatt, seated uncomfortably on these wood chairs from the past. Do they erase these spirits of the persons who swooned here before us? The many lives lost to greed, or lust, or insanity? Surely, the foul-smelling odor of diseased minds, expressing their insanity through their perspiration, can never be removed. I see Wyatt smiling at his old friend and attorney from our Tombstone days together. My husband is always a man's man, no matter if he faces him in a gun duel or a duel of wits. The same chivalrous decorum that makes women come up to him, and makes me turn into an emboldened shrew, is the same demeanor Wyatt wears inside this courtroom.

The prosecutor is holding his lapels as if he were a black-headed mallard, and his footsteps are wide, as a duck walks, and his voice matches the silkiness of his royal blue necktie. I want to hear this supposed revelation, which connects me in a death-grip with my husband.

"We have established that Mr. Earp pulled his gun on the rabbi, Mr. Sonenschein, at 3:37 PM, on May 6, 1888, in Tijuana, Mexico. We have heard from the coroner, and the police at the scene, proving that Mr. Earp's bullet found its mark and is the proximate cause of death. However, it is you, Mr. Hunsaker, who now has new information to assist the State in finding the truth behind an illicit motive in this murder, is it not?"

Honey turns his head toward Wyatt, who sits about twenty feet away, and he nods. "Yes, I suppose so, although it gives me no great pleasure to do so."

"What is your personal and professional relationship with the accused couple, Mr. and Mrs. Wyatt Earp? Could you point them out for the court?"

Honey's head swivels, and he moves his extended right arm and forefinger while looking down his arm's gun barrel, aiming first at Wyatt, and then, at me. His bald forehead glistens with sweat under the harsh overhead gaslights, and I can smell the French cologne he always wears. I picture those pudgy jowls of his, as they rub against my cheek at a party, dance, or shindig.

He brings his hands back toward his chest, and he slowly lowers them into his lap. He takes a deep breath, as he is also a lawyer, preparing himself for his day on the stage.

"I was hired by the State to defend Mr. Earp in Tombstone, Arizona, along with my law partner at the time, Thomas Fitch. I met Mr. Earp, along with his companion, Josephine Marcus, who was then known as Sadie, and we prepared his case, which lasted over a month, as I recall."

Mrs. Foltz rises from her seat. "If the court would rule, what relevance does this have to do with the guilt or innocence of my clients?"

Old Judge Parker cups his left hand to his left ear, and he finally acknowledges her. "What's that Mrs. Fouts? Did you object?"

"Mrs. Foltz, your honor, with a *tz*. Yes, I wanted you to rule on the relevance of the prosecutor's delving into a case that took place over seven years ago." Her voice is much louder this time, and it must be an effort, as her usual tremor is softly lilting, which is no doubt an attempt to flatter the male jurors.

"Well, Mr. Richards, do you have a method to your madness?" Parker raises his owlish brows at the proud duck standing before the witness.

"Richardt, Your Honor. With a *dt*. Yes, your honor, I do. I wanted to establish the fact that the two defendants, even back in Tombstone, were beginning to shape the mental machinations of their nefarious deeds and plans, which would ultimately lead to the demise of the good Rabbi, Jerome Sonenschein, in Tijuana."

"I understand, your honor, but the prosecution fails to get to the heart of this case, which took place on May 6, 1888. The criminal statutes need the State to prove that my clients were in a malicious state of mind toward the victim, not toward the Clanton gang. Their mental plan of malice must be close in time to *this* homicide. Or, perhaps Mr. Richardt has other murders on his mind to convict this husband-and-wife team of committing? If so, then I want to hear from the Grand Jury in those other states."

There is laughter from many inside the courtroom, and I suppose the judge does not hear them because he nods at Archibald Richardt again. "Well, counselor? What do you have to offer?"

"I will continue with my questioning if the good madame can allow, and I shall bring us all up to date. But this malicious intent, as the defense points out with astute clarity, is being proved by what this witness can show us. It comes in the form of affidavits of fifteen madams, including our next witness, Miss Ida Bailey, who will testify that Mrs. Josephine Earp. Or, should I say, common-law wife, Mrs. Earp, for they were never wed inside any church of our Lord …"

"I object! Hearsay and a provocation upon the morals and religion of my client."

"Objection overruled. You may continue, Mr. Richards."

The old judge proves which side he is on.

Mr. Richardt duck-walks across the room to proudly stand in front of his male counterparts, the jury panel of twelve, and he begins waving the papers at them.

"We have women present in this courtroom today, and the subject matter included in these legal affidavits is such that only the jury, the judge, and counsel are going to be privy to them. Suffice it to say, however, they prove, beyond any doubt, that Mr. and Mrs. Earp have invested in houses of ill repute and dens of gambling, drinking, and prostitution. Not only this, but they also make mention of a religious rabbi, the victim, Jerome Sonenschein, who is following them, like a shadow of doom, across state lines, to rouse the towns as to the exact nature of their sinful activities. What more does this court need to prove the malice in their minds against our victim in this case? Think of all the good families threatened by their lust and greed. Think of the future of our children and our schools, and not to mention our beloved churches!"

Mr. Richardt's face is beet-colored, and he is gasping for air. I know just the kind of woman who could soon make Archibald into her plaything. The loudest men are always the whimpering grovelers when they are beset upon by a woman who knows how to use her feminine wiles to capture him in her embraces.

From the front of the courtroom, near the exit double doors, a woman screams. Down the center aisle, a man limps toward the front where we are seated. Dr. Baker gasps and then stands up.

"Fred! What is it? What's happened to you?" Her voice has that panic that every woman experiences. When a child is on the road, running away. A husband is going to a gunfight. A long wait alone at home, and then he walks through the door at one in the morning.

"Oh, my God! Look at his eyes!" A juror yells.

Fred Baker's eyes look like two burning coals. As he fumbles his way down toward his wife, he is drooling, and his arms keep reaching out, scraping the air in front of him. His entire body is shivering as if he has palsy, and then he stops. The entire courtroom is silent.

"I'm so sorry, Charlotte, my love. Venus is before me. She made me go back. Again, and again. The sea winds blew, and the monsters of the deep came for me. Called me into their lair. I cannot go back! Please! Let me stay with you here." He then spins around, as if he is mad. Yes, his mouth is frothing, and he spits forth a gush of blood. It is ghastly! And then, he falls against our table, his tall body jack-knifing, hitting his head on the side of the mahogany edge.

Dr. Baker rushes to him, takes his pulse, but from the staring, vacuous image she strikes, we all believe he might be gone forever. Two policemen come up with a stretcher and carefully lift his body upon it. The whispers begin, and then the shouts.

"Get him checked for the black plague! That man is deathly ill!"

"Our lives are in danger! We must leave here at once!"

And then, the mad scramble begins. As old Judge Parker begins to weakly slam his gavel, people inside the court start to pour out into the aisles, and then they begin to push and shove, moving toward the two doors like lemmings toward the cliffs.

Seizing the moment, I look over and see that our guards are down the aisle, attempting to restore order. I glance over toward Wyatt, and then at Mrs. Foltz. She is preoccupied with Dr. Baker, who is crying, deep sobs wracking her body.

He nods at me. I move toward him.

We are through the back door, into the judge's chambers, and out onto Front Street within minutes. As Wyatt hobbles in his chains and shackles, I follow closely behind, thrusting my handcuffs, holding my wrists forward like a praying mantis.

The crowds outside are enormous. A man in a straw hat, driving a four-horse black carriage, must have recognized us from photographs in the newspapers. He is shouting down at us.

"Wyatt! Marshal Earp! Bobby, get down there and lift them into the back of the rig."

A tall, tow-headed youth springs from the seat next to his father and bounds toward us.

"C'mon, folks. I'll help you get up in there."

This is how we escape after I see the driver, who I am expecting, and I can see the sun going down in the west, down Euclid to the ocean, and the sky looks like Dr. Fred Baker's face, splotched with red and blue, bleeding some kind of monstrous disease all over San Diego.

"Miss Heaven is waiting for you both," says Saul Price, the driver.

I smile over at him. "I wonder if this is the main distraction Miss Riendeau has in mind. It is supposed to be the first act."

I fold my shackled hands, lean my head on Wyatt's arm, and

watch the new electric lights begin to blink on, all along the sidewalks in front of the shops and stores, as our buckboard takes us down the dirt road of Front Street until we turn left onto Broadway.

**

Wyatt tells me the story of Francisco Morta on the way down to Ensenada. He is an old veteran of the Mexican-American War, which ended with the Treaty of Guadalupe-Hidalgo, in 1848. He was given a land grant by his government, and he lived as a ranchero in Rancho Tia Juana until he was forced to move by the Mexico City politicians, who were working more closely with the San Diego politicians to create the businesses and tourist industries across the border. Mr. Morta still employs some Natives to work his small ranch, but he makes his real money doing illicit businesses, such as those which Wyatt and I now pursue to save our own lives.

Heaven Riendeau is at the rancho of Francisco Villegas Morta, in Ensenada, Baja California, about sixty-seven miles from the U.S. border. When we arrive there by Mr. Price's carriage, it is pitch dark, and I can see the gas torch lights in the garden in front of Mr. Morta's collection of low, brick, and stucco buildings. The torches blaze in the blackness like suns.

"*Señor* Earp, and Mrs. Earp, I am so privileged to have you here again." The old man hobbles out to greet us, accompanied by a servant holding a lantern. The servant calls to a smaller, adjoining house, and two young Natives run out and begin retrieving our luggage from the back of the carriage.

"They are from Peru, the rainforests, as a matter of fact," says the old ranchero, hobbling with us in the dark, a long bamboo cane thrust before him.

Heaven is inside, seated before the roaring fireplace. I am very happy to see another woman. Her distraction is working perfectly. She administered the *ayahuasca*, or *yage*, to Fred Baker. This is a vine grown in the Peruvian rain forest and used by shamans to commune with the spirit world. As I sit down next to her, we both begin to stare into the fire, as it crackles and spits back embers. We give ourselves over to its powers, as the men are still talking in the foyer. Wyatt is arguing with the old soldier about something. Wyatt is always arguing, and it is I who gets most of the negotiations done. I wish to talk with Heaven about her drugging of San Diego's leaders, beginning with Charlotte Baker's husband, Fred.

Heaven finally turns toward me. I am wondering why it takes her so long to say anything. She wears her usual crushed velvet, this time red, and her dark hair glistens in the firelight like licorice just out of the oven. Her angelic, oval face frames crimson lips that pucker before she speaks as if she is kissing the air.

"Mrs. Earp. I'm so happy you escaped. Mr. Morta's drugs are quite effective when I put them into the men's drinks at my little opening night soiree. I watched them squirm, at first, chasing after my girls in a trance-like state. The dose is for testing only. When I increased it on Dr. Baker, it put him into a state of stuporous reverie. He will remember nothing afterward." She stops and bows her head, waiting for me to reply.

"Today's appearance in court was quite magnificent. Even Charlotte believed he had succumbed. When will you drug the others? We need to mount our new defense soon."

Wyatt comes up behind me. His voice, although I know it well, startles me.

"Sadie, now what makes you believe we're makin' any kind of courtroom appearance again?"

I can feel the vibration of his deep baritone against my back, as he leans forward. I do not want to bless his countenance with my own, by looking up, so I continue to stare into the fire's blazes.

"Perhaps you want to leave and escape final justice, but I am not of that mind. My people have always believed in finding the truth, and justice is part of the Judaic culture. I want San Diego to know what it has become. If my people must be made to feel guilty about murdering their redeemer, Jesus, then they will feel guilt about who murdered Rabbi Jerome Sonenschein!"

I hear the old man's grunt when I mention the murder of his savior. He is the one who supplies us with this place in Ensenada to keep the underage prostitutes for our contract with Postmaster

General Comstock. He is in this as deeply as we are.

"You men are the ones who wanted to increase the pressure on Mayor Hunsaker. I wanted no part in that. Now that we women have gotten you out of trouble, we all need a way to turn the tables on the prosecution and discover who the real party is behind the murder."

I pick up the iron poker and begin to push a big log in its center. It teeters over, cracking in the middle, spraying embers every which way. Many times I believe men, especially the super masculine types like my husband, should be housed in cages and only let out to do their chores. Leave the big thinking to us women.

"All right then, Sadie. Why did we pay the Foltz woman to defend us? Don't you think she might know who may be behind this? We never got the chance to hear her witnesses and what they have to say."

At these words, I finally do turn around and stare up at Wyatt. He is using that handsome head of his for more than a hat display.

"How far did you think you'd get us away from justice? We did win the war against Mexico, you know. The Mexican government will never shelter us, would they, Colonel Morta?" I turn toward the old soldier. His grizzled gray beard, dark complexion, and owlish eyebrows remind me of my father.

"She is correct, *compadre*. My country is very poor right now. If your country gave any reward for your return, somebody would certainly turn you in, no matter where we hid you."

I look back at Heaven.

"When will you have the other men under the influence? Have they been enjoying your Venus in Furs rituals? I want each of the men on our suspect list so drugged that they will tell us the truth. Mix the hallucinatory drug with opium. That will get them under our powers very quickly."

Heaven smiles and adjusts the white collar under her red velvet dress. "I can do that. They are almost drugged with passion already," she giggles.

"Excellent! I want to hand the guilty party over to the court on a silver platter. Just like Ida Bailey and her drugged dance accomplished that day in Tijuana. Quite frankly, I still believe she is the one responsible for the rabbi's death, but I must prove it. She handed his head over to somebody, as certain as Salome's dance handed John the Baptist's head over to her mother, Herodias. Who is the mother or father responsible for Ida's dance? That's what we must discover."

"You don't reckon one of these men'll rebel and turn Heaven and her girls into the authorities? What happens to your little scheme *then*, Sadie? They'll have her arrested as sure as a fox can capture a fat hen."

Wyatt twists his long mustache end and grins down at me. I hate it when he plays long arm of the law.

"Most of the town will be taken up with hunting us down in San Diego and maybe Tijuana. The newspapers are already on our side, so their search will be half-hearted at best. Hunsaker is up for re-election, and most folks believe he is just trying to get votes with his testimony against us. We'll surely have enough time to find out who is behind the killing of the rabbi."

"If you don't find out, then I will put a bullet in Honey's black heart! That weasel would turn his mother in for votes." Wyatt smirks. "But, you know, there could be something else at play here."

I look up at him. What else is he doing right now to slow me down?

"What do you mean? At play? Did you have something arranged that I don't know about?" I am adamant. "I want to know, Wyatt Berry Stapp Earp!" Only I could ever use his full name. He hates my using it as much as I hate it when he calls me Sadie.

"A little bird told me that another man wants the rabbi dead. Attorney Foltz says she is going to use this fact during our defense."

"What are you saying? Why didn't you tell me? I'm your wife!" I am fuming.

"She told me specifically *not* to tell you." He raises his dark eyebrows. "And, maybe I better keep my trap shut."

I stand up, grab Wyatt by his vest, and pull him toward me until we are face-to-face. I stare hard into his blue eyes.

"You tell me right now, husband, or you will never touch

this body again!"

"Dr. Fred Baker wanted the rabbi killed because he is in love with Ida Bailey. Ida, of course, as we both know, is in love with Sonenschein. That's the love triangle. You know that's why I shot him, Sarah. You know *that* is God's truth! Fred Baker must have wanted me to plug Sonenschein, so his wife and her groups wouldn't help the rabbi shut down the Stingaree."

"If that is true, Wyatt, then we will have to discover how the rabbi was going to kill you on May 6," Mrs. Foltz says.

I want to take some of the *ayahuasca*, but I settle for tequila that the old colonel brings out.

***

It is Lucky Baldwin who brings us news about the second murder. Wyatt, me, and Colonel Morta are talking with Clara Foltz and Dr. Charlotte Baker. Yes, they have discovered where we are in Ensenada, whereas the San Diego prosecution has not. How? They connect the logical dots. Mrs. Foltz has already prepared our witnesses for the self-defense plea, and one of them, Ida Bailey, confesses that Fred Baker pursued her, obsessively, when he learned that Rabbi Sonenschein seduced Miss Bailey. Even though this information hurts Dr. Baker to her core, she is practical enough, after the drugging of her husband by another person, to analyze Fred's blood. When she discovers the hallucinogenic substance, Mrs. Foltz and Charlotte know there is a person behind all of this distraction, so they decide to call Madam Heaven Riendieu at her place of business, the Golden Faun, next door to Bailey's Canary Cottage.

What they find out from Riendeau leads them to our hideout. Why Heaven turns against me so suddenly, and with so much furor, is later discovered when the police report the killing of the young Indian, Anand Prabhakar, by the waitress, Miss Kai Krissy Wong. She poisons the nineteen-year-old immigrant while upstairs in his small room. Krissy, before the police can be notified, confesses to Heaven that she is paid in gold nuggets by a mysterious person at the restaurant.

At the moment, Miss Wong and Miss Riendeau are also here with our defense team of Foltz and Baker. I am anxious to find out why the girl has not been arrested by authorities. I know Foltz needs to discover who this mysterious person is who paid Krissy so much to kill the boy. Perhaps now we can find out why Krissy did it. There must be more than just the money involved. What did Anand know to cause him to be murdered?

Mrs. Foltz is here, she informs us, to create a new investigation team. Therefore, she commandeers the long walnut dining table on Colonel Morta's patio, just outside his ranch house. The Peruvian Natives bring us an assortment of guacamole, fried tortillas, tequila for the men and me, and wine and soft apple cider, for the weaker spirited in our group.

Our attorney is seated at the head of the table, with Charlotte Baker to her right, and Heaven Riendeau on her left. I am next to Heaven, and Wyatt is next to me. On the left side, Colonel Morta sits next to Charlotte and then comes Miss Wong. Finally, Elias Baldwin is on the end, looking for all the world like a misplaced vagabond in a rich man's tuxedo, and who immediately reaches for the tequila and pours himself a long measure into his mug. This is our "magnificent seven."

Does Mrs. Foltz believe we are going to solve both of these murders and save the lives of Wyatt, me, Kai Krissy Wong, and, most likely, Miss Heaven Riendeau? We will need all of Elias Baldwin's luck and more if that is the case.

"I want to first thank all of you for being here. This occasion is such that if I were not in such a quandary, I would immediately allow the authorities to take over and render their decision. This moment, however, is not one of the normal consequences. I will tell you why in a moment. But I first want to say that all of you will be working with me to find the perpetrator of the most heinous crime I have ever investigated."

Most of the people at the table begin to talk to each other, with gasping phrases and shaking heads, and their voices are filled with fear and trepidation. I do not speak. I am stone silent. Even Wyatt is talking nervously to me. He does not know what I know.

"Can you please be more forthright, Mrs. Foltz? We are all

adults at this table. I believe we can process your secret with alacrity and attention." Lucky Baldwin grasps the tequila bottle once more.

Another two of those pours and he will be losing his alacrity and charm. I have seen him shoot up an entire hotel lounge in San Francisco when he gets drunk.

"Miss Wong, please tell the group what you found out about the boy you accidentally killed. It is very important information to add to our inquiry and search for the person responsible for his and, most probably, Rabbi Sonenschein's murder."

Krissy Wong first stares over at Heaven. The young woman's youthful, usually exuberant expression is wan and sorrowful. When Heaven nods at her, she begins in a hesitant voice.

"It wasn't just the gold. It is the letter that came with the gold," she says, her voice trailing off.

"What is in this letter?" The attorney has a tone of urgency in her voice.

Heaven reaches into her crushed velvet handbag and pulls out a piece of paper with typed prose upon it. She hands it to the attorney.

As she reads, her eyebrows rise, and her lips purse in concentration. When she speaks, it is as if she has been converted by some strange religion described by what she is reading.

"This is monstrous and telling information. Kai was acting to inoculate Anand and not kill him. The person who gave her the money included a signed medical form, which explained that the boy has virulent smallpox." Mr. Foltz stares hard at the girl. "Miss Wong. Did this doctor also include the oral vaccine he mentions in this?"

She looks up. "Yes. That's what killed him. I put it in his tea." Tears begin to flow. "I didn't know! It wasn't the money. I believed what this doctor says. In China, we have thousands in our village who contract this. My uncle and aunt had the pox. We have no vaccines. We have to watch them go through the stages of pustules and scabs. My aunt, who is pregnant, dies during her fever. I don't want the boy to infect San Diego. It's a terrible disease!"

"We understand. Nobody is blaming you, young lady.

Heaven, did you keep the vial of poison?" Mrs. Foltz holds out her hand.

"Here it is," Heaven answers, handing the lawyer a small bottle.

"Dr. Baker, please do some chemical analysis on what poison is in this," she tells Charlotte, handing her the little bottle.

"Why is this important news?" Lucky Baldwin asks, his voice slurring a bit from the tequila. "Just one more immigrant. No loss, as far as I can see. I say check him for smallpox. Lousy little curry muncher."

Dr. Baker turns on him like a viper. "Our police will automatically do an autopsy, kind sir. If the poor lad is infected, we will soon be informed."

Kai Krissy Wong is still sobbing. Everybody looks over at her.

"What's wrong?" I ask. "Did something else happen?"

She finally raises her head from her flushed red arms, which now glisten with teardrops, as do her cheeks.

"Anand thanked me so much for the drug. He said he was never told in India he had this disease. He thought he may have contracted it on the trip to San Diego. He said that Miss Heaven gave him a new beginning and that he even attained what he called *moksha*, which is what we Chinese Buddhists call *bodhi* or an awakening to the mystical harmony all-around one. He said each day is a heavenly gift from a woman named Heaven." Her head drops down into her arms again, and Charlotte and Mrs. Foltz get up to console her and caress her shoulders.

"Oh, balderdash! Can't you get to the suspects you have? What is it we have to do now, attorney Foltz? Is this your case or is it not?" Lucky Baldwin is getting riled up by all this attention paid to a young Chinese girl, a waitress at that. An underling, to his way of thinking.

"Shut your trap, Elias," Wyatt speaks up. "Mrs. Foltz says this is an important break in the case, and I, for one, want to hear what she has to say."

"I believe we can now find the culprit behind these killings, but we shall need to work in careful coordination. This new evidence points to the fact that the person behind the death of Anand is either a physician, a nurse, or somebody else who is a health care professional. We may also have a smallpox epidemic on our hands."

Charlotte Baker raises her hand, and Clara points to her.

"You have ruled out my husband, Freddy, I would assume," Dr. Baker says.

"I have, yes. He was drugged to distract the court so the Earp's could escape." Mrs. Foltz stares right at me, and I decide to speak.

"Yes, I confess. My husband and I concocted this method with Heaven Riendeau and Colonel Morta. Dr. Fred Baker was drugged during his visit to Miss Riendeau's evening party, and we appointed Mr. Price to be there at the courthouse when we slipped out the judge's chambers."

"I gathered as much," says Foltz. "I am also aware that you believe it is the other madam, Ida Bailey, whom you believe to be the primary suspect. Is this true?"

I am taken aback. "How did you know this? She *must* be the one. She is in the love triangle with Fred Baker and Rabbi Sonenschein, is she not? This young Indian must have discovered something about this, and Ida needed to dispose of the boy."

"I am well aware that Miss Bailey was under the influence of a drug during her dance in Tijuana. She readily admitted to this. But we have no concrete evidence as yet that she was after Wyatt, or how she is involved in the sex contract between Mayor Hunsaker, the Earps, and Postmaster Comstock."

"Wyatt and I are going to interview her to find out," I say, thrusting my chin out. "We shall prove it to you, I dare say, and this will put an end to all of this cloak and dagger mischief."

"Very well, Josephine. You *shall* visit Miss Bailey and find out what she knows. And Wyatt, in disguise, along with Elias Baldwin, shall visit Mayor Hunsaker." She looks directly at Lucky. "And Mr. Baldwin, I want you and Wyatt, in disguise once more, to search that Canary Cottage to see what you can find in the way of material clues to these murders."

Lucky Baldwin grins from ear to ear. "By all means, Mrs.

Foltz! I know those luxury confines like the back of my hand."

Wyatt laughs. "If you mean the way your hand cheats at poker, then I'd agree with you!"

"The other members of our group shall investigate in this manner. Dr. Baker and I will investigate the involvement of Anthony Comstock, Dr. Fred Baker, and Mayor Hunsaker. Finally, I want you, Heaven, and Miss Wong, to portray nurses and see if you can find any persons who might have initiated the poisoning of Anand Prabhakar. You and Miss Wong are new enough to the community not to be recognized, and Dr. Baker can get you the proper credentials so you can affect your subterfuge without notice. We will all keep in communication and return here when we complete our assigned duties. Mr. Morta will be here to man the fort."

"And please find out if there have been any new cases of smallpox," Dr. Charlotte Baker says.

Everyone stands up, sensing that we will be dismissed.

"This does *not* mean you are all out of suspicion, however. It's just that we are in such a predicament, with the authorities hunting us down already, that I must take drastic measures. If any of you turns out to be a conspirator, then you will be found out. Mark my words. Until then, be on your way, and be very careful."

I take Wyatt's hand as we leave the room. His hand is cold and moist. I feel the opposite, with my flushed face and my mouth like cotton.

***

I have not spoken to Ida Bailey since Tijuana on May 6, when Wyatt killed the rabbi. I am more concerned with this young woman's relationships with Dr. Fred Baker and the rabbi than Clara Foltz seems to be. She seems to be wise about what I was saying before the trial began, but something has happened since then to make her change her mind. Why is she now searching into the Anthony Comstock and Mayor Hunsaker deal with Wyatt and me? I believe we will have had enough of San Diego after all of this transpires.

The Canary Cottage Madam is in her bedroom office when I arrive by Mr. Price's carriage from Ensenada. It is eight in the evening, and I wear black, so as not to be recognized, completing my outfit with a Victorian funeral hat, and a shroud to cover my face. One of Ida's girls greets me, but I do not inform her of my name, just that I have an appointment with Miss Bailey. She points up the spiral staircase to the master bedroom at the end of the second-floor hallway.

After three knocks on the cedar door, Ida opens it. She is smoking a marijuana cigarette, so I immediately wonder how much lucidity I will be able to get from her. Then again, perhaps she will be more inclined to tell me the truth.

I push back the shroud netting and smile. "Ida! I see you've begun your festivities. Speaking of which, are you involved in the murder of a boy named Anand Prabhakar? I already know about you and Fred Baker. Did this boy discover your relationship between your beloved rabbi and Charlotte's husband?"

Her eyes are a deep blue, and she squints at me. She does not seem perturbed at all. She is wearing red Japanese silk pajamas with a tassel around her thin waist.

"The men come and go, Mrs. Earp. You, of all people, must know this. I have no time to discuss the mundane contracts between perverted men. Why should I, then, want to terminate a young man who might have uncovered something untoward about Dr. Baker and Mayor Hunsaker? Weren't you and your husband part of this endeavor as well? If so, why are you asking me? Ask yourself, my lady. Ask yourself."

I take out Wyatt's Bowie knife from my black handbag. Its two sharp edges give me the powerful conviction I need. I grab Ida by her curly-red hair and pull her throat down to my knife. She stares at it as if it were a piece of pineapple upside-down cake.

"My goodness, Grandmother! What big teeth you have!" she smirks.

Can it be this woman wants to die? Is she insane after all?

"Tell me, and I won't report you. I just need to know who wanted my husband dead that night in Tijuana. Answer me, or I'll slit your white throat into a crimson smile. I am an escaped murder defendant, Ida. I have nothing to lose at this point."

She spits in my face.

I slice down the center of her pajamas, and they slip from her body to the floor on both sides, until she stands there nude, her nipples pointing at me. A three-inch cut is bleeding between her breasts. However, she is still smiling.

"If you *are* a murderer, then I would be dead. Since you most likely are not, then I suggest you leave at once. I can scream quite loudly before you can plunge that blade into my heart, or wherever it is you wish to stab me. Do you like women, Mrs. Earp? Many of you older ladies often visit my cottage for just such enjoyment."

The insanity in her eyes tells me everything I need to know. Wyatt and Lucky will be here to search the place, so perhaps we won't need her word about how she may be involved in this case. The mystery of how Anand was poisoned will remain a secret until we all complete our private investigations. I am just sorry I cannot do more to help the effort.

"If you call the police to report you have seen me, Ida, I will come back here and finish what I was going to do. I shall be long gone, nonetheless, so I suggest you get dressed and begin your evening's entertainment."

After I leave the cottage, I do not see Mr. Price's four horses hitched to anything on the street. His carriage has completely disappeared. The person comes up from behind me before I can pull out my knife. I can smell the odor on the cloth instantly. Chloroform. I have smelled it once before. I was fifteen, and I had been raped in an alley in San Francisco. The last thing I thought was that I wished I had gone with Wyatt. That had been our plan in the first place. Now I am being taken somewhere I had not planned to visit.

***

When I awake, I can smell the disgusting odor of soy and noodles, mixed with excrement and urine from the outhouses. I know where I am. Chinatown in the Stingaree. I am bound with hemp rope to an Oriental lounge chair

91

shaped like a dragon. The outer, dragon portion, is gold and the cushions are crimson. My mouth is gagged with a silk scarf, and it tastes like my own vomit. My temperature has increased, and I feel quite ill. It is as if I am in a drug-induced dream world.

The man, whom I can barely see, sits on the other side of the small room at a desk. He is smoking a pipe that smells of cherries and writing in an accounting ledger of some kind. When he hears me squirming, he turns around to face me. Even in my fevered state, I can see who he is. It is Dr. Frederick Baker, one of the most distinguished citizens in San Diego, who is now my captor. Was he perchance hoping for some kind of reward being given by the Mayor's Office for my return?

"Li Wei?" he shouts. "Come in here at once!"

Another man comes into the room, a Chinese gentleman who wears a Stingaree delivery person's uniform. He is rather handsome and clean-shaven. As he takes the gag from my mouth, I stare deeply into his dark eyes, as we Jews have always had a strange affinity with these people. Perhaps because we both enjoy Mahjong, or because we are, as a race, usually despised as immigrants.

"Josephine Earp. I am quite happy to make your acquaintance. Ida has spoken of you often, as you are a major investor in this section of San Diego, the Stingaree, are you not?" His voice is dripping with a sarcastic undertone.

"Business is not on my mind at this moment, Dr. Baker. As you are aware, Wyatt and I are attempting to clear our good name from charges of murder. Why have you done this? Is there a reward you wish the obtain?" The words are difficult for me to get out. The entire room is beginning to undulate in wavy patterns.

"A reward? Why, yes, as a matter of fact, there *is* a reward I am after. And, quite ironically, it involves the clearing of *my* good name. This is the reason I've taken you into my care, good lady. I want you to witness how my actions are beginning to make San Diego into the *santo paraíso* it is meant to be."

Now it is his words that swim before me. Is he insane, or is it my sickness?

"Holy paradise? Have you become delusional?" I manage.

He picks up the ledger at his desk and displays it to me as if he were Moses who has come down from Mount Sinai.

"Are you aware of my work, Mrs. Earp? We are in the early stages of creating the most magnificent display of wild animals on Earth through the Zoological Society and our Marine Laboratories. God has given us this wonderful land to make it into a holy gift to His people. People will come from all over the world to view our zoo and our animals, don't you see?"

"How does this relate to my kidnapping? I am also quite ill, and you are a doctor, are you not? Can you give me something? I am swooning with a fever, and I'm nauseated." My head falls forward onto my chest, involuntarily, and it feels like a steel ball when I raise it once more.

"It is all beginning in Chinatown, right where we are now." He points to one of the names on his ledger. "Did you know that in 1886, David Bruce, a British army surgeon, isolated a coccobacillus from the spleen of a man who had died of Malta Fever? Dr. Bruce named it *Micrococcus melitensis*. This disease is endemic, but it is confused with other diseases, especially malaria."

"Disease? What are you trying to say?" My head again swoons, I am burning up, and my mouth is cotton.

"My injected goats have this coccobacillus, and you were also given an injection, female Judas's goat that you are. Our leader, Rabbi Sonenschein, had the dose meant for you and your husband that evening in Tijuana. It was meant to kill you both right after my betrayer and former love, Ida Bailey, finished her Dance of the Seven Veils."

"After the dance? That was how you were going to kill us? Am I going to … to die?" My heart is pounding in my temples, and I panic.

"Oh, no. Your dose is small. I want you to be the celebrity's name for my first plague, which I shall call the Chinatown Marcus of Sodom Brucellosis Plague, after the gentleman I studied with while I was in Malta. You, of course, are the whore."

I try to scream, but I have no strength. I feel weak, and my body is shivering in the midst of my fevered state. "What are you going to do?"

"I am first cleansing the ethnic scourge, so I may begin my second plague. The doses of brucellosis will, indeed, begin to kill these Chinese, Japanese, and other inferior breeds, just as I poisoned that Indian vermin of your employee, Heaven Riendeau."

He is the medical specialist behind the poisoning of Anand? Of course, he is. "Second plague? This is quite insane. You must desist at once, Dr. Baker!"

"Desist? On the contrary, Josephine Jew. I shall show my love, Ida Bailey, that I can be ten times the man her Jew lover, Jerome Sonenschein, ever was. What she believed he could do with his hocus-pocus; I shall accomplish with science. Darwinian survival of the fittest, and the evolutionary diseases shared between animal and human, shall show the world that I am the future ruler of all species."

I cannot stop myself. I heave up the goat's milk, and it sprays all over the front of my Victorian black dress.

After Li Wei cleans me up, I feel better. The thought of what is happening doesn't make me any better, however. I need to see what Dr. Baker has in store for the citizens, in case I can, by some miracle, escape. He is again writing in his ledger. I decide to mollify him by assuaging his insanity.

"Hello, Dr. Baker? I can see you are mentally deranged. But what of your wife and your children? Have you thought they might not appreciate what you're about to do?" I keep my voice even and calmly reflective. If he is insane, then perhaps he has already invented a rationale to address this problem. In the back of my mind, I keep expecting Wyatt and Lucky Baldwin to break through the door and rescue me. He once again turns toward me, puffing on his pipe and scowling. His long walrus mustaches droop when he does this, giving him the appearance of a Greek Satyr. Will he dare try to rape me?

"Of course, you know about the plagues, as your people are of the older scriptures, and Rabbi Sonenschein, my lover's paramour, has evolved past your mundane beliefs into the mystical realm of Ecstatic Kabbalah. Once I understood that my Ida had fallen in love with the Jew, I realized I needed to do him one better.

Charlotte and her groups of Christian soldiers are attempting to clean up the Stingaree, and I am as well, don't you see?"

I return his frown. "Your wife wants the families in San Diego to live a good life, without the gambling and harlotry that take place in the Stingaree. But she has no reason to kill people to achieve her goals."

This must have agitated him, as he stands up, holding his ledger out toward me.

"Blasted! The plagues I will rain down on this community will teach them a lesson. The second plague shall bring leprosy into their midst. Do you know about the eight-banded armadillos I have delivered to the whore houses?"

"Yes, I saw the young boy and girl messengers bring one to Heaven Riendeau's Golden Faun. It is meant to be an excellent insect eradicator for the grounds. Quite a deplorable-looking creature, I must admit. A rat's head with that scaley, plump body."

"Another irony. Those two messengers are Mrs. Foltz's children trying to spy on your houses. As for the armadillo, it is the best carrier of the leprosy bacterium in the animal kingdom."

"How do you mean? How can it transmit leprosy to humans?" I am interested, and I am appalled, at the same time.

"*Mycobacterium leprae* has a preference for cool temperatures. In man, the lesions manifest mainly on the arms, legs, ears, nose--cooler regions of the body. Although most animals are highly resistant to M. leprae and will rapidly dispose of the organisms, laboratory mice will develop a very limited infection when they are inoculated into the cool temperatures of their hind footpads. Armadillos have an internal body temperature of only 32-35C, and it is this cool body temperature that first attracted the attention of leprosy researchers like myself."

"Cool body temperature? How does this relate to the spread of the horrible infection?" I clear my throat. "Can you give me something more specific?"

"Certainly, since you will be observing some of the victims in a short while. You didn't think my plagues were begun yesterday, did you? Direct exposure to the blood or tissue of an infected animal is probably the highest risk for the spread of M. leprae from armadillos to humans and people eating armadillos as food. And, since the usual incubation takes years, I needed to hasten this for my purposes."

"How?" I am mesmerized, and my mind envisions all the biblical stories I have read about the leper colonies, and the appendages that fall off bodies, like leaves from a tree, and the demolished faces, and the horrible pain and suffering.

"A direct injection from the animal's blood to the human. So, I allowed the working girls to play with the armadillo, but then I took blood from the creature and injected it into the girls at night, while they slept. The disease begins to manifest in weeks, not years, and tomorrow we shall see the results sprouting up, all over the Stingaree, like mushrooms in a loamy forest!"

"That's ghastly! You are a ghoul, not a doctor."

"Wait until you see my final plague. There will be no better, or more horrific, way to show them my power over all of nature!" He begins to laugh, hysterically, until I begin to realize there is little hope of bringing him back from his lunatic fringe.

***

He brings in his "specimens," as he calls them, one by one, for me to witness. I am allowed to bathe and attend to my biological needs, but I am not allowed to cover my eyes. Dr. Baker keeps me tied firmly down in my dragon lounge, so I have to stare straight ahead and gaze at the passing leprous victims—four of them—one after the other. He chooses the ones with the most advanced injuries, including blindness, so they are not able to see me or the doctor who is, supposedly, treating them for their afflictions.

In the typical method of sexist medicine, he blames them for their leprosy. He says they contracted it from their indecent lifestyle, and from their having sexual relations with foreigners from lands where the disease is still running rampant. As they are mostly immigrants themselves, they believe him, the mighty lord and master. For a year, Dr. Baker treats them for their chlamydia and other sexually transmitted diseases, so they have no reason to disbelieve him.

There are large, discolored lesions on their skin, especially around the neck, and lumps on their faces. They have no eyebrows, and the damage of the nerves has led to the blindness and the agonized expression each possesses. One can see they were once beautiful, however, and as they hobble in front of me, I imagine a favorite doll I once had that a neighbor boy had torn asunder to make me cry. Two of the young girls have shortened toes, and they have to walk barefoot, and their noses are lumps of flesh pushed into their faces like bread dough.

What is so abhorrent to me is how Dr. Baker treats them. He keeps up a constant litany of praise and consolation, telling them how they are improving, when they are not, and lying to them about the new remedy he is working on in his laboratory that will cure them. He even has Li Wei translate to the Chinese girls, and it is pitiful watching them attempt to bow in gracious servitude, clutching their ragged dresses in false modesty.

After this grotesque parade is over, and the door is closed behind them, Dr. Baker strides across the room to stand in front of me. He is puffing on that infernal briar pipe like a Southern Pacific steam engine. I have no idea what is next, but I know he is going to give me some kind of horrendous explanation.

He tells Li Wei to take the gag out of my mouth, and the young man does. I am not drugged, so my senses are acute, but I would have preferred that my mind be numbed after that experience. Whatever he is going to tell me can never be explicated away. He is a beast beyond any rational explanation.

"These Chinatown wenches are only the beginning, of course. Don't feel sorry for them. They cannot feel the lesions because of underlying nerve damage and paralysis. It is a fairly humane way to die. The men I have witnessed die without morphine or other pain relief were far worse. The Civil War did not prioritize anesthetics, only weaponry."

I can no longer contain my emotions. "How can you say you're purifying the human race? Those women are tortured!"

He chuckles. "Torture? The disease is God's way of telling

us we are frail creatures. These women would have died in their own countries from some scourge even worse. They receive no advanced care or treatments. Most are dead before they are out of their teen years. In fact, in China, the girls are murdered just because they are females, in their infancy. It is my purpose to show the world how close we are to our animal species. One day, when we've slaughtered the last buffalo, or tortured and burned down the last Native teepee or hut, these creatures will begin to fight back against us."

"Fight back? These women cannot fight back at you! Did you enjoy their bowing and scraping? Are you a gentleman or a monster?"

"We are all only animals, Mrs. Earp. The animals we keep destroying and pushing out of their territories will develop ways of reaching us. They will carry biological destruction in the form of diseases and plagues about which we can only imagine. Their world is vicious. A natural world where most species immediately kill the wounded or sickly in their midst. Lions will eat the runts. The praying mantis female devours her mate to feed her young. Only in captivity can we stop this. I am their lord and master because I have the technology to control them and make them do what I wish them to do. We subdue our lesser species, or they will overpopulate and subdue us! I am the new Adam on Earth to create the new Eden."

"How many more of these women will you infect? How can you report your results to the world and expect not to be condemned and arrested?" I am feeling nauseated once more.

"They will never know it is I who did this, except my anonymous posts to the major newspapers. I am sending out my first letter to the editor at a very local daily in San Diego."

"The *Union*?"

"No, I thought I would give this honor to your attorney, Clara Shortridge Foltz. She owns the *San Diego Bee*, and we have already met. This intellectual woman would appreciate having the first knowledge concerning what I am about to accomplish. My wife, Charlotte, will also come around when she sees how quickly we shall rid ourselves of this Sodom and Gomorrah in our midst.

Our children will be able to live in a town that is, at last, clean and wholesome. No more infestations. No more unholy diseases to treat."

"You don't believe I can stay mute while all of this happens, do you? And, what about Ida Bailey? You say you love her. Can she be trusted to keep your secret?"

"You don't believe you will stay alive, do you, my dear Jewess? After all, your race is one of the sub-species, is it not? You Christ-killers have had to flee every land you ever visited, at one time or another. I will give you a shortcut. You were going to leave San Diego with your stud, the white Aryan, anyway, were you not?"

"How dare you! You are nothing but an anti-Semitic murderer!"

"All of these speculators who come here are simply making hay, drinking, gambling, and whoring about. Until they fill their pockets with riches and move on to the next boomtown down the road. They never care about those who simply want to have a pure and wholesome land in which to raise their children, free of crime, free of decadence, and free of sin! I am giving you a way out of your terrible existence for which you will certainly go to Hell. I am also going to kill Miss Ida Bailey, in a most inglorious manner, tomorrow, during my final plague. As you stated, she knows too much."

My head is spinning. Where are my rescuers? Certainly, they know I am missing. What is keeping them from searching the Stingaree? Mrs. Foltz says she is going to interview this monster. Where is she?

"Put the scarf back in her mouth. I don't want to hear any more from this one." He motions to Li Wei, and I am soon mute once more. I will not see a respite until dinner time, as is the ritual unless I can convince them I need to use the toilet.

The knock on the door surprises Dr. Baker. He is not expecting anyone. He frantically motions to his assistant to push me into the back room, and he does so, as the dragon lounge chair is on rollers. When he closes the door, I am with him in the dark. I can still hear, however, and when I perceive the unmistakable voice of Mrs. Foltz, my heart leaps for joy.

"Aha, Dr. Baker, they told me you might be here. May I have a few words with you? Your wife is coming up the stairs as well if that's all right."

"Of course, Mrs. Foltz. I am just doing some treatments for the young ladies. Come right in. Charlotte will be expecting me for dinner, I would imagine. Have you found the killer?"

"No, I wanted to go over what you knew concerning Ida Bailey and Rabbi Sonenschein. Did you hear about what he wanted to do to save the prostitutes in the Stingaree? I will be honest with you, Dr. Baker before your wife is here. I know you had a sexual relationship with Miss Bailey. Were you jealous of the rabbi's relationship with her?"

"I was not! Ida Bailey is a temptress and a trollop. I never loved her. We had long talks about her religious beliefs, and what that charlatan Sonenschein has taught her about Jewish Kabbalah. I never laid a hand on her. I am married with two children. I have my reputation as a physician and research scientist."

"Both of you. You can stop the pantomime. I know about his affair at the Canary Cottage. And, it wasn't just once, Freddy. Your friend, Lucky Baldwin, saw you there at least five times, and you were enjoying yourself immensely each time. I never told you because I thought, unwittingly, that you would tell me of your own accord. Certainly, I expected you to take care to keep your diseases to yourself for my sake!" Charlotte is shouting, and I can sense the bitterness in her voice.

"Darling! It is nothing. I swear to you. Miss Bailey and I had only an intellectual kinship. Nothing sexual about it at all. I never took one drink. Ask Baldwin. Although, he is usually too inebriated to tell who is drunk and who isn't."

"That woman is a Jezebel. She grew up studying how to seduce men like you. She bragged about it to me. Don't you believe women know these things, you stupid man?" Charlotte is livid.

"Please, both of you. I simply want to know if Ida Bailey wanted Josephine or Wyatt Earp dead." Clara's voice is adamant.

I try to wriggle my hands free, and I bite frantically at the scarf in my mouth. It is plunged far down my throat. Besides, I can hear the breathing of that young Chinaman in the dark. He will, most certainly, stab me, or do something violent if I make enough noise to attract attention in the other room.

I can hear Charlotte sobbing. There are whispers. I hear chairs moving.

"Very well, Dr. Baker. Thank you for your time. As you can see, my client and I are at risk of being taken in by the authorities before we can find out who the real murderer is in this case. I would appreciate it if you can keep quiet until we can reconvene to go over our clues. We have seven in our investigative team. I am hoping you can be the eighth, now that I know you had nothing to do with either murder."

"I will certainly be happy to cooperate, Mrs. Foltz. Injustice is not acceptable. I must first do an important research trial tomorrow for the Zoological Society, but I will meet you after I finish. Where should I go?" His voice is dripping with false conviction.

"I will send my son, David Milton, around on his bicycle. He will give you the exact location where we shall be. Will you still be here in Chinatown tomorrow morning? When are you going to do your trial?"

"I shall be here until ten. If he comes before then, and your meeting is in the late afternoon, then I can do my trial and then meet you all."

"Yes, I can arrange an evening meeting with my investigation group. Around six? David will be here before ten. Goodbye, and thank you again for your help."

"Goodbye, Freddy. I will be there as well tomorrow evening."

I hear the door close, and then I hear Dr. Fred Baker's voice again. It sends chills down my spine.

"Give her the sedative, Li. I don't want to be disturbed the rest of the night. I need to prepare for my unveiling tomorrow."

"Yes, Dr. Baker," says the voice in the dark. "She will not disturb you." They are the first words I have heard come from the Chinaman's mouth, and they sound resigned and emotionless. As if he knows I am not long for this world.

***

I watch the morning sun come up tied to my dragon lounge chair, partially drugged from the sedative, and with a snoring Chinaman on the small bed beside my dragon lounge. I have no idea what is going to occur, but a vision in my imagination gives me the illusion of something my father once told me, while we were stopped at the top of the giant Observation Wheel in Golden Gate Park, San Francisco.

There is a mechanical failure, and we are up there for almost an hour. I have challenged my fear of heights by going on the ride with him. He is proving to be powerless, while my eight-year-old mind begins to panic. When the only person you believe is all-powerful, the way I today feel about my husband, Wyatt, you turn to what they tell you to get you through a difficult situation, such as the one I am in now.

"*Bubeleh*, let go of everything. Don't you know? God is not the big man in the sky who gives us orders. God is the one who needs entertainment. He needs drama. He needs to see you squirm in your seat and be afraid. In His show, so the good ones always win. Always. Give Him a good show, Sarah. You are a good one."

I remember those words because they give me a unique way to view the power that supposedly looks after us during moments of dire straights and frightening consequences coming just over the horizon. When the Chinaman Li awakens, I am prepared to give him a good show.

I discover that Li Wei is an educated man who comes from Hong Kong, and he is studying to become a doctor. He also, quite interestingly, can hypnotize patients. As I am a practitioner of the mesmerist's art, I begin a conversation with him concerning how his technique might differ from my own. I am looking for any chance, however slight, to trick him and escape.

"I find that some persons are not susceptible to suggestion, and to place them into a trance is very difficult and often impossible. Have you found this to be the case, Mr. Li?" He is unwinding the hemp ropes from around my shoulders, waist, and ankles. I am being prepared to watch the grand display by Dr. Baker, and this will require my returning to my dark funereal dress and black shroud, which my caretaker has cleaned.

"Yes, that can often happen, but Dr. Baker has shown me drugs that assist in the suggestion process, such as the hallucinogenic varieties, peyote, psilocybin, and even the marijuana weed can work at times to place the patient under."

"On the night of the shooting of Rabbi Sonenschein, Miss Bailey was under just such a trance." I want to know how much he knows about that night. I gaze deeply into the young man's dark eyes. I can see him begin to go under my suggestive powers. I let go the full force of what my father taught me of Intuitive Kabbalah and its magnetic transmission. I know what he is then telling me will not be remembered.

"Yes, this led to the parting of the ways between Miss Bailey, the town leaders, and Dr. Baker. Miss Bailey did not wish to have drugs given to her girls, and she sought out the rabbi to help her close those brothels where drugs are being used and sold. Although she used them, she is very averse to allowing her women to do the same."

"Indeed, I am aware of this. However, do you happen to know the secret the rabbi possessed, which caused him to become a marked man? Did he know something about Mayor Hunsaker, or perhaps the Post Office General, Anthony Comstock?"

The messenger shakes his head. "No, I am not aware. I do know that both you and your husband are not on good terms with them. When I showed Mrs. Foltz and Dr. Charlotte Baker around the Stingaree, I overheard them saying they are suspicious about the contracts you have with the mayor and Mr. Comstock. Please, I must put the scarf back inside your mouth until this boy messenger comes to give Dr. Baker the information about where they will be meeting this evening."

My mesmerism does not put him under a trance. The silk scarf and I are old friends by now, and when the knock comes at the front door of the other room, I am listening intently. Perhaps the lad, David Milton, will be giving me a signal that they now know I am being held captive, and I will be rescued. I want to hear any clues in his speech that might be informing me of this fact.

However, I can hear nothing the boy says. All I can hear is Dr. Baker's deep voice acknowledging that he will be at the Grand Horton Hotel at six-thirty. I wonder how my group can appear in public, but perhaps it is just a ruse to trap Dr. Baker on the way over there. According to my captors, however, they may be too late to stop what is going to take place this evening, as the display has been moved to sundown. After I witness it, I am to be disposed of forthwith, so what I am to see must be more heinous than the poor leprous girls I saw yesterday.

I follow Li Wei out the door. He has a revolver, and he says he will use it if I try to run or do anything untoward. He also places handcuffs on my wrists and covers them with a black fur handwarmer. What Dr. Baker is going to demonstrate is to take place at the Canary Cottage, as this is where Ida lives. She conspired with the rabbi to stop Dr. Baker from doing what he planned to do for years.

We take a one-horse carriage down to Ida Bailey's place, and the weather is clear and dark. A perfect spring evening in San Diego. The trees are rustling along the street, from the ocean's breeze, and I watch closely for signs of Wyatt or any of the others. They might jump out of a tree or from behind any of the carts or carriages moving along the road. Nothing. We pull up to the cottage next to the Grand Horton. Dr. Baker will not have far to go after his demonstration. Of course, he must first dispose of me.

We find Dr. Baker in front of the cottage. He has nobody with him, but he is smiling broadly, puffing on that infernal pipe of his.

"The display is about ready to begin. Let me explain the genius of what I will now show you. The truth is that Rabbi Sonenschein uncovered my plan when he released the young prostitutes who were going to be working at the hacienda in Tijuana, where Comstock, Hunsaker, and the other men were going to be enjoying their perversions. This is the main reason your husband is marked to die as well, but first I must take care of you, of course."

I am frightened, but my belief that I will be saved overcomes my fear. The reasoning is acceptable. Dr. Baker wanted Sonenschein dead, and both the rabbi and Ida Bailey, for different reasons, wanted Wyatt and me dead.

"What about the Indian boy, Anand? Why did you poison him?"

Dr. Baker smiles and whispers, "He discovered the first free-tail delivering its freight."

"Free-tail? What is that?" I am afraid to hear his answer, but I know it is crucial, in case Clara Foltz or one of the others in our investigation group is lurking somewhere nearby to record his response.

"The largest colony of free-tails found during our zoological expedition is an estimated twenty to thirty million that live in the limestone Ney and Bracken caves near Bandera, in southwest Texas. These little mammals weigh only one-third of an ounce, but they are perfect for my purposes."

"What purposes? What is the cargo this bat delivers?" My imagination tells me it must be carrying something very dangerous, as Dr. Baker's other disease carriers make me cringe at the thought of what it might be.

"Bats are some of the world's best vectors for viral infections, did you know that? I can train these bats to fly to human targets. They are a species that must fly at night. Mexican free-tailed bats can fly up to one-hundred miles round trip in an evening looking for food. They are built for speed with short fur and long narrow wings and can fly up to sixty miles per hour with a tailwind. They have been observed by weather balloons feeding up to ten-thousand feet high while searching for food."

"And what is the virus you have them carry?"

"I shall get to that, and then I will give you my demonstration. I simply visit the whore house and affix the bat's favorite moth to the rear collar of one of the whores I want to infect before she goes to bed for the night. The Indian saw the bat fly inside the Golden Faun that night, and the boy had to disappear. I sent the drug to the Chinese waitress, as I knew of her fear of smallpox."

"But the virus. You did not tell me what it is."

"Rabies virus uses a myriad of strategies to avoid the immune system and hide from antiviral drugs, even using the blood-brain barrier to protect itself once it has entered the brain. It is, therefore, immune from cure. I simply made certain the victim had a cut on her neck where I placed the moth. The tiny bat's saliva transmitted the cargo and the virus did the rest. The woman is dead from rabies as soon as the virus enters her brain."

"My God! What can you show me now? I don't want to see it! Those creatures are infernal."

"On the contrary. The secret that Rabbi Sonenschein had was important to me. We were friends, you see, even when he was following you and your husband around the West buying properties and establishing your whore houses and taverns. At that point, Sonenschein hadn't had his Kabbalah conversion to do good by these prostitutes. He was planting the moths for me, to infect the whores. Once one whore got infected, she would infect the rest of them. Can you imagine the value my bats will have to the military of any country who pays me the right price?"

I am astounded. What Dr. Baker has planned is horrendous and ingenious.

"Tonight, when I go to my meeting with your friends at this hotel, I will give the signal for my men to let loose the trained bats we have inside a cave in Tijuana. We are going to do that to infest your unholy playground for the perverts Hunsaker and Comstock, but your husband shot my rabbi messenger before he could deliver the goods."

"What? You mean, you are going to kill those young women who are working there?"

"Oh, yes. That should have been my first test, but you got in the way. Tonight, however, we have affixed a moth to at least one whore in every bordello in the Stingaree. When my men release the free-tails, rabies will envelop their brains and spread like wildfire. Soon, San Diego will be cleansed of all this human pestilence, once and for all. And now … to show you how it works … Mr. Li, if you please!"

I try to grab the back of my neck to dislodge what I know

must be there, but my hands are manacled. I then hear the whir of tiny wings, and I see the bat about fifty feet above me in the glow of the street light. As it hovers around my head, I think about what my father says. "Let go, Sarah." And, at that moment, I do, and that's when I hear the pistol go off nearby.

From his location in the alley next to the Canary Cottage, my husband's Buntline Special can target this tiny mammal, as it plunges toward my neck to devour the moth affixed there by Mr. Li. It is probably the most accurate and astounding shot he has ever made.

***

Wyatt and I are released, of course, as the entire mystery of who is responsible for both murders is solved. The reality about the activities Dr. Fred Baker is pursuing is not completely understood by all in the community, except by those who are making money off the illicit businesses going on in the Stingaree. Clara Foltz, our attorney, believes the entire economy will eventually suffer because of what has happened, as the horrible truth is that the persons in charge of the government of San Diego, especially the mayor and other people taking advantage of the illegal establishments, do not ever, under any circumstances, want the story of what the doctor, a member of the elite class, is doing. to leak out into the press.

Can you imagine? The horrible truth is so entangled into the very fabric and politics of the community that those in power do not want to admit it is true. Although Clara has uncovered the actual truth of the matter, the establishment in town sees everything detailed in the evidence she has collected quite differently. Even the letter she published in her *San Diego Bee* is disparaged as nonsense, although its contents link Dr. Baker with the use of bats, armadillos, and injected goats. Because he did not sign it, however, the authorities disregard its truth.

However, since Fred Baker is caught attempting to use a trained bat to kill me, which my husband can shoot before it reaches its target, the Grand Jury is forced to drop the murder charges against us. It is simply that the mentally ill research scientist and upstanding medical doctor is "overwrought with passion" for a woman who is obviously "draining the community of its family structure and its Christian values." The Canary Cottage is shut down, as is its next-door neighbor, the Golden Faun. Finally, the death of the Indian immigrant, Anand Prabhakar, is blamed on the victim, as he has circumvented legal immigration authority by coming into our beloved, law-abiding country without a proper medical check.

As for the rest of the Stingaree, and its many more brothels, gambling halls, and taverns, they are allowed to continue, albeit "with much more stringent inspection and other safeguards in place," according to the editorial in the *Union*. Dr. Baker's obvious mental fatigue is addressed by placing him under the care of his wife, Charlotte, which I find quite humorous. That's like placing Wyatt's mental well-being under the care of me!

Although, as we are all invited to Mrs. Foltz's son, Samuel Cortland's wedding in San Francisco, it will be our unique pleasure to hear from Dr. Fred Baker himself report on his "conversion" to Christianity, which this entire case has supposedly brought about. As for Wyatt and myself, we are going to spend a bit of time with my parents while there, but we shall return to San Diego, as we have quite a few investments here. Our reputation is transformed by the major press into something very similar to what the Baker family experiences. Wyatt's bullet can "bring the good family man and respected research scientist, Dr. Frederick Baker, back to his senses," which is partly true, as the disappearance of the Canary Cottage removes a lot of what has kept him under a state of transfixed lust in the first place.

The wedding is taking place at the Bay Cliff House Restaurant overlooking where we land in our steamship from San Diego. I can see the carriages on the beach, parading up and down the sand, and children are rushing back and forth into the waves, playing games of catch, and shouting into the surf. Mrs. Foltz wants us to meet her entire family, as she is especially proud of them, and we are all enthusiastic about the chance to see San Francisco and meet them as well.

The attorney tells us at dinner on board the SS *Goliah*, all about her family, two members of whom are with us on the trip, her daughter Bertha May, and her youngest son, David Milton. She even tells us how she has to lie to the male legal establishment of California about being deserted by her husband, Jeremiah Foltz, a Civil War veteran, whom she later divorced. She has to lie and say he died, and that she is now a widow with five children, instead of living the truth. She can conquer that same legal establishment by convincing the Sacramento politicians to establish the very laws that give her the right to take that exam in the first place, and then after passing the California Legal Bar, on the first attempt, she became the first woman admitted to practice. She does this after spending only one day in law school. The men there ran her and her future law partner, Laura de Force Gordon, out of class because they were "too much of a distraction as women." This is why Wyatt and I chose her to represent us.

I have also fabricated many incidents from my past to protect my honor. For example, Wyatt calls me "Sadie" because of who I was when I was living with Sheriff Johnny Behan in Prescott, Arizona, where Wyatt met me. This was where I first fell in love with Behan when I was sixteen. People later believed I was going by the name of Sadie Mansfield when I lived in Tip Top, a mining boomtown nearby. I "officially" remember it all as a "bad dream," but, the fact is, prostitution is legal there, and women in this profession quite often change their names. I understand very well why Mrs. Foltz has to lie to survive, and why my husband still irritates me to this day by calling me "Sadie."

I have sailed on Lucky Baldwin's yacht out of the San Francisco Bay at Ocean Beach, and today these two love birds are getting hitched inside the luxurious restaurant overlooking that same inlet. It is quite wonderful how history keeps repeating itself, both in the negative ways and in the more beautifully romantic ways, such as this.

There are over two hundred people at the wedding of Samuel Cortland Foltz and Adeline Quantrill. However, at the reception, Mrs. Foltz decides to separate the San Francisco dignitaries and others by placing them in the main dining room away from her private party of family members and us. We are sixteen in number, and I will name them here, as what occurs at this dinner is very important to what I believe concerning the true practice of mysticism and intuitive Kabbalah. Sixteen is double-eight, a number very meaningful to Kabbalistic numerology, as it is even above seven, which is perfection.

At the head of the huge, rectangular table, overlooking the ocean below, are the bride and groom, smiling and toasting us with their glasses of champagne. Seated on their right side are Clara and her mother, Telitha, and her father, Elias Willets, both in their early sixties, who have journeyed from nearby San Jose. Then come the rest of Clara's children, Trella Evelyn, the lovely actress in her twenties and a graduate of Berkeley, Bertha May and David Milton, the two youngest I know from San Diego, and the youngest, Virginia Knox, who is twelve.

Then come the guests from San Diego, Wyatt, and Josephine, Drs. Charlotte and Fred Baker, Miss Kai Krissy Wong, Heaven Riendeau, Miss Ida Bailey, Ah Toy, Mrs. Foltz's best friend and former Chinatown Madam, and Lucky Baldwin. The attorney tells us personally that she has not invited her former lover, Captain of Detectives, Isaiah Lees, as she says they are now separated.

I am especially nervous, as Mrs. Foltz explains that her new daughter-in-law, Adeline, not only has an autobiographical memory, but she is also a clairvoyant with special people with whom she has psychic affinity, and she can converse with the dead. I am certain she can read my mind, so I try to keep my thoughts away from any untoward information about Wyatt and me and our business contracts. This has already put us into dangerous situations, and I know Mrs. Foltz is going to continue to live and practice in San Diego.

"Kind Ladies and Gentlemen. If you please. Your attention!" Mrs. Foltz rises at her place and sends a sharp note into our ears when she strikes her silver knife against the crystal wine glass rim.

The chatter around the table ceases, and we all wait silently for our hostess to speak. We can hear the surf crashing outside. I assume her speech will be about the details of how she solved the mystery we have all been part of, and I am not mistaken … at first. Afterward, however, the events unfold like Tarot cards being placed upon a table, revealing a much more diabolical and sinister prediction underlying these festivities.

"I am so proud of my two children who have brought us together and sealed their holy bonds in matrimony. One might not believe this mystery of ours to be a comedy, which must always end in a wedding, but there are comedic elements that led me to my eventual conclusions to solve it."

"Mother, please tell them about the goat," says Trella Evelyn, as she brushes back a lock of reddish-brown hair from her forehead. She wears a lovely bare-shouldered formal dress, the latest style, and her eyes sparkle with delight. "What you wrote to me that made me fall off my stool laughing."

"Ah, yes. My thespian daughter is referencing the first major clue I obtained pointing to Dr. Fred Baker's involvement in the plot to infect the Stingaree bordellos."

Lucky Baldwin pipes up from the end of the table. "Well, Mrs. O'Leary's cow is said to have started the great Chicago fire of '71. Was it Ida Bailey's goat this time?" He is obviously in his cups already.

Ida also begins to laugh, even though she is banned from doing business in the Stingaree. It is probably doing her well, as she stops drugs and is even taking business classes at the women's school.

"You're not far from the truth, Mr. Baldwin. I was spying around Mayor Hunsaker's office at night, as Charlotte and I were able to get a passkey from a friend in the mayor's employ. Lo and behold, tied to the leather couch in his office was a nanny goat. I tripped on her in the dark, and she let out a banshee wail so loud that it made both Charlotte and I scream to high heaven." Mrs. Foltz says.

There is general laughter around the table.

She continues, "Dr. Baker gave the mayor a goat, but it wasn't poisoned. We had already ascertained that the goats in the Stingaree bordellos had been injected with *coccobacillus*, and the boy Anand's poison contained this bacterium. The only logical persons who could have injected them and provided the bacteria are Charlotte or her husband, and when Charlotte told me about her husband's visit to Malta to research with Dr. David Bruce, the British Army surgeon, the clues began to come together."

"And how did you ascertain that Wyatt and I were marked to be poisoned by Sonenschein?" I ask.

"We found a vial of the poison on the person of the victim, Rabbi Sonenschein. After you were kidnapped, Mrs. Earp. That's when we knew it was Fred Baker behind the poisoning of the goats with Brucellosis. In fact, on the day I visited Chinatown to question him, I was almost completely certain he was our guilty party." Mrs. Foltz can see that Kai Wong has her hand up, and she nods for her to speak.

"I am sorry, but how can they allow Dr. Baker to go free? If it were a poor person who poisoned Anand, he would have been hanged!"

The young waitress is just awakening to the unfairness of real life, and I feel sorry for her. It is Fred Baker who stands up to respond, however.

"I want to tell you all right now that I am the guiltiest devil alive today. I shall be working to help the poor for the rest of my life, in a meager attempt at atonement for what I did. All I can plead to you is for your mercy and the fact that I was driven by my lust and my megalomaniacal insanity." He falls into his chair sobbing.

Charlotte, taking pity on her husband, puts her arm around him. The young Chinese waitress seems consoled for the moment.

Ah Toy stands to speak. At 60, she is tall, thin, and appears distinguished in her flowered azure *cheongsam*.

"If there is a consolation, I think it is that Dr. Baker has begun to work with other researchers around the world to provide vaccines and cures for these diseases, except for rabies, but there may be something to treat that as well if they keep testing."

"Ah Toy is right. We must look to the bright side," the groom Samuel, pipes in. He has worked closely with his mother on enough cases to know she would see the positive results of any treachery.

Clara finishes explaining to all of us how she solved the

mystery after the rest of the group convened back in Ensenada. Only Heaven Riendeau and Kai Krissy Wong seemed reluctant to provide any information about portraying nurses. I soon discover why.

We are in line to congratulate the bride and groom, after the dinner, and the sea breeze is coming in through the open window of the main ballroom. A complete wedding group of over two hundred guests is present. Heaven Riendeau is right behind me in line, and just after I shake Adeline's hand, the young bride begins to go into a trance. Heaven, also, becomes transfixed, staring at the young bride. As the former Golden Faun madame slowly removes her red crushed-velvet dress, we can see she wears multi-colored leotards, with images of what we in Kabbalah call the "Curse of the Evil Eye," which is an image of a blue hand with an eye centered in its palm. Both women's eyes roll back in their heads, and Adeline begins shouting in a deep, masculine voice. When I finally recognize the Jewish accent, I, too, become mesmerized, and I begin to dance.

It is the chanting voice of the dead rabbi, Jerome Sonenschein. Heaven Riendeau, for her part, begins to dance around the bride and removes each of the evil eyes, one at a time, from her leotards, as if they are veils, and she has taken lessons from her cohort, Ida Bailey. Indeed, when Ida also begins dancing, I know something very strange is happening.

Soon, with the chanting bride shouting out in Hebrew, all of the women in the room begin to dance, in a phantasm of passion, around the white bride, stripping the formal outer clothing from their bodies—both young and old—and swooning aloud.

Only *I* know the translated words, however, from Hebrew, and these words are telling us about what is soon to come to San Diego when we return. When the dance macabre is finally over, and Adeline Quantrill Foltz and Heaven Riendeau come out of their trances, I can see that all of the women in the room are breathing hard, and exhausted from their frenzied dance. We women stand in the center of the restaurant's main dining room, and the men stare, standing in an outer circle, their eyes transfixed upon us, so I decide they all need to know what is in store for them.

"That is the spirit voice of Rabbi Jerome Sonenschein, if you want to believe it. He is speaking in Hebrew through this young medium bride. He says there will soon be a murderer in San Diego who shall attempt to kill the first-born male of each family. He quotes the words from our Hebrew scriptures. 'That night, God sent the angel of death to kill the firstborn sons of the Egyptians.' It is the last plague of Passover." This is certainly not a comedy ending to our wedding, but I had to tell them, or I could never live with myself. I did not, however, tell them the real truth: that this passage is actually from our Passover, and in that story, only the Jewish families are spared, and they are the Egyptians. I had to let it all go, just the way my father once instructed me. They will find out whether it is real soon enough. When Heaven Riendeau screams, we all just watch her run, waving her hands in the air, her bare feet patting on the tiles of the floor, her body shaking. Then she is outside, on the balcony. As she climbs up on the chair, and then the wall, we can hear her voice very distinctly, as the fog bank begins to move toward us from out at sea. "I can no longer be part of this! I am pregnant with Elias Baldwin's child. The world is going stark, raving mad!" Heaven grasps her stomach as she jumps into the water.

Wyatt

W hen we arrive in San Diego, I am thirty-nine years old. I've already gained a reputation as a hard-drinkin' gunfighter who tangles with some of the toughest outlaws in the West and wins. But I know I am not a gunfighter, and I rarely drink. I am a gambler and have been a lawman in some of the rowdiest boomtowns in the nation: Wichita and Dodge City, Kansas, and Tombstone. I have courage, and I know how to draw and shoot a pistol without makin' the mistake of hurrying *too much*. But in my long law-enforcement career — at various times I worked as a city marshal, a deputy U.S. marshal, and a stagecoach guard and undercover agent for Wells Fargo — I'd always prefer arresting gun-wielding cowboys without drawing my pistol, because I know that is an insult to them. Most of these fellers fancy themselves infamous gunmen, vicious *killers*, and to be arrested without a struggle, without so much as even having a gun trained on them, is something they would have to live down for a long time to come. I understand that, and I want to insult them because I believe they are cowards and riffraff and that I am a better man than any of them. Confidence is not a quality I ever lack.

I am just over six feet tall, a lean 158 pounds, and have russet-blond hair that I part, using Brilliantine, which my wife hates, and I keep it swept back over my head. My long mustache flows down across my cheeks and creeps back along my jawline toward my ears — "like the overturned horns of a Texas steer," is how Ned Buntline describes it. My eyes are deep-set and blue, and in most of the pictures I've seen of me, I seem to be frowning slightly. Women call me handsome and well-mannered, and often irresistible. I enjoy the attention they often give me, and I admit to havin' secret affairs.

Sadie is my third wife, or rather, the third woman I've lived with. She is in her late twenties when we come to San Diego, and she is brown-eyed, dark-haired, and beautiful, with a quick temper that's often triggered by trivial things. One family friend, and a lifelong bachelor, once commented that the example of Sadie as a domestic partner persuaded him never to marry. But Sadie always shares with me a love of travel and adventure, and despite our occasional spats, we're deeply attached.

I remember when we first get settled here in San Diego. I am sittin' in the living room of my house on Third Avenue, smoking my pipe, recalling with amusement a poker game the previous night that I win with a bluff and a pair of threes. It is almost noon, but I just finished my breakfast of biscuits with butter and strawberry preserves and coffee. In the next room, Sadie is gettin' herself dressed to go out. Mayor Hunsaker has promised to take us to see a few choice lots for sale. Outside, a cover of low clouds is slowly drifting toward the ocean, leaving behind brilliant spring sunshine as it leaves.

We've been in San Diego for a month and were startin' to feel comfortable, even homey. When we first arrive, we get swarmed by the usual gaggle of reporters—the stories about Tombstone and the shootout at the O.K. Corral never die. I kick most of them out with a line I use regular— "I reckon we could talk about something a little more cheerful than that" — but I often have to do significant and lasting bodily harm to some reporters who come to my house to question me. Some want to praise me as a hero, the marshal who helps bring order to the lawless West, but I know this one would be just as quick to paint me as a ruthless killer who shot innocent men if he can confirm the rumors about me that are then being circulated.

That day we meet Honey, I shift in my chair, tapping the contents of the pipe bowl out into a porcelain ashtray. I am thinking of the newspapermen again. They do not know, and in my lifetime never will, that being a lawman to me has always been just another way of making money, good money. They do not know of my lifelong dream of being rich, or of the many enterprises I have tried with mixed success: hunting buffalo, hauling firewood, running saloons, prospecting for gold. Now we've come to the bustling little port of San Diego, where real estate prices are soaring because rail connections have been established to Los Angeles and San Bernardino. There is even talk of San Diego becoming the Santa Fe Railroad company's main terminal on the Pacific Coast. It is the West's latest boomtown, and we came here for the same reason we went to other boomtowns: to make a fortune. If that means buying and selling real estate, or saloons and gambling halls, then that is what we will do.

Sadie enters the living room dressed for the day. She is talkative, as usual, feeling excited about the prospects of buying land. I answer her comments only occasionally, as usual, and when I do, my words are blunt and to the point. As we leave the house with Mayor Hunsaker, I pass the coat rack with my gun belt hanging on it — the cartridge loops stuffed with shells, the eighteen-inch-long-barrel of my walnut-handled Buntline .45 pointing toward the floor. The gun is still hanging there as we stroll down the front walk and turn onto Third Avenue. That day, I never think I'll need it.

But, today, in court, that gun is the reason I am here.

This here courtroom is like the one in Prescott. Small, dingy, and crowded. Can't hardly breathe straight. Our Defense table is facing the judge, an old geezer name of Parker. I think they just might shoot him back of the barn after this trial's over. Put 'em outa his misery. Hackin' and spittin' every five minutes. Deaf as an old mule. Tarnation! He's old.

Mrs. Foltz says the District Attorney over on the other side's name is Richardt. Archie Richardt. Looks to be a dandy to me. Strutin' 'round like a cockwalk rooster. Josie keeps stretchin' her neck to get a gander at me. I ain't about to show her that I'm afeard. Look straight ahead. At that stars and stripes. I count the thirty-eight stars, but we're still growin' fast. I tell Sadie we'll outrun them stars across the West with our business deals. Gambling saloons, whore houses, mining deals, you name it. If we can make a deal, my wife can convince the other party to sign, and I can seal it. Just like I sealed it with my Buntline on May 6, 1888, in Tijuana. Drilled a hole plum in the middle of that rascal rabbi's forehead.

I am asked by Foltz about my recent history in Tombstone after I went on trial in Prescott for hunting down the shooters Frank

McLaury and Billy Clanton. Later, I hunted down Frank Stilwell, and I found him at the train station in Tucson. Some men don't go down by clubbing them with a gun. This man, I believe, bushwhacked my younger brother, Morgan, and shot him in the back. I went on trial for Stilwell's murder also.

No, I tell Mrs. Foltz. I am no stranger to trials or murders. When it's family, they are going down.

"Mr. Earp?"

I turn to face my attorney. I can see Josephine staring at me, as I gaze into the hazel eyes of my defender. "Yes, mam?" Women are always respected, if not served. And if they serve you? You get my point.

"This morning, they'll be calling the policeman who arrested you, who will testify you shot the rabbi with your gun, one bullet in the forehead by a man who is a very efficient shooter. Then the coroner, the forensics expert, and Mayor Will Hunsaker. That will be this morning."

"Yes'm. I know. It's usual."

"Correct. I won't accomplish much of anything this morning with those four witnesses. As you know, we're going after Anthony Comstock this afternoon. He was part of your contract for the sex game in Tijuana, and he's most vulnerable because of his national reputation."

"You mean like cutting out the lead bull in the herd to make the rest calm down?" I need to see what her practical reason is.

"Yes, good analogy. This bull can help us show the jury you could have been a target of someone who needed to prevent you from enforcing that contract. Later, I'll show that Hunsaker and Comstock worked with Sonenschein when they wanted to get their names out of this contract."

"Good thinkin', mam. But don't I need some other reason to kill besides money? The jury didn't like it none that I shot Stilwell, but they changed their minds when they learned I was avenging my little brother."

"Good point. Yes, I need another reason, but I am only obliged to plant doubt and not incontrovertible evidence, the way

Mr. Richardt does. Dr. Charlotte Baker and I have been working on that, so don't fear."

"I see. I ain't afeared." I look over at Josie. She is throwin' bullet eyes at Ida Bailey.

I turn fast and stand up. An all-fired copper is crossin' lots toward my Josie. I try to play Samson and bring my cop bracelets above my head, ready to cow-punch that sow before he can lay hands on her. Mrs. Foltz pushes me back down in my seat. For a lady, she has a pretty strong right arm.

"What's this, Officer?" Foltz is sayin', steppin' betwixt the copper and Josie.

"Judge wants to see you, Mrs. Foltz. Please follow me." The cop is leading my attorney up to old Judge Parker's perch, and the other side wanders up there too. As they squabble together like a hen party, the judge is pointing his bony finger toward my Josie and he frowns. Then he hacks up a good one and spits it into his spittoon.

Josie stands up, as there is now a big gaggle of coppers around these lawyers, and they're all lookin' directly at her. She has the same look on her pretty face that she gets when she sees me sneakin' a drink of whiskey.

"Excuse me, I must see my husband's attorney. Please, let me pass," Josie says. When the ones in her path don't move, she shouts, "Get the hell out of my way or I'll run you down!" That there is more like my wife. "Mrs. Foltz!" Josie yells.

The police still bar her from reaching our attorney. When Mrs. Foltz finally notices her, the lawyer's eyes scan the room like a fox with a hen in its mouth.

"Must you arrest her now?" Mrs. Foltz says, and then one of the policemen breaks ranks and plods his flat feet toward my wife. I strain against the shackles around my ankles, but I know she can handle him. The young squirt tries to grab her wrists, but she pulls them back. He is lookin' back at his *hombres* for help.

Mrs. Foltz strides over to Josie and takes her by the hand. "Let her go, Officer," she tells him. The whipper-snapper holds his empty palms up to show the attorney he don't have hold of nobody.

I can hear Josie shout, "What's happened? Why are you all congregating up here like pigs at a trough?" This weren't no way to treat a lady. My eyes wander over to the exit behind the judge. The door goes into his chambers, I reckon.

Mrs. Foltz, with a big gloomy frown, tells her, "Mrs. Earp, you failed to inform me of your dealings. Now the prosecution has concrete evidence to place you under arrest for being an accessory to murder. Why didn't you tell me about your relationship with Miss Heaven Riendeau from San Francisco?"

Josephine is angrier'n a wet hen, "Riendeau? I don't know what you mean. I have never had any dealings with this woman," she shouts.

The woman attorney is angrier. "Riendeau has not said anything about knowing you. Mayor Hunsaker's office has the proof that you have been running at least twelve bordellos in San Diego, beginning when you were a working girl in Tombstone. You told me yourself that the mayor was your husband's attorney, but you never told me you were running brothel businesses throughout your journeys in California, Utah, and Oregon. Hunsaker knows, beginning in 1874, at the age of 14, Josie Marcus fell in with San Francisco madam Hattie Wells. Late in November 1874, using the alias Sadie Mansfield, you arrived in Prescott, Arizona, and began working in Hattie's brothel."

Oh, now the cat is most certainly out of the bag. Whenever my wife gets caught in her fibs, she turns into an alley cat. "That's a lie! I never worked in a brothel. Honey has gone berserk from the sex parlors he visits. He's trying to protect his investments, by god!"

"You learned the trade, and it seems, according to all the documents Hunsaker has collected, you have perfected the business to a rather high art form. The last agreement came when you spoke to Miss Riendeau in your tavern. Do you not remember your exchange with her?" Mrs. Foltz lowers the boom. "One of your regulars, Mr. Budreaux Randolph, was there, and he works for Mr. Hunsaker's office, part-time. He overheard everything you told Miss Riendeau. However, that's not the last of it."

Josie's face is beet-red. "Last of it? Which *it* do you mean? You're being quite vague for a lawyer, aren't you Mrs. Foltz?" Whoa! Josie is on fire.

"Because you worked these bordellos in absentia, so to speak, you had to create written agreements. Hunsaker has collected all these agreements, and this last oral agreement has caused all your chickens to come home to roost, I am afraid." The woman from San Francisco has some spitfire of her own.

"Agreements? My husband and I have signed hundreds of agreements. We never know what we've signed, most of the time. What does this prove?" That statement surprises me. I thought Josephine reads all those documents.

"The mayor has sworn evidence from several of the bordello madams throughout your travels, ending in San Diego, and including Ida Bailey. In each of these places, you not only became an investor in their duties as prostitutes, but you were always followed by another person who was trying to stop you from these investments."

Another person? What is the prosecution gettin' at? Could it have to do with Hunsaker being on our tails from Arizona? I thought he was too friendly when we landed in San Diego.

"Who was this other person, pray tell?" I guess my wife is reading my mind.

"Rabbi Jerome Sonenschein. He followed you wherever you went. It was his sworn duty to stop you from ruining these women and their lives as children of God. The Grand Jury has written out new charges against you, as a co-defendant in this case, as a murderess in the first degree. They say you wanted the rabbi dead more than Wyatt did, and that you were the main instigator in his assassination because Sonenschein wanted to stop your exploits and bawdy experiments, the likes of which this country has never seen before. Before I can represent you, we must have a very long talk. Is that clear, Mrs. Earp?"

Now both of us are in the hot water of this court tub. I wonder if that little Jew was a threat to Sadie even then? I should've put four holes in that bastard's forehead!

"Hunsaker was behind all of this! I told you about our contract with him to create Comstock's garden of earthy delights in Mexico. Why don't you tell them now? You are not a lawyer. You are a prude and a poor Suffragette. Is Dr. Baker behind this as well?

You and your kind. Always putting the image of society before the truth of the evil that always lurks behind all the prim and proper attitudes and hypocritical religions." Josie shouts as they drag her, kicking like a bronco, across the floor. They shove her in the chair at the Defense table and one of the coppers puts her in steel bracelets. I am afraid to look over at her.

"You will all find out! I shall not stop my investigation until I can show you what was happening here!" Josie screams, and I can see the photographers taking their infernal pictures of her. She will be all over the world's newspapers. Her folks in San Francisco won't like that one bit. My folks are used to me gettin' into trouble.

I watch them walk my wife out of the courtroom. They will put her on ice, I suppose until Mrs. Foltz can gather her wits about her. She keeps nodding at Josie as she passes by her as if she wants her to remember we are all in this together. The one secret I have kept from my wife makes my conscience wriggle like a snake. It will probably have to die with me, or she will become a partner with me in death, as we are life partners.

***

I spend my time between yesterday and today staring at the wall of my cell and picturing my wife on the day we got hitched. She is wearing a purple dress, all's I remember, but her eyes are staring into mine in that way she has. She calls it her "Kabbalah magic." If'n they can bottle that stuff and sell it like snake oil, she could make us rich overnight. I want her to get us out of this one. I've broke out of jails, but that only takes an inside friend or an outside stick of dynamite. That, to me, is practical. What Josie can do is the impractical. The magical. I know she will think of something.

"Hey, Jed! What time's the school bell?" I am calling for the resident jail guard, Jedidiah Ramsey. He fought in the Big War on the reb side, so we laugh and scratch about that for a while, and I tell him about how it happened in Tombstone. He is like a kid inside a candy confectioner.

"School's startin' at seven, Wyatt. Bailiff'll be here for you, so don't worry none." Jed passes my mornin' scrambled eggs, toast, and coffee through the cell's trap-door. It smells good, but I wonder about the coffee. It had the odor of feline yesterday.

He's read the fiction by Ned Buntline, so I explain that this author once sent his Colt pistols, "Buntline Specials," to several lawmen of the West, in 1873, after Buffalo Bill Cody left the author's Iowa stage show. The show was based on one of the writer's stories. Buntline wanted to see if he could lasso a replacement for the famous shooter and showman.

"Buntline's real name is Ezra Zane Carroll Judson. His moniker's almost as long as his ten-inch gun," I laugh. "He sent one of 'em to me, Bat Masterson, Bill Tilghman, Charlie Bassett, and Neil Brown, back in 1876. Heard tell Bill's doin' his own Wild West Shows since a year ago. I only use that danged giant show gun to buffalo drunks, but Buntline lies in those pulp novels and says I always use it."

Jed is impressed by my story. He even asks for my autograph and says I am still a real-life hero 'cause I stood up to those *hombres* in Tombstone. To me, it is all a matter of gettin' my paycheck at the end of the job. I learned to shoot with my five brothers in Pella, Iowa. It was part of life. To hunt for our food and keep those warpaint Sioux away from our horses and women.

After the court bailiff takes me back to the courthouse on Front Street, I am sad to see Josie in her handcuffs. At least they didn't put no ankle bracelets on her. She smiles at me, so's I smile back, but it weren't one of her magic smiles.

Mrs. Foltz looks pretty chipper, considerin' she now has two of us to defend. She is wearin' another fancy bustled dress with a feather in her hat. Ain't seen no lawyer as female as she likes to be in court, but she says it fools the jury when they expect no brains but then gets a lot from her.

"Richardt has changed his key witness," she whispers to me. "They'll be questioning Mayor Will Hunsaker and not Ida Bailey." She sounds happy. "We can turn the tables on the mayor. I'll ask about his contract with you, your wife, and how Rabbi Sonenschein got involved. Of course, I'll call Anthony Comstock as one of our witnesses when it's our turn. It's all about planting that seed of doubt. Remember that when I put you on the stand." She pats my cuffed hands.

"Yes'm," I nod, but I always get stomach growls whenever I think about public speeches.

"I must now speak to Josephine, in my counsel room." She turns and strolls to the back of the court, near the judge's stand, opens a door, and enters. She might as well be out for a Sunday promenade by the ocean, the way the men's eyes follow her.

I begin to think again about that day in Tijuana when I shot the rabbi. I must've told my story a dozen times to the police and Mrs. Foltz. Whenever I'm alone, the visions from that day will repeat in my brain theater like a play is being staged just for me.

On the afternoon of May 6, 1888, I get into a stagecoach and head from downtown San Diego to the Mexican border near Tijuana. I am on my way to referee what is advertised as "The Hundred-Round Fight" — a boxing match.

The event is supposed to take place in San Diego, but me and my promoters are too good at stirrin' up hoopla. Local ministers and then the newspapers start cursin' the pagan practice of pugilism. All of us make arrangements to move the fight to Tijuana, where a man can use his knuckles to knock another man senseless and no one will get upset about it. They choose me as referee for two reasons: one, I have seen more than my share of fights in the mining camps and boomtowns of the West, and I've refereed quite a few of them. Two, I have a reputation for honesty. That's my practicality, Sadie says. At the time, a boxing referee is called upon to hold the purse, decide on a winner, and award the money, too, so his honesty counts for a lot.

As the date for "The Hundred-Round Fight" nears, the promoters give notice that there will not only be two fights but a bullfight and a cockfight as preliminaries to the main events. Then, a few days before the lollapalooza is to take place, the commander of the Mexican army garrison in Tijuana — who is also in charge of the town — realizes that his troops are going to be outnumbered by a crowd of whooping, drunken Americans. And he is shrewd enough to guess that a crowd of whooping, drunken Americans can soon get out of hand and that the melee that might result will not do the career of a Mexican army officer any good. This is how I make friends with Colonel Francisco Villegas Morta, which friendship proves valuable later. Morta decrees that the fights could take place in Mexico, but the spectators will have to stay in the U.S. That's exactly what happens: the contests between men, bulls, and roosters take place in the bed of the Tijuana River while a crowd of some three-thousand people looks on from behind a rope that is rigged up to mark the border.

The National City and Otay Railway have to put on extra cars to take fans from San Diego to the site of the fight, and the cars are full from early afternoon until nightfall. During one trip, a conductor gets into the spirit of the day and pulls an old coot from his seat and begins kicking him in the belly for what onlookers later say is either very slight provocation or no provocation at all. After an account of the incident is published in the *San Diego Union*, the conductor is forced to take a three-month leave.

The bullfight is described by those who see it as mediocre, and the cockfight is said to be worse. In the first boxing match, Gus Brown and Spider Kennedy of San Francisco square off amid a general chorus of boos. I know it ain't good for business, as the fight's been advertised as bare-knuckle, but these two pros wear skin-tight gloves, which results in a little less blood. Kennedy eventually breaks his hand on Brown's jaw, and Brown, a burlier, heavier man, knocks him down decisively in the sixth round.

The second match is betwixt a local blacksmith named Billy McLaughlin and a longshoreman named James O'Neal. I tell everybody they have a grudge against each other, and their hands are truly bare when they went at it. By the fourth round, it is clear that McLaughlin is in trouble, and with one powerful blow, O'Neal finally knocks him into next Tuesday. I have no trouble selecting a winner, of course, but I know I need to fill in time. McLaughlin doesn't regain consciousness for five minutes, so the crowd begins to drift away.

That's when I put Ida Bailey up in the fighters' ring. She doesn't worry none about all the spit and blood. She starts to dance and strip her veils, one by one, just the way she told me she would. I know when Ida eats her two grandma's eyes, her peyote, she can dance for two hours, at least. While she spins around, I have my visions. I keep thinkin' 'bout her doin' that dance for the rabbi, that scrawny little bugger with the numbers all over his black suit like some kinda walkin' roulette wheel.

I know she is seein' him, and I know what she is like in the sack, for me. Not a good picture. She never did no dance for me, in private, but she did tell me once that when she dances for Sonenschein it is a religious experience, not a carnal thing. That gets me mad. It's one thing for a lady to do her business for money, but when she believes her body goes into what she called 'ecstasy,' I get enraged. That ain't normal.

Lucky Baldwin tells me she is a crazy woman, and I should just keep away from her. He says she even knifed some men who manhandled a few of her girls. They was just lowlife miners, but it shows she can kill to protect her own. He then tells me this rabbi is tryin' to get all the prostitutes to join his Kabbalah group to get 'em out of the business of sin for good. Me, Hunsaker, and Sadie get angrier than hornets.

That night, as Ida dances, I keep seein' that little varmint rabbi's head balanced on top of the iron bead at the end of my Colt's ten-inch barrel. Crazy little pecker-head, mockin' me, mockin' Ida, mockin' Sadie. Thinkin' he's too good for all of us. That little Job's turkey is just a runty hugger-mugger. A little man too high for his nut. A bag of big words. Maybe he could trick a woman, but not me. I root out men like him the way a pig roots out truffles.

My shooter's trance during her ballet starts early. Just as the rabbi comes into the tent, and I raise my Buntline to aim, I see Mrs. Foltz come back into my vision inside the court. She is starin' down at me. Hard.

"Mr. Earp, I need to explain something to you," she says, and she sits down beside me in her chair.

I stare into those hazel eyes again. More women and their hypnotic eyes. I guess they're better'n seein' that rabbi's beady ones. "Yes'm?" I speak.

"Your wife told me all about what the State now knows concerning your relationship with the murder victim. You never told me about how Sonenschein was following you both to stop you. Why didn't you tell me that fact?" Her usually feminine voice has taken a sharp tone. "We must now transform our defense, and I need to ask you some key questions before we hear the State's key witness this morning."

"All right, Mrs. Foltz. Shoot." I am ready, but I am also confused. Sadie never told me nothin' about this before. I will play along and talk to her later.

"Josephine told me she made the business arrangements all over the territories and the states you both visited. Is this correct?"

"Yes'm." As per usual. Nothing new.

"The Prosecutor now has a collection of all these contracts. The brothel madams who signed them are also willing to sign affidavits saying you made money from their brothels. Not only that but they will testify that Rabbi Jerome Sonenschein followed you around and attempted to get these women recruited into his Kabbalah group. He wanted to save them. Did you know that?" She presses her hand upon mine. "Your wife knows this fact, and this is the grounds that the prosecution now has to convict her."

"Yes! I shot that little devil! All the folks there, including you, seen me do it. But I never knew Sadie was tryin' to stop sunshine man. She hated him for tryin' to recruit the San Diego girls, and especially the Tijuana thing. But she never said nothin' about wanting him dead because of anything else." I am honest as the tooth fairy.

"Your wife wants us to now question Ida Bailey about her affair with the rabbi. And, to make matters worse, she claims Dr. Charlotte Baker's husband, Fred, was in love with Bailey as well, making it quite the lover's triangle, don't you agree?" Those eyes of hers are stabbin' at me like hot pokers.

"I don't know. You stop now. If'n Sadie says so, then so be it. I ain't never seen proof of this, but if she said it, then you can use it. That's all I can say." I want Sadie to work her magic right then, in the worst way.

"When I question Mayor Will Hunsaker, I will be asking him

about what Dr. Fred Baker said, and what his physician, Dr. Wayne Riley, told me about him."

"What did he say? Is Dr. Fred sick?" I don't want to think what he's sick from.

"Yes, he was. But his illness has a lot to do with what your wife just told me. It concerns Fred Baker's carnal appetite."

"Go ahead. I don't give a hill of beans. This whole town can go to Hades. My wife and me are the ones with our head in the noose. You do what you need to do, Mrs. Foltz, to get us off the scaffold."

"Very well. I just wanted you to know that it could get very personal and very distasteful from here on. I shall do my best." She pats my hands and turns to face the judge, who is climbing into his box like a bent-over organ grinder's monkey.

I take a deep breath, sit back, and try to relax. The picture of that little rabbi's head is now replaced by that of my former attorney, and now San Diego's Mayor, William Jefferson Hunsaker.

My mind again carries me, for some reason, back to Arizona, 1881, when I break away from Celia "Mattie" Blaylock, my common-law wife, and first meet Sarah Marcus, soon to become my next common-law wife. When I get the news about Celia, I am dealing cards for the boys in my new saloon in San Diego, 1888.

I stare for a moment at the stranger in front of me, thank him, and then I call to a dealer to take over for me at the blackjack table. I then walk slowly to my private office in the Copper Queen Casino on Fourth Avenue, step inside, and pull the door shut behind me. Somewhere I find a bottle of whiskey, and the bitter sting of the first swallow hits me like the memory of Celia.

It's news from Tombstone: Celia is dead. Not just dead, but killed herself, because of me. Good God, I think, what a miserable, sordid life I've led. What could be in her mind those last few minutes? Why in the world... The woman is always...

I hang my head. I am unused to the whiskey, and it goes quickly to my head, but that don't stop me from drinkin' it. As numbness spreads slowly through my body, I remember that my thoughts drift from Celia to Sarah, and back to Celia, and then to

Tombstone, that tough, ugly little desert town that people will always associate me with. I recollect the stink of horseshit on the streets, the sweat, and dust on the cheeks of burly miners as they stand at the bar of my Oriental Saloon on Saturday night, the comical young prostitutes tryin' so hard to be sexy. And as the alcohol works deeper and deeper into my brain, the images of Tombstone become darker: the long walk to the yard next to the O. K. Corral that October morning, where the guns of me, Virgil, Morgan Earp, and Doc Holliday, will kill three men; the blood soaking through my brother Morgan's black coat two months later, as he lay dyin' on the floor of a saloon, his spine shattered by an assassin's bullet; the terror in the eyes of Ike Clanton and Frank Stilwell as they realize it is Wyatt Earp who has come up behind them in the darkness, and that he is going to soon kill them for murdering his brother; Celia is shouting at me that day for being gone so much, when the real issue is that we tried so many times to get her pregnant, without success; Celia is weeping and pleading with me as I load my things into a wagon, where Sadie waits patiently for me.

***

I ain't afeared of being arrested. When I pull the trigger, I go into a trance. No, I ain't never been afeard for my life. That's a fact. Have I fears? Oh, yes. I fear my Sadie might leave. She knows me better'n any person on this here Earth. You see, I don't talk much, and I don't read much neither. When I first met Sadie, she is named Mansfield, and she lives with that cheat 'n liar Sheriff Johnny Behan up in Tip Top, where he is keepin' my gal in his saloon. Josephine won't admit it to the public, but I'm a truth sayer. Josie weren't no actress, but I already had me one woman of her kind name of Mattie. Mattie Celia Blaylock, back in Tombstone, and she dies of her laudanum habits. Some say she blames me and she kills herself. I ain't ever seen into that woman's mind, and I never will want to.

I'm behind myself again, so don't mind me. My thoughts and memories get mixed up these days. Sadie always tells me to let her talk about our past 'cause I ain't good at rememberin' nothin'. But I know what I know. I am workin' for my brother, Virgil, who gets appointed Deputy Marshal for the Tombstone Mining District, which includes the whole southeast area of the Arizona Territory. I'm also afeared of losing my kin. That's what drives me into rages, sometimes. When some varmint shows disrespect to family. Only men I ever kill do that. Until this rabbi. They either shoot at or disrespect somebody in my family. You see, Sadie and me can't have no children of our own. But we both love being around families. That is when we ain't lookin' for new places to hang our hats to hunt for quick money.

Quick money. Like quicksilver. It goes through my hands fast. That's why I shot that rabbi at the Hundred-Round Fight in T. J. Weren't no hired killing. Weren't no grudge, like I had with the Clanton's in Tombstone, or how I hunted down Brodus and the McLaury brothers. No siree. Maybe this lady lawyer, Mrs. Foltz, can try to get me off with fancy defenses, but I shot that crazy little bastard Sonenschein because he was rustlin' my wife's women. Just the way a cattle or horse thief does it. Only, with human varmints like the rabbi, you need to be a silver-tongued devil. And he was that—in spades. I could never speak with him. He was too slick. Like my wife, a Jew. Never heard no human varmint speak better'n a Jew. Josephine does all my deals, and if she needs me, I can seal the deal, like I did with Sonenschein.

Now I got this here trial over my killin' the rabbi. When I was young, I stole horses myself, after my first and only church wife, Urilla Sutherland, got the fever and died givin' birth. Had me a great sadness over that. Yep, I stole me a horse in Iowa in the '70s. I escaped jail, I was sued twice, and in '72 I got arrested a few times for being drunk in a house of ill repute in Peoria, Illinois. They called me in the papers a "Peoria Bummer," but I never bummed me nothin'. I gambled, and I whored a bit in my youth, but I always paid my way. I'd hunt buffalo, deliver gold, or gamble for it. Later, with Josie, I learned to invest. She's a woman knows a heap about investing. Never could'a made a thing without her. But no Earp, with or without a companion, was ever a bummer, and there were eleven of us, both male and female. Mostly, we kept in touch, when we could, and we boys traveled and lived together.

My wife gets me into the contract with Mayor Will Hunsaker, Ida Bailey, and Anthony Comstock, the Postmaster-General. It starts as a drunken bet in my tavern when I am tryin' to drum up interest in my Hundred Round Fight. Ida is there drinkin' with the boys, and she hears Comstock's story about his childhood. The man don't drink often, but he is sure as blazes loaded for bear this night. He is sayin' to Ida his best memory is when he plays with a young girl in the woods, and ain't it a shame he can't capture that love again. She says why can't he? He stares at her with a bamboozled look and asks her how. Hunsaker says he also likes the girls a bit on the young side. That's when my Josie pops into it sayin' they should go into the backroom to talk. She puts her arm up to stop Ida from goin' in, and Ida weren't too happy, but she stays out.

Attorney Foltz now says that contract's part of my defense, because Sonenschein, according to what she discovered, was tryin' his darndest to stop that contract from bein' carried out. Said the rabbi's group of Kabbalists wanted to get all the ladies out of our brothels, even the under-age ones in Mexico that we created, like this one for Hunsaker and Comstock. I guess I don't care nothin' about it much. If it keeps my neck out of a noose, it must be worth a try. There weren't to be no naked things going on in this place, anyways. At least, that's what Josie told me she put in this here contract. Like I say, my wife does all the contracts, not me.

Funny how I thought about Celia again, and the whole business in Tombstone. Here I am on trial for my life. Why is my mind playing tricks on me? This courtroom seems like a prison today. With my wife on trial with me, it makes me feel like the rooster demoted to the hen house. Will that judge ever make it into his seat up there? Good gravy! The prosecutor walks like Doc Holliday on a drunken spree. Like a duck in a suitcoat. Mrs. Foltz tells me he's about to prove how my Sadie's connected to this murder by questioning Mayor Hunsaker. My duck's ass!

"We have established that Mr. Earp pulled his gun on the rabbi, Mr. Sonenschein, at 3:37 PM, on May 6, 1888, in Tijuana, Mexico. We have heard from the coroner, and the police at the scene, proving that Mr. Earp's bullet found its mark and was the proximate cause of death. However, it is you, Mr. Hunsaker, who has new information to assist the State in finding the truth behind an illicit motive in this murder, is it not?"

Now that dirt bagger is lookin' right at me. Is he nodding as if asking me for permission? Go to hell, Honey.

"Yes, I suppose so, although it gives me no great pleasure to do so."

No pleasure? Then why you up there, jackass?

Richardt is smiling at him. Two peas in a pod. Two snake oil salesmen. "What was your personal and professional relationship with the accused couple, Mr. and Mrs. Wyatt Earp? Could you point them out for the court?"

Oh, that's a fancy move. Will points us out by puttin' his straight arm on his horizontal left arm, and stares down the right one as if it's a gun. First, he points at me. Swivels. Then he points at Josie. Looks like a pointin' setter with a bald head.

I always forget Hunsaker's a lawyer. When he defended me in Arizona he was different. I also spotted him whisperin' to Sadie about what he was going to do next. She told me he was a fine lawyer, and, I guess he was. I got off. But now he seems just like all lawyers. They are only good if they are on your side of the fence. I reckon Mrs. Foltz might be right about him bein' part of the conspiracy agin' us.

"I was hired by the State to defend Mr. Earp in Tombstone, Arizona, along with my law partner at the time, Thomas Fitch. I met Mr. Earp, along with his companion, Josephine Marcus, who was then known as Sadie Mansfield, and we prepared his case, which lasted over a month, as I recall."

Mrs. Foltz stands up and raises her right hand at the old coot judge. "If the court would rule, what relevance does this have to do with the guilt or innocence of my clients?"

Parker puts his palm against his right ear and stretches his turkey neck out. "What's that Mrs. Fouts? Did you object?"

"Mrs. Foltz, your honor, with a *tz*. Yes, I wanted you to rule on the relevance of the prosecutor's delving into a case that took place over seven years ago." Clara Foltz's voice gets louder this time.

"Well, Mr. Richards, do you have a method to your madness?" I wonder if the old man is inventing new people I don't know about.

"Richardt, Your Honor. With a *dt*. I do. I wanted to establish the fact that the two defendants, even back in Tombstone, were beginning to shape the mental machinations of their nefarious deeds and plans, which would ultimately lead to the demise of the good Rabbi Jerome Sonenschein in San Diego."

My lawyer sashays her way up to stand in front of the judge. Smart move. He can hear her better. "I understand, your honor, but the prosecution fails to get to the heart of this case, which took place on May 6, 1888. The criminal statutes need the State to prove that my clients were of a malicious state of mind toward the victim, not toward the Clanton gang. Their mental plan of malice must be close in time to *this* homicide. Or, perhaps Mr. Richardt has other murders on his mind to convict this husband-and-wife duo of committing? If so, then I want to hear from the Grand Jury in those other states."

Folks in the court start laughing then. Can't blame 'em none. It is pretty danged funny. All of it.

"Well, counselor? What do you have to offer?" Parker stares down the prosecutor.

"I will continue with my questioning if the good madame can allow, and I shall bring us all up to date. But this malicious intent, as the defense points out, with astute clarity, was being proved by what this witness can show us. It comes in the form of affidavits of fifteen madams, including our next witness, Miss Ida Bailey, who will testify that Mrs. Josephine Earp ... or, should I say, common-law wife, Mrs. Earp, for they were never wed inside any church of our Lord ..."

Foltz shouts. "I object! Hearsay and a provocation upon the morals and religion of my client."

"Objection overruled. You may continue, Mr. Richardt."

The prosecutor marches over to stand in front of the twelve jurymen. He scowls and pulls at his earlobe. He waves the papers he holds in his hands at them.

"Although we have women present in this courtroom today, the subject matter included in these legal affidavits was such that only the jury, the judge, and counsel are going to be privy to them. Suffice it to say, however, they prove, beyond any doubt, that Mr. and Mrs. Earp have invested in houses of ill repute and dens of gambling, drinking, and prostitution. Not only this, but they also make mention of a religious rabbi, the victim, Jerome Sonenschein, who was following them, like a shadow of doom, across state lines, to rouse the towns concerning the exact nature of their sinful activities. What more does this court need to prove the malice in their minds against our victim in this case? Think of all the good families threatened by their lust and greed. Think of the future of our children and our schools, and, not to mention our beloved churches!"

Richardt's face is turning blue-red. He looks like a fish out of water.

I can hear some commotion at the front of the courtroom. The double doors open, and a woman screams. Staggering down the aisle comes a man who limps. When he gets halfway, Dr. Charlotte Baker stands up and seems to recognize him.

"Fred! What is it? What's happened to you?" She moves toward him as he is staggering toward her. I remember when I came back from the Tombstone gunfight. Celia had the same look in her eyes.

A juror stands up and points at Dr. Fred Baker. "Oh, my God! Look at his eyes!"

The man's eyes look swollen and inflamed like red ants had got to 'em. His mouth is drooling, and he keeps reaching out toward his wife. His whole torso shakes like he is in his own earthquake. Then he stops. All of us in the court are waiting, silent as a tomb.

When he finally speaks to her, his voice sounds like it is inside a casket and he is already dead. "I'm so sorry, Charlotte, my love. Venus was before me. She made me go back. Again, and again. The sea winds blew, and the monsters of the deep came for me. Called me into their lair. I cannot go back! Please! Let me stay with you here." He then begins to spin, like a dervish or a madman. His mouth froths like a dog's and he spits out blood onto the floor. Then, when he reaches our table, his body pitches forward and he grazes his head against the end of the table before he hits the ground.

His wife rushes over and stoops down to feel his pulse. Two coppers come up with a stretcher and lift his body onto it. I can hear the whispering and then the shouts begin.

"Get him checked for the black plague! That man is deathly ill!"

"Our lives are in danger! We must leave here at once!"

The people begin to panic and run toward the exits. Old Judge Parker keeps up a feeble banging of his gavel, but the folks keep pushing and shoving, shouting out like ghosts in a cemetery.

Mrs. Foltz is comforting Dr. Charlotte, as she is crying like a banshee. I look over at Sadie. She has the Kabbalah magic look in her dark eyes. I nod at her, and we both take off, headed toward the back of the judge's stand. The old man has flown the coop, so we are alone. I try to keep up with her, my shackles keep me dragging behind like a ghost in that Dickens story at Christmas. She keeps looking back at me as we walk through the back door, into the judge's chambers, and then out onto Front Street. The sunshine blinds us, at first, but then we see the rush of traffic and people running every which way down the street.

The crowds are big. I can see a man wearing a straw hat up in a four-horse carriage. He looks down at me and grins.

"Wyatt! Marshal Earp! Bobby, get down there and lift them into the back of the rig."

A red-haired youngin' jumps down from the seat next to him and runs up to us. He is about nineteen or twenty.

"C'mon, folks. I'll help you get up in there."

When we finally climb into the cab, the man shouts down at us.

"Miss Heaven is waitin' for you both."

Josephine smiles at him, so she must know him. I do not. I also don't know who that Miss Heaven is. Were we to be shot instead of hanged?

"Who's this Heaven?" I poke Sadie with my hands.

She turns to look at me. Then, she leans out to shout up at

the driver. "Is this the main distraction Miss Riendeau had in mind? It was supposed to be the first act."

The driver starts his horses into a trot, and we take off until we get to Broadway, and then we turn left.

***

We decide to travel to Ensenada. Mr. Price contacts our attorney, Mrs. Foltz, so she knows about our hide-out, and she will come out to tell us what we all need to do next. Old Colonel Francisco Villegas Morta's rancho is about seventy-six miles from the border. He's an old veteran of the Mexican-American War, which ended with the Treaty of Guadalupe-Hidalgo, in 1848. He was given a land grant by his government, and he lived as a ranchero in Rancho Tia Juana until he was forced to move by the Mexico City politicians, who were working more closely with the San Diego politicians to create the businesses and tourist industries across the border.

Colonel Morta still employs some Natives to work his small ranch, but he makes his real money doin' crooked businesses, which me and Josie are now pursuin' to save our hides.

Morta has the gas torch lights glowin' when we arrive in Mr. Price's carriage. His rancho consists of three low, brick, and stucco buildings, and as we come up to the center house, I can see the old man waitin' in the path with one of his servants.

"*Señor* Earp, and Mrs. Earp, I am so privileged to have you here again." Morta limps out with his cane to greet us, accompanied by a servant holding a lantern. The servant calls out to a smaller, adjoining house, and two young Natives run out and begin unloading our luggage from the back of the carriage.

"They are from Peru, the rainforests, as a matter of fact," he points out, guiding us through the cactus garden and up into his hacienda. His cane makes a hollow sound in the dark, and it gives me a memory of pistols being cocked. Josephine heads on into the main room, where the fire is roaring, and I can see a woman seated in front of it on the divan. That must be Miss Heaven Riendeau who

136

works for my wife.

Colonel Morta stays with me in the foyer to talk a bit. I enjoy the smell of a rancho, the burning wood, the corn tortillas frying somewhere, and a feeling of hospitality. Always hospitality. *Mi casa, es su casa.*

"I don't want you spreading those drugs around, Francisco. They were for the hacienda in Tijuana only. Now that the rabbi is dead, we don't serve that place at all. Is that clear?"

The old man smiles with a crooked lurch of his right lip.

"*Sí, Señor* Earp. My natives have taken it all back. The *ayahuasca* is now safe with me."

I smile down at the short man who's got cragged wrinkles and a scar along his right cheek from a skirmish against the *Norte Americanos*. We've made many deals together in the West, mostly for drugs, but sometimes for land. He is a trusted old friend.

"Do you think we could stay here for a spell? The courts are after us, and Mr. Price has taken the carriage back to San Diego."

"As long as you need to stay, my friend. You know that." Francisco grins up at me.

I can hear Josie squawking in the other room, so I decide to interrupt her. I want to meet this new woman she's employed at what they were calling the Golden Faun, next-door to Ida Bailey's Canary Cottage. I can feel the rush of warm air as I walk into the parlor. I stand behind my wife and know she'll feel my presence. We have that kind of almost spiritual affinity. I love that word. Affinity. Sadie told me what it means. "Attraction beyond words," she said. The ability to sit and feel close to each other without mouthin' one single syllable. She is talkin' about appearing in court again.

"Sadie, now what makes you believe we're makin' any kind of courtroom appearance again?" I tell her.

I lean forward, knowing she'll feel the energy of my voice upon her back. She doesn't lookup. She keeps starin' into that blasted fire. The fire doesn't interrupt her mind because she decides to speak to the fire.

"Perhaps you want to leave and escape final justice, but I am not of that mind. My people have always believed in finding the truth, and justice is part of the Judaic culture. I want San Diego to know what it has become. If my people must be made to feel guilty about murdering their redeemer, Jesus, then they will feel guilt about who murdered Rabbi Jerome Sonenschein!"

Francisco grunts like a pig when he hears her mention Jesus. He is, after all, a Catholic. She needs to remember how much we owe him for keeping the ladies we use in our contracts in Mexico. Old Francisco might be dragged into our problems also. For the drugs. For the women. For lettin' us stay here. But old Sadie keeps her mouth waggin', as usual.

"You men were the ones who wanted to increase the pressure on Mayor Hunsaker. I wanted no part in that. Now that we women have gotten you out of trouble, we all need a way to turn the tables on the prosecution and discover who the real party is behind the murder."

Now she wants to be the investigator and forget we ever paid Mrs. Foltz to represent us. She picks up the iron poker and pierces the center of the hell-red log. It sprays a shower of sparks. Glad that log ain't my heart.

"All right then, Sadie. Why did we pay the Foltz woman to defend us? Don't you think she might know who might be behind this? We never got the chance to hear her witnesses and what they have to say."

I put my hands on her shoulders, and she finally turns to stare up at me. I can see the flames from the fire reflect in the pupils of her brown eyes. She is still a very beautiful woman to me.

"How far did you think you'd get us away from justice? We did win the war against Mexico, you know. The Mexican government will never shelter us, would they, Colonel Morta?" She turns her head to gaze at the old man standin' beside me.

His sproutin' gray eyebrows rise, as he turns toward me and speaks. "She is correct, *compadre*. My country is very poor right now. If your country gave any reward for your return, somebody would certainly turn you in, no matter where we hide you."

I look back over at Sadie. I wonder how much we should trust this Riendeau woman. She ignores me and looks over at the woman.

"When will you have the other men under the influence? Have they been enjoying your Venus in Furs rituals? I want each of the men on our suspect list so drugged that they will tell us the truth. Mix the hallucinatory drug with opium. That will get them under our powers very quickly."

Now there's somethin' new. The Riendeau woman sits fancy in her red velvet dress and those innocent eyes. Those two have cooked somethin' up, sure as I'm standin' here.

"I can do that. They are almost drugged with passion already." Heaven laughs.

They want to use drugs to get these men to confess. Not a horrible idea, but I want to voice my disapproval anyway.

"You don't reckon one of these men'll rebel and turn Heaven and her girls into the authorities? What happens to your little scheme *then*, Sadie? They'll have her arrested as sure as a fox can capture a fat hen." I finish my speech with a twist of my handlebar. I know she hates when I'm smug.

"Most of the town will be taken up with hunting us down in San Diego and maybe Tijuana. The newspapers are already on our side, so their search will be half-hearted at best. Hunsaker is up for re-election, and most folks believe he is just trying to get votes with his testimony against us. We'll surely have enough time to find out who was behind the killing of the rabbi."

That does it! I want to get my words in. "If you don't find out, then I will put a bullet in Honey's black heart! That weasel would turn his mother in for votes." I grin. "But, you know, there could be something else at play here."

She looks up at me. Her face is flushed and not from the fire.

"What do you mean? At *play*? Did you have something arranged that I didn't know about?" She thrusts her chin out like a Sunday School teacher. "I want to know, Wyatt Berry Stapp Earp!"

When she calls me that I know I am about to get thrown to the wolves. I decide to switch my tactics.

"A little bird told me that another man wanted the rabbi dead. Attorney Foltz said she was going to use this fact during our defense." I twirl the old mustache.

Then she explodes. "What are you saying? Why didn't you

tell me? I'm your wife!"

"She told me specifically *not* to tell you." I raise my eyebrows. "And, maybe I better keep my trap shut."

She responds by standing up, grabbing me by my vest, and pulling me toward her face until we're at a steer and heifer stand-off.

"You tell me right now, husband, or you will never touch this body again!"

I decide at that moment to tell her the truth. It might mean the death of both of us, in the long run, but I have to confess.

"Dr. Fred Baker wanted the rabbi killed because he was in love with Ida Bailey. Ida, of course, as we both know, was in love with Sonenschein. That's the love triangle. You know that's why I shot him, Sarah. You know *that* is the God's honest truth! Fred Baker must have wanted me to plug Sonenschein, so his wife and her groups wouldn't help the rabbi shut down the Stingaree."

"If that is true, Wyatt, then we will have to discover how the rabbi was going to kill you on May 6," Mrs. Foltz says.

The lawyer, along with Lucky Baldwin and Dr. Charlotte Baker, has just entered the parlor.

Josie is so frustrated she reaches for Francisco's bottle of tequila on the table, pours herself a big drought in the wine glass, and drinks it down like a black swan standin' in the April rains, her long neck stretchin' out, takin' in the liquid from the God Zeus hisself.

***

We discover from Lucky Baldwin that there's been a second murder, although it's complicated. Me, Josie, and Colonel Morta are talking with Clara Foltz and Dr. Charlotte Baker. Attorney Foltz already has her defense prepared for us, so she has the witnesses. Ida Bailey, the Canary Cottage madam, one of her witnesses, has confessed to Dr. Charlotte Baker that her husband, Fred, pursued her romantically after finding out that Rabbi Sonenschein was sleeping with Miss Bailey. Dr. Charlotte is, quite properly, angry at Fred's betrayal, but she's a practical woman. She performs the blood analysis on her husband after he passes out inside the courtroom.

As we all discover from this blood analysis, Dr. Fred Baker's blood contains the hallucinogenic drug given to Heaven Riendeau by Lucky Baldwin. Riendeau is performing the drugging of the men at her whore house. As a result, Dr. Charlotte Baker calls Miss Riendeau at the Golden Faun, located next door to the Bailey's Canary Cottage. That's when they find out about the murder of the Indian boy, Anand, which leads them all to our hideout, as Colonel Morta's *ayahuasca* was being used as some of the drugs.

The practical answer to this second murder, according to Mrs. Foltz, is that Heaven Riendeau has turned against Josie and Ida Bailey when my wife tells her to "create a distraction" during the trial. However, Riendeau takes it one step farther by uncoverin' the fact that the waitress, Kai Krissy Wong, has poisoned the young Indian, Anand Prabhakar. Wong kills the young immigrant while she is upstairs with him in his room at the Golden Faun. Before the police can be notified, Krissy confesses to Miss Riendeau that she's been paid in gold nuggets by a mysterious person at the restaurant.

We now can ask both Miss Riendeau and Miss Wong what's happened, and so Foltz and Charlotte Baker bring them to our hideout to do just that. I, for one, am anxious to discover who this mysterious person is who wants a boy dead. What did this Indian know? It must be a reason more than just murder for hire. Common sense tells me that much.

Mrs. Foltz tells us she's here to create a new investigation group. When she tells the old colonel to get his servants to move the big walnut table to the outside patio, I know we're in for an explanation and orders from Mrs. Foltz about what our duties will be. I hope she doesn't ask me too many questions. Outside, the Peruvian fellers bring out big bowls of spicy guacamole, fried tortillas, tequila for the men, and wine and soft cider for the ladies.

Our lawyer perches herself at the head of the table, and Charlotte Baker is seated on her right, and Heaven Riendeau is on her left. Josie is next to Riendeau, and I'm next to Josie. On the other side, Colonel Morta is sittin' next to Charlotte Baker, and then comes Miss Wong. Finally, Lucky's on the end, in his tuxedo, stickin' out like a weasel in a hen house. He's already reachin' for the tequila bottle, which is usual for him. He pours hisself a big drought in a clay cup, sniffs it once, and bolts it down, and his face twists into a grimace.

We're supposed to solve two murders and protect me and my wife from the gallows? The chances of that are slim and none, as far as I can see. The attorney clears her throat and begins her lecture.

"I want to first thank all of you for being here. This occasion is such that if I were not in such a quandary, I would immediately allow the authorities to take over and render their decision. This moment, however, is not one of the normal consequences. I will tell you why in a moment. But I first want to say that all of you will be working with me to find the perpetrator of the most heinous crime I have ever investigated."

What's she mean by heinous? Everybody gets to mumbling.

I turn to Sadie. "What do you think she means?"

Lucky's big jaws let out a tipsy roar from the end of the table. "Can you please be more forthright, Mrs. Foltz? We are all adults at this table. I believe we can process your secret with alacrity and attention." He reaches again for the tequila.

If he drinks much more, I know he'll get ornery. I've been on a few drunken toots with him in San Francisco. He can shoot up a fancy restaurant as quick as a Clanton Cowboy.

Mrs. Foltz points at the young Oriental waitress.

"Miss Wong, please tell the group what you found out about the boy you accidentally murdered. It is very important information to add to our inquiry and search for the person responsible for his and, most probably, Rabbi Sonenschein's murder."

I am waitin' for that answer myself. The girl first looks over at her boss, Miss Heaven. The girl looks like a beat dog. Her dark eyes appear sullen as a box turtle. When the older woman nods for her to answer, the girl's voice answers in a high-pitched whine.

"It wasn't just the gold. It was the letter that came with the gold," she says.

The attorney pops up from her seat like a jack-in-the-box. "What was in this letter?"

I watch Miss Riendeau reach deep into her velvet purse and pull out a folded letter. She unfolds it, stares down at it, and finally hands it over to the waiting attorney standing next to her.

Mrs. Foltz's readin' voice sounds like a preacher's sermon. Through pursed together lips, she speaks in a sing-song, Holy Joe, spiritual sound.

"This is monstrous and telling information. Kai was acting to inoculate Anand and not kill him. The person who gave her the money included a signed medical form which explained that the boy had virulent smallpox." The attorney glares at the girl. "Miss Wong. Did this doctor also include the oral vaccine he mentions in this?"

The young woman looks up at the attorney, and her voice sounds more confident.

"Yes. That's what killed him. I put it in his tea." Tears begin to pour. "I didn't know! It wasn't the money. I believed what this doctor said. In China, we had thousands in our village who contracted this. My uncle and aunt had the pox. We had no vaccines. We had to watch them go through the stages of pustules and scabs. My aunt, who was pregnant, died during her fever. I didn't want the boy to infect San Diego. It's a terrible disease!"

"We understand. Nobody is blaming you, young lady. Heaven, did you keep the vial of poison?" Mrs. Foltz holds out her hand to Heaven Riendeau.

"Here it is," Heaven answers, handing the lawyer a small bottle with residue in the bottom.

"Dr. Baker, please do some chemical analysis on what poison is in this," she tells Dr. Charlotte, handing her the bottle.

"Why is this important news?" Lucky Baldwin asks. Elias is gettin' his drunk on now. "Just one more immigrant. No loss, as far as I can see. I say check him for smallpox. Lousy little curry muncher."

"Our police will automatically do an autopsy, kind sir. If the poor lad was infected, we will soon be informed." The doctor is havin' none of his back-talk.

We all look at the waitress, as she's still cryin' her little heart out.

My wife's the first to talk to her. "What's wrong?" Josie asks. "Did something else happen?"

She finally raises her head from the prone position, and her arms shine with teardrops, as do her cheeks.

"Anand thanked me so much for the drug. He said he was never told in India he had this disease. He thought he may have contracted it on the trip to San Diego. He said that Miss Heaven had given him a new beginning and that he had even attained what he called *moksha*, which is what we Chinese Buddhists call *bodhi* or an awakening to the mystical harmony all-around one. He said each day was a heavenly gift from a woman named Heaven." Her head drops down into her arms again, and Charlotte and Mrs. Foltz get up to pet her and caress her shoulders.

"Oh, balderdash! Can't you get to the suspects you have? What is it we have to do now, attorney Foltz? Is this your case or is it not?" Lucky doesn't enjoy gettin' upstaged by this Chinese servant girl. Elias is known to hate the Chinese because he caught two of 'em stealin' from one of his silver mines.

I know what to do, and I do it. "Shut your trap, Elias," I bark at him. "Mrs. Foltz said this was an important break in the case, and I, for one, want to hear what she has to say."

"I believe we can now find the culprit behind these killings, but we shall need to work in careful coordination. This new evidence points to the fact that the person behind the death of Anand is either a physician, a nurse, or somebody else who is a health care professional. We may also have a smallpox epidemic on our hands." Mrs. Foltz sits back down. She looks frustrated.

Charlotte Baker raises her hand, and Clara Foltz points at her.

"You have ruled out my husband, Freddy, I would assume," Dr. Baker says.

"I have, yes. He was drugged to distract the court so the Earp's could escape." Mrs. Foltz looks at Josie, and my wife speaks. I reckon this is our Alamo.

"Yes, I confess. My husband and I concocted this method

with Heaven Riendeau and Colonel Morta. Dr. Fred Baker was drugged during his visit to Miss Riendeau's evening party, and we appointed Mr. Price to be there at the courthouse when we slipped out of the judge's chambers."

Josie makes me angry. I never know about her plans, but she always adds me. What's she tryin' to do now?

"I gathered as much," says Mrs. Foltz. "I am also aware that you believe it is the other madam, Ida Bailey, whom you believe to be the primary suspect. Is this true?"

My wife's feathers are ruffled. "How did you know this? She *must* be the one. She was in the love triangle with Fred Baker and Rabbi Sonenschein, was she not? This young Indian must have discovered something about this, and Ida needed to dispose of the boy."

"I was well aware that Miss Bailey was under the influence of a drug during her dance in Tijuana. She readily admitted to this. But we have no concrete evidence as yet that she was after Wyatt, or how she was involved in the sex contract between Mayor Hunsaker, the Earp's, and Postmaster Comstock."

Josie is quick on the draw to the lawyer's response. "Wyatt and I were going to interview her to find out," she says, pushin' her chin out. "We shall prove it to you, I dare say, and this will put an end to all of this cloak and dagger mischief."

"Very well, Josephine. You *shall* visit Miss Bailey and find out what she knows. And Wyatt, in disguise, along with Elias Baldwin, shall visit Mayor Hunsaker." The lady lawyer looks directly at Elias, who is beginning to sway a bit. "And Mr. Baldwin, I want you and Wyatt, in disguise once more, to search that Canary Cottage to see what you can find in the way of material clues to these murders."

Lucky grins. "By all means, Mrs. Foltz! I know those luxury confines like the back of my hand."

I guffaw. "If you mean the way your hand cheats at poker, then I'd agree with you!"

"The other members of our group shall investigate in this manner. Dr. Baker and I will investigate the involvement of Anthony Comstock, Dr. Fred Baker, and Mayor Hunsaker. Finally,

I want you, Heaven, and Miss Wong, to portray nurses and see if you can find any persons who might have initiated the poisoning of Anand Prabhakar. You and Miss Wong are new enough to the community not to be recognized, and Dr. Baker can get you the proper credentials so you can affect your subterfuge without notice. We will all keep in communication and return here when we complete our assigned duties. Mr. Morta will be here to man the fort."

"And please find out if there have been any new cases of smallpox," Dr. Baker pipes in.

We all stand up, believin' it's time to *vamanos*.

"This does *not* mean you are all out of suspicion, however. It's just that we are in such a predicament, with the authorities hunting us down already, that I must take drastic measures. If any of you turns out to be a conspirator, then you will be found out. Mark my words. Until then, be on your way, and be very careful."

Josie takes my hand as we depart. I know she's tryin' to make-up for her lie on my behalf. We're goin' into the pit of darkness now, and my partner has to be Lucky Baldwin. Am I cursed? Could be.

***

Before we leave Ensenada, I instruct Lucky on what we're going to do. Josie and me get what we needed from her trunk, which she'd brung with us from San Diego. That woman keeps everything.

I tell Baldwin we need to go on foot when we spy on Hunsaker. We need to go when it's dark, and we have to wear disguises. He agrees, although he laughs and says it's kind of a lark. I also tell him if he drinks, I'm not takin' him.

"I don't need a drunk stumblin' around in the dark. If we get caught, I go to the gallows, not you!"

He sneers back at me and says, "I know, Wyatt. How long we been friends? I'm not about to risk our friendship over a bottle of hooch. I just think you get too serious, sometimes. I like to have fun when I do things, don't you?"

"Look. We both like to gamble, right?"

"Right."

"And, we both like to win. right?

"Right."

"Finally, we both come here to San Diego 'cause it's a boomtown, right?"

"You are correct, good sir!"

"We need to stop the evil forces at work here so's we can return to what we enjoy. If truth be told, I plugged that rabbi 'cause he was snoopin' in my family's business too much. You know, like that varmint you had killed in Frisco? The one-eyed gunslinger who lost a mining claim because of you?"

"Yes. William Lusk. That man threatened me in the lavatory of the Palace Hotel. I'm no gunslinger, Wyatt. I'm a lover. I had to hire somebody."

"Now I *will* laugh. Lover. My Josie says we should wear these Jewish uniforms and two false beards. We wore 'em for Halloween. You're about my wife's height, and they're robes, so no problem with torso size."

I hand Lucky the black robe and the beard, which is stuck on the jowls with bone glue.

"Also, we got these two round fur hats. *Shtreimel* is what Sadie said they are. The Orthodox Hasidim wear 'em."

When we'd finish our dress-up, we really look the part.

"Let me talk if'n we need to. Josie taught me some Yiddish words I can use."

Lucky laughs. "Don't you worry. I wouldn't say anything in this get-up. Unless they aim to shoot me for being a bear. Or worse. A Jew bear."

I push him. "Hey, keep your trap shut about Jews. My wife is one."

"Oh. I'm so sorry, rabbi! I thought you were about to hang for shooting a Jew in the forehead."

"That's different. Climb up in the surrey. We need to *vamanos*. Keep your hat next to you. They can blow off." I climb up into the driver's side, and Lucky follows me on the passenger side.

Of course, I take along my insurance policy. My Colt .45, to be exact. Not the Buntline, as it'd certainly give me away. The ride is rickety but passable. I'm used to ridin' solo. We look to be two wandering Jews out on the town, and I'm enjoyin' my role as head rabbi. I don't believe Lucky's happy, as he keeps squirmin' in his seat like a Sunday School teacher inside a saloon. I drive us to Ida Bailey's Canary Cottage near Broadway. It's Sunday, so there's nothin' much going on. Ida's place has a few lights on, so there may be some entertainment goin' on inside. I hitch the two horses up, and we walk down the garden path to the cottage. The usual red lantern is shining on the porch, and Lucky, even in his robe and fur hat, reaches up to touch the lantern for good luck.

The Chinese house boy, Peng Shi, lets us in, and his eyes grow wide, as we take off our fur hats and hold 'em in the crooks of our arms like they's pet beavers. Finally, he takes them from us, but he holds 'em gingerly, maybe afeared he might get bit.

Ida comes sashaying into the parlor, wearing a silver, low-cut evening dress, and a wide crystal glass of champagne in her hand. At first, she doesn't recognize us, but when Lucky goes up to her, pinches her rear-end, and lets out a war-whoop, she breaks into surprised laughter.

"Lucky Baldwin, this is not masquerade night! What are you doing here? And who is this tall fellow with you?"

I put my forefinger up to my lips. "Shh! This is our disguise, Ida. It's me. Wyatt. We need to ask you some questions about the rabbi and your affair with Dr. Fred Baker. We don't have much time."

"I see. The police have been through this already. I'm so tired of their impositions." She dabs her eyes with the handkerchief she plucks from between her breasts. "It's all so horrible! Will you and your wife survive this ordeal?"

"I reckon. If we can find out who might be behind these murders. My lawyer sent us here. She believes we might find some new clues."

Ida perks up. "Oh yes! I have spoken to her myself. I was there when you shot that poor rabbi in Tijuana, as was she. Aren't you afraid the police will arrest you both now?"

Lucky puts his arm around Ida's waist. "Not if you keep that pretty mouth buttoned, my dear. Wyatt and I are playing detective to save his and Josephine's life. Please show us the rooms in this house."

"No business tonight. I believe there is something very sinister going on in San Diego. I have been having strange dreams. In every one, I am flying above, and when I look down at my town, I see all the ladies of the Stingaree in peril. They are running about, and it is dawn. But they are afraid of the rising sun. And, well they should be. Because in my dreams, each time, when the sun comes up it is not the bright, glorious ball of fire we see each day, but it has transformed into a gigantic, human eye! It casts an eerie dark glow from its single, radiating pupil, and the rays from this eye hit my girls, and they are struck down, each and every one! That's when I awaken. Is this an omen?"

I am used to these kinds of mysterious dreams, and even daydreams, from my wife and her magical Kabbalah.

"Ida. Did you have a special relationship with Dr. Fred Baker?" I want to get at what we are supposed to ask about their love triangle. I believe Baker wanted Sonenschein dead because he was tryin' to close down the whore houses in the Stingaree. Baker loved Ida, and Ida loved Sonenschein, but they were at odds.

"No. Dr. Baker was helping us out, just like his wife, Charlotte. He gave us milk goats and other animals from his work for the Zoological Society. And I was involved with the rabbi only because of his religion. I am enthralled with mysticism. I believe it can be the answer to all we need in this world."

As we climb the stairs, I wonder if she's tellin' us the truth. Could she also be behind the death of the Indian feller, Anand?

Just as Ida puts the key inside the lock of the storeroom door, there's a scream. It's comin' from downstairs. We both follow Ida. She rushes into one of the rooms where the screams are comin' from.

After she turns the lamplight on, we can see the young woman. She's sittin' up in bed, in her nightgown, clutching the back of her neck. The window's open, lettin' in a draft, but it's warm outside. The girl has her right hand on her neck. When she brings it from behind her head, we can see it. The blood's unmistakable, even in the dim gaslight.

"Penny, what happened? Why are you bleeding?" Ida's voice is frantic.

The girl continues to cry as she stares down at the streak of blood on her palm.

"I don't know! I was asleep, and then I was awakened, when I felt a sting on my neck."

"Let me look," I say, and I pull her head toward me, so I can see the back of her neck in the light. There's blood oozin' from a cut inside the indentation at the base of her skull. I feel it, and it's not deep.

"Maybe some insect bit you? The window's open." She seems to calm down a bit after I say this.

"Yes, my dear. I will get a bandage. Then you can go back to sleep. Let me close this window for you."

After Ida closes the girl's bedroom window and then bandages her, we all leave the room.

I decide we need to go, as Hunsaker's office still needs to be investigated. I don't know what this event means, but I'll certainly report it to Mrs. Foltz when we return to Ensenada.

As we stand in the vestibule at the front door, I decide to tell Ida what we need.

"If this Penny becomes ill for some reason, would you please notify our attorney, Clara Foltz's office? She's in the Nesmith-Greely Building on Fifth Avenue."

"Of course, Wyatt. I hope you can find out what you need to know. Take care of yourselves."

"Thank you, Ida. I'll be back when this is over," says Lucky, winking. "And I won't be wearing my bear hat." He laughs as he places it on his head.

When we're back inside the surrey, I turn to Lucky, as my thoughts are beginning to whirl around like tumbleweeds. I'm worried we might be part of somethin' much bigger'n what I thought when all of this began.

"Partner, do you ever wonder if the whole shootin' match is

rigged against us? I mean, what if I *am* guilty of these here murders, just because of somethin' me or Josie might have signed? Or, somebody more powerful wants me to be guilty?"

Lucky looks out at the passing lights on Broadway. I seen him reflect like this a few times before. Like the time he decides to put all his gold into silver mines at just the right time. After the market changes, when he gets back from huntin' in India, the Comstock Ophir Mine stock shares he owns explode sky-high, and he earns his nickname. This is the way this country always plays the game of investments. Those who know when to risk it all become the winners. But what makes that difference? Why does one person have value or luck over another?

"Wyatt, I have always respected you because you're practical. You told me, the first time I met you, that nobody ever understood that about you. They always thought you were a big risk-taker, just the way all us gamblers tend to be. You told me, as a straight shooter, that you never made any decision unless you believed it would keep you safe in the long run. The thing was, you took the chance when others wouldn't."

I'm surprised he remembers that. Lucky has fifty times more money and properties than I do. He's a world traveler, he owns banks, a yacht, and he makes money mostly through his investments. He gambles a lot more than I would ever risk. Yet, he's out here with me, alone, no bodyguards to protect him. He trusts me, and he enjoys adventures more than safety.

"You don't understand, my friend. After you told me about divorcin' Sarah, in '62, when she lost both your children in childbirth, you also told me you never wanted to marry again. But then, after you struck it rich in the Comstock Lode, you started hitchin' up with the young gals. Remember? Two divorces, and then you married Jennie Dexter, and she was just sixteen. When she died of consumption, you married another sixteen-year-old who looked just like her. Lillie Bennett. You called me that night after her father bought you that honeymoon cottage in San Francisco. Remember? 'Never again,' you told me. 'Lillie's the one.' No, she was just the beginning. You got sued by four more young women, and by then you was in your sixties! In '83, that youngin' shot you in your hotel, and you didn't even remember who she was! You may have had a lot more luck than I've had, Elias, and you may have all the hotels, properties, mines, banks, and a big theater. But you can't keep your pecker in your pants. Especially when there's young girls around."

Lucky scratches his false beard. He's squirmin' in his seat.

"Damned your hide, horse thief! You got your Colt in that belt beneath the rabbi robe. I also have *my* insurance. And now I need a belt of it from *my* belt." He reaches inside his robe and pulls out a silver flask, unscrews the top, and brings it to his mouth. He tosses his head back, and he drinks a full measure of the contents. I can smell the whisky.

"Didn't I tell you about the booze?" I say, but I know he's off to the races. Just the way he does when we go to the track together in San Francisco, Golden Gate, and in Los Angeles, at his Arcadia thoroughbred park.

He tucks the flask back into his belt, belches, and laughs. "Ha! Wyatt, you may be quick on the draw, but you don't understand life. I hire niggers from North Carolina, chinks from China, and a lot of other riffraff right off the boat. The press calls me a great example of integration and opportunity for immigrants. But, I'm also practical, just like you. I know what to call these workers when I talk to the newspapers. But I hire them because they're cheap labor, and I save money. That's the bottom line. They get to work. And they're good workers. Who else will give them the work? Nobody. Especially when the railroads are on strike. We both win because we risky businessmen are the only game in town!"

It's three in the mornin' when I shoot the lock off Will Hunsaker's office door. I have a few belts from Lucky's flask, and I'm feelin' no pain. I'm also losin' my traction. If somebody hears my shot, like a copper, we'll both be arrested. I make my own luck, so I get the answer on top of my head. I put my fur hat between the lock and my gun's muzzle before I fire. It sounds like I've shot into Lucky's big stomach at point-blank range. We stagger inside.

It smells like old cigars and leather inside the mayor's office. I can't quite remember what Mrs. Foltz wants us to look for. I know I need to turn a lamp on, and I do, but when I hear Lucky trip over somethin' near the desk, I know we're in for trouble.

"Bwaaaaaa!" It sounds like a demon escapin' from Hell.

Lucky's sprawled on the wood floor next to it. A nanny goat. She's tied to the desk, and her lips vibrate as she spits on Lucky's spats.

"She spat on your spats!" I laugh and point at his shoes.

Baldwin looks down at them, sees the goat's spittle, and he starts laughin'.

"Leastways, I didn't get her other end," he croaks, belches, and tries to stand up. But he again trips over the goat, and she lets out another loud bleat.

"Shh! Pumpkin! I can't marry you if you keep talkin' back to me," Lucky begins to roar with laughter, bends over, holding his sides.

That's when we hear the commotion outside. Someone's tryin' to enter the office.

I pull out my Colt, run over to the front door, and stand there behind the door frame, waitin' for the door to open. I can hear Lucky wrestlin' with the nanny in the office.

My friend then breaks wind, and the goat bleats in response. I cover my mouth with my left hand to keep from laughin'.

When the door opens, I can see by the silhouette that she's female. I won't buffalo her, so I grab her around the neck and draw her into me, closin' my hand over her mouth.

"It's Wyatt Earp," I whisper into her hair.

"I'm Heaven Riendeau, Mr. Earp. Please let me go."

I let go of her just as Lucky staggers into the foyer.

"What are you doing here?" I half-laugh, as I'm still drunk.

"Mrs. Foltz sent me over to check on you two. She expected you might not be up for the task. By the looks of things, she was right."

"No, Miss Heaven. It ain't all bad. We found out that a young prostitute was bit by something in her bed over at Ida Bailey's house. And Lucky just tripped over the mayor's goat."

We all can't help it. The laughter begins, and it escalates until Heaven shushes us.

"Be quiet! That is actually good news. It means Hunsaker

received a goat from somebody, just like I did at the Golden Faun, and Ida did at her establishment. It must be Dr. Fred Baker's doings."

"Is that so?" I stop giggling. "What you think the girl gettin' bit in her bed means?"

"Yes, Miss uppity," Lucky says, takin' another snort from his flask. "You got our goat figured out, so how 'bout hooker bites?"

"Funny you should ask. I had the same thing happen the other night at my place. One of my girls, Janice, woke up screaming. And she had a bite on the back of her neck. Was that where Bailey's girl was bitten?"

"That's correct. Right on her neck in the back, in that little indent. A small cut, but it was bleedin' a lot." I place my forefinger on the back of Heaven's neck, and she shivers.

"Only I saw something else that night in the Golden Faun. I never told anybody, as I thought it might be one of those free-tailed bats."

"Free-tailed bats? Why'd you think that?" I am sure interested.

"I found part of a moth on the floor near her bed. It was sliced in half, with blood all over its wings. Sure enough, when I felt the back of Janice's neck, there was the fuzzy powder from the moth's wings on her skin, near the bite. I thought maybe one of those bats came in through the open window, and a moth may have landed on her neck. Those bats are very small. They can get in and out of a room like a hummingbird."

"Do tell. Sounds like too much coincidence to have the same thing happenin' next-door to each other's place." I am sobering up. "We need to tell Mrs. Foltz all about this."

"Don't forget Pumpkin!" Lucky blurts out. "What's the mayor doin' with a nanny goat in his office?"

"Yes, Lucky, we'll tell her about the goat," I say, and I open the door. "Come, we'll give you a ride back to your place, Miss Riendeau."

"Why, thank you, Mr. Earp," she smiles and takes my arm. "Would you both like to come in and have a drink before we go back to Ensenada? Maybe even stay over?"

I think about it. A little bit of heaven on earth might not be too bad, after this strange night of tomfoolery.

***

W e're both itchin' to get back to Ensenada to find out if our information helps the case. I decide to skip the invitation by Heaven, though we do stay over at her place, as she needs the ride back to Mr. Morta's rancho. She completes her assignment with Kai Krissy Wong. They have some information about who's been treated for diseases in the last few weeks. Also, who might've had access to the drugs found in Fred Baker's bloodstream?

Miss Wong meets us inside the Golden Faun, as she lives upstairs at the Moonbeam Café and Tavern, next door. All four of us feel like pieces in a giant and mysterious jigsaw puzzle. The women want to wait until we get to the ranch before they deliver their pieces, so me and Lucky keep our curiosity to ourselves.

Heaven grins at us from the back seat of the surrey, as we pass the checkpoint into Mexico, at the San Ysidro border crossing. She's wearin' another outfit of her favorite crushed velvet cloth, a green dress with matching hat, topped with an ostrich feather. Miss Wong's wearin' her waitress uniform.

"We talked it over, Mr. Earp. We don't really know yet who the suspects might be. One of us might still be suspected, even at this late hour." Heaven glances over at Miss Wong, who nods in agreement.

We're still wearin' our Hasidim costumes, 'cause we need to cross the border without bein' recognized. I am itchin' to get my Colt back into my holster, as the muzzle rubs against my belly, which is still queasy from our drinkin' last night.

"My wife wanted us to stay and fight this here case, so that's what I'm doin'. If one of us inspectors is behind the murders, then why would he or she want to show up after we all brung in our evidence?"

Old Lucky laughs. "If they're the murderer, then maybe they

want to get rid of those who know about their guilt. We could all have targets on our backs."

"No, Elias, I have a strong hunch Mrs. Foltz knew who the guilty party was before she assembled us. She just wanted to find out for certain. We just might have the last hatchet to cut the head off this chicken."

Lucky's drivin' the rig, so he hands the gate guard his identification. The guard waves us through.

"I, for one, don't understand who would want to kill a young boy. I truly hope Mrs. Foltz can put all these clues together at last." Heaven heaves a big sigh. "I haven't slept much at all for the last week."

"Neither have I," says Kai Wong. "What if *you* killed them both, Mr. Earp? You killed before. Why not again?"

I turn around to stare at the young Chinese woman. I never hate the chinks, the way a lot of my friends do who work for the railroads. The Chinese never cut into my business none. They gamble in their own place, and they whore in their own place. I even understand when the government decides to ban them from comin' here from China. They work for less and put whites outa work. Mrs. Foltz tells us her best friend in San Francisco is a former Chinatown madam name of Ah Toy. Nice name for a madam.

"Don't worry none, young lady. If I use somebody for target practice, then I have a good reason. You ain't on my list today." I watch her eyes grow wide with the usual fear I've seen hundreds of times. "And if this old codger aims at you, then it won't be to shoot you." I point to Baldwin. "It'll be somethin' much worse!"

Lucky spits his tobacco out the window and laughs.

I ain't afeared when women take over. I am prepared for it. My Josie is the same kind of woman as Mrs. Foltz, but this lawyer knows a lot more about how people act when they get cornered, so we're all payin' close attention sittin' around the patio table. If I can get my darlin' wife back in one piece that's all I want.

Dr. Charlotte Baker, Heaven Riendeau, Kai Wong, Lucky, and me are there. Only Dr. Baker's husband, Fred, Ida Bailey, and of course, my wife are missin' this little tea party. Francisco Morta has food for us, but no booze. Mrs. Foltz, by the looks of her, is not here for the opera. She's here to get down to solvin' our mystery.

"Ladies and gentlemen, thanks for returning to our little Mexican hideaway. I have done some more discovery work on this case, and now that you're here, we can begin to assemble what we have collected together. You are all part of my family now, so I want you to feel that way. Let's begin with Wyatt and Mr. Baldwin. What did you gentlemen discover? I had to send Heaven to see if you were all right when I heard about what went on at the Canary Cottage."

"Yes'm. There was quite a scene there. Lucky and me were about to search around the place, with Ida as our guide. Then we heard a scream from one of the ladies' bedrooms."

All the women at the table sit up straighter and stare at me.

"One of Ida's girls had a bite on the back of her neck, about right here." I point to the cleave at the base of Lucky's skull. "Later, Heaven said she found half a miller moth on the floor by the bed of her girl. There was also moth wing powder on her neck. We reckoned somebody fixed that miller on her neck."

Heaven speaks up. "As I told Mr. Earp, I believe somebody might have used free-tail bats to get in and out of the rooms."

"Yes, that actually comports with what Charlette and I discovered." Mrs. Foltz is writin' something down on the pad of paper she has on the table in front of her. "Anything else?"

"The goat in Mayor Hunsaker's office," Lucky says. "I nearly broke my neck trippin' over the danged thing!"

"You nearly broke your neck 'cause you was drunk," I add.

There are some laughs. I want to get to the heart of the matter. Time's crawlin' slower'n a one-legged drunk dog.

"The goat was a nanny, correct?" Foltz asks.

"That's right, mam. In the dark, she sounded like a banshee. What do y'all think it means?" I hope her investigatin' mind has figured somethin' out.

Mrs. Foltz turns toward the madam of the Golden Faun. "Heaven, what did you discover in your search of the hospital wards?"

"Krissy and I searched the wards for drug prescriptions and if there were any new cases of anything, like smallpox, which was what Anand had. No smallpox. But we did find several inpatients who had two other kinds of diseases."

"Oh yes? What diseases were those?" Mrs. Foltz asks, her pencil poised above her pad.

"Two women had been admitted with leprosy, and five had been treated for *Micrococcus melitensis*"

Dr. Charlotte hits her fist on the table. "Brucellosis! I knew it. Freddy's goats were injected with it."

"Be calm, Charlotte. I told you not to become emotional. There must be some explanation, and we shall discover it." Clara Foltz turns toward me again. "Wyatt, do you know what this means?"

I know, but I didn't want to say it out loud. My best friend in Tombstone, Doc Holliday, the old dentist and gambler, has a name for what we're gettin' ourselves into. He calls it the "curse of Hamlet's Father." It's when we find out the guilty one is a close relative. In this case, it's Dr. Charlotte Baker's husband.

"Fred Baker, like you said before. He was courtin' Ida Bailey. And Ida, bless her heart, loved the rabbi. I reckon Dr. Baker wanted to get even somehow with Sonenschein and Bailey. Is that about it?"

I can hear Dr. Charlotte begin to sob. It tears into me just as if it was Josie sittin' there.

"I am afraid you're very close to the answer. We spied on Hunsaker and Comstock, and we discovered that Fred Baker was putting pressure on them to stop the little garden of earthly delights in Tijuana. There were letters between them that became escalating in their threats and anger. The last letter Charlotte found in Hunsaker's desk. You didn't look in that drawer, Wyatt. That letter was an anonymous threat concerning a new plague being visited upon all the women in the Stingaree."

"A new plague? Is that about the bats?" My voice trembles, as I can picture my Sadie with a bite in her lovely neck.

"Yes, I'm afraid it is. We have reason to believe Dr. Fred Baker has been using the bats from his research to give these women one of the most deadly and contagious diseases known to mankind.

Rabies. There is no cure, and it can be passed on to other animals and, of course, to other humans."

"My God!" Lucky gasps. "You mean to say we could have those lovely girls drooling and biting folks like mad dogs?"

Dr. Charlotte has composed herself. "The bat doesn't always bite. Sometimes the saliva will drool onto you, and you could have a minor open cut. Or sometimes a bat will lick on the skin and, again, transmit the virus that way."

Kai Wong stands up as if she's ready to run out the door. "But that's how those poor women got it! They got bit from the moths attached to the backs of their necks. The saliva got into those cuts."

"Yes, I'm afraid that's right. We have only one chance right now, I am afraid. We need to hope we can stop Fred Baker before he lets all those bats he has loose out in San Diego." Mrs. Foltz also stands up. "We must leave right away. My son David Milton told us he overheard Dr. Baker's plan to show Josephine Earp his great plague at the Canary Cottage, just before his meeting with us at six-thirty PM. Charlotte and I confronted him in Chinatown about his relationship with Ida Bailey." Mrs. Foltz looks down at her pad. "And the other disease, the leprosy. The delivery of the armadillos was the cause of that horrible disease."

"But I need to find out how my husband was able to cause the incubation of the *M. Leprae* from the armadillos in such a short amount of time." Charlotte follows Mrs. Foltz out the door.

We all follow behind them. I don't have time to change from my rabbi's costume, but I do swipe my holster from Mr. Morta's rack in the hall. My Colt Buntline Special slides inside it, and I'm ready for my Annie Oakley act if need be.

We take the big carriage down to San Diego. Mr. Price drives the rig, and he drives those four horses at a pretty fast clip. The women folks bounce up and down like marionettes. When we pull up to the Canary Cottage, it's still pretty early, and Dr. Fred Baker and my wife haven't appeared. We have time to figure out our plan.

We all stand around on the street like lost souls, as the traffic moves past us to go to dinner, or into the Stingaree. Some even stop at the cottage, with men pouring out of their dark carriages like phantoms, gigglin' like school girls, and pounding each other on the backs as they light their stogies and pipes.

Mrs. Foltz takes charge. "We need to get ready for the most logical occurrence. Charlotte, you know about your husband's work with bats. What would you assume he would do to use them as some kind of plague vector? What would be his physical position and what should we prepare to do to stop his attempt?"

Charlotte sighs. "I really can't say, Clara. All I know is that he was working with them in Texas and that the species is very small. Perfect for getting in and out of small places at great speeds. They can also fly great distances, so I would assume he could keep them stored just about anywhere near here. Even across the border."

"All right. We shall have to wing it if you'll excuse my expression. I do want to place our best marksman in a place out of sight but within firing range. Wyatt, would you be more comfortable in a tree or upon terra firma?" The lawyer certainly doesn't know much about target shootin'.

"I reckon I'll stay out of view until they get here," I say. "That's where ya'll will be too, I suppose."

"Quite right. We need as many eyewitnesses as we can manage," Clara points out.

"Quickly!" Dr. Charlotte whispers. "Here comes Freddy!"

We all high-tailed in different directions, but lawyer Foltz motions for us to follow her. We see Dr. Fred Baker step out of his one-horse surrey and stand in front of the Canary Cottage. He seems to be starin' at it as if he can make Ida Bailey, his lover, magically appear in front of him.

We are all out of sight from the street, tucked into the alleyway between Canary Cottage and the Grand Horton Hotel. When we see the one-horse carriage pull up, about fifteen minutes later, Dr. Charlotte whispers, "It's Li Wei. My Stingaree messenger."

Indeed, it is a Chinaman, and when he opens the carriage door, I see the sight I've been waitin' so long to see. My beautiful wife, Sadie, steps down, her hands hidden in front of her by some furry muffler so that Li Wei has to carefully guide her and hold onto both her arms. It's all I can do not to plug that feller right away, the way I done the rabbi so long ago. I see the Chinaman has a gun, so I would be in my rights.

Fred Baker is puffing on his pipe as the two visitors come up to him. I have my Colt ready, and I aim at him. I can, if need be, quickly pivot to the Chinaman for a second shot. Baker grins, and we can hear him from our places in the alley. He sounds like some kind of preacher.

"The display is about ready to begin. Let me explain the genius of what I will now show you. The truth is that Rabbi Sonenschein uncovered my plan when he released the young prostitutes who were going to be working at the hacienda in Tijuana, where Comstock, Hunsaker, and the other men were going to be enjoying their perversions. This is the main reason your husband was marked to die as well, but first I must take care of you, of course."

My finger circles around the trigger of my gun when I hear these words. I know Foltz wants proof, so I hold back my anger.

My Josie is courageous. It's like she knows we're here listenin' to her.

"What about the Indian boy, Anand? Why did you poison him?"

"He discovered the first free-tail delivering its cargo." His voice is a whisper, so I have a hard time hearin' what he says.

"Free-tail? What is that?" Sadie makes him answer. That's my girl!

"The largest colony of free-tails found during our zoological expedition was an estimated twenty to thirty million that lived in the limestone Ney and Bracken caves near Bandera, in southwest Texas. These little mammals weigh only one-third of an ounce, but they are perfect for my purposes."

"What purposes? What is the cargo this bat delivers?"

We know what that cargo is.

"Bats are some of the world's best vectors for viral infections, did you know that? I was able to train these bats to fly to human targets. They are a species that must fly at night. Mexican free-tailed bats can fly up to one-hundred miles round trip in an evening looking for food. They are built for speed with short fur and long narrow wings and can fly up to sixty miles per hour with a tailwind. They have been observed, by weather balloons, feeding up to ten-thousand feet high while searching for food." Dr. Baker waves his hand around in the air as if he's pointin' out the bats for us.

Josie comes in for the kill. "And what is the virus you have them carry?"

"I shall get to that, and then I shall give you my demonstration. I simply visited the whore house and affixed the bat's favorite moth to the rear collar of one of the whores I wanted to infect after she went to bed for the night and was fast asleep. The Indian saw the bat fly inside the Golden Faun that night, and the boy had to disappear."

Again, I feel my itchy trigger finger. My wife is itchy too.

"But the virus. You did not tell me what it was."

"Rabies virus uses a myriad of strategies to avoid the immune system and hide from antiviral drugs, even using the blood-brain barrier to protect itself once it has entered the brain. It is, therefore, immune from cure. I simply made certain the victim had a cut on her neck where I placed the moth. The tiny bat's saliva transmitted the cargo and the virus did the rest. The woman would be dead from rabies as soon as the virus entered her brain."

Our worst fears are exposed. Just what Baker's wife told us.

"My God! What can you show me now? I don't want to see it! Those creatures are infernal."

"On the contrary. The secret that Rabbi Sonenschein had was important to me. We were friends, you see, even when he was following you and your husband around the West buying properties and establishing your whore houses and taverns. At that point, Sonenschein had not had his Kabbalah conversion to do good by these prostitutes. He was planting the moths for me, to infect the whores. Once one got infected, she would infect the rest of them. Can you imagine the value my bats will have to the military of any country who pays me the right price?"

That's how he does it! I hope Mrs. Foltz has that down. But

he isn't finished.

"Tonight, when I go to my meeting with your friends at this hotel, I will give the signal for my men to let loose the trained bats we have in a cave in Tijuana. We were going to do that to infest your unholy playground for the perverts Hunsaker and Comstock, but your husband shot my rabbi messenger before he could deliver the goods."

Charlotte is correct again. The bats are comin' in from Mexico.

"What? You mean, you were going to kill those young women who were working there?"

"Oh, yes. That would have been my first trial, but you got in the way. Tonight, however, we have affixed a moth to at least one whore in every bordello in the Stingaree. When my men release the free-tails, rabies will envelop their brains and spread like wildfire. Soon, San Diego will be cleansed of all this human pestilence, once and for all. And then, I shall give the word to do the same in all the other brothels in other states and territories. And now … to show you how it works … Mr. Li, if you please!"

The Chinaman signals to somebody in a room behind us up in the Horton.

Josie knows something's afoot, 'cause she's tryin' to get her manacled hands up above her head to reach the back of her neck. I know this is my shot. My eyes peer into the sky, and I can hear the whir of wings. Frantically, I search in the lit space just above us, tryin' to spot the little varmint. I'm about to give up when I finally spot it. I line my bead up with the hovering demon, with my gun's muzzle restin' on my forearm. It's a good sniper pistol, at 10 inches long, and so I hold my breath and squeeze the trigger slowly, slowly. All I can see in my fantasy is that bat biting my wife's neck. But it never reaches its target, because my bullet meets it before it reaches her.

"Damn you to hell!" I shout.

***

The court lets me and Josie go. When they discover how involved the city leaders are in the Stingaree, I guess they want no more of us. My wife says it's 'cause Dr. Fred Baker is one of 'em that he got off also. I agree. When they say he's sufferin' from the "diabolical clutches of a femme fatal and a Jewish cult leader," I know. Ain't no way the truth of the matter would be uncovered. Back in Tombstone, it would be solved by gunslingers gettin' even. In boomtowns and big cities, it's solved with politics and Christian forgiveness. The rest of the Stingaree, and its many brothels, gambling halls, and taverns, are allowed to continue, but "with much more stringent inspection and other safeguards in place," according to the editorial printed in the *Union*.

Ida Bailey's Canary Cottage is shut down, for now, as is Heaven Riendeau's Golden Faun. They blame the kid, Anand Probhakar, for his own murder by sayin' he is in San Diego illegally without a proper medical check. All the poor gals who get leprosy and goat milk poison, not to mention rabies from the bats, are swept under the courtroom's rug, so to speak. Dr. Fred is put on probation with required treatment from his wife, Charlotte. That's a rip-snorter!

It's very nice of our lawyer, Mrs. Foltz, to invite us to attend her son, Samuel Cortland's wedding in San Francisco. Me, Josie, and Lucky are excited to see our old digs again. Josie wants to see her folks again while we're there, but we decide to come back to San Diego after the wedding. We still have all our new properties to look after.

We experience the same magical change of reputation as the Baker's. My "bat bullet" is written about in the press so much that they put the damned bat, with the bullet next to it, in a glass case inside the Grand Horton for visitors to gawk at. I guess I went from murderer to hero in their eyes, which is typical in my experience.

When we arrive by the steamship *SS Goliah*, into Ocean Beach Bay, San Francisco, we can spot the restaurant on the top of the hill where the weddin' is going to be. The Bay Cliff House is where Lucky once chased a waitress into the kitchen, is all I can remember of the place. The attorney tells us on board the ship, at dinner, all about her family. Two of them are with us on the trip, her daughter Bertha May, and her youngest son, David Milton. She even tells us how she has to lie to the men lawyers in California about being deserted by her husband, Jeremiah Foltz, a Civil War veteran when she divorced him. She lies and tells them he dies, and that she's a widow with five children instead of the truth. She's able to later convince that same legal establishment, the Sacramento politicians, to establish the very laws that give her the right to take that exam in the first place. Then she passes the California Bar, on the first shot, to become the first woman admitted to practice. This is why Josie and I chose her to represent us.

When we are dressing to attend the wedding, Sadie is in a romantic mood. She grabs my waist, pulls me toward her, and asks me if I remember bein' out on Lucky Baldwin's yacht in this same harbor. I tell her I do and that Lucky tells me he wants to get us hitched on his yacht in the future.

"It is quite wonderful how history keeps repeating itself, both in the negative ways, and in the more beautifully romantic ways, such as this," she says, and then we kiss.

There are over two hundred people at the wedding of Samuel Cortland Foltz and Adeline Quantrill. However, at the reception, Mrs. Foltz decides to separate the San Francisco bluebloods and others by placing them in the main dining room away from her private party of family members and us. We're sixteen in number, and I will name them here, as what occurs at this dinner is very important to what Josie and me believe is the true practice of mysticism and intuitive Kabbalah.

At the head of the huge, rectangular table, overlooking the ocean below, are the bride and groom, smilin' and toastin' us with their glasses of champagne. Seated on their right side are Clara and her mother, Telitha, and her father, Elias Willets, both in their early sixties, who have journeyed from nearby San Jose. Then come the rest of Clara's children, Trella Evelyn, the lovely actress in her twenties and a graduate of Berkeley, Bertha May and David Milton, the two youngest we know from San Diego, and the youngest, Virginia Knox, who is twelve.

Then comes us guests from San Diego, Josie and me, Drs.

Charlotte and Fred Baker, Miss Kai Krissy Wong, Miss Heaven Riendeau, Miss Ida Bailey, Ah Toy, Mrs. Foltz's best friend and former Chinatown Madam, and Lucky Baldwin. The attorney tells us personally that she hasn't invited her former lover, Captain of Detectives, Isaiah Lees, as she says they are now separated.

My wife tells me she's nervous, 'cause Mrs. Foltz explains that her new daughter-in-law, Adeline, not only has an autobiographical memory, but she's also a clairvoyant with special people she has psychic affinity, and she can talk with the dead. "I think she might be able to read my mind," Josie says. She tells me she'll try to keep her thoughts away from our business contracts. This already puts us into dangerous situations, and we know Mrs. Foltz is going to continue to live and practice in San Diego.

"Kind ladies and gentlemen. If you please. Your attention!" Mrs. Foltz stands at her place and strikes her silver knife against the crystal wine glass rim.

The talk around the table stops, and we all wait for our hostess to speak. We can hear the surf crashing outside. I assume her speech will be about the details of how she solved the mystery we had all been part of, and I am not mistaken … at first. Afterward, however, the events unfold like poker cards bein' dealt to us, revealin' some magic hands underneath these festivities.

"I am so proud of my two children who have brought us together and sealed their holy bonds in matrimony. One might not believe this mystery of ours to be a comedy, which must always end in a wedding, but there certainly are comedic elements that led me to my eventual conclusions to solve it."

"Mother, please tell them about the goat," says Trella Evelyn, as she brushes back a lock of reddish-brown hair from her forehead. She wears a lovely bare-shouldered formal dress, the latest style, and her eyes sparkle with delight. "What you wrote to me that made me fall off my stool laughing."

"Ah, yes. My thespian daughter is referencing the first major clue I obtained pointing to Dr. Fred Baker's involvement in the plot to infect the Stingaree bordellos."

As usual, Lucky Baldwin pipes up from the end of the table.

166

"Well, Mrs. O'Leary's cow was said to start the great Chicago fire of '71. Was it Ida Bailey's goat this time?" He's drunk already.

Ida Bailey also starts to laugh, even though she's been banned from doing business in the Stingaree. It's probably good for her, as she's stopped using drugs, God love her, and she's even takin' business classes at the women's school.

"You're not far from the truth, Mr. Baldwin. I was spying around Mayor Hunsaker's office at night, as Charlotte and I were able to get a passkey from a friend in the mayor's employ. Lo and behold, tied to the leather couch in his office was a nanny goat. I tripped on her in the dark, and she let out a banshee wail so loud that it made both Charlotte and I scream to high heaven."

Folks laugh all around the table. I'm laughin' 'cause the same thing happened to Lucky and me in that same office. I'm not about to tell 'em about it.

"Dr. Baker gave the mayor a goat, but it wasn't poisoned. We had already ascertained that the goats in the Stingaree bordellos had been injected with *coccobacillus*, and the boy Anand's poison contained this bacterium. The only logical persons who could have injected them and provided the bacteria were Charlotte or her husband, and when Charlotte told me about her husband's visit to Malta to research with Dr. David Bruce, the British Army surgeon, the clues began to come together."

"And how did you ascertain that Wyatt and I were marked to be poisoned by Sonenschein?" Josie asks. I love it when she uses big words to impress educated folks like these.

"We found a vial of the poison on the person of the victim, Rabbi Sonenschein. After you were kidnapped, Mrs. Earp. That's when we know it was Fred Baker behind the poisoning of the goats with Brucellosis. In fact, on the day I visited Chinatown to question him, I was almost completely certain he was our guilty party." Mrs. Foltz sees that Kai Wong has her hand up, so she nods for her to speak.

"I am sorry, but how can they allow Dr. Baker to go free? If it were a poor person who poisoned Anand, he would have been hanged!"

This young waitress is just wakin' up to the unfairness of

real life, and I feel sorry for her. It's Fred Baker who stands up to answer.

"I want to tell you all right now that I am the guiltiest devil alive today. I shall be working to help the poor for the rest of my life, in a meager attempt at atonement for what I did. All I can plead to you is for your mercy and the fact that I was driven by my lust and my own megalomaniacal insanity." He slips down into his chair and cries.

Charlotte, taking pity on her husband, puts her arm around him. The young Chinese waitress seems calm for the moment.

Ah Toy, the Chinese Madam stands up. At 60, she is tall, thin, and wears a flowered blue *cheongsam*.

"If there is a consolation, I think it is that Dr. Baker has begun to work with other researchers around the world to provide vaccines and cures for these diseases, except for rabies, but there may be something to treat that as well if they keep testing."

"Ah Toy is right. We must look to the bright side," the groom Samuel, pipes in. He has worked closely with his mother on enough cases to know she would see the positive results of any treachery.

Clara Foltz finishes explainin' to all of us how she solved the mystery when the rest of us come back to Ensenada. Only Heaven Riendeau and Kai Krissy Wong don't want to give any more information about bein' nurses. I soon discover why.

We are in line to congratulate the bride and groom, after the dinner, and the sea breeze is comin' in through the open window of the main ballroom. A complete wedding group of over two hundred guests is present. Heaven Riendeau is right behind Josie in line, and just after she shakes Adeline's hand, this young bride begins to go into some kind of a trance. Heaven, too, becomes transfixed, starin' at the young bride like a huntin' cougar. As the former Golden Faun madam slowly removes her red crushed-velvet dress, we see she wears multi-colored leotards, with images of what Josie whispers to me are called the "Curse of the Evil Eye," which is an image of a blue hand with an eye centered in its palm. Both women's eyeballs roll back into their heads, and Adeline begins shoutin' in a deep, manly voice. When I see my wife, and all the other women, begin to dance, I know they're either jokin' or possessed by the devil.

I know that language. Josie uses it when she lights candles on Friday nights. It's Hebrew. Heaven Riendeau, for her part, begins dancin' around the bride and removes each of the evil eyes, one at a time, from her leotards, as if they're veils, and she took lessons from Ida Bailey. When Ida also begins dancin', I know somethin' very strange is afoot.

Soon, with the screamin' bride shouting out in Hebrew, all of the women in the room start to dance, in a wide circle, around the white bride. They all strip the formal, outer clothes from their bodies—both young and old—and begin to swoon, rockin' back and forth.

All of the women finally stop. They stand in the middle, breathin' hard and sweatin' like stuffed pigs, and all us men folks are around them, starin' at one another. My wife is the one who speaks first.

"That is the spirit voice of Rabbi Jerome Sonenschein, if you want to believe it. He is speaking in Hebrew through this young medium bride. He says there will soon be a murderer in San Diego who shall attempt to kill the first-born male of each family. He quotes the words from our Hebrew scriptures. 'That night, God sent the angel of death to kill the firstborn sons of the Egyptians.' It is the last plague of Passover."

When Heaven Riendeau screams, we just watch her run, wavin' her hands in the air, her bare feet hittin' the tiles of the floor, her body shakin' like a Shaker, and then she's outside, on the balcony. As she climbs up on the chair, and then the wall, we can hear her voice, as the fog bank begins to move toward us from out at sea.

"I can no longer be part of this! I am pregnant with Elias Baldwin's child. The world is going stark, raving mad!" When Heaven jumps, I look at Lucky. He is grinning.

Ida

The Prosecutor, Mr. Archibald Richardt, subpoenas me to testify, so here I am, seated in front, on the right-hand side of the courtroom. Mr. Earp is over on the other side with Mrs. Foltz and Dr. Charlotte Baker. He is manacled around his legs and he is handcuffed, which should be the way we keep all men, in my mind's eye. Most of the world's corruption takes place because men are given free rein to war, pillage, rape, and destroy Nature's blessings. I know this as a fact even before I meet the victim, Rabbi Jerome Sonenschein.

Observing wealthy men throughout my development years as an orphan in San Diego gives me a bird's eye view of them and what makes them lustful sentient beings. Not only am I able to create my persona and "tricks of the brothel trade," I am also able to chisel the personas of my ladies in waiting. If there is one idea that binds all of us madams in the Stingaree together, including Josephine Marcus, it's the fact that men want docile, weak-minded, and artistically performing ladies at home, but they want women they can pay for, who can pretend to appreciate their much more superior intellectual status, as well as their uniquely masculine ability to woo in a most ribald manner.

I must certainly clarify the last statement. Most men are not "intellectual," in the literary sense. They are usually saturnine and fit into the categorical metaphor I like to use from Jonathan Swift's satirical novel *Gulliver's Travels*, as belonging from the Land of the Houyhnhnms. These creatures are, of course, horse-like beings who pride themselves on their practical reasoning based on eugenics or racial and ethnic superiority, as demonstrated by their ability to monetize Nature for selfish value, including the control of the wild naked men called Yahoos, who they drive like cattle to do the back-breaking work in the fields.

Men today pride themselves on their "horse sense," and this is what I mean when I state they are "intellectuals." Few of them have read any literature, and even fewer understand the spirit world all around us, or the mystical realm of reality if it's not based upon a firm foundation of logical cause and effect. If I tell a man that my breasts can provide him with milk developed in the Garden of Eden, he may scoff at me. However, once I show him these breasts, he will soon become quite a devout believer, especially if I can croon a holy tune from his Bible School days, such as "We Shall Gather at the River," or some other such innocent refrain. It is this juxtaposition of what the great poet William Blake calls the "Songs of Innocence and Experience" that gets to them almost every time. Even the lowest grade of Houyhnhnm appreciates such declarations of Edenesque love.

I detest the American system of criminal justice. First of all, they allow only men to serve on the jury, and then they have the audacity to call it a "jury of one's peers." Even in the case of Wyatt Earp, the defendant *du jour*, none of these jurists is a former gunslinger or marshal, and he most certainly doesn't make most of his money from investing in saloons, gambling halls, and brothels. At least, not directly.

Therefore, how are any of these men a peer of Mr. Earp? Furthermore, how is Capital Punishment supposed to deter other humans from killing again? Most murders are committed when the shooter is not in his or her right mind, correct? Either the person is under the influence of a substance, or under the influence of poverty, greed, or passion. How are any of these specific conditions related to the State murdering you by hanging? Perhaps I might think twice before easily pulling the trigger, but chances are much more in favor of my still doing the dastardly deed because of the "mental stress" conditions I just mentioned, which have nothing to do with making me fearful about being hanged. Such illogical reasoning makes me abhor men and all their games of injustice.

I am surprised I am called as a witness for the prosecution. I've already explained how I was under the influence of peyote during my dance after the Hundred-Round Fight in Tijuana. However, this District Attorney, Richardt, insists that I have many "keys to his victory," as he phrases it. My testimony is based on what I know concerning the victim, Rabbi Sonenschein, and how involved I am in his Kabbalah group. Also, it's based on my work in the Canary Cottage, where I have my relations with Wyatt, Mayor Hunsaker, and others. He tells me Wyatt is jealous of Sonenschein's involvement with his wife, Josephine Marcus, and this is the main reason Earp killed him.

There will be four witnesses who will present this morning, and I will be the last, as the key witness, testifying in the afternoon. The policeman at the scene of the murder will testify that my beloved, the rabbi, was unarmed, and he was shot from point-blank range, a bullet in the forehead by a very efficient shooter. I cannot say I saw this happen, as I was having a hallucination at the time. As far as the forensics expert, the coroner, and even Mayor Will Hunsaker were concerned, I was to play no part.

The court is packed with as many humans as can legally be sequestered inside one domicile of this size. There are newspaper reporters, photojournalists, and even two Western Union wire transmitters, who hunch over their telegraph keys like cats guarding a prized mouse. The rest are mostly male and female townspeople. I recognize many of the men who visit the Stingaree quite often, but there are also gallery attendees from other counties, states, and territories. The oppressive atmosphere is eating me alive. I have always experienced claustrophobia in such confined quarters. Thus, my consumption of drugs creates the unreality I need to see this crowded world in the specter of distortion I believe it deserves.

Here's that Archie fellow again. He smells like Whistler's Mother, with some kind of cologne, which reeks of distilled apples. His somber suit fits him loosely, and, with its dark color, he could be an undertaker's double if it wasn't for that ungodly royal blue floppy necktie. His walruses droop with caked wax from some fly-specked jar in his toilet. His pinched eyes behold only straight lines and geometric shapes, and I am merely one more block of wood. A little piece, not even human, to fit into his grand design. His goal is the direct path leading poor Wyatt onerously to the gallows outside.

The judge is on the bench in front of us all. Judge Parker. Up above, assuming the pose of a gray-haired ghost god as from the ceiling above, in the Sistine Chapel, he is leaning toward Adam, the prosecutor. I saw this image in a photograph in the San Diego Library. There seems to be a ruckus up near his tower. Policemen have gathered there, and the old barrister is motioning for both of the lead attorneys to visit him. Mrs. Foltz and Mr. Richardt march up to their god. The old man is pointing to somebody behind the defense table, behind Wyatt. It is Josephine. She stands up and tries to bypass several reporters who have congregated in her path.

"Excuse me, I must see my husband's attorney. Please, let me pass." They hold their places, their cameras poised. "Get the hell out of my way or I'll run you down!" That is much better. She makes her way through and now stands before the attorneys and the policemen. "Mrs. Foltz!" Josie's attorney is conferring and is ignoring her for the moment.

When she finally spies her client, Mrs. Foltz's face turns as red as the fashionable bustled dress she wears. "Must you arrest her now?" Clara Foltz is speaking to a young policeman at the front of the pack. He hesitantly moves toward Josephine, as one would approach a mountain lion. His attempts to grab her wrists are rebuffed in stealth motions from the wildcat. "Let her go, Officer," the attorney instructs him, and he does so. He fades back into the circle of his companions near the judge's bench.

"What's happened? Why are you all congregating up here like pigs at a trough?" Josephine is now very loud. I do believe her Jewish dander has been raised. I have seen her this angry once before, as she walked in on Jerome Sonenschein and me. He was teaching me a special Hebrew chant to call forth the *Ein Sof.*

Mrs. Foltz addresses her with composed authority. The journalists are scribbling madly in their notebooks.

"Mrs. Earp, you failed to inform me of your dealings. Now the prosecution has concrete evidence to place you under arrest for being an accessory to murder. Why didn't you tell me about your relationship with Miss Heaven Riendeau, from San Francisco?"

Now, what could this be concerning my new neighbor and competing madam? I am aware Josephine has employed her, but I could not guess what this specific inquiry might be referencing.

"Riendeau? I don't know what you mean. I have never had any dealings with this woman."

Does she lie to her husband's attorney? Oh my!

"Riendeau has not said anything about knowing you. Mayor Hunsaker's office has the proof that you have been running at least twelve bordellos in San Diego, beginning when you were a working girl in Tombstone. You told me yourself that the mayor was your husband's attorney, but you never told me you were running brothel businesses throughout your journeys in California, Utah, and Oregon. Hunsaker knew, beginning in 1874, at the age of 14, when Josie Marcus fell in with a San Francisco madam Hattie Wells. Late in November 1874, using the alias Sadie Mansfield, you arrived in Prescott, Arizona, and began working in Hattie's brothel."

The attorney has made her accusation clear to her. Will she become a second defendant next to Wyatt?

"That's a lie! I never worked in a brothel. Honey has gone berserk from the sex parlors he visits. He's trying to protect his own investments, by god!" Josie's jugular veins were quite prominent when she yelled.

"You learned the trade, and it seems, according to all the documents Hunsaker has collected, you have perfected the business to a rather high art form. The last agreement came when you spoke to Miss Riendeau in your tavern. Do you not remember your exchange with her?"

What could these negotiations entail? Mrs. Foltz is getting to the heart of the inquest.

"One of your regulars, Mr. Budreaux Randolph, was there, and he works for Mr. Hunsaker's office, part-time. He overheard everything you told Miss Riendeau. However, that's not the last of it."

"Last of it? Which *it* do you mean? You're being quite vague for a lawyer, aren't you Mrs. Foltz?"

Ah, poor Josie. Sarcasm will get you nowhere with this intelligent attorney.

"Because you worked these bordellos in absentia, so to speak, you had to create written agreements. Hunsaker has collected all these agreements, and this last oral agreement has caused all your chickens to come home to roost, I am afraid."

The mayor seems to have been one busy fellow. His interest, in this case, goes far afield from what I know about his efforts with my girls. It may have something to do with the contract these men made with the Earps. Anthony Comstock, the Postmaster-General, was the main benefactor in this contract, but Hunsaker was also there. I saw them all go into the back room together that day.

"Agreements? My husband and I have signed hundreds of agreements. We never know what we've signed, most of the time. What does this prove?"

Josie is still playing ignorant. Was it any wonder she is now seen as a possible conspirator?

"The mayor has sworn evidence from several of the bordello madams throughout your travels, ending in San Diego, and including Ida Bailey. In each of these places, you not only became an investor in their duties as prostitutes, but you were always followed by another person who was trying to stop you from these investments."

That must be the *coup de grâce*.

"Who is this other person, pray tell?"

Poor wife. Indignant to the end.

"Rabbi Jerome Sonenschein. He followed you wherever you went. It was his sworn duty to stop you from ruining these women and their lives as children of God. The Grand Jury has written out new charges against you, as a co-defendant in this case, as a murderess in the first degree. They say you wanted the rabbi dead more than Wyatt did, and that you were the main instigator in his assassination because Sonenschein wanted to stop your exploits and bawdy experiments, the likes of which this country has never seen before. Before I can represent you, we must have a very long talk. Is that clear, Mrs. Earp?"

This contract they made in the backroom must have involved the mayor directly. Now Josephine has to pay for her bad negotiation. They are fitting a hangman's noose for a lady.

"Hunsaker is behind all of this! I told you about our contract with him to create Comstock's garden of earthy delights in Mexico. Why don't you tell them now? You are not a lawyer. You are a prude and a poor Suffragette. Is Dr. Baker behind this as well? You and your kind. Always putting the image of society before the truth of the evil that always lurks behind all the prim and proper attitudes and hypocritical religions."

She is still shouting at Mrs. Foltz as the police drag her out of the courtroom.

To her benefit, the attorney nods at her client, to acknowledge that she will still be defending them both.

"You will all find out! I shall not stop my own investigation, until I can show you all what is really happening here!"

Her own investigation? Could it be that Mrs. Earp has others in her employ? I will do some snooping of my own. She will never find out about the rabbi and I because we made a sacred pact! It held until he was torn from me, like my own heart, on that horrific day. If you hang for this betrayal, Josephine, it shall be your just desserts.

***

I live an interior life. My appreciation of the world around me is always lackluster unless I can see something that improves my lot. This is the way we are, those of us from poverty and the lower depths of this spinning world. I teach my girls the natural order and a logical process in their relations with men. I color code them to make it easier for our clients to properly call for them. I show them how to make a man reach his climax faster, to save us all time, which is money. It is like eating at the Moonbeam Café. I never allow drunken men to partake of their beauty inside our Canary Cottage. I establish firm rules in here, and, as I look around inside this home, where I and my ladies spend most of our days, the furnishings are respectful and decorous. Polished maple furniture from France. Colorful rugs from the Far East. The best paintings of San Diego's harbor and ocean. Relaxation. Intelligence in the form of the posters of my favorite Romantic poets in their art and their own words. Keats, Shelley, Wordsworth, and Lord Byron.

In the parlor, where my ladies first meet with their guests, I have a print of William Blake's pen and watercolor of his famous "Lovers' Whirlwind," depicting the words from Canto V. of "The Inferno" in Dante's *Divine Comedy*: "The infernal hurricane that never rests carries along with the spirits in its rapine; whirling and smiting it molests them. When they arrive before its rushing blast, here are shrieks, and bewailing, and lamenting; here they blaspheme the power divine." However, I tell my ladies that Blake disliked any organized religion. He showed these lovers on their circuitous way into heaven, instead of remaining in Hell, which was where Dante wanted to keep them, as he was writing his book for the Roman Catholic Church.

"You ladies are to be respected. Didn't Jesus save a prostitute and send her to heaven? Mary Magdalene? Keep your chins up! Our day of salvation will come just as hers did."

In reality, before I met Jerome, I thought about brothels as being the sequestration of women who could prove to be much more efficient and intelligent about carnal affairs than men could ever be. This was before I had to take drugs to make the world as misshapen as my inner misanthrope. Indeed. My intellect had been hewn by myself, alone, inside the San Diego Library, and within the libraries of bachelor attorneys, and men of the world, who would happen upon our town the way the rabbi did. They were vagabonds and nomads, just like the Earps.

The one major distinction, of course, between these Christian men of the world and my Jerome Sonenschein is that they have the money to depart and sail on to the next port or boomtown. Not Jerome. As he told me, on the first day we met, "I am provided for only when I can provide for others. When I look at you, my lovely, I never see a woman." I was aghast at such a statement. Never before had I seen such a man who beheld life as being a game of equal and fair distribution of deeds. "My goodness! What do you see, pray tell?" I was already smiling, as he wore that clown's suit with all the numbers, anagrams, and formulas covering it as if it had been sketched upon by Isaac Newton experiencing a grand mal seizure.

An oversized black felt fedora adorned his black head. It covered most of his wide forehead, and his long *payot* sideburns snaked down like curtains to cover the matching, tight-curled, full black beard. To me, he was the antithesis of Saint Nicholas, the fat red elf who came to the orphanage each Christmas to hand us girls our candies, stockings, and dolls. Sonenschein had a swarthy complexion and murky eyebrows that seemed to animate whenever he spoke. His eyes! They were of two different colors. The right one, a common brown, but the left was sliver-gray, the shade of a corpse's pallor, and it was this one he told me that had been burnt by anti-Semites in his native Ukraine. They exiled him from Brody, his birthplace, for his interpretation of Kabbalah scriptures. When he spoke that day in the Canary Cottage, I became his forever.

"I see Asherah." And then he took off his hat and marked it with a piece of yellow chalk he extracted from his coat pocket where his watch fob should have been. אֲשֵׁרָה were the letters he inscribed.

"You are the queen of the sea, the wife of Yahweh, and the mother of all. They see you as a town seducer, one who would break apart family, but I know your true source. For this was why I was banished from my homeland. I worship her which gives Israel her true soul and divinity. The elders attempted to banish her to become the national emblem of *Shekinah*, for Israel, but they can never banish my queen! As Jeremiah wrote, 'On every high hill and under every spreading tree you lay down as a prostitute.' I am here to save you all, and convert you back into what you were meant to be! Temple goddesses who will care for you, my Asherah, in this new land of the Canaanites!"

The rabbi explained that he was forming a group of followers who believed he could call upon the powers of the *Ein Sof* to cleanse us and to keep us worthy of our stature as temple goddesses rather than sinful whores. He said Solomon and David kept many concubines, who served their sexual needs, and this was a common practice in ancient Israel. It changed when the men banished all worship of Asherah, under Josiah, the sixteenth King of Judah. Jerome said the *qadishtu* were these temple women, and they were once considered high priestesses until the men decided they wanted all the power.

"In my group, you will remain in power as prostitutes, and I shall return you to your former selves, respected as priestesses of sensual Kabbalah."

His words make complete logic to me. I always believe our profession is not profane or evil. We serve a higher purpose than what the Christians say we are. The rabbi explained that with the Jews it was because of the same jealousy of our feminine sensuality and carnal knowledge that they decided to drive us away. "Why else would the women of ancient Judah and Israel have worshipped Asherah, and built statues of her, and prayed to her likeness inside their homes? We were the true source of fertility for them. We were closer to God, as we worked inside the male dominion, the temple, and these men learned from us about all the ways of pleasing a woman. The men took this knowledge back home and made their wives fertile with a new passion. We, the temple priestesses, when we became fertile, had children who served the priests, who did not remain without family, the way it was with the Christians, who limited sexual experience to marriage and eventually forbade it for their priests."

I know we deserve more respect from this male-dominated world. We lost our power to them thousands of years ago. We now hide our faces in public, and when our birth control fails, we abort our fetus or lose employment, and then we sell or give away our children to orphanages, the way I grew up. This is not justice.

I believed Rabbi Soneschein, and I soon learned from him how to love in many different ways. He was also a man of the world, but his new Kabbalah took him into many brothels around the world, and I gained all his knowledge of how to perform coitus, which he had learned from being with women of many different cultures. Jerome also said that we could lift ourselves and form a union. He said, in other countries, our lot was not disrespected. These women were given a living wage and could hold their heads high in the communities in which they served a useful purpose. "Where else could lonely and perhaps ugly men go? We gave them a taste of passion and relief from how society tortured them." And thus, the rabbi explained, the society paid them respect for their public service, and doctored them for free, kept them healthy, and did not arrest them. Of course, I told him. This should be the way of the world!

I believe that Wyatt Earp is just another jealous man, envious of this rabbi and all he knew about the passions of women. The big man. The gunslinger and marshal, Wyatt Earp, is just another jealous Josiah, trying to get rid of a man who wants to better our lives and give us new hope. When he shot Rabbi Jerome Sonenschein, Earp might as well have shot me and all the other prostitutes in San Diego, or the world, for that matter. Perhaps I sensed that this murder would happen on that day. Why else would I have ingested my grandmother's eyes, my name for peyote buttons, before I danced my magical dance of the seven veils? I did not want to see what would happen to the only man who had ever truly given me and my sisters the respect we deserved.

I have never confessed this love of the little rabbi to anybody. Certainly not to the police, when they questioned me, and not to District Attorney Richardt or Attorney Clara Foltz. This will be the secret I will take to my grave. It was our pact. Unless it is I who is being tricked. I need to find out if the rabbi was telling me the truth about what he was doing that day in Tijuana. Was the pact he made with me authentic? I shall first listen to what Earp's lawyer says on this topic. Then, if I discover any doubt, I will do my exploration into whether what Clara Foltz posits is true. As it now stands, in my mind, Wyatt Earp murdered my lover because he was jealous and because the rabbi was attempting to give us prostitutes some respect and value. If the worm turns, however, and I find out differently, I may be the one who next murders someone.

I will return to the courthouse and hear the testimony. Perhaps the time is at hand for the truth to reveal the connections I need to know.

How are they able to pack even more people into this horrible house of tortured minds? Perhaps I should take something to ward off all these evil spirits clustering about? Ghosts are siphoning the thoughts being created by these creatures gathered here to listen to the accusations against a similar woman of my fallen ways. Josephine Earp looks so pitiable chained at the wrists. Her blue dress is wrinkled from jailhouse wear, and she frequently turns to look over at her husband, on the other side of the defense table, but he continues to stare straight ahead, his masculinity is never interrupted. Why are men so stoic in public? Do they believe showing emotion makes them vulnerable to attack? Don't they know the worst attack comes from within?

William Jefferson Hunsaker is on the stand. I have been usurped as the key witness. District Attorney Richardt hastily explained to me that he had changed his tactic and I shall be interviewed later. I suppose it's because of the arrest of Josephine. According to the earlier discussion between Clara Foltz and Josie, the mayor now holds most of the proof he needs to convict and show a conspiracy existed between her and her husband to terminate Rabbi Sonenschein's life.

"Do you swear to tell the truth, the whole truth, and nothing but the truth, so help you God?" The short bailiff is now swearing in the mayor. District Attorney Richardt appears prevailing and studious, grasping his lapels and rocking on his heels, awaiting his big moment. A few cameras explode in the gallery, taking in the scene of the mayor raising his right hand, and he places his left palm on the Bible as if it were the derriere of one of my ladies.

Honey, as Josephine calls him, is staring at this inquisitor with collegial rapport, as they are both barristers, complicit in this duty dance with the truth, as they see it. Mr. Richardt begins.

"We have established that Mr. Earp pulled his gun on the rabbi, Mr. Sonenschein, at 3:37 PM, on May 6, 1888, in Tijuana, Mexico. We have heard from the coroner, and the police at the scene, proving that Mr. Earp's bullet found its mark and was the proximate cause of death. However, it is you, Mr. Hunsaker, who has new information to assist the State in finding the truth behind an illicit motive in this murder, is it not?"

The mayor turns his head toward the defense table. His eyes are now upon the man he once defended in Arizona, in another murder trial. How quickly the legal tables can turn. Now he is testifying against Wyatt and his common-law wife.

"Yes, I suppose so, although it gives me no great pleasure to do so."

"What is your personal and professional relationship with the accused couple, Mr. and Mrs. Wyatt Earp? Could you point them out for the court?"

Hunsaker's balding head glistens with perspiration, as he gestures toward the couple, first Wyatt, and then Josephine, aiming his forefinger at them as if it were a gun. "I was hired by the State to defend Mr. Earp in Tombstone, Arizona, along with my law partner at the time, Thomas Fitch. I met Mr. Earp, along with his companion, Josephine Marcus, who was then known as Sadie, and we prepared his case, which lasted over a month, as I recall."

Richardt's counterpart, attorney Foltz, stands up. "If the court would rule, what relevance does this have to do with the guilt or innocence of my clients?"

The elder Judge Parker places his cupped right hand behind his right ear. "What's that Mrs. Fouts? Did you object?"

"Mrs. Foltz, your honor, with a *tz*. Yes, I wanted you to rule on the relevance of the prosecutor's delving into a case that took place over seven years ago." She is speaking much louder now.

"Well, Mr. Richards, do you have a method to your madness?" Parker's hearing suffers to understand the prosecutor's last name also.

"Richardt, your Honor. With a *dt*. Yes, your honor, I do. I wanted to establish the fact that the two defendants, even back in Tombstone, were beginning to shape the mental machinations of their nefarious deeds and plans, which would ultimately lead to the demise of the good Rabbi Jerome Sonenschein in San Diego."

This attempt is going back to their lives in Tombstone? What kind of evidence can they provide to show this is true? Wyatt Earp gambles a lot, and I doubt they have that kind of money.

"I understand, your honor, but the prosecution fails to get to the heart of this case, which took place on May 6, 1888. The criminal statutes need the State to prove that my clients were of a malicious state of mind toward the victim, not toward the Clanton gang. Their mental plan of malice must be close in time to *this* homicide. Or, perhaps Mr. Richardt has other murders on his mind to convict this husband-and-wife team of committing? If so, then I want to hear from the Grand Jury in those other states."

People laugh. The old judge turns on Richardt again. "Well, counselor? What do you have to offer?"

"I will continue, with my questioning, if the good madame can allow, and I shall bring us all up to date. But this malicious intent, as the defense points out, with astute clarity, is being proved by what this witness can show us. It comes in the form of affidavits of fifteen madams, including our next witness, Miss Ida Bailey, who will testify that Mrs. Josephine Earp. Or, should I say, common-law wife, Mrs. Earp, for they were never wed inside any church of our Lord ..."

"I object! Hearsay and a provocation upon the morals and religion of my client."

"Objection overruled. You may continue, Mr. Richards."

Although still getting the prosecutor's name wrong, the judge's bias is showing.

The prosecutor marches over to stand before his jury. He is ready for a grand speech of some kind.

"We have women present in this courtroom today, and the subject matter included in these legal affidavits is such that only the jury, the judge, and counsel are going to be privy to them. Suffice it to say, however, they prove, beyond any doubt, that Mr. and Mrs. Earp have invested in houses of ill repute and dens of gambling, drinking, and prostitution. Not only this, but they also make mention of a religious rabbi, the victim, Jerome Sonenschein, who was following them, like a shadow of doom, across state lines, to rouse the towns of the exact nature of their sinful activities. What more does this court need to prove the malice in their minds against our victim in this case? Think of all the good families threatened by their lust and greed. Think of the future of our children and our schools, and, not to mention our beloved churches!"

If this attorney hopes to corroborate his balderdash with my testimony, he will be quite surprised with what I tell him. Jerome Sonenschein was accomplishing the exact opposite unless he was lying to me all along.

It is time. I get up from my seat and excuse myself. Four other people let me pass, and I reach the aisle. A few people glance at me as I walk toward the double doors of the court entrance. The bailiff opens them for me, and I go out into the vestibule. There he is, still perusing all the photos of judges. I grasp his shoulder with my right hand. He looks at me, and his eyes are ghastly. Charlotte Baker will love him. I push him toward the courtroom entrance. His mouth begins to drool, as he staggers forward into the courtroom and begins to limp down the aisle. I move into a small cul-de-sac in the rear of the court to observe.

A woman screams. Dr. Fred Baker, my zombie, walks toward the defense table. Dr. Charlotte Baker stands up.

"Fred! What is it? What's happened to you?" Her voice is full of panic.

"Oh, my God! Look at his eyes!" Another voice proclaims.

Charlotte's husband has eyes like a demon's, red-rimmed and bulging. He staggers forward; his arms thrust toward his wife in a pleading gesture. When he finally stands before her, his mouth is dripping with saliva as he speaks.

"I'm so sorry, Charlotte, my love. Venus was before me. She made me go back. Again, and again. The sea winds blew, and the monsters of the deep came for me. Called me into their lair. I cannot go back! Please! Let me stay with you here."

His body pitches over and his forehead grazes the table when he falls.

Mrs. Baker takes his pulse, but from her vacant expression, it can't be a good sign. Two policemen come through the doors carrying a stretcher. They lift the poor doctor and set him gingerly upon it. Charlotte follows him out, holding onto his hand. I can hear her weeping.

"Get him checked for the black plague! That man is deathly ill!"

"Our lives are in danger! We must leave here at once!"

The gallery of visitors becomes quite boisterous. I want to get out of this madhouse. My claustrophobia is beginning to set in once more.

I follow a man in a straw hat as he exits, as the people push and shove behind us until we are outside the courthouse. These recent developments make me aware that I need to do some investigating into whether what Hunsaker says is true. Is Jerome implicated in some way with Wyatt and Josephine Earp? Did he lie to me? If so, perhaps the Earps *are* guilty. Or, if I can keep my sacred pact, then another murder may be in the offing. If I am Asherah, as my rabbi proclaims me, then I will call upon my ladies to do my bidding. I cannot allow us to be punished for the sins of these others, these impure ones.

I do hope Freddy Baker feels better. I did what Heaven Riendeau wants. Simply one madam doing a favor for her next-door neighbor. I even allowed him to see me and my ladies dance inside the White Lady Cave, just before I took him to court. He was hallucinating so much; I hope he's not seriously injured.

This married man who lusts for me is not going to remember anything.

***

he headlines of the evening edition of the *Union* tell the story about why Heaven Riendeau wanted me to drug Dr. Fred Baker, "Accused Murderers Have Escaped!" The two defendants, Mr. and Mrs. Wyatt Earp, have "fled together through the Judge's chambers and into the night. Their whereabouts are at present unknown, but police are searching for them both within San Diego and across the border areas into Mexico."

I need to act at once if I want to determine what may have been behind the rabbi's subterfuge. I decide that the sacred pact we have means more to me than my safety and even the safety of those for whom I am presently responsible. The only way to discover how involved Jerome had been with the Earps, or anybody else, for that matter, will be to investigate the property we purchased together, the Hotel New Canaan, located on the La Jolla Cliffs. Our transactions there and down in the caves below will lead me to the answers.

When I suggest to my ladies of the Canary Cottage that we visit the La Jolla Caves, where Rabbi Sonenschein practiced his Kabbalah, all of them refuse to go. They view his murder as a curse upon everything he and his group attempted to do. I remind them we had over three hundred women who belonged to our group, and it has not disbanded entirely.

"Jerome was murdered by a man who may have been hired by the same wealthy men who use us as their spermatozoa savings banks. Don't you want to protect his memory and all he's done for us?"

"Miss Bailey, you plum crazy! Those feral women livin' in them caves are not human, now that he's gone." June was always the one to speak up first. A lithe and superstitious Negro woman from New Orleans, she was the first to say the rabbi's murder put a voodoo curse on the Canary Cottage.

"You best keep out of it, mum," Sarah Goldstein put in. As one of my three Jews, she is the most threatened, personally, by the Kabbalah. Jerome had once frightened this girl from London by insisting that she offer her menstrual blood on the Sabbath rather than wine. I knew he was jesting, but she never forgot it, and she did not trust him again.

"You women are so cowardly. What about your new status as *qadishtu*? The rabbi promised you all that you could be temple priestesses. The pact I had with him goes beyond death. I am Asherah. This is the new Canaan. Remember?"

However, when I see none of them is going to come with me, I set out alone. I need to discover if Sonenschein lied to me, and this could be a matter of life and death.

Facing north towards La Jolla Shores, the seven sea caves of La Jolla are etched within a seventy-five-million-year-old sandstone sea cliff that sprouts forth along a thousand yards of coastal beach and the Pacific Ocean. I always consult the surf and tide charts to be certain I can access the caves without being drowned in my small sailboat.

Before getting my Canary Cottage chauffeur, Peng Shi, to drive me out to the caves, I want to stop at the Hotel New Canaan. Perched on the La Jolla Cliffs, it overlooks the La Jolla Shores cove below. Rabbi Sonenschien purchased the hotel, previously owned by Alonzo Horton's brother-in-law, William Wallace Bowers, who was responsible for designing and outfitting the Horton House, and who went on to great success as the collector of the port, state senator, congressman, and promoter of San Diego. Mr. Bowers, coincidentally, was also a frequent visitor to my establishment.

Along with my help, we cater to mostly consumptive males of substantial wealth coming to San Diego by the thousands during our boom years. The reason we choose males is that our maids and housekeepers are members of Sonenschein's Kabbalist group, chosen from women in the various brothels in town. He convinced these women to work for him because he told them, they would be "rehabilitated and begin to integrate successfully back into society."

This rehabilitation was not to be free of the sex trade, as these women would perform massages, upon request, with extra duty fellatio added into the bargain for an additional charge. My women were told by me that they were being endowed with spiritual power as *qadishtu,* and they would take part in weekly mystical ceremonies, whereupon I would show them the Dance of the Seven Veils and explain my role as their spiritual leader, the reincarnated Asherah. They learned quickly, and they performed admirably.

Of course, there are other such hotels and even one hospital, which caters to the same clientele as we, and they can solicit new visitors to San Diego through frequent advertisements in newspapers on the East Coast. For example, here is one such ad from the first consumptive hospital established by Drs. Remondino and Stockton and is a very simple structure on the block fronting Columbia and F streets.

The United States has a small section away off in its southwestern corner, which will give a man a life of ease, comfort, luxury, and besides allow him at the same time to accumulate wealth to any amount. If you have any doubt about this just look at the early

Americans who came here in the period following the annexation of California. They are endowed with Falstaffian paunches, Bonifacial noses, and Teutonic complexions of roses; never sick; with digestions to be envied by the ostrich or alligator; lungs like a blacksmith's bellows and hearts as tough as that of a turtle. Their muscles are firm and their frames sturdy and their bank accounts are . . . unlimited . . . their main occupation being the clipping off of coupons from their stores of bonds. There is evident proof of the physical and financial effects of our climate which cannot be gainsaid—as the Horton House porch is always more or less ornamented by a number of these living witnesses of the wonderful effects of our incomparable climate.

Not to be outdone, Jerome Sonenschein ran his ad, which is more adventurous. It alludes to the main feature of his hotel, and he calls it "The Asherah Treatment":

Kabbalist Rabbi and Mystical soothsayer, Jerome Sonenschein, welcomes the weary vagabond to his New Canaan Hotel and Sanitarium. Atop the cliffs of seaside La Jolla, you can bask in the morning's ocean breezes, and feel the strong, yet soft hands of our qadishtu, who are trained by their Asherah, the female goddess of the Far and Middle East, to administer the healing salves and ointments of The Asherah Treatment, to open your breathing passages all over the body, not just in the lungs. Also, the Sonenschein *drink, called posca, which was given by the Ancient Roman Emperors to their victorious soldiers, is combined with the fresh garden fruits and vegetables, and grain-fed chickens and cattle, to enliven your body with new energies. The sunshine of the beach and the surf below will tan your skin to a healthy brown. Come one, come all, to bask in this passion fruit of San Diego: The New Canaan Hotel, Resort, and Spa.*

The *posca* is vinegar or spoiled wine. And the foods we give them are obtained from Mexican farms at a very reduced rate. We, of course, raise the wholesale prices ten times and make a very nice profit. Our ladies bring in the most money, with the heart of The Asherah Treatment, and I perform my mystical Seven Veils Ballet every Saturday night following the gambling the men do in the basement of the hotel. We find the men are more generous with their money if we have our ladies do the massages while I am dancing. I arrange it so that the stage is in front of the twenty-five isolation booths, with one man on each table, gazing out at me, as their oiled bodies are being treated by our *qadishtu* damsels.

As Peng Shi pulls our carriage up to the front of the hotel, I stare down the cliff's steep terrain to the cove below. The wind is out of the southwest, and it is relatively dry and sunny for May. We have our rain mostly in winter months, not spring, and the only way I can circumnavigate the caves below is to have my Chinese driver use the boat at just the right time, which, according to my pocket watch, is in about one hour, when the tides are out. I inhale the divine aroma of the clean air, which is one of the major sales points in all our literature for the hotel. I wear a spring frock of royal blue, the color of the District Attorney's tie, as I recall. Shiny satin material, with no bustle, long sleeves, and buttons down the front. I am sans hat because of the nature of my expedition down to the caves.

I can see several of our residents sitting and smoking (not encouraged, yet permitted) their pipes and cigars on the front porch of the hotel. They are rocking, back and forth, wearing the red robes we issue to all our consumptive guests, with the monogrammed "NCH" in gold lettering on the right front pocket. Several of them recognize me from my dance, one would assume, and their eyes careen over my body, remembering my bare appendages during their massages, and the message my naked form gives to their imaginations. Although I have had many flowers, candies, and even passionate poetry delivered to me here and at the Canary, I refuse to mix business with their pleasure. My *qadishtu* women always take care of that part of our enterprise.

"Good morning, gentlemen," I say, opening the wide front door of the house and stepping inside. My chauffeur has already started down the cliff to get our boat ready for its voyage. He will retrieve me following my inquiry with the manager of New Canaan, Esteban Ruiz.

Mr. Ruiz has been manager of our hotel since the beginning, as the rabbi knew him from his frequent journeys to Mexico, where he did our shopping for the discounted produce and meat. The hotel is four stories tall, an A-frame building with ornate Asian and Middle East furniture, lamps, paintings, and rugs, to highlight our theme of Kabbalah practices and mystical cures.

The hotel is dug out and set back into the cliff itself, and there is, consequently, no open rear side on the structure. The main dining area and foyer have two huge electronic chandeliers, one on the ceiling of each room, which are shaped like pyramids. They mechanically revolve in multi-colored patterns, giving off constant waves of luminescence, spreading all over everything and everyone below. Each room also has a smaller version of these lights. The rabbi told all our guests that hypnotic pyramid shapes hold the secrets to eternal life, even after the body has failed to function.

Esteban is front and center, as I had called him beforehand about our visit. He wears his ruby frock coat and trousers, with golden lapels, with the New Canaan patch on his pocket, and his shiny black Mexican Army boots. Mr. Ruiz had served in the Mexican-American conflagration, and, like many new American citizens, he is passionately conservative and patriotic. His English, interestingly enough, has a French accent, as he has also been educated in France during Emperor Maximillian's occupation years of 1861-67.

Esteban is now fifty-eight, and his heels click together when I greet him. His gray, Parisian Van Dyke mustache and swarthy complexion gives him the humorous appearance of a French aristocrat visiting North America.

"*Bonsoir mademoiselle* Bailey! We have thirty-two guests at present, and I have just ordered supplies for the rest of the month."

"Thank you, Esteban. Could we adjourn to your office to discuss a private matter? I need to get down to the boat shortly." I do not wait for his escort. I proceed to the office ahead of him.

I lean forward in the red chair as Esteban settles into his. If anybody knows about whom Jerome Sonenschein may have met or had dealings with, before he was murdered in Mexico, it will be our manager.

"Do you know if anybody conferred or spoke to the rabbi before he traveled to Mexico on May 6? The Earps have escaped, and I need to know some things, as a murderer who may kill again is now wandering loose in San Diego and, most likely, Mexico."

Esteban rubs his chin whiskers. "I understand. Were you aware of the new madam hired by Mrs. Earp? Her name is Miss Heaven Riendeau. A lovely French name, no?" He smiles.

"I believe her name was mentioned during the trial. What about this woman?" Could this be another woman Jerome might have been pursuing without my knowledge?

"There is a Mexican officer who tells me about this woman. Colonel Francisco Villegas Morta. He has done work for the Earps before, and I have purchased some drugs from him for our hotel. He told me that Miss Riendeau now runs a new brothel next door to you. The Golden Faun. Were you not aware of this?"

"No. I have been very busy at the courthouse. I believe one of my regular clients, Elias Baldwin, may have mentioned her name during one of his visits. How is she involved with the rabbi?"

"Colonel Morta told me he sold *ayahuasca* to Mr. Baldwin. One of his Peruvian servants said he saw Baldwin deliver it next door to your new neighbor. Morta also told me Riendeau was at his rancho in Ensenada, and this is where the Earps and their attorney were ... *Tambien*."

This is amazing. "He is hiding them at his rancho? Why would he tell you this?"

"He told me he is worried about the authorities. He does not trust the *gringos*. He wants me to report them if one of them is the murderer, including his old *amigo*, Wyatt Earp."

That sounds reasonable enough. "But how is the rabbi involved?"

"Morta told me he overheard that the rabbi was part of, how do you say? *Ménage à trois*?" Esteban lowers his head.

"A romantic threesome? With whom?" The truth of this might be part of the revelation I am searching for.

"Mr. Earp believes Dr. Frederick Baker was in love with you, and then Baker discovered you were in love with Rabbi Sonenschien. He stated that Baker, as a result, wanted to kill the rabbi. Also, Miss Riendeau drugged Dr. Baker so he could provide the distraction at the trial."

"Yes. They were able to escape, but what about Earp killing Jerome?" Was this the answer I needed?

"Morta said Wyatt Earp believed Dr. Baker paid the rabbi to kill him in Tijuana, so he and his wife would have to close down the brothels involved in the contract between Mayor Hunsaker and the Postmaster-General of the United States."

Astounding. "They had a contract? How was Jerome going to kill a professional gunman like Earp? You know the rabbi was a pacifist. He would never hurt anybody."

"The lawyer, Mrs. Clara Foltz, then told her client, Mr. Earp, that if what he said was true, she would need to find out how the rabbi would be able to kill the former marshal on that day. *Ooh, la la!*" Esteban flails his hands. "That is all I know."

"Esteban, do you have peyote?" I want to become a visionary during my visit to the White Lady. Not only did I now understand what my women had become, but I also understand why we chose that specific cave for our spiritual practices.

"*Oui, mademoiselle,*" he says, and he extracts two of my "grandmother's eyes" from his watch pocket and hands them to me. I swallow them without liquid, and their bitter-tasting reality scrapes the back of my throat like a kind of curse.

***

As Peng Shi brings our sailboat toward the White Lady Cave, he lowers the sails and takes hold of the oars. The surf is down, as it is now low tide, so we are going to make it easily through the narrow passageway, which, so the dreamy myth says, is "formed into the outline of the romantic white lady."

Jerome and I first learn this starry-eyed version of her story from an old sea captain, Horatio Griswold, who is now waving at us while he stands on the shore. His black watch cap and grizzled white whiskers are left from his ten years as a captain on several fishing boats out of San Diego Harbor. He then became the lighthouse keeper on Point Loma for another five years. Today he is serving as the unofficial host of the seven sea caves.

Griswold has stories about all the caves, and he named them, but we chose the White Lady because it is the largest, most curious cavern, and it is rumored to have once been a hideaway for pirate treasures. It is also the last of the caves on the northern side of the sand cliffs, out of view from the main beach. As my peyote begins to weave its visions, I understand this is my final chance to save the rabbi's Kabbalah magic.

As I stand in front of her entrance, the small waves lap against my calves, and I recall the old man's romantic story about how our cave got its name. I can hear his scratchy baritone, as I step through the shape of the white lady and into her spiritual core.

"She and her new husband were on their honeymoon in La Jolla. They were from Los Angeles. One day, the woman, named Mrs. Hathaway, went hunting for seashells along the beach and near the sea caves. The waves were seven feet high that day. Although her body was never found, her brother claimed to have seen the ghost of his sister inside this cave, where she was swept away while they were outside searching for her. He said she was wearing her silver wedding gown and an orange wreath in her hair."

How sweet. As I watch the seagulls careen overhead, and I feel the staring eyes of the cormorants, perched on the ledges just inside our cavern, I finally understand that our lady Hathaway has not been swept out to sea. Peng Shi tells me that the gangsters trap these cormorants and use them to dive for fish. They keep a long rope taut around their necks, so they cannot swallow the fish. I understand now. The white lady is just like a cormorant. She has been used by men to do their bidding. I walk inside, and I can hear her voice echo off the walls, and the diving birds scream and fly out of the cave.

"Don't believe their stories," she screams. "I was a prisoner of *his* love, not mine!"

I can see her now, her back to the entrance, standing on the sand in her pure white dress. As she steps toward the surf, she drops the shells, and she spreads her arms out wide to greet the onrushing tidal wave. In my vision, her form dissolves into the mist coming off the crashing waves in the distance.

Horatio informed us back on that first day that the town of La Jolla wasn't named for the Spanish word *joya*, meaning "jewel," as many of the town's elders believe. Instead, the name originally came from an Indian word, *mut-lah-hoyyah*, meaning "the cave place." Gradually, the "mut" became lost and the Kumeye Indian word was shortened to "lah-hoy-yah." "The current spelling is likely a product of Spanish influence," the old man says.

After Jerome paid the old man to reserve the White Lady for our exclusive use, we began our Kabbalah recruitment and training. Griswold also makes money from the Chinese businessmen who are transporting opium, and they store it inside the other caves, from where they later move the drug into town by railroad pack mules. Old Griswold, of course, does not have any official deeds of ownership. He simply keeps watching so that police, tourists, or other wanderers don't decide to boat or swim into the caves. He employs a crew of fifteen men, mostly Mexican divers and swimmers from down the coast in Baja, California, who keep a constant canoe and armed watch over the entrances to these seven caves.

I keep paying the old man, and today we are going to see what happened to all the women who formed their group after Wyatt killed the rabbi. Before he was shot, they were charged with maintaining the storage of the secret Kabbalah tabernacle and statue of Asherah. We bring each prostitute we recruit from the brothels in the Stingaree down here to be initiated into the Mystical Society of Asherah.

But now, old man Griswold informs me, one of these renegade women, Marjorie Van Fleet, a Dutch whore from Amsterdam, has become the leader of the group of some twenty or thirty former prostitutes who are presently living inside the cave. To show the others she is the leader, he says, she fights them all and is victorious. As a reward, Marjorie today makes her residence inside the smaller and more private cave near the White Lady, which is called Little Sister.

As we enter the cave, the familiar odors of the sea and its tidepools fill my nostrils with memories of my ancient grandmother, the one I often see when I take peyote. I see her now. She stands in the shadows, her scraggly gray hair knotted with seaweed, a necklace of writhing, tiny octopi around her neck. She whispers to me of the supremacy we women possess, and how I can meld into the walls of this cave to extract its millions of years of knowledge. The cavity's bulwarks and roof glow with colors from mineral deposits and vegetable matter, from the red of iron oxide to the pinkish-purple of iodine found in kelp. These are the moments I become the true vision of Jerome's Goddess, Asherah, capable of anything, giving birth to the feminine power that the world understands but had long forgotten to respect.

Up ahead, I see the flaming torches of the altar. They have moved Asherah's statue deeper into the cave. I motion for Peng Shi to follow me into the darkened stomach of the White Lady, but his eyes widen as we near the lit grotto. Suddenly, he turns on his heels and begins sprinting back to the entrance, shouting in Chinese over his shoulder. This is not for him to see, and he knows it.

I enter the outer perimeter of the cathedral-shaped grotto, and a naked woman bolts across my path and races further back into the depths of the cave. She must be real, as I feel the sand spray against my face as she runs by. She is swift, so she must have been doing this for many weeks. I feel the rounded stones on the floor as they push into the soles of my boots. I look up into the dark shadows of the cave all around me, expecting other women, or perhaps even Chinese gangsters, to jump down on me.

I soon realize I am on an emblematic journey meant solely for women, and it began at the entrance, with the vision of that suicidal lady in white. She represents how women have been relegated and trapped into mere gatherers, child-bearers, and romantic playthings of men. But then, the ocean waves and their authority gradually change us, giving us layers upon layers of new strength, and nature begins to carve her more powerful patterns into the sandstone and us, providing a new, majestic tidal flow, during the millions of years in which the waves bombard and suck out the sand, giving us the indestructible energy of the sea and its feminine creative force. The moon controls the tides, and we soon learn to control the moon and her mysterious magic of birth, creativity, and madness.

"Marjorie!" I shout into the grotto of our mother cave, the White Lady. Perhaps June is correct. These women have gone insane after hearing of the rabbi's murder, and they became animals, foraging for clams and mussels, making love to passing strangers in the night, forgetting their powers of female Kabbalist magic, now that their master is taken from them. Maybe they are taking opium from the Chinese and are now addicted, doing the bidding of the Tong gangsters and their Goddess, Mazu, who is also a goddess of the sea.

As I enter the Asherah temple, what I see makes my heart begin to pound, like the surf outside. All the women have circled Marjorie, and they are also nude, and their leader is dancing around the carved statue of their goddess. It was engraved by Rabbi Sonenschein into my likeness, and he promised it would one day radiate the magic we need to conquer any human entity to make it our slave. I can feel the pounding bare feet of the dozens of *qadishtu* as they dance circles around the statue and their screaming leader. Marjorie sprints toward me, her small breasts bouncing under the torch lights, her wide eyes and flying red hair pierce my consciousness, and I can again hear my ancient grandmother calling me.

"Asherah! You are now home! Take the power they give you, and use it against our enemies."

Marjorie, her chest heaving with passionate adulation, explains what has occurred.

"We have crossed over into the future, oh Asherah! You may now take back what is rightfully ours. The rabbi was just another sacrifice. Like Jesus and all the other prophets, he was meant to leave us, so we could finally evolve. He was the second Jesus to die, only to leave us to regain our rightful place in Creation. Go back to them. We shall wait until that moment you command us. We will forever be under your spell, oh Asherah, wife of Yahweh, and Goddess of the Sea!"

All of the women begin to flail their arms wildly over their heads. Spinning on the sand, they begin circling me, chanting, and I feel their energy inside me, and my breastbone vibrates. I can feel the torch flames enter my brain, and I know the tide will begin to move toward us once more to quench our passion. I need to escape to dry land before I am devoured by my power, which is increasing every second I breathe this new and miraculous magic of Wildlife and the divine metamorphosis. We control the moon, the waves, and the ocean itself. We can force the tides to fill the land and their cities, destroying, once and for all, the lusting negativity of their patriarchal greed.

Marjorie escorts me back to the entrance. Peng Shi is waiting for me inside the sailboat. The sun is descending into the waves as we sailed our way around the sandstone caves back to shore. He knows not to ask me questions. Instinctively, I feel her at my back. As the ball of red-orange sinks into the Pacific, I step out of the boat and turn directly east where she rises behind the La Jolla Cliffs. A full and radiant white ball of mystical magic meant just for us. The true White Lady.

When we return to the Canary Cottage, and my ladies tell me there was another murder, which had taken place next door, I am not surprised. I have taken my grandmother's eyes, my peyote, and I know anything is possible.

"Who was it?" I ask.

"An immigrant named Anand Prabhakar. He was Heaven Riendeau's house boy from India."

Sarah Goldstein wraps her arm around my shoulders. She knows I am in my shamanic hallucinogenic trance again. And, as she begins to change into my grandmother, I understand that I could have murdered them all. Rabbi Sonenschien, this Indian boy, even Jesus Himself. I am an ancient creature, a woman of perpetual vengeance, ready to conquer them all.

As I begin to dance, adorned in my seven veils, my ladies of the Canary simply dance with me, sipping their champagne, greeting our new male clients, bidding them enter our domain. Whether at the ocean and inside her caves or under the full moon's radiance of the Stingaree—it is all the same truth. It is now ours for the taking, and so we drink, we laugh, we sing, and we gambol. I know we will always frolic, even on their graves, and the night is forever ours to possess, along with their lustful minds, and their shaking, quivering orgasmic bodies.

"Come in, my brave men! My prospectors. My city idols. My men of vast fortunes and limited means. The boom can go bust at any moment, any second, and we shall always be here to catch you! To hide you away against our bosoms and inside our grottos of hidden treasures."

***

When I receive word from hotel manager Esteban Ruiz that Colonel Morta called him about the new investigations being done by Attorney Foltz and her group, I am astounded. Ruiz says, "Wyatt and Josephine Earp are going to contact you about Rabbi Sonenschein and your relations with him and Dr. Fred Baker."

What I fear most is that I might be implicated in the murder of Jerome. I have no true memory of that day in Tijuana. My hallucinations were so damaging to my psyche that I may have had a black-out during some of these times. Now that I discover Dr. Fred Baker was drugged by Heaven Riendeau to allow the Earps to escape from authorities, I am also implicated in the crime. Freddy is supposedly in love with me and he hated his rival, the rabbi. Could things become any more complicated?

At about four in the evening, I have company. They are very strange men, indeed. Peng Shi takes their tall fur hats and escorts them into the drawing-room. I wear my low-cut silver sequined gown, and I brandish my first glass of champagne of the evening. I am prepared, and I know who these two men, disguised as Jews, actually are.

When the shorter one comes up to me and grabs my derriere, he lets out an Indian war cry. I want to tell him he has the incorrect tribal affiliation, but I hold my tongue. Instead, I decide to play along with their poses, even though I know them.

"Lucky Baldwin, this is not masquerade night! What are you doing here? And who is this tall fellow with you?"

Wyatt Earp puts his forefinger up to his lips. "Shh! This is our disguise, Ida. It's me. Wyatt. We need to ask you some questions about the rabbi and your affair with Dr. Fred Baker. We don't have much time."

"I see. The police have been through this already. I'm so tired of their impositions." I reach between my breasts to bring out a kerchief for affectation. I am now on stage for them. "It's all so horrible! Will you and your wife survive this ordeal?"

Wyatt peels off his false beard. "I reckon. If we can find out who might be behind these murders. My lawyer sent us here. She believes we might find some new clues."

I decide to attempt to frighten them. "Oh yes! I have spoken to her myself. I was there when you shot that poor rabbi in Tijuana, as was she. Aren't you afraid the police will arrest you both now?"

Old Lucky curls his arm around my waist. "Not if you keep that pretty mouth buttoned, my dear. Wyatt and I are playing detective to save his and Josephine's life. Please show us the rooms in this house."

Two of my girls, June and Sarah, poke their heads inside the salon. I shake my head and frown at them. They disappear. I decide to go into my Sarah Bernhardt impression.

"No business tonight. I believe there is something very sinister going on in San Diego. I have been having strange dreams. In every one, I am flying above, and when I look down at my town, I see all the ladies of the Stingaree in peril. They are running about, and it is dawn. But they are afraid of the rising sun. And, well they should be. Because in my dreams, each time, when the sun comes up it is not the bright, glorious ball of fire we see each day, but it has transformed into a gigantic, human eye! It casts an eerie dark glow from its single, radiating pupil, and the rays from this eye hit my girls, and they are struck down, each and every one! That's when I awaken. Is this an omen?"

Wyatt frowns. "Ida. Did you have a special relationship with Dr. Fred Baker?"

I walk out of the room and head up the stairs. The two men

follow me. I look back at Wyatt. "No. Dr. Baker was helping us out, just like his wife, Charlotte. He gave us milk goats and other animals from his work for the Zoological Society. And I was involved with the rabbi only because of his religion. I am enthralled with mysticism. I believe it can be the answer to all we need in this world."

As I put the key into the lock of the storage room, there is a scream. It comes from downstairs. It is Penny Worthington's room. I race down the stairs, throw down my champagne glass, and thrust open Penny's door. She is sitting up in bed. I turn the gas lamp on, and I can see she is grasping the back of her head with her right hand. When she brings her hand around, it has blood inside her palm. It frightens me.

"Penny, what happened? Why are you bleeding?"

The girl continues to sob. "I don't know! I was asleep, and then I was awakened, when I felt a sting on my neck."

"Let me look," says Wyatt, who is now standing near the bed beside Lucky. He pulls her head down toward him. There is blood oozing from a cut between the tendons at the base of her skull. He feels inside, and it isn't a deep wound. "Maybe some insect bit you? The window's open."

Penny seems to relax a bit. "Yes, my dear. I will get a bandage. Then you can go back to sleep. Let me close this window for you." After I close the window, I obtain the bandage from the dresser drawer and wrap it at the base of her skull. I turn off the gaslight, and Penny lays back down on her pillow. We leave the room.

Back in the vestibule, the men put their false beards and hats back on. I am glad they are leaving. I know Wyatt's wife, Josephine, will be coming shortly.

"If this Penny becomes ill for some reason, would you please notify our attorney, Clara Foltz's office? She's in the Nesmith-Greely Building on Fifth Avenue." Wyatt says.

"Of course, Wyatt. I hope you can find out what you need to know. Take care of yourselves." I open the door.

"Thank you, Ida. I'll be back when this is over," Lucky

winks at me. "And I won't be wearing my bear hat." He laughs, and I close the door.

Josie Earp arrives at five. We have all eaten dinner, and I am inside my office bedroom upstairs. June comes up to tell me.

"Mam, Mrs. Earp is downstairs to confer with you," she says.

"Thank you, June. Please keep this meeting confidential." I nod at June, and she nods back.

I decide to smoke one of my special cigarettes of marijuana, so I get it from my desk drawer and put it inside my red Egyptian holder. I am not going to get up to welcome her. I know her visit is not a friendly one. I wear my red Japanese pajamas with a tassel on the waist.

As she knocks on my door, I light my smoke with the silver ignitor in the shape of an asp that Lucky Baldwin gave me. The wisps rise in the air, dispersing the unique odor I know she will recognize as soon as she enters.

"Come in!" I shout. It feels like the times I smoked in the Catholic orphanage. The nuns burst in unannounced.

"Ida! I see you've begun your festivities. Speaking of which, were you involved in the murder of a boy named Anand Prabhakar? I already know about you and Fred Baker. Did this boy discover your relationship between your beloved rabbi and Charlotte's husband?"

Her dark eyes and blue eyeshadow match her shady purpose. She also wears that gloomy Victorian outfit, adorned with bustle and silk top hat, including a bone-white cameo brooch at her neck. Women like Sadie Earp attempt very hard to portray a royal persona when they come from the same lower classes as I. She even has a dark shroud of netting that covers her nose and mouth like a mask.

I start to feel the marijuana's blissful and mesmerizing effect, which always makes me much more vocal and down to earth. I stand up. When she pulls the netting away from her face, I am ready for her.

"The men come and go, Mrs. Earp. You, of all people, must know this. I have no time to discuss the mundane contracts between perverted men. Why should I, then, want to terminate a young man who might have uncovered something untoward about Dr. Baker and Mayor Hunsaker? Weren't you and your husband part of this endeavor as well? If so, why are you asking me? Ask yourself, my lady. Ask yourself."

Josie takes advantage of me by quickly extracting a double-bladed Bowie knife from her handbag. Before I can escape, she grabs my hair and pulls my head down near the blade clutched in her right hand. My throat is now within two inches of both sides of the blade. She is, quite obviously, not there to discuss the progress of Women's Suffrage.

I smile at the blade. "My goodness, Grandmother! What big teeth you have!"

"Tell me, and I won't report you. I just need to know who wanted my husband dead that night in Tijuana. Answer me, or I'll slit your white throat into a crimson smile. I am an escaped murder defendant, Ida. I have nothing to lose at this point."

Suddenly, I feel the power from the White Lady Cave course through me. I spit in her face.

She slices down the center of my pajamas, and they slip from my body to the floor on both sides, until I am standing there nude, my bare nipples pointing at her. A three-inch cut begins to bleed between my breasts. However, I am still smiling.

"If you *are* a murderer, then I would be dead. Since you most likely are not, then I suggest you leave at once. I can scream quite loudly before you can plunge that blade into my heart, or wherever it is you wish to stab me. Do you like women, Mrs. Earp? Many of you older ladies often visit my cottage for just such enjoyment."

I must have called her bluff, as she backs away, tucking her knife back into her bag. She holds onto the doorknob and inhales deeply, staring at me as if I were some kind of patient at the mental asylum.

"If you call the police to report you have seen me, Ida, I will come back here and finish what I was going to do. I shall be long gone, nevertheless, so I suggest you get dressed and begin your evening's entertainment."

I feel an intuitive rush as I hear her leave and go down the stairs. When I hear the front door close, I run over to my bedroom window, which faces the street traffic. I can see her black mourning dress below as she stands near the curb. She is looking up and down Broadway at the passing steed traffic, consisting of buggies, delivery wagons, and men on horseback.

When a shadowy phantom appears behind her, I can see that his right-hand holds some kind of handkerchief. As his right arm reaches around her head, and his hand presses the kerchief against Josephine's face netting, I cannot stop myself. I scream. As I see her being pulled up into a black carriage that is parked at the curb, I stare, in hallucinated shock, as the horse draws the carriage away from the curb and down the dark, busy street.

***

Instead of notifying the police, I decide to call Attorney Foltz's office to tell them what I'd seen. I know I may be putting Josephine's life in jeopardy, but I also realize she is probably being closely watched by her investigation group in Mexico. With this in mind, I also call Esteban, my manager, so he can call his contact at the Ensenada rancho, Colonel Morta. One way or another, the attorney shall be informed about what happened.

The art of living is based on rhythm--on give and take, ebb and flow, light and dark, life and death. By accepting all aspects of life, good and bad, right and wrong, yours and mine, the static, defensive life, which is what most people are cursed with, all is converted into a dance, "the dance of life," metamorphosis. One can dance to sorrow or joy; one can even dance abstractly. … But the point is, by the mere act of dancing, the elements which compose it are transformed; the dance is an end in itself, just like life. The acceptance of the situation, any situation, brings about a flow, a rhythmic impulse towards self-expression. To relax is, of course, the first thing a dancer has to learn. It is the first thing anyone has to learn to live. It is extremely difficult because it means to surrender, full surrender.

I understand the power I witness inside the White Lady Cave. This sensual strength always infuses me, even as an orphan living in San Diego. Whenever I begin to dance, the men around me become transfixed. That power I have over them matures, later, into what I have today, and what those women believe, who worship me as Asherah, Goddess of the Sea and wife of Yahweh. The only doubt I have is who controls the dance. Part of me believes it is merely the drug, peyote. Another part of me believes it is Rabbi Jerome Sonenschein, my lover. A final part of me, and the part that has recently arisen, after my baptismal resurrection at the La Jolla Caves, believes it is the collective power of all women, throughout history. Common sense tells me if I have any power, it is this final cause that is the actual source.

Can I use this power of dance for good and evil purposes? Did I possibly use it to inflame the mind of Wyatt Earp on May sixth in Tijuana? Could my dance have inadvertently caused him to shoot my love, my only source of true Kabbalah wisdom? As I sit smoking the last of my marijuana, gazing down from my window at where I saw Josephine Earp disappear into the night, I finally believe my powers are real, and when I choose to use them again, they can also be fatal to someone else. With this potential mystical and phrenetic lightening, how can one ever believe the usual science of cause and effect again? I certainly cannot maintain the status quo any longer. From that moment forward, until we discover what is causing this pandemonium of murderous mayhem, I vow to keep my rhythm in abeyance. Until, of course, I need it to continue our female control over these patriarchal and greedy demons.

I know that the only person who wants to kidnap Josephine Earp is Dr. Fred Baker. She is correct about the love triangle. My love for Jerome was common knowledge all over the Stingaree, as he had been collecting women to join us in our secret rendezvous out at our New Canaan Hotel and the White Lady Cave, where we initiated them into our society. It is our goal to control all the ladies and gradually work them into our plans. I must now find out where Dr. Baker has taken Josie and what he is going to do to her. The last time I saw him, he was trying to convince me to be his permanent mistress. He says he will pay whatever it costs to have me stay true to him. That is where he is! He told me he would buy me a place over in Chinatown, where I can stay and meet him each week. That is where I will go now to save Josephine

As Peng Shi drives the surrey out to Chinatown, I think about how the Indian boy working for Heaven Riendeau might have been murdered. If he discovered how the Rabbi was blackmailing Dr. Fred Baker, then Jerome may have poisoned him. He certainly had access to all the drugs he needed. One fact I never told Josephine was that when I was dancing and sleeping with Fred as part of his regular visits to my cottage, we both took some hallucinogens that Lucky Baldwin had, something from Peru, I believe. Yes, that day in court, I recall, when Dr. Baker staggered down the aisle to his wife. He mentioned Venus, sea winds, and some monsters of the deep. He must have recalled seeing me do my dance in the White Lady Cave, and Venus, the goddess of love, was what he thought I was. I don't know the exact date we were there, as I was under the influence as well, but it must have been very close to when he came into court. He had been drugged, and it was Josephine Earp that was behind it all. Yes. I remember. Heaven Riendeau came over that evening to get the drug from Lucky Baldwin. I volunteered to give it to Dr. Baker that day he appeared in court. That was why Dr. Baker kidnapped her.

"Stop here!" I pound on the glass, and Peng Shi pulls the surrey up to the two-story building apartments Dr. Baker had shown me during our time together. He is probably there with Josephine.

As I step down out of the surrey, a passing newspaper carrier is waving headlines for the evening edition on the sidewalk.

"Women in San Diego Afflicted with Strange Ailments!" the young Chinese boy yells.

I pay him a nickel and take a copy. The cover story explains what is happening:

Many ladies are complaining to their physicians of strange discomforts. Most of these women are employed in the brothels and gambling houses in the seedier neighborhoods of our fair city. The hospital and medical professionals have yet to explain the exact nature of these afflictions. However, when pressed to explain, they say these women often have discolored patches on their bodies, small nodules, or bumpy growths, and some have lost their eyebrows and eyelashes. Many others have also complained of vomiting and diarrhea after drinking goat's milk.

As I look up at the building, I become very frightened about what I just read. If Dr. Fred Baker is attempting to stop the prostitution from which I and the Earps are making our profits, then he may be behind this sudden infliction raging through San Diego. If I interrupt whatever he is going to do to Josephine Earp, I have no doubt he could turn on me. I need to seek help from much higher authorities to stop this. Attorney Foltz has not appeared yet, and perhaps they have been arrested. I know not who the murderer is, but if Dr. Baker is the culprit, then he will not hesitate to murder me.

"Peng Shi, take me to the Mayor's office!" I order, and my driver assists me up into the surrey, and we are off. "Please, go as fast as you can," I add, gripping onto the front rail behind him.

As we pull up to the building on Front Street, near the courthouse, I can see there are police formed all around the area, directing traffic and answering questions of the people crowding the sidewalks and inside the passageways of the town's governmental seat, such as it is. This is, of course, the first real mayor San Diego has ever had, so I imagine he is being bombarded with questions concerning the disappearance of his past client, Wyatt Earp, and his wife, Josephine. Also, there is this new development concerning the women becoming struck with strange physical maladies, and the foreigner from India who is murdered next door to my cottage. Many of these people wear masks over their faces and are looking up into the night sky all around them.

As I come up to them, I can hear parts of their conversations.

"He had vampire bats attack women in their sleep?"

"No, they were carrying poisons. That's how these women were stricken with diseases!"

"Is it the End of Days? Let us pray it is not so!"

I can see Mayor Will Hunsaker standing in the center of a group of reporters. I know him from that Stetson he always wears to my cottage. If anybody knows what is truly happening, it should be he.

"Mayor! Please, I have important information for you!" I push my way through the crowds toward him. Several reporters flash their cameras at me, but I care not. This is a matter of life and death.

"Gentlemen, make way for this woman," the mayor instructs. "Ida, what are you doing here? What news have you?"

"I have news about Josephine Earp and where she is at this moment. I witnessed her being kidnapped in front of my cottage, and it is my belief Dr. Fred Baker is holding her captive in Chinatown. I can give you the exact building address."

He takes my hands and slowly shakes his head. "No, that can't be so, Ida. In point of fact, we now have all three persons in custody. Wyatt and Josephine Earp and Dr. Baker."

"In custody? Did they murder again?"

"No, there was no homicide, but you were correct about Dr. Baker holding Josephine captive. We believe these crimes took place because the doctor has deranged mental faculties. I need to speak about this with you, in private. Please walk with me to my office." He begins pushing through the crowds, and he motions to a man standing on the sidewalk. "Ben, please tell these reporters and citizens what we know right now. I must confer with Miss Bailey about this case."

As we walk together through the corridor to his office, the reporters are taken outside by two policemen. "I want this to be completely private, Ida. This is very critical to our case." He opens the door and holds it for me to walk through. I sit down in the smaller leather chair in front of his maple desk. After he reclines in his much larger chair and lights his pipe, I am ready to respond.

"I may as well tell you what happened tonight, as you have been part of this from the beginning." He clears his throat. "You were aware of the contract made between the Earps, me, and Post Office General Anthony Comstock, were you not?"

"I was forbidden from attending this meeting in Wyatt's saloon, but I was there, yes."

He nods. "Yes, and you had a regular agreement of an intimate variety with Dr. Fred Baker. Is this also true?"

I feel myself being questioned by an attorney, which he has been. "Do I need representation, Mayor? Am I accused of any wrongdoing?" I try to make my voice sound as confident as I can, but I am also wondering whether he knows about my dealings at the New Canaan Hotel and, most especially, about the White Lady Cave down the La Jolla Cliffs.

"No, you are not under arrest. I told you, I needed to ask you questions concerning Dr. Baker and the Earps."

"Very well, yes. I saw Fred Baker at regularly appointed times, but it all took place in my Canary Cottage," I say.

"The reason I ask is that we believe Dr. Baker committed his illegal activities because of a fit of enraged jealousy he had concerning your previous lover, Rabbi Jerome Sonenschein. Is it also a fact that Dr. Baker wanted you for himself?"

I feel my head spin for a moment. I take a deep breath. "Yes, but I was sworn to the rabbi. Dr. Baker was just a business arrangement. Like you, Mayor, and the other men in this town." I take out my kerchief and wipe my brow.

"Were you aware that your former lover, and the victim in Tijuana, Rabbi Jerome Sonenschein, was working for Dr. Baker?" He puffs on his pipe, and I feel a wave of nausea course through my body.

"No, I did not," I say.

"The reason I am letting Wyatt Earp and his wife go is that Sonenschein was going to poison Wyatt when he came to the Hundred Round Fight on May sixth. We found the vial of cyanide poison sewn into the inseam of his numbered jacket, just where Dr. Baker told us it would be."

I gasp. "That cannot be! Jerome was there to stop my ladies from being taken to work in those Tijuana bordellos. He wanted to recruit them all to work for us and learn a legal trade."

"No, I am afraid Jerome Sonenschein was a fraud, Ida. Dr. Baker was risking it all for you. He was attempting to infect the entire Stingaree with rabies, using the free-tailed bats he had trained to do the job. I assumed you knew your Miss Penny Worthington had died last evening. If you had been at the Canary Cottage tonight, you might have also become one of the victims."

All I can see is the face of my dearest, the rabbi, as he makes love to me inside the White Lady Cave. When I feel nauseated, I know for certain it is true. I am, indeed, impregnated with his child. Then, like the waves outside, the other male faces begin to enter my dream cavern. The hundreds of consumptive men, watching me dance, the other men from my childhood, paying me, smiling at me, perspiring on their upper lips, on their chests, on their loins, shivering with joy at my wounded youth, my spoiled virginity. My body is supine, my breathing is rapid, and I fall into a swoon from which I will probably never recover.

***

When they release Wyatt and Josephine Earp, I know I must enact my revenge. The only person I can trust now to assist me is Miss Heaven Riendeau, my next-door neighbor. The mayor closes down my Canary Cottage, acting upon instructions from the court to clean up the Stingaree of the likes of me and my "den of temptresses," as the *Union* has phrased it in their headline the next day. Naturally, they release Dr. Fred Baker, as he is judged to be mentally deranged, and the victim of my feminine wiles. After all, what do the lost lives of the ten whores mean when they are infected by what they now are calling his "experiments"?

I find it hilarious when that same court places him under the care of his wife, Charlotte, who is now leading the female crusade to shut down the entire Stingaree forever. The men, including our beloved mayor, secretly believe this is not necessary, of course. As a result, I become the sacrificial lamb for their continuing profits. However, because I still pay the taxes and underhanded profits from my cottage and hotel, Hunsaker tells me I can continue my brothel once the community has been sufficiently "healed."

I invite Heaven to meet me at my La Jolla hotel, so we can go over my plans for revenge. She informs me over the telephone that she took the money from Josephine Earp only because she had it to give. After she found out the details about the Earps' perverted contract to use under-age children in Tijuana for the Postmaster-General, and how they were close friends with the Bakers and Mayor Hunsaker, she became quite angry. When I tell her about how Fred Baker was released after killing ten women in the Stingaree, including her Penny, and how the town had made me the scapegoat, she says she will do anything I need to get even with them.

Esteban greets us at the hotel that evening, and we go directly to my office. We drink champagne, and I tell her about my ingenious plan. It is based on what occurred in San Diego, and I also want information from her about how we can create the grand deception that will lead to our becoming very wealthy if we can accomplish it.

"Are you familiar with St. Vitas' or St. John's Dance?" I ask, sipping from my glass.

"Wasn't that the affliction people had in the Middle Ages? They began to dance uncontrollably, often passing out from exhaustion?"

I am impressed by her knowledge. We, prostitutes, are often said to be unintelligent and from lower-class backgrounds, but Heaven and I are, quite obviously, an exception.

"Yes, it was classified as a mania. It was a mass hysteria brought on by the stress of living in those backward days when living was dangerous, and no science had been established to prevent diseases such as the Bubonic Plague. I want to discuss this with you, as it pertains to an idea I have been going over in my mind, ever since that day in Tijuana, when Rabbi Sonenschein was gunned down by Wyatt Earp."

She leans forward with interest, sipping from her glass. "From what you've told me over the telephone, I have also been thinking about those two, especially Josephine. She is one of the greediest and most irritable women I have ever met."

"Did you notice the frenetic atmosphere in San Diego after the truth about what Dr. Baker could do with those animals—especially those bats—came out in the newspapers?" I want to be certain she can establish the same mental impression I have concerning my plan.

"Why, yes. I saw the men were quite anxious about entering my house. They clustered outside for the longest time, and my clientele numbers have shrunk to very small proportions. One, two, or three each night, and most of them are sailors or other riffraff."

"What I mean concerns the dance mania. When I left the mayor's office, after he explained what had happened in front of my cottage, when Wyatt shot the bat that was attacking his wife. As I approached Canary, I saw a scene that might have come directly from the drawings I had seen in the library of people under the influence of St. Vitus mania."

Her eyebrows rise. "Do tell. Were they dancing?"

"Yes, but it was much more than just a dance. In fact, they were not moving about in any kind of orderly rhythm at all. For example, when I dance, I am filled with a natural energy that comes from everything and everyone around me. I feel infused with a synchronous, flowing motion that enjoys life, and I want to display my body in the most passionate and fluid manner possible. But these people were like lonely puppets on strings. The puppeteers were invisible demons, each one making the dancer a separate tool of motion and of a demonic, shaking frenzy I have only witnessed once before in my life."

"What do you mean?" She asks.

"I was attending a meeting of so-called Shakers, a religious group. They had these same types of separate, energetic movements, their arms flailing about, their legs pounding the ground with no rhythmic beat, just an absurdly crushing motion. Also, those Shakers were doing what they later told me was speaking in tongues, inspired by the Holy Spirit."

"Yes, I've heard of that," she says.

I now want to emphasize my point. "There were no such oral stimulations or singing in the group I saw in front of my cottage. They were silent, and upon their faces was a contortion of different spasms and twists in face muscles, as if they were in pain and agony. They behaved just the way those people in the drawings looked. They were responding to an inner sickness or plague of some kind."

"I see. What do you make of it all, and how does this fit into your plan for revenge?"

"These were not men waiting to enter my brothel. There were women and children there as well. They were all possessed. Some wore masks. Some had blank expressions on their faces. But they all had different motions in their dances. No rhythm. No collective energy of joy. Nothing but painful contorting and spasms of anguish. Also, they kept gazing up at the sky, as if they expected some catastrophic punishment from God."

"From God? Are you certain it wasn't because of the fear of the bats of Dr. Baker?"

"Possibly, but they seemed more frightened, as though they expected the end of something. Perhaps even life itself. Or, the Apocalypse of End Times." I gulped down the rest of my champagne and set the crystal down hard on my desk top. "Tell me, Heaven. Were you invited to San Francisco by that woman attorney, Mrs. Clara Foltz? To attend her son's wedding at the Bay Cliff House Restaurant?"

"Why, yes, I was. I was rather surprised, as I am new to the community. Although, from what I learned, Mrs. Foltz and her children are also new to San Diego."

"I will plan to put a drug into the women's drinks at dinner at this restaurant. It is called *aliento del diablo*, or devil's breath, by the natives in Columbia. It is from the nightshade family of plants, and in low doses, combined with alcohol, makes one very compliant and suggestive. When I begin to dance, you shall follow me and dance also. The result should cause all the women to dance with us. It won't be exactly like the St. Vidas form, as we want them to follow our motions, but when we take off our clothes, they should follow us."

Heaven laughs. "Take off our clothes? Are you being serious?"

"I am. I want these women to understand the power we can have over them. We will not be completely nude. Just our overclothes will be removed. In truth, before we leave for San Francisco, I want to initiate you into my female group. I call it the Asherah Society. You will have to come with me down below at the cove. I will take you at low tide inside one of the seven caves."

"This all sounds rather enchanting. I love it!"

"Yes, and I want you to do one more thing for me at the wedding restaurant."

"What is that?"

"After we finish our dance, I want you to run outside and jump into the bay. I will have Peng Shi down there to retrieve you from the water. I want you to shout the following before you jump, so everyone can hear you."

"What words are these?" Heaven's eyes are very large and round.

"I can no longer be part of this! I am pregnant with Elias Baldwin's child. The world is going stark, raving mad!"

She stands up. "It sounds quite mad, but I shall do it!"

***

Mrs. Foltz pays for our fares both ways on the SS *Goliah*, and Heaven and I stay close together throughout the voyage up the coast to San Francisco. We learn about the lawyer's family during the dinner we have together on the ship. The two children who came with us, Bertha May and David Milton, sit at the table and smile when she introduces them. I saw them both in the Stingaree delivering medical and grocery supplies. She explains she has five children and that she had to lie about being divorced from their father. She said he died, and then she worked with her future legal partner, a woman named Laura, to get the law passed so that women could go to law school and become lawyers. She passed her Bar Examination of the first attempt, with her five children standing in the alley outside on that memorable day.

I whisper to Heaven, "Perhaps she can get them to pass a law to get all these husbands, like Dr. Baker, from cheating on their wives."

Since this is the first time I have been out of San Diego, I am anxious to see San Francisco. When we arrive, Heaven and I take a tour along Ocean Beach where we can see the Bay Cliff Restaurant perched high above us, as we stroll, hand in hand, feeling the mist from the waves against our faces, and nodding to the people who pass us, who wear their finest clothes and whose children race into the waves and run back out again, cheering loudly whenever they get their shoes, dresses, and pants wet. All I can remember are my trips down to the San Diego Bay with the other children from Our Lady of Guadalupe Catholic Mission Orphanage. We were not free to roam, as these children are, and my life then was taken up by strict discipline and by my studying the ways to control men and to get out of my prison.

Over two hundred people are attending the wedding between Mrs. Foltz's son, Samuel Cortland, and his bride, Adeline Quantrill. When I discover that Miss Quantrill is, like me, an orphan, I vow to speak to her. I also learn that the lawyer's best friend, Ah Toy, is also a former Chinatown madam, who earned enough money to become an art dealer and real estate investor. Heaven speaks with Ah Toy at length, as they knew each other from Heaven's days in San Francisco.

Heaven comes running up to me, out of breath. "Ah Toy says Adeline is a psychic and can read minds," she tells me. "One of Mrs. Foltz's biggest cases concerned wives who were murdering their husbands while they slept. The women had been mesmerized to kill by a man the Foltz family eventually captured. Ah Toy said that Adeline was able to exchange thoughts with Osiris, the young son of Dr. Paschal Beverly Randolph, the author of *Magia Sexualis*. I have his book. The girl's psychic genius saved them all when they were being held prisoner inside that San Jose mystery house owned by Mrs. Sarah Winchester."

We can place the drug in the eighty-some wine glasses of all the women invited to this wedding, as the dose of devil's breath is so tiny that it is hardly noticeable. Heaven and I go around to all the placements, which have a name at each seat and drop the dose into each glass. It takes us thirty minutes, and we finish in the private dining room where our immediate family group of sixteen will be seated.

At the head of the huge, rectangular table, which overlooks the ocean below, are the bride and groom, Adeline and Samuel, smiling and toasting us with their glasses of champagne. Seated on their right side are Clara Foltz, the attorney, and her mother, Telitha, and her father, Elias Willets, who are both in their early sixties. They journeyed from nearby San Jose. Then come the rest of Clara's children, Trella Evelyn, the beautiful actress in her twenties and a graduate of Berkeley, Bertha May and David Milton, the two youngest I know from San Diego, and the youngest, Virginia Knox, who is twelve.

Then come the guests from San Diego, Wyatt, and Josephine Earp, Drs. Charlotte and Fred Baker, Miss Kai Krissy Wong, Heaven and I, Ah Toy, and Lucky Baldwin.

Mrs. Foltz stands up at her place to address us.

"Kind ladies and gentlemen. If you please. Your attention!" She strikes her wine glass sharply with her knife's handle. I hope she consumed her drink, along with all the other women in the restaurant.

"I am so proud of my two children who have brought us together and sealed their holy bonds in matrimony. One might not believe this mystery of ours to be a comedy, which must always end in a wedding, but there are comedic elements that led me to my eventual conclusions to solve it."

"Mother, please tell them about the goat," says Trella Evelyn. "What you wrote to me that made me fall off my stool laughing."

"Ah, yes. My thespian daughter is referencing the first major clue I obtained pointing to Dr. Fred Baker's involvement in the plot to infect the Stingaree bordellos."

Infect? Not murder women? I find it disturbing that she can be so cavalier about the lives of my women. What if it were her daughter who died from Fred Baker's poisons?

"Well, Mrs. O'Leary's cow was said to start the great Chicago fire of '71. Was it Ida Bailey's goat this time?" I can see the old goat, Lucky Baldwin is drunk already. The next time he comes to visit my cottage I will have a special surprise for him. Despite myself, I begin to laugh.

"You're not far from the truth, Mr. Baldwin. I was spying around Mayor Hunsaker's office at night, as Charlotte and I were able to get a passkey from a friend in the mayor's employ. Lo and behold, tied to the leather couch in his office was a nanny goat. I tripped on her in the dark, and she let out a banshee wail so loud that it made both Charlotte and I scream to high heaven." The attorney says.

Everybody is laughing, except for Lucky Baldwin.

Clara Foltz continues, "Dr. Baker gave the mayor a goat, but it wasn't poisoned. We had already ascertained that the goats in the Stingaree bordellos had been injected with *coccobacillus*, and the boy Anand's poison contained this bacterium. Finally, we found a vial of poison on the person of the victim, Rabbi Sonenschein. The only logical persons who could have injected them and provided the bacteria were Charlotte or her husband, and when Charlotte told me about her husband's visit to Malta to research with Dr. David Bruce, the British Army surgeon, the clues began to come together."

Josephine raises her hand, and Mr. Foltz nods at her to speak.

"And how did you ascertain that Wyatt and I were marked to be poisoned by Sonenschein?"

"We found a vial of the poison on the person of the victim, Rabbi Sonenschein. After you were kidnapped, Mrs. Earp. That's when we knew it was Fred Baker behind the poisoning of the goats with Brucellosis. In fact, on the day I visited Chinatown to question him, I was almost completely certain he was our guilty party."

The waitress, Kai Wong raises her hand. Mrs. Foltz acknowledges her. "I am sorry, but how can they allow Dr. Baker to go free? If it were a poor person who poisoned Anand, he would have been hanged!"

The girl certainly makes an excellent statement.

I am surprised when Dr. Fred Baker stands up to address her.

"I want to tell you all right now that I am the guiltiest devil alive today. I shall be working to help the poor for the rest of my life, in a meager attempt at atonement for what I did. All I can plead to you is for your mercy and the fact that I was driven by my lust and my own megalomaniacal insanity." He falls back down into his seat. His eyes are tearful. His wife, Charlotte drapes an arm around him.

Sixty-year-old Ah Toy then stands to speak.

"If there is a consolation, I think it is that Dr. Baker has begun to work with other researchers around the world to provide vaccines for these diseases, except for rabies, but there may be something to treat that as well if they keep testing." She speaks excellently enunciated English.

"Ah Toy is right. We must look to the bright side," says the groom, Samuel.

When we finish, everyone adjourns to the main dining room where the tables have been pushed back to make room for the over two hundred guests in the wedding party. Heaven and I get in line to congratulate the bride. We notice the women around us are acting rather strangely subdued. They are not talking. Instead, they look straight ahead and listen. The drugs must be starting to work. Josephine Earp first takes the bride's hand and shakes it. When Heaven reaches Adeline Quantrill, standing in her long white wedding dress, my compatriot begins to rhythmically sway and shake her body, the way I instructed her in the White Lady Cave. I also notice the bride seems to go into some kind of a trance as Heaven begins dancing. Adeline's eyes roll back into her head, and she also begins to sway along with Heaven.

As my partner begins to pick up her tempo, she also starts taking off her outer dress. First, her red velvet jacket, and then her long dress of the same material. As she does so, her body keeps swaying, and I notice all the women in the room slowly begin to circle her. Upon Heaven's undergarment, multi-colored leotards, are the images of what we in Kabbalah call the "Curse of the Evil Eye," which is an image of a blue hand with an eye centered in its palm. It's a nice touch.

When Adeline starts to channel a deep baritone voice, which is spoken in Hebrew, all the women are dancing around both her and Heaven. I can feel the floor vibrate, and the men are transfixed, staring and watching us dance in the center circle.

I am horrified, as I soon recognize that the voice Adeline is chanting is my lost lover's voice. Jerome is being channeled by the young psychic bride. Heaven must believe I know this would happen, as she continues to do her part. She strips each of the evil eyes from her leotards so that one can see her pink flesh beneath.

Finally, after Adeline and Heaven come out of their trances, and all the women are exhausted from their St. Vidas dance, Josephine steps forward to speak.

"That was the spirit voice of Rabbi Jerome Sonenschein, if you want to believe it. He was speaking in Hebrew through this young medium bride. He says there will soon be a murderer in San Diego who shall attempt to kill the first-born male of each family. He quoted the words from our Hebrew scriptures. 'That night, God sent the angel of death to kill the firstborn sons of the Egyptians.'"

We have certainly not planned for this, but Heaven continues with our ruse. She runs toward the balcony outside the restaurant's double doors. We watch, as she climbs the wall and turns back toward us. As she speaks, I mouth the words along with her.

"I can no longer be part of this! I am pregnant with Elias Baldwin's child. The world is going stark, raving mad!"

When she jumps, many people gasp, but I understand that we have been outdone by a curse much more horrible than our meager attempt to frighten the elite. I no longer feel my role as Asherah, Goddess of the Sea and bride of Yahweh means anything. Instead, a much darker curse is prophesied by my lover from his grave, both upon San Diego and upon my own body. My hand reaches down to grasp my stomach, and I pray for the first time in my life. I ask God to protect my child.

Heaven

As one might imagine, being named "Heaven" makes my tasks in life more difficult than most children and adults. What more ultimate purpose is there for humans than to reach an afterlife foretold in a child's bedtime prayers? "Now I lay me, down to sleep, I pray the Lord, my soul, to keep. If I should die, before I wake, I pray the Lord my soul to take." Take? Take my soul where? I would ask, staring at the ceiling of my crowded bedroom, with six of my older siblings snoring all around me.

Once when I hear my name whispered by my grandmother, as she lay dying, I think she is calling me over. It is not me she wants. It is that cursed promised land she has prayed to every day she is alive with us in our San Francisco apartment in North Beach. We live in squalor with all the other Mexican, Italian, and French immigrant families, working in the factories, plowing on farms, and fishing on the boats to make a living.

My mother finally tells me it is my grandmother who suggests naming me Heaven. My grandmother, who suddenly catches her strict Catholicism, as one catches the flu, after her drunken husband, Francois, leaves her for an eighteen-year-old bartender's daughter on the Barbary Coast. She comes to live with us shortly thereafter, just before I am born. Like a barnacle on the hull of a ship, my grandmother, Antoinette Marie Marquette, becomes the holy conscience of our family, and I become her prime candidate to become a nun, one might suppose, although I soon have a much different idea about where I shall go. My future, I vow, after she dies, will be invested in what my grandmother always calls "Mammon," or the material world that persecutes the poor so much. I reason that if this material world holds all the power to persecute, then it must also hold all the power that one could take from to enjoy life.

Thus, it is, in my second year of Catholic high school at Sacred Heart Cathedral, I learn I can make my living by using my body and my mind. The sailors who go on liberty on the docks of the Barbary Coast, where my grandfather found his prize, are the ones I earn from and learn to manipulate, and where I find out how to ply the trade which takes me around the world, sailing with Elias Lucky Baldwin, and, ultimately, into the boomtown of San Diego, working for another female refugee from the Gold Coast up north, Sarah Josephine Marcus, the common-law wife of the Wild West gunslinger, sheriff, and U. S. Marshal, Wyatt Earp.

Women, who have to face the reality of a society that does not protect them, or give them any rights, unless they behave correctly under the yoke of their lords and masters, come to me to learn how to use their bodies to make a living. One does not succeed in the game of prostitution unless one finds a place where she can be protected, both mentally and physically. Just as my grandmother's church gives our family some assistance when we give our assistance in return, so it is with the society that uses women as their playthings. While renting my own body as a young girl of sixteen on the Barbary Coast, I quickly see that the women who rent their bodies to men are, quite often, swept up by those men who keep them working.

These men are called "pimps," as they speak for these "fallen" women, who have been trained not to do any kind of contract negotiations in life. Many of these women, I discover, have been raped by their fathers or uncles, or deserted by them, so they lose the male spokesperson who is charged to legally represent them to society. In higher class society, the families, dominated by the men, allow their daughters to come out to the aristocratic public in the form of the French *Debutante*. So it is that I want to serve my debutante women of the lower classes with the same care and respect given to women of those aristocratic families. It becomes my goal, therefore, to get in touch with women who understand how men treat us if we give them power over us. The brothel madams in San Francisco are the ones who give me the schooling I need to begin my first house.

The women I take into my first house are called "crib girls." Crib girls are women who work in narrow stalls that line certain alleyways, and they have it particularly bad, some entertaining as many as eighty or one hundred customers in a single day. Maiden Lane is one of those alleyways, its name an unintentional tribute to a time when it reigned as San Francisco's most racially diverse assemblage of prostitutes. Syphilis is widespread, and the hazards and rigors of the job generally make for a short, unhappy lifespan.

Therefore, I make it my job to hire medical contacts to give my women the prevention and treatment they need. It is also my job to hire the staff who can serve as bouncers and protectors in my house, lest any customer becomes rowdy or attempts to harm one of my women. As I learn from the international madams, like Miss Ah Toy, in Chinatown, there are men in the street gangs who can serve this duty as protector very well. These are not evil men, as depicted in the Christian press, they are simply men who want to shield women from harm. Is it evil that they see how the world works? Without protection, these women will be beaten, robbed, and possibly killed. These so-called "gangsters" hear how these young women arrive in the streets, and listen to their stories of family abuse and poverty, until these men understand them, as they came from the same poverty.

I also learn, as time progresses, that the more we keep our house sophisticated and safe, the more money we make, and our clientele increasingly comes from high society, and they expect such care and refinement as a matter of ritual. They have more money to purchase women with expertise in the manner of love-making, so I can pay out more money to keep my house stable and healthy. We call it the "golden circle of prosperity." Only when the economy takes a bad turn, such as the railroad strikes in 1877, do we need to take more innovative methods to stay solvent. It is during this time that I begin my private escort service, catering to the wealthy businessmen who stay in the best hotels. This requires political contacts, of course, and this is how I first met Elias Baldwin.

I get word that a gentleman at the Palace Hotel has been chasing after a sixteen-year-old girl of mine with the business name of Candace Darling. The man is so smitten with her that he is chasing her all over the hotel, throwing his money at her, as she runs from the bar, to the billiard room, and even into the ladies' powder room. He is so wealthy and powerful, however, that the hotel's security detectives do not dare do anything to the inebriated Baldwin. As I discover, this Mr. Baldwin, in his fifties, owns the Palace Hotel, as well as many other real estate holdings in San Francisco. From my experience working with drunken sailors on the Barbary Coast, I know men in their cups are pretty much the same, except for perhaps their vocabulary.

When I come into the salon portion of the Ladies' Room, I see that Mr. Baldwin has Candace pinned against the tall mirror in the back. He has in his right hand a riding crop, one that's used at the race track. Each time the girl attempts to break away in one direction or the other, he lunges in that direction with his whip to keep her trapped. The hotel detective, a Mr. Salvador, tells me that his employer is a gambler, and the press has given him the name "Lucky" as a result of a fortuitous wager he makes when buying silver stocks. Armed with this knowledge, I decide I know a way I can out-maneuver this man and keep my girl's dignity intact.

"Well, Lucky Baldwin, the most fortunate man in San Francisco. I'm so pleased to make your acquaintance!" I sidle up to them, keeping my voice calm yet encouraging. I see some real fear in Candace's eyes, and Lucky is perspiring heavily. He doesn't turn around. He keeps playing with his prey as if I am not here.

"You know, Mr. Baldwin, you own this hotel, and you've been so kind to allow my escort girls work here, one with whom you seem to be quite entranced at the present moment. I am a businesswoman, just like you, and I have a gambling proposition that could make us both some money."

His long walrus mustaches twitch on the right side of his face as he raises his right eyebrow and turns his head slightly in my direction.

"Huh? Money, you say? You that whore they call Heaven?" He chuckles to himself. "I betcha use that name in your business, too, am I right? Can't you see I'm just trying to get this little filly into my corral? C'mon, sweetheart. You don't need to be afraid of me. My whip won't hurt."

"Yes, a lot of money. With times so difficult, people want to make money quickly at the track, and I know you own the one out at Golden Gate Park. Here's my idea. What if we have a special race that we'll advertise in the papers and this hotel. Each horse that runs in that race will be matched up with one of my fillies, as you call them. Candace here, for example, could be matched with the number two horse. If the male or even female better wins first, second or third place with a horse that matches my girls, then they'll not only win the odds for that wager, but they'll also get the gal as an escort at your fine hotel. They get to win twice. You get business for your hotel and race track, and I and my girls get some publicity for future dates with all these winners. How does that sound, Mr. Baldwin?"

Lucky stops pursuing Candace. He takes off his gray Stetson and wipes his brow with a handkerchief he brings out of his suit coat pocket. Finally, he turns full around to face me, staggers a bit, but he is smiling. Candace takes off running out of the ladies' salon.

"Heaven, honey. I like the way you think. We can do this. If there's anything I like more than a young tart, it's a gambling wager that I can be certain to win. Let's you and me go get a drink and talk this out some more." He cracks the whip in his hand at me, and I play as if I were scared. I follow him toward his tavern, knowing I have him in the palm of my hand.

That is how I first met Lucky Baldwin. We have ourselves a fine relationship in San Francisco, and he takes me on a world cruise on his yacht, just before I decide to follow him down to San Diego, when it begins to grow into the boomtown it is today. I learn from him that with a little creative merchandising, my business can cater to the wealthy classes, and men like Baldwin have the contacts to keep me on a money streak for a long time. San Diego is also becoming a playground for the rich and famous, so my trip there is almost a predestined journey. Although my grandmother Antoinette never approves, my family in San Francisco enjoys the five hundred dollars a month I send them. As Lucky often says, "Luck never happens to those who aren't willing to risk it all." When I come down to San Diego, I am, in a way, risking it all.

When Lucky tells me that he is good friends with Wyatt and Josephine Earp and that they are also investing in my line of work, I know I need to look her up when I come down to San Diego, and, as a result, she gives me the money to begin my own house right next to the biggest bordello in the Stingaree, Ida Bailey's Canary Cottage. From what I hear about Bailey, she has a bit of a problem with her drugs, and the result is that she often gets too far into her mystical beliefs and away from her business. I plan to take advantage of that as soon as I can.

When Wyatt Earp is arrested on May 6, 1888 down at the Hundred-Round Fight he is promoting in Tijuana, complications between Ida Bailey and me begin to get worse. However, even with her husband on trial for murder, Josephine Earp decides she wants to meet with me again about another loan. When she agrees to my proposal to establish a new type of bordello, which caters to wealthy men who enjoy bondage, leather dresses, and whips, I become focused on that rather than on other things in town. Besides, now that I have the extra money, I can also establish the Indian Tantric services that can be taught to me by my new house boy, Anand Prabhakar.

But first, I need to provide the distraction which I agreed to create for Mr. Earp. She wants me to get some narcotic from Lucky Baldwin, who is often at the Canary Cottage. Having done this, I am going to put the drug, *ayahuasca*, in the men's drinks tonight. Hopefully, they will be so incapacitated that they won't be able to attend the trial. Many of these men are journalists and policemen. I even get Mayor Will Hunsaker and Dr. Fred Baker over here from time to time, although Baker still seems to prefer Ida's place.

I am about ready to take a bath to get ready for the evening's festivities when the front door opens. It is Rosie Daniels, the woman who pretends to be Joan of Arc for our clients. She is out of breath, and her pretty face is flushed, as she comes from today's murder trial of Wyatt Earp at the courthouse down on Front Street.

"Miss Riendeau! I must tell you what happened today. Mrs. Earp has been arrested as an accomplice to the murder of Rabbi Sonenschein!" She wipes her perspiring forehead with a kerchief she extracts from her bosom. "That lady lawyer of Wyatt's, Mrs. Foltz, told her the mayor found out what you and Mrs. Earp discussed when you met at her place."

I wonder what she told me that day, which would have implicated her in that murder by her husband. "Did she give any more details about what was said and who overheard us talking?"

"It was the mayor who had his assistant, a Mr. Budreaux Randolph, there. He overheard your conversation about the loan and about the secret contract concerning the bordello in Tijuana to entertain the visiting Postmaster General, Anthony Comstock."

"Comstock? Did they know about that? What else did the lawyer say?" I am now quite afraid for my employer's fate.

"She said Mayor Hunsaker did more investigating into Mr. Earp's contracts with other bordello madams all over the West and in the Territories. It seems the victim, Rabbi Sonenschein was also following them and trying to stop these madams from doing business. He wanted to save those women from their new employment. Therefore, she said, Mrs. Earp was complicit in the murder of the rabbi because he was also trying to stop the bordello from being created in Tijuana, about which the mayor had personal information."

"I see. That traitor! Wasn't the mayor a lawyer for Wyatt in Arizona in 1881?"

"Yes, he was. It was all in the newspaper. Look, they wrote all about the two Earps who are now on trial for murder." Rosie hands me an evening edition of Mrs. Foltz's paper, the *San Diego Daily Bee*. "It says that even though Mrs. Earp is now being tried as an accomplice, Mrs. Foltz is still going to be defending both husband and wife."

"I see. That's good. Isn't it?" Rosie's eyes are wide.

"I suppose so. Please go prepare for this evening and tell the other girls they also need to be ready." I wave her away.

I realize I must do something to provide an even larger distraction than I was first going to accomplish. Josephine needs time to do something inside the courtroom that will help her win the case. I need to think about this as I take my bath. There is only one way to provide a sufficient distraction to allow the Earp's time to do something inside the court tomorrow. I know what I have to do. The only man, besides old Judge Parker, the mayor, or one of the jurors, important enough to this case to cause a distraction, is the husband of Mrs. Foltz's assistant, Dr. Fred Baker.

When I arrive next door at the Canary Cottage, Ida is her usual gadfly self, flitting from one of her gentleman guests to the another, like a spring butterfly. She is already aware of my new methods of attracting clients, as I know she is escalating the competition by parading her ladies in broad daylight down Broadway. It looks like a whore's Easter Parade, but she gets away with it because she knows even more public officials than I do.

"Is that Miss Heaven Riendeau?" She turns away from the man I came over there to see, Elias Baldwin, and she nearly begins to skip over to see me.

I extend both my hands, which she takes gingerly into her own. Almost instantly, she turns my palms face up and examines them closely. It feels like Grandmother Marquette checking me to be certain I haven't been in the cookie jar lately.

"Oh, your lifeline is very long indeed! However, this extended crease means you need to start taking life less seriously, my dear. Whips, leather, and boots? Goodness gracious, what will the gentlemen think of us?" I can see by the size of her pupils that she, most likely, has been in her psychedelic cookie jar. If her dress were any lower in front, she could charge parking fees for men's noses.

"Ida, thank you for your prognostications, but I must speak with one of your regulars over there," I say, pointing toward Lucky, who is telling some bawdy joke to his companion.

She nods. "Of course. Just don't be a stranger. I want to talk with you about your merchandising ideas. I am told you have initiated quite a few innovations in your Golden Faun."

"Yes, and I was told you contracted with some important people to initiate your ideas across the border," I say, leaving her with something to reflect upon from the real world.

I march over to Lucky, wave my hand at him to follow me, and he does. We stand together within the vestibule near the front door.

"I assume you know Mrs. Earp's been arrested?"

He nods. "Yes, we're working on it."

"I've been instructed to do my part as well. I need some more of that drug from Wyatt's friend in Mexico."

"Colonel Morta. Yes, I can give you some. What are your plans to use it?"

"I am going to drug Dr. Fred Baker. I believe I saw him in there ogling Ida If I'm not mistaken. He's going to provide a distraction in the courtroom tomorrow."

"You understand, of course, that this drug is very unpredictable and quite dangerous." Lucky frowns.

"I do. But this is an emergency, and the lives of our friends depend on my acting quickly."

He reaches into his frock coat inside pocket and pulls out a felt bag. He hands it to me. "There you go, little lady. Doc Baker will probably not remember much of what he experiences, so I hope that's one of your goals."

"It is. The other goal is that he needs to be taken over to the courthouse tomorrow after he takes it."

I can see a shadow coming out of the light of the parlor into our dark vestibule. It is Ida Bailey.

"My hearing, when I am partaking of my cannabis, is quite acute. I overheard your conversation, and I want to help. Don't you trust me, Heaven?" I can feel her grinning at me, even though I can't see her face.

"I wasn't aware you wanted to help," I mutter.

"I believe most of the Stingaree is aware of the fact that Dr. Baker goes out of his way to help me. Some rumors are that he enjoys my company above all others. But, let's not tell Mrs. Dr. Baker, shall we? She's working with Mrs. Foltz on an important case right now, is she not?"

She is attempting to be her usual sarcastic self while serving a purpose.

"Very well," I say, "please give it to him before he goes to court tomorrow. I have a dose here that will make him enough of a distraction to help the Earps in their present predicament." I start to hand the *ayahuasca* to her, but she raises her hand to stop me.

"Don't worry, Heaven. I am probably the most knowledgeable white person in the United States concerning these hallucinogens. I will have just the proper dose for Dr. Baker, and I will escort him personally to the courthouse tomorrow."

"Very well, I must be off now." I nod to them and open the door. "I have my party to attend," I smile and step outside. Lucky will be proud of my risk-taking in this instance, but I am not certain I have made the correct decision with Ida. If there is a conspiracy afoot to kill the rabbi, and if Mayor Hunsaker is correct about Sonenschein wanting to stop the prostitution contracts of Wyatt and Josephine Earp, then they are guilty of murder. And I am assisting not one, but two murderers.

***

Many of the men who come to my house that same evening are court officials, and their conversation concerns what is happening during the murder trial. There are also three newspapermen. When I slip the small doses of *ayahuasca* into their drinks, they speak even more interestingly, as their connections with the different topics become wider and more deeply probing. Two of them have the usual problem of vomiting and diarrhea, which I learn when I take the drug while visiting Peru with Lucky Baldwin on our world cruise. Even Josephine Earp does not know about my shaman abilities.

The shaman we meet teaches me how to guide the people, who are using the drug, to instruct them how to become more conscious of their present lives and, most especially, of their past lives and relationships. My personal experience taking *ayahuasca* has been quite revealing, as I begin to understand my associations with members of my family, and in the world, and how I repress some of the more wonderful moments with them because of my selfishness and desire to escape their poverty.

The Amazonian shaman, an Incan Q'ero, when he learns I am a madam, and that I supervise women who have sex with men for money, becomes quite animated, saying that it is good that I want to learn how to administer it to my girls and my patrons. When I ask his name, he says he has no name, as his "old self has disappeared and melds into Mother Earth's Energy." He says the drug opens the mind to "all kindness and respect for our human bodies and souls." Unlike our culture, in the Americas and Europe, the shamanic and tribal cultures have religious leaders who live outside society, to get in touch with their inner world, and the world of nature, instead of being trained to be ordained by a hierarchy of clergy, which is the way of our world. The shamanic way makes for more acceptance of individuality and intense respect for a person's connection to their surroundings and each other.

For example, when we live close to nature, as we have done before the Industrial Revolution, we are more open to its influences, as it is practical to do so, and it means our very survival. This is why respect for the power that nature has over us is encouraged, and what we often call "superstition" and "myth," in derogatory ways, are ways of opening one's mind to accepting many different interpretations of life around one. I find that this is what *ayahuasca* can do, and when my clients take it, they also are more receptive, for the most part, to the experiences I invent, such as the so-called "sadomasochism" of powerful women, like my Rosie Daniels and her persona as Joan of Arc, and the other ladies, who wear their costumes of leather and utilize bondage techniques. The shaman says that his tribal sexual rituals often take on this same game of aggressiveness; the hunt and the chase, which are quite common in the jungles and with the animals in their everyday lives. The experience is not hurtful or disturbing. It is enlightening and jubilant.

However, there is also a dark side to administering or using the drug, and he admonishes me. He is not merely referencing using too much of the drug, which is what we are going to do to Dr. Baker, it is *how* it is used. If the person using it or administering it believes he or she is more powerful or wants to control others, then the positive aspects of the drug will vanish, and the people using it can become quite violent and controlling, thinking they are a god or some other magical power. He invites us, instead, to walk in the *Qapac Ñan*, the Royal Road, or spiritual path, toward our consciousness of a living world where we respect and protect both humanity and nature.

He says it is better to be guided by the animal spirit guides like the Condor, the Puma, the great Serpent, and the Hummingbird, instead of the human gods. "Why is that?" I ask, just before spending three nights being initiated into the drug's experience. The no-name shaman looks deeply into my eyes and rolls them as he speaks. The translator tells me what he says, "You can see the truth of yourself. Man is not honest like the animals around him." This complete honesty is what I fear most of my life, and it is something my entire society is never able to give me. We are, in effect, each tricked into believing what other people tell us is what we must be. This is what we become. An image of what our society says we are, not our true self.

Without an animal totem to guide us, I realize, we become so obsessed with how we appear to others, so self-conscious of our societal personas that we ignore what makes us individuals. In reality, it is this uniqueness that makes us interesting to each other, creates bonds that change with time, and gives us an appreciation of our foremost and most enduring quality. This quality is what we have when we first grow out from the comfort of our Mother Earth: human compassion. We are not created by some omnipotent Father in the sky who tells us His Commandments. We are flexible, roaming animals, who know when to appreciate what is happening around us, but who also intuits that our best actions are based on loving-kindness. We must learn to see past all of society's protective and greedy images, to keep power and destruction, to control us.

Although it is my purpose to allow my women, and any of my clients, to participate in the ritual of *ayahuasca* to find the Royal Road, my financial reality is such that I need to first do what my employer, Josephine Earp, wishes of me. However, it makes me angry to do this when I know that right next door, Ida Bailey is using this drug, and many other drugs, in a selfish way. How can Mrs. Earp be so accepting of Miss Bailey's dangerous use of hallucinogenic drugs, when she has me, who has been taught how to administer them to cleanse the mind of selfishness forever? I need to find out more about what Ida is doing and how she might be involved in the relationships between her, Dr. Fred Baker, and Rabbi Sonenschein. There is also the secret contract with Mayor Will Hunsaker concerning the bordello in Mexico for Postmaster General Anthony Comstock.

In my effort to find out what Mayor Hunsaker is doing, during the trial, I have given him a larger dose of my drug. After he vomits, I know I can approach him and isolate him in another room. Under the trance of this drug, most people became very compliant. They are susceptible to suggestion, can be mesmerized, and they, quite often, speak the truth when questioned.

The parlor is filled with many men who are participating in the trial of Wyatt and his wife. There are four newspapermen, two court reporters, two alternate jury members, and, of course, Mayor Hunsaker. Each is sitting in a separate sofa or chair, with one of my girls attending to him, as I have instructed them to do so. My girls know about my shamanic rituals, as they have experienced them as well. The mayor is with Rosie Daniels, away from the others, as he enjoys being given orders from such a tall and physically imposing woman who wears the armor of a French Soldier in the Battle of Orleans in 1429.

"Joan, how is your lowly serf doing? Is he ready to be disciplined in the boudoir?" I smile as I stride up to the two of them. They are cuddling on the wide sofa near the fireplace. The mayor has his head in Rosie's lap, as she has opened her breastplate armor to prevent his head from discomfort. At the sound of my voice, he gazes up at me. His balding head and diminutive body make his trance seem rather ludicrous. His tie is undone, and I can see some flecks of vomit on his chin.

"William is quite ready, Miss Heaven," says Rosie, smiling down at her man.

The new leather costumes, with whips and bondage tools to use during our Venus in Furs rituals, are proving quite popular with my clientele. As I glance around the parlor, I can see Rosanne, Michelle, and Fern adorned in their variety of chosen outfits. Rosanne, as the Circus Lion Tamer; Michelle, as the Head Mistress of the private school; and Fern, my Chinese, as the female pirate captain.

Hunsaker smiles up at me. He looks rather like a pet dog in the lap of his master.

"I hear you have become the prosecution's main witness, William. How did this come about?" I ask, sitting down on the small armless settee next to the sofa. This fact must be why Josephine wants Dr. Baker drugged as a distraction during tomorrow's continuing trial.

"Oh, yes! We have those two murderers right where we want them. I have proof that Josephine wanted the Rabbi dead as much as her husband did. Did you know she is financing many more brothels than yours?" He points his forefinger at me. "She is an accomplice to murder!"

"No, I did not. How is this important to your case against them?" I expect as much, as most people understand that Josephine Marcus Earp is behind all the negotiations the Earps make. She is a sharp businesswoman.

"Come here," he whispers, moving that same forefinger to beckon me closer. I lean toward him.

"Rabbi Sonenschein followed the Earps all over the Southwest to attempt to stop them from financing these bordellos. He was a very holy man, don't you know? His Kabbalist teachings told him to purify women and get them out of these sinful ways of theirs." He giggles and looks up at Rosie. "Although, there are always exceptions when the woman is in charge."

"Is the attorney, Mrs. Foltz, still representing the Earps?" If Hunsaker is telling the truth about this new evidence, it might seem the defense could change its tactics or even resign.

"Yes. I'm afraid she is. So is that bothersome assistant of hers. Dr. Charlotte Baker. But I have proof that her husband has been having an affair with Ida Bailey, so I don't suppose Charlotte will be valuable to Foltz much longer." He laughs.

"Is that so? Well, I wish you success tomorrow, Mayor. May justice prevail." Little does he realize that we will have Dr. Fred Baker in a haze of oblivion by the time court convened tomorrow morning.

I get up from the settee to call Colonel Morta in Ensenada. I now have the information I need to put another, more important, plan into action.

"Goodbye, madam. Don't call me by that name. Mayor. I am a child of the ever-present and universal love," Will Hunsaker tells me, grinning up at me, as I walk away.

***

My plans to create the new Tantric Yoga wing in the Golden Faun are going well. My new house boy, Anand Prabhakar, is teaching three of my ladies the method and process of having sexual relations to create the powerful result of *moksha* and God Consciousness through a meditation using the different *chakras* of the Kundalini inside the body. Janice, Alexa, and Bobbie are the chosen ones, as they have the most intelligence to learn something that has so much ritual importance. They, in turn, need to be able to convince the wealthy suitor clients that the magical process will produce the reward they expect. Although Josephine Earp knows about both the Venus in Furs sadomasochistic role-playing games, and this newer mystical game for the wealthy, I am going to take it upon myself to learn first-hand what this Tantrism can do. It is time this young man experiences the joy of what a real woman can do for his personal life.

I already know my girls are vying for him between themselves, as this is the way of the bordello lifestyle. Unless I act upon this and possess the lad for myself, I might have some real problems in the future with morale and discipline. From what I observe in the Canary Cottage, Ida Bailey keeps her ladies believing that she is a mystical creature to be adored and even worshiped if one were to believe what she says concerning her Kabbalah relations with the murder victim, Jerome Sonenschein. I want to find out for myself what her business relations are, as this is what concerns me most. If I am to survive in the Stingaree, financially, I need to know exactly what my biggest competition is doing to make money.

My previous tour of the rest of the Stingaree bordellos show me the usual riffraff and bounders. Men run their saloons and employ whores to get the patrons inebriated, mostly sailors and other working-class roustabouts, and so these clients are similar to those patrons who came to my taverns back when, as a teenager, I began in this business on San Francisco's Barbary Coast. These are the lowly places the police often shut down. They arrest the owners and the prostitutes, as they never cater to any of the city officials or wealthier investors in the community. They believe enticing a policeman or two will work. I learn very quickly, however, during my year living with Lucky Baldwin, that unless one plays one's cards right, even these upper-class officials can turn against your business, unless you keep them happy.

This is why I want to establish my entertainment for the cultured elite. Once they know my bordello is catering to the wealthy, and they can collect a percentage of the receipts for their participation in my entertainments, the more inclined they are to keep the police and citizens' groups at bay. I believe Miss Ida Bailey will soon be headed for ruin, as her methods are based on her mythology instead of on the character of her patrons.

Soon, I will be able to siphon from her clients until the Golden Faun becomes the place for all the wealthy men in San Diego. However, there is, indeed, some other means of income Ida is earning that I need to discover. She has something that keeps the likes of Lucky Baldwin and Wyatt Earp coming back, again and again. I know it has something to do with that dead rabbi and his Kabballah cult, which gets him killed on May 6.

"Anand!" Standing at the foot of the stairs, I shout up into the confines of the second floor where the boy's room is located. It is the supply closet, into which I have added a cot and a dresser of drawers. He is so grateful that he kisses my hand and says he has achieved *moksha* the first night he sleeps there. I am going to make him even more grateful, as I want to introduce him to the most sensual experience of his life in my bedroom.

Michelle comes out of the parlor to my right. "Miss Heaven, I let Krissy go up there this morning. She had a package for him. I think they might be busy."

That little tart? Is this how I am repaid for my kindness? Is he getting his love and affection from another immigrant whore? I am going to put an end to this!

I stomp up the stairs, and I take the skeleton key out of my pocket, as I come up to the supply room at the back-end of the second-floor landing. I can hear nothing inside, so I open the door.

"What happened to him?" On the floor, next to the cot, lay the body of Anand. Ms. Wong is standing near the dresser, a bottle of some kind in her hand. There are also the remnants of a torn package on the floor near her feet. Her eyes are large and round.

"Miss Heaven, honestly. I don't know what happened. I was working, and another waitress told me a package was left for me at the hostess station. It also had an accompanying letter. The letter was from a doctor from India who said that Anand had virulent smallpox. I was to give him the enclosed vaccine to stop the spread of the disease and cure him at once."

"There must have been more to this. Why has he passed out?"

She lowers her head. "He's not unconscious. I'm afraid … he's … he's dead."

"Dead?" I stoop down and feel the young man's neck for a pulse. Nothing. "You just gave him this poison because of a letter? Are you insane?" My anger causes the girl to weep. "Kai, what else was in that envelope?"

She raises her head and wipes tears from her eyes. "A payment. Two gold nuggets." She cries more.

I know I must tell somebody about this. Whoever wants this boy dead might be the same person behind the Sonenschein murder. What causes the rabbi to enter the hundred-round fight that day in Tijuana? Does he mean harm to the Earps because of their contract with Postmaster Comstock? Perhaps Anand knows something about this from one of the women in my house, and this person wants him dead.

Rosie Daniels comes to the door. "Miss Heaven? Y'all better come downstairs. Dr. Charlotte's on the telephone."

I motion for the waitress to follow me. I need to call the police.

Hello, Heaven?

When I hear Dr. Baker's voice, I think that whoever wrote this letter may also be a physician, and it sends a chill through me as I listen.

"Yes, this is she."

I'm at the office, but Mrs. Foltz told me to contact you. Has anything happened at your house?

I quickly summarize the poisoning of Anand and the fact he might have smallpox. I also read the letter to her.

You must come out to Colonel Morta's rancho in Ensenada right away. Mrs. Foltz wants you both here. I will contact the police and tell them it was not Miss Wong who killed the boy. They will perform an autopsy. Also, bring that bottle of whatever she administered to him. Then, I will meet with you all, and bring Mr. Baldwin with me. Is that clear?

"Yes, doctor. We shall be there this evening." I hang up and tell Kai that Dr. Baker is going to talk to the police and that she isn't in any danger. Dr. Baker will probably have to get Elias Baldwin from next-door at Ida Bailey's, as he has probably begun his evening's drinking gambit already. It is over sixty miles to Ensenada, so I will have to drive the carriage myself. My heart grieves for the poor boy, and I feel guilty about lusting after him for my own selfish needs. Some kind of karmic retribution will, most likely, be visiting me, sooner or later.

***

The waitress Miss Wong is still emotionally distraught on our long drive down to Ensenada. I keep reassuring her that Dr. Baker will take care of things with the police. However, I know we need to prepare for the meeting with the attorney, Mrs. Foltz. I explain that the case against Mr. and Mrs. Earp rests upon how well the defense can prove doubt that preparation and anger occurred on May 6 in Tijuana.

"Even if Wyatt shot the rabbi in the head, with witnesses, it does not mean there were no extenuating circumstances involved." I want her to be ready for the legal questions of Mrs. Foltz, as she is a bit resentful of the wealthy, and she might say something untoward about them.

"What do you mean? Extenuating? If a gunman shoots another man in front of others, isn't that murder?" She is not looking at me. She is watching the passing scenery on the road. Sporadic cacti, a few palms, and some agave, the spined plants, which the Mexicans use to create their tequila, spread across the desert landscape as the sun begins its descent in the Pacific Southwest.

"Let me explain to you this way. Dr. Baker is going to tell the police that you acted because you believed a doctor paid you to do so. Also, the letter showed he had a contagious disease. You could not have foretold what happened, so that is an extenuating circumstance. It is not a deliberate poisoning of Ananda."

She nods, but she still looks away.

"I understand, but what does Mrs. Foltz believe are the circumstances that will free *her* clients?" Kai finally turns toward me. Her lips are tightly pursed, and her hands are folded tightly in her lap.

"I was not inside the court, but from what I've read in the newspapers, and from what Rosie Daniels told me, this rabbi was attempting to close down the brothels in the Stingaree, especially the newly created place in Tijuana. Some underage prostitutes may have been provided to the men there, and the rabbi was angry. However, the extenuating circumstance is that the law is quite different in Mexico. Humans are considered consenting adults at sixteen years of age in our country, but in Mexico, children can consent to sexual congress at twelve. As you can see, this contract was legal, but the rabbi, who was a very religious man, may have thought differently."

She unfolds her hands, and her frown disappears.

"I see. But the lawyer must get people who can verify this fact to show how the rabbi was acting to threaten the Earps, no?"

I am happy to hear she has a logical mind. "Yes, and it can be any kind of threat. If, for example, the rabbi was in love with Wyatt's wife. Or, if there were any other people involved to put pressure on the legal agreement, which meant the livelihood of the Earps was in danger."

"And, what I will do will be to explain exactly what happened, and nothing more?'"

"Correct. You must tell the truth to the best of your ability."

Three hours later, I pull our surrey into the rancho of Colonel Francisco Villegas Morta. I can see he has lit torches all along the road, and there are no other buggies or carriages parked in front, so I assume we have arrived before the others. I am not going to tell the others, but I have also visited this rancho before to speak with one of Mr. Morta's employees, a Peruvian named Carlos, who is also a shaman. We speak about using the *ayahuasca*, and I tell him what I have learned in the Amazon from the shaman in the Q'ero tribe.

The old ranchero greets us at the door, and he leads us into his parlor where there is a roaring fireplace. He has a limp and a cane, and he is short. His face has taken the toll of his many years in the Mexican Army, and I can see a raised wound that spreads down his cheek. But his welcoming smile makes the scar superfluous.

"Miss Heaven, it so kind of you to visit *mi casa*. Your friends will be here in a few minutes, I would assume. *Por favor*, make yourselves comfortable next to the warm fireplace."

Kai Krissy Wong sits on a cat seat next to the wall, and I take the sofa in front of the big fire. The room has a few deer heads and a big grandfather clock near the entrance to the dining room. The patio lights are seen in the back of the dining room. It smells of warmed tortillas, and the odors feel very comforting.

About fifteen minutes go by when I hear voices in the other room near the front entrance. The Earps have arrived. Josephine comes into the parlor immediately, and her husband tarries a bit to discuss something with Colonel Morta in the vestibule. I know she will want to know about how the *ayahuasca* drugs worked, especially on Dr. Baker. It is at this moment that I decide to lie to her. I keep staring into the fire, watching the flames lick at the air like my guilty conscience. However, I know I need to protect Ida Bailey from suspicion, as my plan will require my working with her.

I finally turn toward her, purse my lips, and wet them, and I smile. "Mrs. Earp. I'm so happy you escaped. Mr. Morta's drugs were quite effective when I put them into the men's drinks at my little opening night soiree. I watched them squirm, at first, chasing after my girls in a trance-like state. The dose was for testing only. When I increased it on Dr. Baker, it put him into a state of stuporous reverie. He will remember nothing afterward."

I bow toward her, looking deeply into her dark eyes. Her raven hair is silky and radiant, and she wears a dark blue frock with a medium bustle. When she speaks, her tone continues the familiarity we established when I visited her in her tavern to entreat her for the loan.

"Today's appearance in court was quite magnificent. Even Charlotte believed he had succumbed. When will you drug the others? We need to mount our new defense soon."

Excellent! She has no suspicion about Dr. Baker and Ida Bailey drugging him. Before I can respond, her husband comes up from behind her and grasps her gently by the shoulders.

"Sadie, now what makes you believe we're makin' any kind of courtroom appearance again?"

She continues to stare into the fire. I can tell by how she turns down the corners of her mouth that she is not pleased by his statement.

"Perhaps you want to leave and escape final justice, but I am not of that mind. My people have always believed in finding the truth, and justice is part of the Judaic culture. I want San Diego to know what it has become. If my people must be made to feel guilty about murdering their redeemer, Jesus, then they will feel guilt about who murdered Rabbi Jerome Sonenschein!"

Colonel Morta makes a guttural sound, and Wyatt squeezes Josephine's shoulders before she answers.

"You men were the ones who wanted to increase the pressure on Mayor Hunsaker. I wanted no part in that. Now that we women have gotten you out of trouble, we all need a way to turn the tables on the prosecution and discover who the real party is behind the murder."

She squirms out of his grip, bends down, and picks up the fireplace poker. She thrusts it deep into the largest log and it cracks in the middle, shooting sparks all over. She is still ignoring him as he speaks. His blue eyes glare above his long blond mustaches.

"All right then, Sadie. Why did we pay the Foltz woman to defend us? Don't you think she might know who might be behind this? We never got the chance to hear her witnesses and what they have to say."

Finally, Mrs. Earp turns around to look up at her husband. Her own eyes have that same squinted firmness that one sees quite frequently between husband and wife. It is one of the main reasons I want to stay unmarried.

"How far did you think you'd get us away from justice? We did win the war against Mexico, you know. The Mexican government will never shelter us, would they, Colonel Morta?" She turns to look over at the old colonel standing next to him.

"She is correct, *compadre*. My country is very poor right now. If your country gave any reward for your return, somebody would certainly turn you in, no matter where we hid you."

Josephine turns to look at me again.

"When will you have the other men under the influence? Have they been enjoying your Venus in Furs rituals? I want each of the men on our suspect list so drugged that they will tell us the truth. Mix the hallucinatory drug with opium. That will get them under our powers very quickly."

She will never know how far I have progressed with my drugging of these men. I smile at her. "I can do that. They are almost drugged with passion already," I say, giggling, and I adjust the collar under my velvet dress.

"Excellent! I want to hand the guilty party over to the court on a silver platter. Just like Ida Bailey and her drugged dance accomplished that day in Tijuana. Quite frankly, I still believe she is the one responsible for the rabbi's death, but I must prove it. She handed his head over to somebody, as certain as Salome's dance handed John the Baptist's head over to her mother, Herodias. Who is the mother or father responsible for Ida's dance? That's what we must discover."

Wyatt twists the ends of his mustaches and stares down at us.

"You don't reckon one of these men'll rebel and turn Heaven and her girls into the authorities? What happens to your little scheme *then*, Sadie? They'll have her arrested as sure as a fox can capture a fat hen."

"Most of the town will be taken up with hunting us down in San Diego and maybe Tijuana. The newspapers were already on our side, so their search will be half-hearted at best. Hunsaker is up for re-election, and most folks believe he was just trying to get votes with his testimony against us. We'll surely have enough time to find out who was behind the killing of the rabbi."

I wonder what she might think if she knew where Mayor Hunsaker was just last night?

"If you don't find out, then I will put a bullet in Honey's black heart! That weasel would turn his mother in for votes." Wyatt frowns. "But, you know, there could be something else at play here."

She glares up at Wyatt. "What do you mean? At play? Did you have something arranged that I didn't know about?" She is adamant. "I want to know, Wyatt Berry Stapp Earp!"

"A little bird told me that another man wanted the rabbi dead. Attorney Foltz said she was going to use this fact during our defense."

Their confrontation is getting quite interesting. They are discussing even more extenuating circumstances than I can invent.

"What are you saying? Why didn't you tell me? I'm your wife!"

"She told me specifically *not* to tell you." His eyebrows arch. "And, maybe I better keep my trap shut."

Does Wyatt know about Ida Bailey and her drugging of Dr. Fred Baker?

Josie stands up, grabs Wyatt by his jacket lapels, and glowers at him. "You tell me right now, husband, or you will never touch this body again!"

"Dr. Fred Baker wanted the rabbi killed because he was in love with Ida Bailey. Ida, of course, as we both know, was in love with Sonenschein. That's the love triangle. You know that's why I shot him, Sarah. You know *that* is the God's honest truth! Fred Baker must have wanted me to plug Sonenschein, so his wife and her groups wouldn't help the rabbi shut down the Stingaree."

Has Fred Baker confessed to Wyatt about his relationship with Ida? That can't be. Ida told me she never told anybody about their love affair. Besides, she knew that Josephine Marcus had her relationship with the rabbi. Perhaps it wasn't romantic, but she certainly had learned everything should could about what he did in his Kabbalah group.

"If that is true, Wyatt, then we will have to discover how the rabbi was going to kill you on May 6," Mrs. Foltz says.

The lawyer, along with Lucky Baldwin and Dr. Charlotte Baker, enters the parlor.

***

Dr. Charlotte Baker had informed Mrs. Clara Foltz about what had happened. She had also called the police, as she said she would do, to get Kai Krissy Wong released from any possible arrest warrant. It is Elias Baldwin who informs them all when he arrives, in his usual brash manner, as if he were in charge of the questioning, instead of lurking over at the Canary Cottage with Ida Bailey.

I watch the lawyer as she takes over the proceedings. I know I have to be careful not to speak about my secret plans, but I also need to give enough information to convince Mrs. Foltz that I am part of her investigation. She gets Colonel Morta to open the patio, and we all sit down around the table. The Peruvian Natives bring us an assortment of guacamole, fried tortillas, tequila for the men, and wine and soft apple cider for the others.

"I want to first thank all of you for being here. This occasion is such that if I were not in such a quandary, I would immediately allow the authorities to take over and render their decision. This moment, however, is not one of the normal consequences. I will tell you why in a moment. But I first want to say that all of you will be working with me to find the perpetrator of the most heinous crime I have ever investigated."

Why does she mention just one crime? Isn't she informed about Anand Prabhakar's death?

Everyone begins to talk at once. This lawyer is quickly becoming controversial. Only Josephine Earp seems nonplussed.

As is his habit, Elias Baldwin reaches for the tequila bottle and pours a large amount into his glass. "Can you please be more forthright, Mrs. Foltz? We are all adults at this table. I believe we can process your secret with alacrity and attention." His voice is still lucid, but that will not last too long.

"Miss Wong, please tell the group what you found out about the boy you accidentally murdered. It is very important information to add to our inquiry and search for the person responsible for his and, most probably, Rabbi Sonenschein's murder."

Kai turns toward me. Her lower lip quivers. I nod at her and smile. She turns back to look at Mrs. Foltz.

"It wasn't just the gold. It was the letter that came with the gold," she managed to blurt out. She was still concerned about her possible guilt.

"What was in this letter?" The attorney has been informed by her assistant, Dr. Charlette Baker.

I reach into my velvet purse and extract the letter. I pass it over to Mrs. Foltz, who begins reading it immediately. Her eyebrows rise as she continues until she finally looks over the top and speaks to all of us.

"This is monstrous and telling information. Kai was acting to inoculate Anand and not kill him. The person who gave her the money included a signed medical form which explained that the boy had virulent smallpox." Mr. Foltz's gaze moves over to the girl. "Miss Wong. Did this doctor also include the oral vaccine he mentions in this?"

"Yes. That's what killed him. I put it in his tea." Kai begins to cry again. "I didn't know! It wasn't the money. I believed what this doctor said. In China, we had thousands in our village who contracted this. My uncle and aunt had the pox. We had no vaccines. We had to watch them go through the stages of pustules and scabs. My aunt, who was pregnant, died during her fever. I didn't want the boy to infect San Diego. It's a terrible disease!"

She has never told me about her life in China. This is a revelation.

"We understand. Nobody is blaming you, young lady. Heaven, did you keep the vial of poison?" The attorney reaches out to me. I nod, and I reach into my purse to extract the bottle. "Here it is," I say, as I hand it to her. I know what she will be thinking concerning the possible suspect.

"Dr. Baker, please do some chemical analysis on what poison is in this," she instructs her legal assistant, handing her the bottle.

"Why is this important news?" Elias asks, and his voice is now slurring a bit from the tequila. "Just one more immigrant. No loss, as far as I can see. I say check him for smallpox. Lousy little curry muncher."

"Our police will automatically do an autopsy, kind sir. If the poor lad was infected, we will soon be informed." Dr. Baker is vehement, even toward this wealthy gentleman.

Kai Wong begins to sob again. I grasp her arm to comfort her.

"What's wrong?" Josephine Earp asks her. "Did something else happen?"

Does Mrs. Earp know about my relationship with the boy?

Kai's arms are moist with tears, as she has been crying with her head cradled inside them on the table. She sits up and turns to address Josephine.

"Anand thanked me so much for the drug. He said he was never told in India he had this disease. He thought he may have contracted it on the trip to San Diego. He said that Miss Heaven had given him a new beginning and that he had even attained what he called *moksha*, which is what we Chinese Buddhists call *bodhi* or an awakening to the mystical harmony all around one. He said each day was a heavenly gift from a woman named Heaven."

I feel my deep guilt rise in my throat, and my eyes fill with tears. I join Mr. Foltz, who has moved over to where Kai is seated to console her, and I gently stroke the back of her head, which has again sunk into its cradle of tears.

"Oh, balderdash! Can't you get to the suspects you have? What is it we have to do now, attorney Foltz? Is this your case or is it not?" Elias is drunk now. It reminds me of the nights he tortures me on board his yacht with his drunken curses about the women in his life, including me, as it turns out.

"Shut your trap, Elias," Wyatt shouts. "Mrs. Foltz said this was an important break in the case, and I, for one, want to hear what she has to say."

Mrs. Foltz is not fazed by the masculine bravado. "I believe we can now find the culprit behind these killings, but we shall need to work in careful coordination. This new evidence points to the fact that the person behind the death of Anand is either a physician, a nurse, or somebody else who is a health care professional. We may also have a smallpox epidemic on our hands."

She knows what I suspect. This narrows the suspect list quite a bit, one imagines.

Charlotte Baker is also concerned, and she raises her hand like a schoolgirl in class. The attorney points to her.

"You have ruled out my husband, Freddy, I would assume," Dr. Baker says.

"I have, yes. He was drugged to distract the court so the Earps could escape." Foltz turns to look at Josephine. They both are not aware of my secret. Ida Bailey drugged Dr. Fred Baker, not I.

That does not deter Mrs. Earp from speaking about it. "Yes, I confess. My husband and I concocted this method with Heaven Riendeau and Colonel Morta. Dr. Fred Baker was drugged during his visit to Miss Riendeau's evening party, and we appointed Mr. Price to be there at the courthouse when we slipped out the judge's chambers."

Correct drug. Wrong house. I am not certain where Miss

Bailey may have drugged him that morning before the court was in session.

"I gathered as much," says Mrs. Foltz. "I am also aware that you believe it is the other Madam, Ida Bailey, whom you believe to be the primary suspect. Is this true?"

How can Josephine believe that? The medical connection is the better clue.

"How did you know this? She *must* be the one. She was in the love triangle with Fred Baker and Rabbi Sonenschein, was she not? This young Indian must have discovered something about this, and Ida needed to dispose of the boy," Josephine explains.

"I was well aware that Miss Bailey was under the influence of a drug during her dance in Tijuana. She readily admitted to this. But we have no concrete evidence as yet that she was after Wyatt, or how she was involved in the sex contract between Mayor Hunsaker, the Earps, and Postmaster Comstock." The lawyer responds, and Josephine's neck reddens.

"Wyatt and I were going to interview her to find out," Josephine says, as she thrusts her chin out. "We shall prove it to you, I dare say, and this will put an end to all of this cloak and dagger mischief."

"Very well, Josephine. You *shall* visit Miss Bailey and find out what she knows. And Wyatt, in disguise, along with Elias Baldwin, shall visit Mayor Hunsaker." Mrs. Foltz stares directly at Elias. "And Mr. Baldwin, I want you and Wyatt, in disguise once more, to search that Canary Cottage to see what you can find in the way of material clues to these murders."

My former lover is exuberant. He raises his fist in the air. "By all means, Mrs. Foltz! I know those luxury confines like the back of my hand."

Wyatt strikes his friend on the back and laughs. "If you mean the way your hand cheats at poker, then I'd agree with you!"

"The other members of our group shall investigate in this manner. Dr. Baker and I will investigate the involvement of Anthony Comstock, Dr. Fred Baker, and Mayor Hunsaker. Finally, I want you, Heaven, and Miss Wong, to portray nurses and see if you can find any persons who might have initiated the poisoning of Anand Prabhakar. You and Miss Wong are new enough to the community not to be recognized, and Dr. Baker can get you the proper credentials so you can affect your subterfuge without notice. We will all keep in communication and return here when we complete our assigned duties. Mr. Morta will be here to man the fort." Mrs. Foltz is quite organized in her instructions. I shall be working with Kai. This will give me a way to bring my plan to fruition.

"And please find out if there have been any new cases of smallpox," Dr. Charlotte Baker points out.

Everyone stands up. We all look at one another warily. We know the guilty party could be among us, and I know Clara Foltz knows this as well and will be keeping an eye out for us.

As if she hears my thoughts, the attorney addresses us again.

"This does *not* mean you are all out of suspicion, however. It's just that we are in such a predicament, with the authorities hunting us down already, that I must take drastic measures. If any of you turns out to be a conspirator, then you will be found out. Mark my words. Until then, be on your way, and be very careful."

I leave the room with my arm around the young Kai, who now seems clear-headed. She will be privy to my thoughts on the way back to San Diego. However, she shall not be informed of my master plan, which will make me much more powerful than even this murderer, whomever she or he was.

***

My master plan has to do with my involvement with another immigrant, a twenty-year-old young woman by the name of Louise Eugénie Alexandrine Marie David. She is from Belgium, but she has, at even that very young age, traveled extensively, and her visit to San Diego has occurred at the behest of her current teacher and fellow anarchist and feminist, Élisée Reclus, who was visiting a relative in New Orleans. Louise, as Mr. Reclus's protégé, is also rebellious enough to understand the problem of being a brothel madam in the Wild West, and this is what we begin to discuss together inside the Moonbeam Café, shortly after they arrive by steamship.

They both speak English very well, and what we exchange by letter over the past three years, especially when I work in San Francisco, leads to my conversion. This conversion is known presently as Anarcho-Communism, by its detractors, but we see it as the more mystical and feminist force for equal rights and the Free Love Movement. I became initially aware of this struggle while I am with Elias Baldwin. As he is a man known to employ many immigrant laborers, in his variety of mining and industrial businesses, the various political groups that represent workers are constantly a thorn in his side. He tells me he employs Pinkerton Guards and other private police to break their efforts at establishing labor unions and other, what he calls "socialist anarchies."

This effort to establish a woman's right to do with her body what she wishes, and a worker's right to be paid a living wage and to labor under safe and reasonable hours and conditions, leads to the topic we are going to discuss. Namely, the recent Haymarket Square bombing and riots in Chicago on May 4, 1886. What I learn from my friends from Belgium is the fact that our murder trial in San Diego is directly connected to these international groups, around the world, who are struggling to be free. Some of them have become victims in Chicago.

The local political establishment in San Diego, which includes both sides of the legal representation of the Earps and the State of California, believes they are trying a simple case of felony Murder in the First Degree. Therefore, one might assume, the task is to prove the guilt or innocence of those directly responsible for the deaths of Rabbi Jerome Sonenschein and, later, immigrant Anand Prabhakar. Therefore, they believe, when this case is decided, then the problems of the community shall be solved.

The fact is, however, that even though the three women at the center of this trial, who seem to be romantic and business adversaries, are, on the contrary, vicious and conspiring enemies, plotting against each other to support causes far beyond that which the establishment believes to be the case at hand. As a result, I am meeting with these two representatives, both European anarchists, to plot our method of causing a great and violent revolution, right here in San Diego, which will ultimately make the Haymarket Workers' Riots seem innocuous and childish in comparison.

The gentleman who stands at the booth table in the back has a full beard, graying throughout, and his hair is long and over the collar of his simple frock coat. "Mademoiselle Riendeau! It is so marvelous to meet you in the flesh. I must say, you are quite an attractive exemplar of the female anatomy. This is my assistant, and spiritual advisor, Mademoiselle Alexandra Marie David. I would use her complete name, but she tells me you have become friends in your correspondence."

The woman who sits inside the booth is dressed in a flower-print dress with a Gypsy- sequined vest, a bell-shaped, crocheted blue peasant hat, and live blossoms of white peonies thrust into the sides of her lovely, dark-brown hair. Her gaze is, in fact, other-worldly and spiritual, and I nod to her as I sit down.

Kai Krissy Wong appears, and I whisper to bring us a bottle of champagne.

"Are you traveling up the coast after it's over?" I ask, realizing that my next move in our plan is to conspire with Ida Bailey about what will occur in San Francisco when this murder case resolves itself in the method, we approved beforehand, when I was still living in San Francisco.

"*Oui*, Miss David will be conferring with Miss Adeline Quantrill, the psychic bride and future daughter-in-law of attorney Clara Shortridge Foltz. It seems they are both telepathic, and Miss Quantrill has been reading minds ever since her parents were killed by Apaches, in the desert, when she was a young girl on a train coming to San Francisco. As you know, our organization employs whomever we need to carry out such intricate ruses. They need not know what the exact nature of our plan is, as this is not important." He smiles and twirls the ends of his mustaches.

Kai comes toward us with the champagne and three glasses. She pours a sample for Mr. Reclus, he tastes it, nods his approval, and she pours three glasses. When Kai leaves, Miss David continues with what she has to say.

"As I explained in my recent letter, I will enlighten the girl that we are a world feminist organization, which wants to cause a stir in the press so that our cause can become better understood. No person will be harmed. It will simply be an experiment in group enchantment or mass hysteria. We have done this before in France and, most recently, in England. It works out very well, as we can be interviewed by the newspapers right away following such demonstrations of organized spiritualism. I have already prepared the speech, in the Hebrew tongue, that she will deliver during the wedding reception at the Bay Cliff House Restaurant."

The young lady would make a wonderful temptress in my Golden Faun. I can envision her in a similar outfit, a riding crop in hand, the same serious expression on her countenance. I decide to toy with her in a manner I have not done in my letters.

"I see. But what will happen if she can read *your* mind, Miss David? Won't that cause a problem?" I raise my eyebrows for effect.

She laughs. "Oh my, no! You see, I have studied Eastern meditation techniques. I can clear my mind of any thoughts. At any moment I choose. It's quite simple. I can teach you some time if you wish."

"I see. That should be sufficient." I turn to her teacher. "I understand you will not tell me what the world leaders of the movement will do once we accomplish our ruse. Isn't it enough that we have created this competition between the Earps and your representative, Rabbi Sonenschein?"

They are both staring at me, and my heart races, but I will continue to the end.

"You told me you simply needed to take revenge on May 6, in memory of the Haymarket martyrs. Did the boy have to die also? Just so you can now do this, a much grander, publicity stunt? I know my part in this effort. And yours, I assume, will be to reap the rewards of turning San Diego into a Transcendental farming community like Brook Farm, Fruitlands, and Oneida. Your masterpiece volume, which I've read, creates scientific, self-determined bioregions, with no industrialized overseers, or central government. This book has already caused you to be imprisoned once. Are you not afraid of more imprisonment? You defended the Paris Commune of 1871. Is this your new cause?"

He frowns, and I can envision him as a slave owner, perhaps during our Civil War, overseeing the simple yet useful plantation life of his free slaves.

"Unless we work together on this, Miss Riendeau, our plan will never succeed. If you have been doing what we instructed, then you are now an accomplice. Are you ready to finally participate in something much bigger than your selfish little whore house? Your women are being held to become sex slaves. Even married women are being held under the uncivilized yoke of a sexist oppressor, the husband, who impregnates them at will, without so much as any woman being given a right to refuse him in his lusting habits. The town's mayor, the Earps, and the Post Office General, who claims to keep your country pure of pornography and sex, they were all going to frolic with twelve-year-old children in Tijuana! Can you abide this?"

I have never heard this argumentative tone in his letters. He is being a feminist crusader after all. I remember all the street girls I take in, give food, health care, and shelter. He is correct. These San Diego voyeurs and purveyors of injustice need to be taught a lesson!

"I just want to be certain my employees and I are cared for, that's all. I shall do as you instruct, and that includes working with Ida Bailey. Like me, she will become a comrade for this worldwide effort to liberate women and free the workers from a life of drudgery at the hands of people like Elias Baldwin, the Earps, and Mayor William Hunsaker. In fact, with her drug-induced life, Ida will believe she is the center of attention as Goddess Asherah."

"*Mais oui*! Perhaps her magic will help us as well. I believe in these things, but my teacher does not," Alexandra says.

"Of course, our lives will be placed in jeopardy, but our plan has gone well thus far. At this very moment, the victim of Ida Bailey's affections, Dr. Fred Baker, has kidnapped Josephine Earp. And, as we are well aware, the two immigrants, Rabbi Sonenschein and the Indian boy, Andand, have already served their purposes. I pray Ida and I do not have to become martyrs for us to succeed in our final grand plan!"

"*Oui*, Dr. Baker was converted to our cause when he worked under Dr. David Bruce, a loyal anarcho-communist. We have just returned from England. He is doing well, and he is using the ruse of being in love with Ida Bailey to carry out the experiments. In the coming years, we shall assassinate kings, kidnap corporate leaders, bomb buildings, inflict plagues, and do anything we can to destroy the world capitalist stranglehold on our freedoms!"

I stand up, raise my fist above my head, and begin to sing the "Internationale," but our waitress, Kai Wong, approaches to serve us once more.

"Put this on my account, Kai," I tell her, and I escort my friends out of the café and into the warm, San Diego sunshine. Now that I know Dr. Fred Baker is carrying out his end of our plan, Ida Bailey will soon be contacting me, in desperation.

When I return to the Golden Faun, I discover I am correct. In addition to the newspapers being filled with panicked headlines about being attacked from the skies by rabid bats, I know I must meet with Ida Bailey to put the last part of our grand plan into motion. The *Tribune's* front page reports that Dr. Fred Baker has been arrested for the death of at least ten prostitutes in the Chinatown section of the Stingaree. Wyatt and Josephine Earp have been arrested again, and their fate is yet to be determined.

On the telephone, Ida tells me she wants me to meet her at her La Jolla hotel called, quite appropriately enough, the Hotel New Canaan. It is interesting to know the rabbi gave her an interest in such an enterprise. I assume it is some kind of consumption cure ruse to bilk wealthy men, from the East Coast, out of their money. This, of course, is at the heart of our anarchist war against the Lucky Baldwins of the world, who use any disease, drug, obsession, or malady to make a profit.

"I will go there immediately," I tell her. "I only took money from Josephine because she had it to loan. When I discovered her contract with the Post Office General to provide underage children, as young as twelve, for his sexual enjoyment, I became enraged. I will do anything you wish to get even with them!" I conclude, hanging up the telephone. I pat the stomach of my new and very green crushed velvet dress and instruct Rosie Daniels to drive me out to the La Jolla Cliffs at once.

Her hotel manager greets us when we arrive, and I instruct Rosie to wait for me and to entertain herself in the hotel. The structure is built into the cliff and has only three sides. The hotel is four stories, an A-frame building with fancy Asian and Middle Eastern furnishings, lamps, paintings, and rugs, to feature the Kabbalah practices and mystical cures inside. These furnishings include many mechanical and electronically lit chandeliers, which cast a continuous and hypnotic aura of color and shadow beneath its revolving specter.

Ida wears a low-cut evening dress, much like twenty-year-old First Lady, Frances Cleveland wears and makes fashionable, and she motions for me to follow her into her back office. Her office contains a smaller version of the hypnotic chandelier, as well as a mahogany business desk and leather chairs in front. I sit in one of these and await her instructions.

"Are you familiar with St. Vitas' or St. John's Dance?" Ida asks me.

I can see her idea is working nicely with ours. We assume that her proposal will utilize the wedding and hypnotic drugs in some way, as Ida is also quite enamored with the supernatural powers of dance, as she exhibited on that fateful day in Tijuana when Wyatt Earp shot the rabbi and ruined our plans.

I know exactly what to tell her. "Wasn't that the affliction people had in the Middle Ages? They begin to dance uncontrollably, often passing out from exhaustion?"

"Yes, it was classified as a mania. It was a mass hysteria brought on by the stress of living in those backward days when living was dangerous, and no science had been established to prevent diseases such as the Bubonic Plague. I want to discuss this with you, as it pertains to an idea I have been going over in my mind, ever since that day in Tijuana, when Rabbi Sonenschein was gunned down by Wyatt Earp."

Yes, you idiot, I think. *There is a very good reason Sonenshein was there that day. He was there to kill Earp.* I lean forward to feign interest, taking a sip from my glass.

"From what you've told me over the telephone, I have also been thinking about those two, especially Josephine. She is one of the greediest and most irritable women I have ever met."

She nods. "Did you notice the frenetic atmosphere in San Diego after the truth about what Dr. Baker could do with those animals—especially those bats—came out in the newspapers?"

This is the moment I need to convince her of the fear Dr. Baker has caused. "Why, yes. I saw the men were quite anxious about entering my house. They clustered outside for the longest time, and my clientele numbers have shrunk to very small proportions. One, two, or three each night, and most of them are sailors or other riffraff."

She sips and moistens her lips. "What I mean concerns the dance mania. When I left the mayor's office after he explained what had happened in front of my cottage when Wyatt shot the bat that was attacking his wife. As I approached Canary Cottage, I saw a scene that might have come directly from the drawings I have seen in the library books of people under the influence of St. Vitus mania."

I raise my eyebrows in mock surprise. "Do tell. Were they dancing?"

"Yes, but it was much more than just a dance. They were not moving about in any kind of orderly rhythm at all. For example, when I dance, I am filled with natural energy that comes from everything and everyone around me. I feel infused with a synchronous, flowing motion that enjoys life, and I want to display my body most passionately and fluidly as possible. But these people were like lonely puppets on strings. The puppeteers were invisible demons, each one making the dancer a separate tool of motion and of a demonic, shaking frenzy I have only witnessed once before in my life."

Her drug-enthused imagination was again taking hold. "What do you mean?"

"I was attending a meeting of so-called Shakers, a religious group. They had these same types of separate, energetic movements, their arms flailing about, their legs pounding the ground with no rhythmic beat, just an absurdly crushing motion. Also, those Shakers were doing what they later told me was speaking in tongues, inspired by the Holy Spirit."

I can believe she might have been converted on the spot.

"Yes, I've heard of that," I say.

"There were no such spastic stimulations or singing in the group I saw in front of my cottage. They were silent, and upon their faces was a contortion of different spasms and twists in facial muscles, as if they were in pain and agony. They behaved just the way those people in the drawings looked. They were responding to an inner sickness or plague of some kind."

Now I can see how her observations and subsequent idea can fit into our plan.

"I see. What do you make of it all, and how does this fit into your plan for revenge?"

"These were not men waiting to enter my brothel. There were women and children there as well. They were all possessed. Some wore masks. Some had blank expressions on their faces. But they all had different motions in their dances. No rhythm. No collective energy of joy. Nothing but painful contorting and spasms of anguish. Also, they kept gazing up at the sky, as if they expected some catastrophic punishment from God."

Dancing is very good. It is excellent. But I want to see how she connects this event.

"From God? Are you certain it wasn't because of the fear of the bats of Dr. Baker?"

"Possibly, but they seemed more frightened, as though they expected the end of something. Perhaps even life itself. Or, the Apocalypse or End of Times." She swallows the remainder of her champagne and sets the crystal down hard on the desk top. "Tell me, Heaven. Were you invited to San Francisco by that woman attorney, Mrs. Clara Foltz? To attend her son's wedding at the Bay Cliff House Restaurant?"

There it is! We are now on the same path.

"Why, yes, I was. I was rather surprised, as I am new to the community. Although, from what I learned, Mrs. Foltz and her children are also new to San Diego."

"I will plan to put a drug into the women's drinks at dinner at this restaurant. It is called *aliento del diablo*, or devil's breath, by the natives in Columbia. It is from the nightshade family of plants, and in low doses, combined with alcohol, makes one very compliant and suggestive. When I begin to dance, you shall follow me and dance also. The result should cause all the women to dance with us. It won't be exactly like the St. Vidas form, as we want them to follow our motions, but when we take off our clothes, they should follow us."

The Belgians will be pleased. Ida Bailey's ego has consumed her plan just as we expected.

However, I laugh to keep her guessing. "Take off our clothes? Are you being serious?"

"I am. I want these women to understand the power we can have over them. We will not be completely nude. Just our overclothes will be removed. In truth, before we leave for San Francisco, I want to initiate you into my female group. I call it the Asherah Society. You will have to come with me down below at the cove. I will take you at low tide inside one of the seven caves. The White Lady Cave."

Rabbi Sonenschein was quite good. He had her convinced that she was Asherah.

I clap my hands. "This all sounds rather enchanting. I love it!"

"Yes, and I want you to do one more thing for me at the wedding restaurant."

What could this mean? "What is that?"

"After we finish our dance, I want you to run outside and jump into the bay. I will have Peng Shi down there to retrieve you from the water. I want you to shout the following before you jump, so everyone can hear you."

I make my eyes as big as saucers. "What words are these?"

"I can no longer be part of this! I am pregnant with Elias Baldwin's child. The world is going stark, raving mad!"

How can she know my secret? I have told no one. Is she also a psychic?

I stand up. "It sounds quite mad, but I shall do it!"

***

When I return to the Golden Faun, I get a call from Clara Foltz. She wants me to walk over to Mayor Hunsaker's office to check on the two men, Wyatt and Elias. She fears they might be in some trouble.

When I arrive, I can hear some commotion inside the office, so I know they must be inside. The door's lock has been shot off, and so I open the front door quite easily. As soon as I step into the dark foyer, a big arm reaches around my neck and pulls me into him.

"It's Wyatt Earp," he whispers into my hair.

"I'm Heaven Riendeau, Mr. Earp. Please let me go."

He releases me just as Lucky staggers into the foyer.

"What are you doing here?" Wyatt laughs. Do men take anything seriously?

"Mrs. Foltz sent me over to check on you two. She expected you might not be up for the task. By the looks of things, she was right." I tell them.

"No, Miss Heaven. It ain't all bad. We found out that a young prostitute was bit by something in her bed over at Ida Bailey's house. And Lucky just tripped over the mayor's goat."

They begin to guffaw like schoolboys again, so I shush them.

"Be quiet! That is good news. It means Hunsaker received a goat from somebody, just like I did at the Golden Faun, and Ida did at her establishment. It must be Dr. Fred Baker's doings."

"Is that so? What you think the girl gettin' bit in her bed means?" Wyatt says.

"Yes, Miss uppity," Lucky says, and he takes another drink from his flask. "You got our goat figured out, so how 'bout hooker bites?"

"Funny you should ask. I had the same thing happen the

other night at my place. One of my girls, Janice, woke up screaming. And she had a bite on the back of her neck. Was that where Bailey's girl was bitten?" I enjoy leading them on about this entire plan by our operative.

"That's correct. Right on her neck in the back, in that little indent. A small cut, but it was bleedin' a lot." Wyatt puts his finger upon the nape of my neck, and I shiver.

"Only I saw something else that night in the Golden Faun. I never told anybody, as I thought it might be one of those free-tailed bats." This information should keep them guessing.

"Free-tailed bats? Why'd you think that?" Wyatt asks.

"I found part of a moth on the floor near her bed. It was sliced in half, with blood all over its wings. Sure enough, when I felt the back of Janice's neck, there was the fuzzy powder from the moth's wings on her skin, near the bite. I thought maybe one of those bats came in through the open window, and a moth may have landed on her neck. Those bats are very small. They can get in and out of a room like a hummingbird." This, of course, is what poor Anand sees that gets him poisoned by Dr. Baker.

"Do tell. Sounds like too much coincidence to have the same thing happenin' next door to each other's place. We need to tell Mrs. Foltz all about this." Wyatt moves toward the door.

"Don't forget Pumpkin!" Lucky blurts out. "What's the mayor doin' with a nanny goat in his office?"

"Yes, Lucky, we'll tell her about the goat," says Wyatt, and he opens the door. "Come, we'll give you a ride back to your place, Miss Riendeau."

"Why, thank you, Mr. Earp," I smile and take his arm. "Would you both like to come in and have a drink before we go back to Ensenada? Maybe even stay over?"

***

Kai Wong and I drive back with Wyatt and Lucky to Ensenada to find out if our information helps the case. We've finished our assignment, and it didn't take long. We have a list of those who were treated for strange diseases and who might have access to the drugs found in Dr. Fred Baker's bloodstream.

I smile at the two men from the back seat of their surrey, as we pass the checkpoint into Mexico, at the San Ysidro border crossing. I have on my favorite crushed velvet green dress with a matching hat, topped with an ostrich feather. Kai still wears her waitress uniform.

"We talked it over, Mr. Earp. We don't know yet who the suspects might be. One of us might still be suspected, even at this late hour." I look at Kai, and she nods in agreement.

The two men are still in their Hassidim disguises, as we need to cross the border. Wyatt turns around to address us.

"My wife wanted us to stay and fight this here case, so that's what I'm doin'. If one of us inspectors is behind the murders, then why would he or she want to show up after we all brung in our evidence?"

Lucky laughs. "If they're the murderer, then maybe they want to get rid of those who know about their guilt. We could all have targets on our backs."

"No, Elias, I have a strong hunch Mrs. Foltz knew who the guilty party was before she assembled us. She just wanted to find out for certain. We just might have the last hatchet to cut the head off this chicken." I hope the lawyer is still falling for our ruse.

Lucky is driving, so he hands his identification to the guard at the crossing gates.

"I, for one, don't understand who would want to kill a young boy. I truly hope Mrs. Foltz can put all these clues together at last." I sigh. "I haven't slept much at all for the last week."

"Neither have I," says Kai Wong. "What if *you* killed them both, Mr. Earp? You killed before. Why not again?"

Wyatt turns around to stare at the young waitress.

"Don't worry none, young lady. If I use somebody for target practice, then I have a good reason. You ain't on my list today. And if this old codger aims at you, then it won't be to shoot you." He points at Elias. "It'll be somethin' much worse!"

Lucky spits his tobacco out the window.

Dr. Charlotte Baker, Kai Wong, me, Lucky, and Wyatt are assembled inside Colonel Morta's ranch house. Only Dr. Baker's husband, Fred, Ida Bailey, and kidnapped Josephine Earp, are missing. The old Mexican has food for us, but no liquor. Mrs. Foltz looks very serious as she addressed us.

"Ladies and gentlemen, thanks for returning to our little Mexican hideaway. I have done some more discovery work on this case, and now that you're here, we can begin to assemble what we have collected together. You are all part of my family now, so I want you to feel that way. Let's begin with Wyatt and Mr. Baldwin. What did you gentlemen discover? I had to send Heaven to see if you were all right when I heard about what went on at the Canary Cottage."

"Yes'm. There was quite a scene there. Lucky and me were about to search around the place, with Ida as our guide. Then we heard a scream from one of the ladies' bedrooms."

All of us women at the table stare at Wyatt.

"One of Ida's girls had a bite on the back of her neck, about right here." Earp points to the nape of Lucky's neck. "Later, Heaven said she found half a miller moth on the floor by the bed of her girl. There was also moth wing powder on her neck. We reckoned somebody fixed that miller on her neck."

I want to clarify this remark. "As I told Mr. Earp, I believe somebody might have used free-tail bats to get in and out of the rooms."

"Yes, that comports with what Charlette and I discovered." She's writing it down. I think she believes me. "Anything else?"

"The goat in Mayor Hunsaker's office," Lucky says. "I nearly broke my neck trippin' over the danged thing!"

"You nearly broke your neck 'cause you was drunk," Wyatt says.

There is general laughter.

"The goat was a nanny, correct?" Foltz asks.

"That's right, mam. In the dark, she sounded like a banshee. What do y'all think it means?"

Mrs. Foltz turns toward me. I feel a lump in my throat. "Heaven, what did you discover in your search of the hospital wards?"

"Krissy and I searched the wards for drug prescriptions and if there were any new cases of anything, like smallpox, which was what Anand had. No smallpox. But we did find several inpatients who had two other kinds of diseases."

"Oh yes? What diseases were those?" Mrs. Foltz asks, her pencil raised.

"Two women had been admitted with leprosy, and five had been treated for *Micrococcus melitensis*"

Dr. Charlotte slams her fist down on the tabletop. "Brucellosis! I knew it. Freddy's goats were injected with it."

"Be calm, Charlotte. I told you not to become emotional. There must be some explanation, and we shall discover it." Clara Foltz turns toward Earp. "Wyatt, do you know what this means?"

"Fred Baker, like you said before. He was courtin' Ida Bailey. And Ida, bless her heart, loved the rabbi. I reckon Dr. Baker wanted to get even somehow with Sonenschein and Bailey. Is that about it?"

Charlotte begins to sob.

"I am afraid you're very close to the answer. We spied on Hunsaker and Comstock, and we discovered that Fred Baker was putting pressure on them to stop the little garden of earthly delights in Tijuana. There were letters between them that became escalating in their threats and anger. The last letter Charlotte found in Hunsaker's desk. You didn't look in that drawer, Wyatt. That letter was an anonymous threat concerning a new plague being visited upon all the women in the Stingaree." Mrs. Foltz is putting her puzzle together in the wrong manner.

"A new plague? Is that about the bats?" Wyatt asks, his voice shaky.

"Yes, I'm afraid it is. We have reason to believe Dr. Fred Baker has been using the bats from his research to give these women one of the most deadly and contagious diseases known to mankind. Rabies. There is no cure, and it can be passed on to other animals and, of course, to other humans." That's not the only reason he's experimenting, however.

"My God!" Lucky gasps. "You mean to say we could have

those lovely girls drooling and biting folks like mad dogs?"

Dr. Charlotte is not crying anymore. "The bat doesn't always bite. Sometimes the saliva will drool onto you, and you could have a minor open cut. Or sometimes a bat will lick on the skin and, again, transmit the virus that way."

Kai Wong stands up, and I have to hold onto her dress to keep her from fleeing. "But that's how those poor women got it! They got bit from the moths attached to the backs of their necks. The saliva got into those cuts."

"Yes, I'm afraid that's right. We have only one chance right now, I am afraid. We need to hope we can stop Fred Baker before he lets all those bats he has loose out in San Diego." Mrs. Foltz stands. "We must leave right away. My son David Milton told us he overheard Dr. Baker's plan to show Josephine Earp his great plague at the Canary Cottage, just before his meeting with us at six-thirty PM. Charlotte and I confronted him in Chinatown about his relationship with Ida Bailey." Mrs. Foltz looks down at her writing pad. "And the other disease, the leprosy. The delivery of the armadillos was the cause of that horrible disease."

"But I need to find out how my husband was able to cause the incubation of the *M. Leprae* from the armadillos in such a short amount of time." Charlotte follows Mrs. Foltz out the door.

We all follow behind them. I notice Wyatt takes his long gun and holster.

We take the big carriage down to San Diego. Mr. Price drives the rig, and he drives the four horses fast. When we pull up to the Canary Cottage, it's early, and Dr. Fred Baker and Josephine Earp have yet to appear. It will be over soon.

As we wait, the brothel males wander around, smoking, laughing, and discussing investments.

Mrs. Foltz addresses us. "We need to get ready for the most logical occurrence. Charlotte, you know about your husband's work with bats. What would you assume he would do to use them as some kind of plague vector? What would be his physical position and what should we prepare to do to stop his attempt?"

Charlotte sighs. "I really can't say, Clara. All I know is that he was working with them in Texas and that the species is very small. Perfect for getting in and out of small places at great speeds. They can also fly great distances, so I would assume he could keep them stored just about anywhere near here. Even across the border."

"All right. We shall have to wing it if you'll excuse my expression. I do want to place our best marksman in a place out of sight but within firing range. Wyatt, would you be more comfortable in a tree or upon terra firma?" Our plan will now become complete, one way or another.

"I reckon I'll stay out of view until they get here," Wyatt says. "That's where ya'll will be too, I suppose."

"Quite right. We need as many eyewitnesses as we can manage," Clara Foltz says.

"Quickly!" Charlotte whispers. "Here comes Freddy!"

We all move in different directions, but lawyer Foltz motions for us to follow her. We see Dr. Fred Baker step out of his one-horse surrey and stand in front of the Canary Cottage. He seems to be staring at the cottage as if he's hypnotized. I know he understands we're here.

We are all hiding in the alley between the Canary Cottage and the Grand Horton Hotel. When we see the one-horse carriage pull up, about fifteen minutes later, Dr. Charlotte whispers, "It's Li Wei. My Stingaree messenger."

Li Wei, Dr. Baker's assistant gets out, walks around, and opens the passenger door. Josephine Earp, her hands hidden by some kind of muffler, is guided by Li Wei, who has a gun. I can see Wyatt has a bead on him from the shadows of the alley.

Fred Baker is puffing on his pipe as they come up to him. He clears his throat and smiles as he addresses Mrs. Earp. He could do no better had he been in a play by Shakespeare.

"The display is about ready to begin. Let me explain the genius of what I will now show you. The truth is that Rabbi Sonenschein uncovered my plan when he released the young prostitutes who were going to be working at the hacienda in Tijuana, where Comstock, Hunsaker, and the other men were going to be enjoying their perversions. This is the main reason your husband was marked to die as well, but first I must take care of you, of course."

Josephine is not afraid. "What about the Indian boy, Anand? Why did you poison him?"

"He discovered the first free-tail delivering its cargo."

"Free-tail? What is that?"

"The largest colony of free-tails found during our zoological expedition was an estimated twenty to thirty million that lived in the limestone Ney and Bracken caves near Bandera, in southwest Texas. These little mammals weigh only one-third of an ounce, but they are perfect for my purposes." That's our story all right.

"What purposes? What is the cargo this bat delivers?"

"Bats are some of the world's best vectors for viral infections, did you know that? I was able to train these bats to fly to human targets. They are a species that must fly at night. Mexican free-tailed bats can fly up to one-hundred miles round trip in an evening looking for food. They are built for speed with short fur and long narrow wings and can fly up to sixty miles per hour with a tailwind. They have been observed, by weather balloons, feeding up to ten-thousand feet high while searching for food." Fred Baker waves his hands around.

"And what is the virus you have them carry?"

"I shall get to that, and then I shall give you my demonstration. I simply visited the whore house and affixed the bat's favorite moth to the rear collar of one of the whores I wanted to infect after she went to bed for the night and was fast asleep. The Indian saw the bat fly inside the Golden Faun that night, and the boy had to disappear."

Nicely dramatized.

"But the virus. You did not tell me what it was."

"Rabies virus uses a myriad of strategies to avoid the immune system and hide from antiviral drugs, even using the blood-brain barrier to protect itself once it has entered the brain. It is, therefore, immune from cure. I simply made certain the victim had a cut on her neck where I placed the moth. The tiny bat's saliva transmitted the cargo and the virus did the rest. The woman would be dead from rabies as soon as the virus entered her brain."

Charlotte has certainly corroborated this information.

"My God! What can you show me now? I don't want to see it! Those creatures are infernal."

"On the contrary. The secret that Rabbi Sonenschein had was important to me. We were friends, you see, even when he was following you and your husband around the West buying properties and establishing your whore houses and taverns. At that point, Sonenschein had not had his Kabbalah conversion to do good by these prostitutes. He was planting the moths for me, to infect the whores. Once one got infected, she would infect the rest of them. Can you imagine the value my bats will have to the military of any country who pays me the right price?"

This should plant the fear of God into all of them.

"Tonight, when I go to my meeting with your friends at this hotel, I will give the signal for my men to let loose the trained bats we have in a cave in Tijuana. We were going to do that to infest your unholy playground for the perverts Hunsaker and Comstock, but your husband shot my rabbi messenger before he could deliver the goods."

"What? You mean, you were going to kill those young women who were working there?"

"Oh, yes. That would have been my first trial, but you got in the way. Tonight, however, we have affixed a moth to at least one whore in every bordello in the Stingaree. When my men release the free-tails, rabies will envelop their brains and spread like wildfire. Soon, San Diego will be cleansed of all this human pestilence, once and for all. And then, I shall give the word to do the same in all the other brothels in other states and territories. And now ... to show you how it works ... Mr. Li, if you please!"

The Chinaman signals behind us up in the Grand Horton.

We all watch the bat come down in a flash of dark-brown fury, flapping its wings furiously. Then comes the gunshot, and the bat falls to the pavement, just behind Josephine Earp.

"Damn you to hell!" Wyatt Earp shouts from the shadows.

***

Thankfully, the attorney, Mrs. Foltz, is paying for our round-trip fare to San Francisco for the wedding of her son. After being officially initiated into Ida Bailey's Asherah group inside the White Lady Cave, I know for certain we made the correct decision to use her in our plan. I immediately wire Élisée and Alexandra, who will be staying at the Palace Hotel. However, I do not inform them about my pregnancy with Elias Baldwin's child. They would certainly ask me about this new development following our dance at the wedding reception, and I plan to keep it a secret from them. They have such strange ideas about having children that they frighten me.

Besides, I want to keep my options open concerning Lucky and myself. He may, indeed, welcome the news, or he may not. That will, most likely, be open to negotiations, if I know him as well as I believe I know him. It is the coincidental knowledge of my pregnancy by Ida that concerns me much more. During her dance in the La Jolla cave, she at one point began to cavort around my body and touch my stomach with her hands, which put quite a fright into me.

We all have dinner together on board the steamship *Goliah*, and Mrs. Foltz introduces Ida and me to her two children living with her in San Francisco, David Milton, and Bertha May. David, I notice, wears female attire, and this is surprising, but not outrageous, as my experiences in the brothel business have introduced me to many more and wide-ranging psychological aberrations. He is a very intelligent and courteous young man, nonetheless, as is the girl. Mrs. Foltz presides over the dinner, with the captain of our vessel playing a gracious host.

Mrs. Foltz explains she has five children and that she has to lie about being divorced from their father. She says he died, and then she works with her future legal partner, a woman named Laura Gordon, to get the law passed so that women can go to law school and become lawyers. She passes her Bar Examination on the first attempt, with her five children standing in the alley outside on that memorable day.

Ida whispers to me, "Perhaps she can get them to pass a law to get all these husbands, like Dr. Baker, from cheating on their wives." I find this amusing, as neither Ida nor Josephine Earp knows the *real truth* underlying Dr. Baker's alleged dalliance with Ida, or its purpose, and neither does Ida. If Mrs. Earp believes she created a distraction so she could escape a courtroom, then imagine what she would think if she knows Dr. Fred Baker is working for a world anarchist group?

When we finally anchor in Ocean Beach Bay, Ida and I take the passenger barge to shore. I spend most of my time, inside our cabin at night, researching information I need to know about the Foltz family. I read newspapers and magazines that cover the attorney and her exploits, both in San Francisco and elsewhere. Ida and I then stroll along the beach, holding hands, and she points up to the Bay Cliff Restaurant. I tell her I have been there many times during my life in San Francisco and that she will enjoy its luxurious confines immensely. While we walk, I am quite distracted, and I pay little attention to my surroundings, which I have experienced many times in the past, both as a lonely prostitute wandering the sands alone and as a brothel madam, escorting gentlemen of leisure to my house of ill repute.

I keep wondering about what my European cohorts are planning. They insist upon never telling any of what they term "cell members" throughout the world exactly what shall take place and that we must simply "follow instructions to the letter," and leave the resulting consequences to them. However, I have read one of the main doctrines of the Paris Commune of 1871, about which Mr. Reclus and Miss David so often refer, and it is written by two Germans, Karl Marx, and Friedrich Engels. The so-called *Communist Manifesto* of 1847 directly leads to the revolutions of 1848. Why? Because, in it, they espouse continuing revolts against the "ruling classes" and "nobility," which supposedly will lead to a "dictatorship of the working class." It is this word "dictatorship" that frightens me most, along with the authors and their continuous call for violence in the name of freedom. The revolutions that occur, in fact, in the years 1847 and 1848, lead to more violence and death of these revolutionaries and the imprisonment of thousands more. Is this new revolt planned by them just another method of our comrades getting arrested or killed?

This is Mr. Reclus's answer to my doubts, in his wire back to me, which I read as we waited for the wedding dinner to begin inside the Bay Cliff Restaurant:

As the Greeks knew long ago, Ms. Riendeau, there must always be a ruling class to control the people who cannot control themselves. Capitalists rule by violence, do they not? They will insist upon keeping their power, so we must insist upon keeping property under our control, as we have the best motives. We want to bring freedom to women, power to the workers, and the control of property and the means of production for the common good. What more admirable goals are there? Just wait. Our plan will get the notoriety we need. Be patient. Follow your instructions. And may our cause be victorious!

Of course, I have not informed my leaders about Ida's private plan to drug the women in their drinks. I am also concerned that her plan will not function in our best interests. There are over two hundred persons in the main dining room, so we need to place the doses into some eighty females' wine glasses. Luckily, there are name cards at each place setting.

I can meet briefly with the bride, Adeline Quantrill, and she informs me that Miss Alexandra David has given her the information about the ingenious ruse to get publicity for the worldwide Suffrage Movement. She is a beautiful bride, with a white satin gown that has a long train of cloth decorated with sunflowers, which are, she tells me, the symbols of the suffragettes and the Temperance Movement. She is unconventional in her beauty, as she wears dark eyeshadow, and her eyebrows are red smudges above her glistening gray eyes. She shaved them, and the red smudges contrast, in a very Japanese fashion, with her almost porcelain complexion.

"I have memorized the Hebrew perfectly, and I shall go into my trance when you come through the reception line," she tells me.

"Thank you so much, Adeline. This will mean a great deal to our cause," I say to her, and I turn on my heels to run back to inform Ida of something else. I want her to believe I have spoken with all of the attorney's friends and family.

Thus, I run up to my compatriot, out of breath, and say, "Ah Toy says Adeline is a psychic and can read minds. One of Mrs. Foltz's biggest cases concerned wives who were murdering their husbands while they slept. The women had been mesmerized to kill by a man the Foltz family eventually captured. Ah Toy said that Adeline was able to exchange thoughts with Osiris, the young son of Dr. Paschal Beverly Randolph, the author of *Magia Sexualis*. I have his book. The girl's psychic genius saved them all when they were being held prisoner inside that San Jose mystery house owned by Mrs. Sarah Winchester."

I obtain all of this information from the newspapers, and I have not spoken to any of Mrs. Foltz's family other than Adeline. My biggest news source, ironically, is Mrs. Foltz's very own *San Diego Bee*, which I find quite humorous.

At the head of the massive table, which overlooks the ocean below, are the bride and groom, Adeline and Samuel, who are smiling and toasting us with their glasses of champagne. Seated on their right side are Clara Foltz, the attorney, and her mother, Telitha, and her father, Elias Willets, who are both in their early sixties. They journeyed from nearby San Jose. Then came the rest of Clara's children, Trella Evelyn, the beautiful actress in her twenties and a graduate of Berkeley, Bertha May and David Milton, the two youngest I know from San Diego, and the youngest, Virginia Knox, who is twelve.

The guests from San Diego are next: Wyatt and Josephine Earp, Drs. Charlotte and Fred Baker, Miss Kai Krissy Wong, Ida and I, Ah Toy, and Elias Baldwin.

Mrs. Foltz stands up at her place to address us.

"Kind ladies and gentlemen. If you please. Your attention!" She strikes her wine glass with her knife's handle. I assume she has her drugged drink, along with all the other women.

"I am so proud of my two children who have brought us together and sealed their holy bonds in matrimony. One might not believe this mystery of ours to be a comedy, which must always end in a wedding, but there are comedic elements that led me to my eventual conclusions to solve it."

"Mother, please tell them about the goat," says Trella Evelyn. "What you wrote to me that made me fall off my stool laughing." That goat seems to be the "butt" of humor in more than one escapade inside Mayor Hunsaker's office, as I was there as well, but with Wyatt and Elias.

"Ah, yes. My thespian daughter is referencing the first major clue I obtained pointing to Dr. Fred Baker's involvement in the plot to infect the Stingaree bordellos." Dr. Baker's activities are certainly heinous, but he is part of our plan as well.

"Well, Mrs. O'Leary's cow was said to start the great Chicago fire of '71. Was it Ida Bailey's goat this time?" Elias points to Ida and guffaws. He is well into his frolic for the evening, just he was on that night, aboard his yacht, when I became pregnant.

"You're not far from the truth, Mr. Baldwin. I was spying around Mayor Hunsaker's office at night, as Charlotte and I were able to get a passkey from a friend in the mayor's employ. Lo and behold, tied to the leather couch in his office was a nanny goat. I tripped on her in the dark, and she let out a banshee wail so loud that it made both Charlotte and I scream to high heaven." Mrs. Foltz explains.

Everybody begins to laugh, except Elias, who is, no doubt, remembering his confrontation with the nanny.

"Dr. Baker gave the mayor a goat, but it wasn't poisoned. We had already ascertained that the goats in the Stingaree bordellos had been injected with *coccobacillus*, and the boy Anand's poison contained this bacterium. Finally, we found a vial of poison on the person of the victim, Rabbi Sonenschein. The only logical persons who could have injected them and provided the bacteria were Charlotte or her husband, and when Charlotte told me about her husband's visit to Malta to research with Dr. David Bruce, the British Army surgeon, the clues began to come together."

When I hear about Dr. Bruce, I let out a sigh of relief. She has not done any research about the *real* connection between him and Dr. Baker.

Josephine wishes to speak. The lawyer nods to her to do so.

"And how did you ascertain that Wyatt and I were marked to be poisoned by Sonenschein?"

A prescient question indeed.

"We found a vial of the poison on the person of the victim, Rabbi Sonenschein. After you were kidnapped, Mrs. Earp. That's when we knew it was Fred Baker behind the poisoning of the goats with Brucellosis. In fact, on the day I visited Chinatown to question him, I was almost completely certain he was our guilty party."

Ah, but it was not merely Dr. Baker, don't you see?

My little rebel, the waitress, Kai, wants to speak. "I am sorry, but how can they allow Dr. Baker to go free? If it were a poor person who poisoned Anand, he would have been hanged!"

That statement seems to dislodge Dr. Baker's conscience, as he stands up to address the gathering.

"I want to tell you all right now that I am the guiltiest devil alive today. I shall be working to help the poor for the rest of my life, in a meager attempt at atonement for what I did. All I can plead to you is for your mercy and the fact that I was driven by my lust and my own megalomaniacal insanity." Dramatically, he fell back down into his chair and his wife draped her arm around him.

Yes, and he did his experiments to assist the poor workers of the world! Dr. Baker may want to ask Trella Evelyn Foltz about a part in one of her plays.

Sixty-year-old former Chinatown madam, Ah Toy, then stands up.

"If there is a consolation, I think it is that Dr. Baker has begun to work with other researchers around the world to provide vaccines for these diseases, except for rabies, but there may be something to treat that as well if they keep testing." She speaks in excellently enunciated English.

"Ah Toy is right. We must look to the bright side," said the handsome young groom, Samuel.

When we conclude, everyone leaves the small dining area to go to the main dining room where space has been cleared to make room for the over two hundred guests. Ida and I get in line to congratulate the bride. I know our plan will now begin. The women are starting to feel the drug's effects. They are not talking. Instead, they look straight ahead. Josephine Earp first takes the bride's hand and shakes it. Adeline smiles. When I reach Adeline, I begin my best rendition of what Ida showed me in the White Lady Cave initiation. I begin to rhythmically sway and shake my body. I also watch as Adeline begins to go into her hypnotic trance. Her gray eyes roll back into her head, and she also begins to sway along with me. We are dancing in tempo to our inner spirits.

As I begin to pick up the tempo, I start taking off my outer dress. First, the red, crushed velvet jacket, and then the long dress. As I do so, I keep my body swaying, and I notice all the women in the room begin to circle us. This must be mass hysteria. Upon my multi-colored leotards, I have placed the images of what in Kabbalah they call the "Curse of the Evil Eye," which is a picture of a blue hand with an eye centered in its palm. This is Ida's idea from what she learned from our Rabbi Jerome Sonenschein.

When Adeline finally begins to channel a deep baritone voice, which is speaking Hebrew, all the women begin dancing around both the bride and me. I can feel the floor vibrate, and the men look hypnotized, staring and watching us, over eighty women, dance within this center circle.

Now I shall hear what those Hebrew words mean, and I am listening intently for Adeline's translation. They will tell me what the next phase of our world revolutionary plan shall be. I begin to strip each of the eyes from my leotards, one by one, and cast them into the crowd, until my pink under flesh is exposed.

It is not Adeline who translates, it is Josephine Earp, who naturally understands our secret message being delivered for the masses, so she steps forward. Her dark-brown eyes are wide and fearful as she speaks:

"That was the spirit voice of Rabbi Jerome Sonenschein, if you want to believe it. He was speaking in Hebrew through this young medium bride. He says there will soon be a murderer in San Diego who shall attempt to kill the first-born male of each family. He quoted the words from our Hebrew scriptures. 'That night, God sent the angel of death to kill the firstborn sons of the Egyptians.'"

THE DANCING MURDERS

There are screams and gasps from the audience. Murder of children? This must be the grand hoax the Belgians have promised. Two dead martyrs in San Diego, and now our cause will receive the international coverage it needs? How? By putting the fear of God into the City of San Diego? I must wire them for a complete explanation. I look back at Dr. Baker, and he nods at me. If I don't follow my instructions, he will certainly report me to them. To fulfill my final part, I begin, barefoot, to run across the tiles. Clutching one hand on my growing fetus, I sprint out of the dining room, through the double doors, and up to the wall overlooking the Pacific Ocean. I climb carefully upon the wall, and I stand, facing my audience, who is peering at me from the interior of the restaurant. I can see that Dr. Fred Baker is smiling at me and nodding his head. "I can no longer be part of this! I am pregnant with Elias Baldwin's child. The world is going stark, raving mad!" I know Ida has her man, Peng Shi, down below in his sailboat, ready to take me on board. Little do they all know, however, that I, true to my word, hold inside my body a child who could be an intended first-born victim or a child born into new freedom. If my anarchist comrades are true to their word, I and my child will need protection. If they are simply attempting to gain international notoriety, then I shall continue my role in their patriotic and feverish plot to gain freedom for women and workers all over the world. As I jump into the bay and hit the water, I feel newly-baptized. I am a woman of a new kind of faith. Beyond religion, beyond patriarchal greed, and beyond anything the world expects. If my comrades, including Dr. Baker, are serious about killing children, then my fate will be in another direction, and I may go insane, or die, attempting to defend my precious love child.

Historical Notes

My town of San Diego, in 1888, was a boomtown, just like many other towns up and down the California coast, and throughout the great Southwest states, and into other U.S. Territories. I used my imagination to shine a mirror of present society and its problems back into the past by asking the question, "What if an entire community were in psychological denial concerning tragic events that occur in their most notorious neighborhoods, which cater to prostitution, gambling, and medical chicanery to treat tubercular (consumptive) patients?"

Some current (2021) events you may want to use to compare/contrast with these fictional activities are 1. The COVID-19 crisis, infections, and treatments. 2. Human sex trafficking problems in the USA, including the specific case of Jeffrey Epstein. 3. Treatment of new immigrants and refugees coming into the USA.

Most of the setting details describing San Diego in 1888 were obtained at the San Diego Historical Society and from many public and private libraries in California. The biblical references were found in research done by my deceased wife, Ellen Bernabei-Musgrave, for her course "The Bible as Literature." The information about Judaic Kabbalah and Mysticism was researched, but a lot of the applications and rationales of these practices are fictionally created and applied to fit my plot and its characters.

The three of the four suspect characters are historical, as well as my Portia of the Pacific series attorney/detective, Clara Shortridge Foltz, and her partner for this mystery, Dr. Charlotte Baker. Their life histories were researched, but their historical details were woven into my completely fictional plot, so nothing that happens in this mystery, including the murders, the fictional names of the minor characters, and the locations of these murders ever took place. Finally, three characters in this novel are the actual names of three readers, who won a raffle to become characters, which I also did in the third mystery in my series *The Stockton Insane Asylum Murder*. Their names are Heaven Riendeau, Kai Krissy Wong, and Anand Prabhakar. They were all very good sports to allow me to use their identities in my plot.

Next Mystery in the Series

Now that our school system, in 2021, has taken the foot off the pedal in the Liberal Arts, especially Literature and analysis of people (Sociology), the population is losing sight of what makes a profound and interesting story. This especially concerns the belief today that any mention of our current society's "taboos" (race, religion, gender, and many other hot-button political issues) should be carefully analyzed for their potential "impact" on the society at large. Except, of course, the lens that is being used by whichever biased group attempting to gain power, whether on the left or the right, who uses its wits and rhetoric as the sole "expert" to negate all others.

Why I mention this is because this is what, in the 1920s and 1930s, became the breeding ground for totalitarian powers to come to the forefront and claim the mantle of "nationalist pride." The people were so afraid of losing even more power than they had already lost during World War One and the following Great Depression that they began mistrusting their neighbors and listening to the special interest groups and political parties, who either wanted power for themselves, or who wanted to take power from others and claim they had done it for the benefit of all, while it was, in truth, the nationalist populism which had done it.

Why? Because mobs and violence bring power from the "barrel of a gun," as both the Communists and Fascists said, in one form or another. And the liberal democracies at the time understood that rhetoric also, and they believed in the biblical commandment of "an eye for an eye," without caring about the possible result of "making the whole world blind."

In my seventh mystery of the Portia of the Pacific Historical Mysteries, "The Evil Eye Murders," I will be showing the much earlier, Nineteenth Century roots of this same nationalist rhetoric

276

and manipulation, which was passed on to the "wisdom" of those in the future who used these techniques to create a much deadlier and vaster world conflict.

My microcosm, once again, will be my current hometown, San Diego, as these powers will be shown in stark contrast to the idyllic beauty of the countryside and seaside splendor. Just as the idyllic lands around the concentration camps in Germany, during World War Two, camouflaged the atrocities going on, just as the wealthy boulevard in Tel Aviv today hides the atrocities inside Gaza (for perhaps different but still nationalist reasons), so did San Diego and other places hide seeds of violence and fear of each other and what our "special interests" proclaim to the world.

Again, this book will not be enjoyed by people who see themselves in the characters and who hate any kind of literature that explores the realpolitik of acquiring the power and the will to kill your enemy, whomever you proclaim them to be. For, as Franz Kafka and others knew so well, in the final analysis, to twist a saying of our current gun rights advocates in the USA, it is not "the machines and the guns" who kill people, it is the "love and worship of those machines and guns" that kill people and who become your sworn enemies.

The symbol of the little group who takes power in my mystery can be twisted, by manipulating a few letters, into a terrorist group that took power in Gaza, much later in history, and who are still causing problems for everybody. The "good guys," featuring my attorney and detective, Clara Shortridge Foltz, and Russian aristocrat and mystic, who has become a leader of a group called the Theosophist Society, in 1875, Madam Helena Petrovna Blavatsky, join forces to fight this "enemy" special interest group, and the new killer in town, which follows the credo of philosophers Friedrich Nietzsche, who wrote *Thus Spoke Zarathustra*, and the authors of the book *The Communist Manifesto*, Marx and Engels. But it is this new leader and killer's love and worship of the Greek God, Dionysus, which ultimately makes him or her a murderer, even of children.

Ironically, Blavatsky's group would later, in "real history," be accused of racism, nationalism, and feeding into the credo of the

Nazi Party, because she references the "swastika symbol," in her book, *The Secret Doctrine*, which is an ancient symbol of the Hindus. In Hinduism, the right-facing symbol (卐) is called swastika, symbolizing *surya* ("sun"), prosperity and good luck, while the left-facing symbol (卍) is called *sauwastika*, symbolizing night or tantric aspects of Kali. Just as the symbol of "Hamsa," is not the name of the terrorist group "Hamas," it still became the symbol of the murderers and the murders committed in San Diego in 1889 in my little mystery.

About the Author

James Musgrave's work has been featured in *Best New Writing 2011*, Eric Hoffer Book Awards, Hopewell Press, Titusville, N.J. He was semi-finalist in the Black River Chapbook Competition, Fall, 2012. He was also in a Bram Stoker Award Finalist volume of horror fiction, *Beneath the Surface, 13 Shocking Tales of Terror*, Shroud Publishing, San Francisco, CA. Both of his historical mystery series were curated and selected as "featured titles" by the American Library Association's Program for Independent Authors at biblioboard.com. The first mystery in his series, *Forevermore*, won the First-Place blue ribbon for Best Historical Mystery, in the Chanticleer International Clue Book Awards, 2013. James lives in San Diego, and is the publisher of EMRE Publishing, LLC. Visit the Author's website at emrepublishing.com

www.ingramcontent.com/pod-product-compliance
Lightning Source LLC
Chambersburg PA
CBHW060859250626
47159CB00008B/2804